Tiffanie DeBartolo was born in Youngstown, Ohio, on November 27, 1970, just 22 minutes after Thanksgiving Day ended. Until she was eight, she thought all the food and festivities that took place on Turkey Day were all about giving thanks for her.

Before she started writing novels, she penned three screen-plays including *Dream for an Insomniac* – which she also directed – starring Ione Skye and Jennifer Aniston.

She divides her time between Boulder, Colorado and New York City. *The Shape of My Heart* is her first novel.

# ACKNOWLEDGMENTS, SAPPY DRIVEL, AND AN EMAIL ADDRESS:

I am supremely grateful to the following people:

Two of the classiest men I know—my agent, Albert Zuckerman, and my editor, Hillel Black, for opening their hearts to Jacob, Trixie, and to me. I am forever in their debt.

Ruth Danon, April Krassner, Catherine Barnett, and everyone at the NYU summer intensive writing workshop, for giving so much of themselves. And to Tim O'Brien for his priceless advice and encouragement.

Chris Cornell, for combining fifteen little words in such a way as to instigate ninety thousand other ones.

Richard Weiner, Bob Shook, Fay Greenfield.

Ben Heldfond, Eddy Midyett, Troy Reinhart, and Corrine Clement, as well as all my dear friends and relatives who influence and nurture me. You know who you are.

My grade school and high school English teachers, especially Miss Canavan, Mr. Antognoli, and Mrs. Shattuck.

Above and beyond: to four of the five most important people in my life: my parents, Candy and Eddie DeBartolo, and my sisters, Lisa and Nikki, for not only accepting but encouraging my unusual imagination, and for their unconditional love and support.

Lastly, to Scott. The coolest, most noble man I know. I thank him for *everything*.

If you'd like to communicate with me, send an email to: BeatriceJordan@aol.com. I'll answer the nice ones. I might even answer the psychotic ones. But if you write to tell me how much you hated the book, don't think you're going to get a response.

# The Shape of My Heart

## Tiffanie DeBartolo

PIATKUS

Copyright © 2002 by Tiffanie DeBartolo

First published in the United States in 2002 by Sourcebooks, Inc.

First published in Great Britain in 2002 by
Judy Piatkus (Publishers) Ltd of
5 Windmill Street, London W1T 2JA
email: info@piatkus.co.uk

This edition published 2003

'Preaching The End Of The World'
By Chris Cornell
© 1999 Disappearing One Music (ASCAP)
All rights reserved. Used by permission.

'Two Out Of Three Ain't Bad'
By James Steinman
© 1977 Edward B. Marks Music Company
All rights reserved. Used by permission.

**The moral rights of the author has been asserted**

*A catalogue record for this book is available from the British Library*

ISBN 0 7499 3378 X

Printed and bound in Great Britain by
Mackays of Chatham Ltd, Chatham, Kent

*For Jeff*
*Because your truth was a soul-truth.*

*So to thank you*
*and to never forget that you happened.*

# PRELUDE

When I was twelve, a fortune-teller told me that my one true love would die young and leave me all alone.

Everyone said she was a fraud, that she was just making it up.

I'd really like to know why the hell a person would make up a thing like that.

I remember the whole horrendous scene, more or less, like it was yesterday. A splashy dinner party in Hollywood the week of my seventh-grade Christmas vacation. My dad was a piss-faced entertainment lawyer—he ran one of the biggest firms in town—and he was always dragging us to one god-awful party after another, purely for show of course, to appear as if we were the quintessential family, which was a big crock of vomit. We were sitting at a large round table overpopulated by too many wine glasses and an empty bread basket. Me, my parents, my brothers Chip and Cole; along with a made-for-TV movie star; his wife, who was a famous TV star herself; and another guy who I was told was a pitcher for the Dodgers. He's the one who ate all the bread.

Apparently the people throwing the party thought it would be fun to have a fortune-teller working the room, as a sort of bohemian novelty, I imagine. I watched her roving. She had deeply etched lines around her eyes, though everything else about her seemed young. Her hair looked like cotton candy and was the same shade as her lipstick. I tried to figure out how old she was but it was impossible to tell. She seemed both ancient and ageless. Maybe a vampire, I thought. She was dressed like a gypsy, with a heavy shawl, lots of lace, and huge hoop earrings. They were gold and they touched her shoulders. I recall thinking that I could probably get my fist through one of them if she'd let me try, but I didn't mention it when she came over because something about her scared the shit out of me.

As soon as she hit our table she made a beeline to where I was sitting, as if no one else were there. She smelled like cigarettes. Even at that age I had a delicate nose. Smells formed the basis of my first and most critical impressions, and the nicotine compounded my already negative hunch about her.

"My name is Madra," she said. "What's yours?"

"Beatrice," I said. But what I thought was, Hey, if you're so psychic you'd already know my name. I didn't say that though. I was shy back then.

"And how old are you, twelve?" she said.

Wow. Okay. Maybe she was clairvoyant after all. Because I didn't look twelve. Especially with my hair the way it was. I had long, thick black hair, and instead of trying to deal with it, my mother used to pull it up really tight into a ponytail on top of my head. I looked like I'd had a facelift. Couple that with my skin, which has always been the color of a bleak winter, and my rawboned little chicken legs, it's a wonder I passed for double digits at all.

"That's right, I'm twelve," I told Madra.

"But you have a very old soul, my dear. You are almost at the end of your cycle. You have lived many lives and are reaching nirvana."

I sat there, hypnotized. She might as well have been speaking Swahili, that's how little sense she made to me. She took my hand, turned my palm face up, and studied it.

"You are an artist," she said. "You will have a long life. And a great love."

My brother, Chip, who's five years older than I am, said, "What a load of crap." Madra acted like she didn't hear him; she just kept going.

"You will also know much sadness, but you are strong."

She frowned, and I thought I detected a tear in her eye when she broke the last bit of news. "You will lose your soulmate to tragedy. Not enough time, not enough time." She shook her head, lurid. "Bless you, Beatrice."

Madra put my hand down. She walked to the next table where Warren Beatty was sitting. She sat down on his lap, examined his right ear, and told him he was going to have lots of children. He laughed and said she had the wrong Warren Beatty.

Back at our table, my family was reeling from my predicted future. They had petty lives and thus found my fated misfortune hilarious. I was greatly distressed. It was 1984. That year, my true love was John Taylor from Duran Duran. He played the bass and wore eyeliner. I was sure he'd be dead by morning.

He survived.

# ONE

*If your intentions are pure*
*I'm seeking a friend*
*for the end*
*of the world*

That's all the ad said. That, plus a phone number.

It was the biggest one under the section titled MEN SEEKING WOMEN in the *LA Weekly*. I didn't usually even read the *Weekly*. I never liked going out all that much. Reading it only reminded me that I lived in L.A., and no one with any sense would want to be reminded of that. With its constant contradiction of sunshine and violence, going out in Los Angeles was like offering yourself up as a sacrifice to the god of hellfire. It just brought me down.

But for some reason that day, I felt an urge. Was it claustrophobia of my apartment, or of the couple-hundred mile radius I helped populate? I had my suspicions. Either way, it all screamed *Get me out of here!*

I picked up the *Weekly* right in front of the natural food market two blocks from my apartment. It was only six o'clock and I didn't feel like spending the entire evening alone, nor did I feel like succumbing to a knock on the door from Greg, my neighbor-slash-ex-boyfriend, who deep down I loathed to all hell but who also, conveniently, lived right down the hall. When he was bored he came looking for sex, and I wasn't in the mood to endure the wrestling match of my conscience versus my libido. I was feeling weak and wanted to see what my other options were.

I was flipping the pages, looking for movie listings, when it caught my eye.

*Seeking a friend for the end of the world*

I couldn't have put it better myself. Except to add one question: Where the fuck have you been all my life?

I read the ad over a few more times and then, for some nonsensical reason I'll probably never be able to explain, I did it. I skipped the movie, went up to my apartment, and called the number. Sometimes the most consequential moments in my life originate from a state of completely witless human auto-pilot.

After four rings an answering machine picked up and a computer-generated voice asked me to leave my name and number. It caught me off-guard. I didn't know what to say and didn't want to sound asinine. I hung up.

Ten minutes later, after jotting down exactly what I would tell him to make myself sound enchanting, I called back and left a floundering message that wasn't even close to what was written on the Post-It note I held in my hand.

"Uh, hi. My name's Beatrice. I'm twenty-seven years old and, well, I don't know what else to say. I saw your ad in the *Weekly*. I was intrigued. Call me if you want. I mean, I don't know, I've never done anything like this before but, anyway…here's my number."

Like I told the machine, I'd never called a personal ad before, and hadn't ever planned on calling one. As a matter of fact, I made fun of people who had to advertise for dates, and I usually prefer my own company to any old idiot, unless I'm really horny. But I wasn't too proud to admit that in a city where women choose men by the kind of car they drive, and men choose women by the size of their breasts, I'd become moderately despondent.

I'm only a B cup.

Besides, the ad seemed different, inspiring in a way. I asked myself if any of my former lovers would have ever thought of something that provocative to write in a personal ad, and because the answer to my question was a resounding no, I figured it was worth a shot.

I didn't hear from anyone for almost two weeks, and I had all but forgotten about it until I answered the phone and heard his voice.

He said, "Trixie?"

I paused. "Do you mean…Beatrice?"

Chuckling a little, he said, "Isn't Trixie short for Beatrice?"

If it was, I said, I'd sure as hell never been called it.

I knew it was the guy from the ad as soon as he spoke. Whoever he was, that is. The tone of his voice was smooth and rich, like freshly ground coffee. And he spoke softly, deliberately, as if every word he uttered were a self-portrait.

He told me his name was Jacob Grace, and he apologized for not calling me back sooner, although he gave no explanation as to why it took him so long. He said he was twenty-nine, that he was a writer—currently working part-time at the *Weekly*—and that he'd very much like to meet me as soon as possible. He said all this as if he were in pain, as if I were a lost love he never got over. Or maybe that was the dreamer in me. I try to find meaning anywhere I can. It's the only way I know how to validate my existence.

Jacob and I arranged to meet for lunch the next day at Fred's on Vermont. It wasn't too far from where he worked, he explained. He ate there a couple times a week.

"They have corn dogs and pop-tarts on the menu," he said boyishly.

I asked him what he looked like, pretending I needed to

know in case it was crowded. I really just wanted to make sure he wasn't some kind of Quasimodo.

"What do you look like," he said back to me, more a statement than a question.

"I have long black hair, and I'll wear a topaz stone around my neck."

"You were born in November," he said. "So was I."

"How do you know that?"

"Topaz is the birth stone for November. I have brown hair. See you tomorrow."

# TWO

I got to Fred's a few minutes early and stood outside, peering in through the slats of the wooden blinds. The place was like a time warp, with brown and yellow leather booths, caricatures of old movie stars on the walls, and vintage white toasters on every table. I'd never been to a restaurant where they let you toast your own bread. There was a jukebox in the corner, and a massive cappuccino machine behind the counter. But what really caught my eye was something on the wall. I could see it from where I was—a painting of a rocky beach with a raging sea crashing down upon it. In big letters across the front was scribed the phrase: NOT NOW.

It was a kitschy piece of shit but something about it made my heart hurt.

I was going to walk in and get a table, then I spotted Jacob. He was in the booth right under a bad likeness of Lauren Bacall. Don't ask me how I knew he was the guy, I just did. It was a typical spring day: warm, clear, a predictable bore, with the temperature reaching the mid-seventies, but he was wearing a black, ratty, old wool coat that looked like it had been through a war. He was smaller than I'd pictured him— a little taller than me, but he looked fragile somehow, sitting alone with his head down. He hadn't shaved that morning, I could tell because there was a hint of scruff across his delicate jaw. And his hair was brown, like he said, but a fiery brown, as if it were flecked with cinnamon. It was disheveled and still a little damp. My guess was that he'd washed it before he left his house but probably didn't own a brush—it stuck out and around in all directions. He reminded me of a puppy from the pound.

I watched him as I entered, hoping he would spot me. He never raised his gaze. He was reading what looked like a foreign newspaper when I walked over.

"Jacob?" I said, feeling as if I were interrupting something.

Only then did he look up, and I caught sight of his eyes. They were deep-set, so much so that they almost appeared in shadow, a watery version of his hair color, like liquid leather. And they were older, wearier than his age let on. But I sensed in them a splash of irony, too; a proud acceptance of the fact that life can be a bitch sometimes, that some people feel things too deeply. I always felt like that myself, that I didn't marry into the landscape of the human world like others did, that I was on the outside looking in. I imagine it's much easier not to take things so seriously, to just *blend*, but I'd long ago given up trying to live in vain and I knew I had to suffer for it. I was just sick, beaten, in a city of millions, of suffering by myself. I was twenty-seven going on sixty-five. I should have received Social Security for my misery.

I'd never seen that look on another face before, had never identified it in another person. I'd met with it only in fiction. But everyone falls in love with Holden Caulfield when they're sixteen. They read *The Catcher in the Rye* and don't feel so alone. The problem is, they get over it. They forget that grief. Or they bury it. I never could.

So I was instantly attracted to Jacob, mainly because he had that look, like he still remembered. But the contentment on his face said he found value in it, wasn't plagued by it like I was. As far as I was concerned, that made Jacob the smarter one between the two of us, and who couldn't use someone who'd maybe teach them a little something about life and how to live it, the only problem I could foresee was that my attraction to him began to manifest itself as a feeling, a specific part of my body was melting, and I hoped I could sit down in case anything started to drip—I was wearing a skirt.

Jacob's face softened and he stood up. His fingers were thin and kind, and he grasped my hand with both of his. He smelled like an exotic wood.

"Trixie," he said. "Do you mind if I call you Trixie?"

"No, I like it."

He asked me to sit down, and we sat in silence as he studied me, his head resting on his fist. I felt a bit uncomfortable, but was made to feel less so by the fact that Jacob seemed completely at ease, as if it were the most common thing in the world to sit and stare at someone you'd never met. I noticed his newspaper was French.

Finally, he spoke.

"You know, you're really beautiful," he said. "You kind of have, I don't know, the face of a Henry James heroine."

That might sound like the biggest line of Velveeta you've ever heard, but trust me, it didn't come out like cheese at all. He wasn't flirting—not intentionally anyway. He was simply being honest—a rare quality I would soon come to know was typical of Jacob Grace. I found his compliment embarrassingly romantic, as I had more than once thought of becoming some neo-metropolitan version of Isabel Archer; had ached to leave the city of bright lights and ill-fated dreams, drained and confused, but still headstrong enough to embark on a literal and metaphorical journey of discovering all of what life might really hold for me.

I have a lot of lame-ass daydreams like that.

I felt my cheeks blush.

"I'm sorry. I didn't mean to make you self-conscious,"

Jacob said with a gentle smile on his face.

"I just never think of myself that way."

"I like the Victorian look: porcelain skin, raven hair, sort of refined features. It gives you a certain uniqueness here among the acres of sun-kissed blonds. It gives you depth."

I motioned to Jacob's newspaper. "You speak French?"

He shrugged. "*Un peu*," he said. "I'm trying to learn."

I nodded and we were silent again.

I got the impression Jacob was an odd person, and I mean that as the best possible compliment I could give a guy. He had the most sincere face I'd ever seen, and it seemed he put on absolutely no pretenses whatsoever. Something about being with him made me warm, like I was sitting in front of a fireplace whose embers were barely flickering, yet still giving off heat. It made me feel safe.

"Jacob, can I ask you something?"

"Sure."

"Your ad, you must've had dozens of calls. Why did you call me back?"

He squinted. "I didn't get dozens of calls. Six maybe, but not dozens. That's why it took me so long to call you. You were the last of them." He paused, making little dots on the tablecloth with his fork. "The truth is, I placed the ad as sort of a joke. I was in the office one day complaining about never finding any decent women in Los Angeles, and a coworker of mine cooked up the idea."

"Have you met all of us now?"

"Five of you. One I chose not to meet."

"Why's that?"

"Transvestite," he said. "Too much make-up."

"What were the other ones like?" I wanted to know if I had any competition.

"They ran the spectrum," he said. "Suicidal gothic, older

than my mother, on anti-depressants and loving it, and lastly, the one I was the least impressed with, a woman who thought Henry Miller was a police sitcom from the seventies. You're the only normal one so far, normal being a relative term, of course."

"You have no idea how relative," I said. "I went to Catholic school for twelve years."

That made Jacob laugh.

"I thought it would be a great idea for a story," he said. "So if nothing else, I'll get work out of it. I've never placed a personal ad before either. And I kind of figured this whole thing would turn out to be just something to write about. Well, I mean, until now, maybe."

"You know," I said, "I don't even read the paper much. I just happened to pick one up that day. The ad was the first thing I saw."

"If that isn't fate, I don't know what is," Jacob said, grinning as if he'd won the lottery.

He had pointy canine teeth. Like a wolf.

We ordered cappuccinos and grilled cheese sandwiches, and told each other our life stories.

Jacob was born in Tennessee but moved to California before he was a year old. He grew up in Pasadena, the only child of a single mother who worked as a dance instructor. He described her peculiarly in the plural as "really good people."

"What happened to your father?" I said.

"He took off a few months after they got here. He was kind enough to keep in touch for a year or two, but that was about it. We haven't seen him since."

"Have you ever tried to contact him?"

"No," Jacob said. "Someday I'd like to be able to talk to him face to face though, the fucking piece of trash."

I got the feeling his father was still a raw subject for Jacob; it was the only time I saw his smooth ride wane to minor turbulence.

Jacob was passionately obsessed with his writing. I could tell by the bonfire in his eyes when he spoke about it. It was everything to him.

"If I didn't have my work," he said, "I'd probably be dead by now."

He told me about a year-long stint in a university writing program that he summed up as a complete waste of time. Not long after he quit, he wrote a short story that was published by *Esquire* magazine, and consequently optioned for a nice chunk of change by a local film studio. Jacob declined the offer to actually write the screenplay.

"That's not my gig," he said.

As far as he knew, the screenplay had never been written or made. But he lived off of that exploit for a few years, in the meantime writing stories here and there for various publications, as well as his work at the *Weekly*. Most recently, he said, he'd been working on a novel.

"It's a story about a kid from Hollywood who longs for his southern roots, obsessing over rainstorms, the blues, and the crazy woman in his building who thinks she's Scarlett O'Hara."

"Does it have a name yet?"

"I call it *Hallelujah*," he said, as if it were a beloved pet.

I'd told Greg—my previous boyfriend—that I was an orphan because, from the start, I could never foresee the relationship going anywhere and I didn't want to have to introduce him to my mother. It became a real pain in the ass. I had to talk like an idiot when I answered the phone and Mom was on the other end. Holidays were a problem as well. The guy I dated before Greg, I told him my parents were South African expatriates, and that we didn't speak any longer because they'd supported apartheid. But for some reason, when Jacob asked, I couldn't bring myself to lie. On the contrary, I had the very atypical impulse to tell him everything.

"I grew up in the Hollywood Hills. I have two brothers and a set of parents that I have virtually nothing in common with. My philandering father left my mother nine years ago and I haven't spoken to him since. My mother, who now lives in Santa Barbara, means well but is criminally materialistic. I studied fine art in college, and I design jewelry for a living. That's me in a nutshell."

"Somehow I doubt that," Jacob said, his eyes shining. "But it's a good start. Tell me about the jewelry you make."

"It's the kind of stuff that looks fairly inexpensive, but sometimes costs a whole paycheck. I like to mix precious stones and gems with crude, organic materials. So things look a bit off."

I told him about a piece I'd sold the week before. It was one of my all-time favorites—an exquisite little Burmese ruby that, instead of placing on an ordinary chain, I secured to a piece of brown twine wrapped around heavy-duty wire, then encircled it in tiny pearls. It was extraordinary looking, completely unrefined and beautiful. The woman who bought it paid quite a bit, even after I tried to talk her out of it.

"Why did you try and talk her out of it?" Jacob said.

"Because the horrible smell of department store cologne oozed from her pores. And she called the necklace 'cute.' I knew she was going to wear it once to show her friends how cool she thought she was, then stuff it in a drawer and never put it on again."

I could tell by the look on Jacob's face that he found me amusing. I kept talking. "I told her the necklace was fragile.

And that it didn't match her skin tone. She just wouldn't give up. I guess you could say I get a little sentimental about my pieces. And truthfully, I never thought this whole business would take off, but people here will buy anything, thank God; it's one of the only things in life that makes me happy. So far, I've only discovered four things that make life worth living for me. My work is one of them."

"What are the other three?" Jacob wanted to know.

"Music, books, and sex," I said. "Not necessarily in that order."

His eyebrows rose an inch and he smirked. "What else do you need?"

Jacob said he could tell I was an artist by the way I held my spoon. I didn't quite understand what he meant, but I liked that he was paying attention. He asked me if I would give him something I made, that he could wear around his neck.

"I'll make something for you."

We talked for a while longer, then we wandered down the street and stopped at a used record shop. We walked in and began pointing out the music we liked and didn't like, assessing all the vinyl we thought life wasn't complete without owning. We both concurred that anyone not in possession of *Blood On The Tracks*, *Exile On Main Street*, and anything by U2 didn't know diddley about rock 'n' roll. We were also together on the fact that any band, song, or solo work that a guy named Paul Weller had been even remotely connected to was cool, even though 98 percent of the world's population outside of Britain has never heard of him. The one thing we did disagree on was the genius of Prince. Jacob liked him; I put him in the over-rated, egomaniacal-freak category. But I scored an extra point with Jacob by being a Fugazi fan, even correcting him on the pronunciation of the singer's last name.

"MacKaye. I'm told it rhymes with pie, not pay."

"How the hell do you know so much about music?" Jacob said.

I explained to him that, as with most things in my life, it was because of and despite my mother. Growing up, she constantly nagged me that if I knew my homework as well as I knew the words to every song on the radio, I'd be a genius. She wouldn't let me watch MTV while I ate breakfast, and forbade me to turn on my stereo anytime after dinner.

"Beatrice, I'm afraid you're going to turn into a pothead. Then everyone will think I was a bad mother."

That's what she used to say to me. Lucky for her, my nose is too acute for pot. Nothing that smells like a burning piece of vegetarian shit goes anywhere near my nasal passages.

"But," I said to Jacob, "I had a pair of headphones my mother didn't know about. And I ended up valedictorian of my class. That finally shut her up."

Jacob nodded slowly. "What do you say we mark this day—the day we met—by buying each other a record? Something we think reflects our perceptions of each other."

It sounded like a great idea to me. We both began to browse the racks with concentrated intent. I walked up and down every aisle and looked in every bin, hoping something would strike me. Finally I came across an old Nick Drake album called *Five Leaves Left*. I discovered Nick Drake when I was in school but hadn't listened to him for years. His music was full of grief and torment and truth. I knew Jacob would love it.

Jacob had been outside waiting for me for five minutes. He'd walked directly to a bin, found what he was looking for, snuck up to the register, and purchased it. When I met up with him on the sidewalk he handed it to me. It was a record called *Seven Steps To Heaven* by Miles Davis. He told me that if it didn't bring tears to my eyes when I listened to it, he couldn't be my friend.

"I'm kidding," he said. "But you'll dig it, I know you will. Especially the third track. It's one of my favorite songs *ever*." He stressed the "ever" like it hurt.

I gave him the Nick Drake and he said he couldn't wait to listen to it. Then he glanced at his watch, apologized, and said he had to go. With his hands in his pockets, he looked at me and breathed deeply. For the first time all day I got the impression he was nervous. Staring at his shoes, he said, "Not too long ago, I broke up with someone I was with for a long time. I haven't done this in a while."

I took a step toward him, to let him know that anything he wanted to do was okay by me. He looked up, leaned in, touched his forehead to mine, and kissed me.

His lips were full and soft and he tasted like coffee.

"I'll call you later," he said, then he caught himself. "I mean, *can* I call you later?"

I didn't have to answer that.

I stood watching him until he turned the corner and I couldn't see him anymore. I went home, put on *Seven Steps To Heaven*, and spent the next six hours with Miles Davis, constructing a necklace for my new friend. I played the third song, his favorite, over and over, and swore I could smell Jacob Grace in the sounds emanating from my speakers.

# THREE

Jacob called me that night and we talked for a long time. He told me all about Nina—the ex-girlfriend. Their relationship had always been rocky, he said, though they managed to stay together for three years.

"I met her in traffic school," he said, as if that explained why he'd been with her for so long.

Jacob told me Nina was some kind of amazingly talented photographer by trade. "And, by the end of our relationship, a junkie."

I asked him if that's why they broke up.

"There were a lot of reasons," he said. "After a while, we sort of lost our ability to communicate. I went looking for her at a party one night and found her passed out on the laundry room floor with a belt tied around her arm and a needle sticking out of her vein. Unbeknownst to me, it'd been going on for weeks. It's not a good sign when your girlfriend's a heroin addict and you don't even know it."

Jacob said he tried to snap her out of it. She told him he was a drag and started sleeping with someone who shared her habit.

"She left me for a crack-head," he said. "Last I heard, she's now a lesbian."

A lesbian. Cool. One less woman to worry about, I thought.

"What did you do after she left?"

"I got in my car and drove. I ended up in Costa Rica. I

spent two months there, just writing. For hours on end. You know what it's like when you're working and everything just clicks. Six hours go by and it feels like seconds. I love that. It was one of the most exhilarating and most painful times of my life. I didn't want to come back."

"Why did you?"

"I was running out of money. And I knew I had a job waiting for me at the paper. Otherwise, I wouldn't have. My roots are somewhere else. I've never felt like I belonged here."

I asked him where he thought he belonged.

"Someplace more intimate, with more soul. Los Angeles signed a pact with the devil and lost its soul a long time ago, you know? It flourishes, but it's doomed. I'm planning on getting out of here as soon as I can."

"Where to?"

"To the south. Mississippi, Georgia, Tennessee, I don't know. As soon as I sell my book, I'm going to buy a little house somewhere down there, one with a porch. I'm going to spend my days writing and my nights making love in the sweltering southern heat. Set my spirit free."

Jacob talked like no one I'd ever met. I wondered if he talked that way because he was a writer, or if he was a writer because he talked that way.

I asked him when he knew he wanted to write. He told me about how, when he was in high school, he and his buddy, Pete, who was still his best friend, used to skip class and sneak off to Hollywood Park, where he'd met Charles Bukowski.

"He was there all the time. It was obvious we were too young to gamble, so he used to take our money and go bet on horses for us. Then he'd buy us beers and try to get us dates with the waitresses. But he also gave me books. I didn't know real men wrote poetry until I met him."

As far as women went, Jacob told me he'd dated a few girls

since Nina, besides the ones who answered the ad, that is, none of which he had any intention of seeing again.

"What about you, Trixie?"

I told him about some of my mistakes, most recently Greg the neighbor. We went out for almost a year and broke up just before Thanksgiving. Up until about a month prior to meeting Jacob, Greg and I were still having sex on occasion, though I eventually put a stop to that as well. Greg made his living as a professional surfer, and I tend to have a weakness for men who manage to get through life without having to hold down a real job, probably because my father worked a hundred hours a day and I never saw him. What's worse, anytime I complained about my father's absence, my mother tried to make *me* feel like the guilty one.

"Mom, why doesn't Dad ever eat dinner with us?"

"Beatrice, your father works hard so that you can live in a nice house and have everything you want. Don't whine."

"What if what I *want* is for him to eat dinner with us once in a while?"

"Drop it, Beatrice."

That's my excuse for even speaking to Greg—a blond beach bum with a bowl-shaped haircut, who smelled like coconut, occasionally referred to me as "Dude," and thought monogamy was the practice of sewing your initials onto a set of towels. I used to catch him traipsing the halls with random surfing Betty's, and he'd offer me no explanations. He'd just greet me by jutting out his chin, as if I were the building superintendent. I suppose I should have stuck up for myself a little, but I didn't care enough to fight about it. It's not like I wanted to marry him. Hell, I could barely stand him. Yet it wasn't until after Valentine's Day that I finally cut him off once and for all. He gave me a card with my name written really big on the envelope. Not only had he decorated it with lightning bolts, but he'd spelled it wrong. Like this: *Beatress*.

Game over, man. He had a dick the size of a baseball bat anyway. I don't care what it looks like in porn, a salami like that sorely limits excessive positional experimentation.

"You have issues with your father," Jacob said.

"No kidding," I said sarcastically. Of course I have issues with my father. Everybody does. Even Christ had an issue with his father. The same one as me, I think. And the same one as Jacob. Abandonment. Why the hell have you forsaken me?

"I hope that doesn't offend you," Jacob said. "It's just that women who put up with that kind of shit from men usually have major father hang-ups, you know, abuse, dependency, whatever. Don't feel bad. Along with all his other faults, my father's an alcoholic, or so I've been told."

"My father's not an alcoholic," I said. "A workaholic is more like it. And when he wasn't working, he was wining and dining and kissing his client's asses. Or he was with one of his girlfriends. Then once a year he would take us on a family vacation and think that made up for lost time. The funny thing was, the vacation spots were always places he had business, so we still barely saw him. Now he lives in Malibu with his new wife. She's not much older than I am, and he bought her boobs for their first wedding anniversary."

"Upper-class white trash," Jacob said.

"Is upper-class a problem for you?" I said sheepishly, feeling a bit self-conscious about my lifelong economic state in an above-average tax bracket.

"I'm not a communist, Trixie."

There was so much I wanted to tell Jacob, and so much more I wanted to know about him, but it was late and I didn't want to seem needy by keeping him on the phone all night. Before we said good-bye we made plans for dinner the next day. Jacob wanted to take me to some little dive up on Pico that had all-you-can-eat sushi for the astounding bargain price of twelve bucks a person. He and his friends met there every Saturday night and he wanted me to come. Normally, raw fish on sale would make me nervous, but Jacob probably could have claimed he had the ability to turn water into wine and I would have believed him. When we hung up it was one o'clock. I dozed off wondering if Jacob got an erection that afternoon when he kissed me on the street. Moments later, I was awakened by the phone ringing.

"Trixie," Jacob said. "Did I wake you?"

"Not really."

"I know it's late but," he paused, "would it be all right if I came over?"

"Right now?"

"Yeah."

"Jacob," I said, "how long have you been waiting to ask me that?"

"Who knows?" he said, more to himself than to me. "Maybe all my life."

# FOUR

I lived in Santa Monica, in the Charmont apartments at Fourth and California—just a stone's throw from the beach if you happen to be Nolan Ryan. The building was practically ruined beyond repair during the Northridge quake in '94. A major renovation then took place, and by the time I moved in it looked like new, on the outside anyway.

The exterior was redone to resemble a sort of Mexican-inspired Art Deco hotel, like how I imagine it probably looked when it was first built; with a stucco finish on the front façade, white bricks everywhere else, and a small quad in the middle, separated from the street by a stone wall and a black iron gate. It was my own pseudo-paradisiacal Alamo. There was a fountain in the courtyard, and the landlord had set up strands of white lights on all the trees. They came on when it got dark and made it look like Christmas all year long, which was really nice until Christmas actually came, then it was a letdown because nothing changed.

The inside of my apartment exuded the faded glamour of old Hollywood. The floors were dark oak, there was glass hardware on all the fixtures, and I had what I lovingly referred to as booger-green tile in the bathroom. In the small living room, I kept a television, a brown velvet couch, two red floor pillows, and an old pine coffee table that I'd painted black due to Greg's tendency toward leaving wet glasses on it. There was a tiny white kitchen down the small hallway to the left, then the bathroom, then my bedroom, which was just my bed, plus a cool Heywood-Wakefield dresser that I splurged on when I moved in. Across from there was a second, smaller bedroom that I occasionally used as an office, but I didn't work at home much. I shared a studio with a group of designers about a dozen blocks away in a more industrial part of town.

Jacob lived in a run-down apartment off of Pacific Avenue in Venice. During the middle of the night, it would only take him a few minutes to get from his house to mine. I had to go downstairs to let him in because on that day the buzzer in my apartment wasn't working. I could ask who was there, but I couldn't open up the door.

After I got off the phone with Jacob, I gathered up the tools I'd been using to make his necklace, washed the dirty cereal bowl I'd left in the sink, and headed to the lobby. In the elevator on the way down, I looked at myself in the reflection of the mirrored-brass panel in front of me. I was still wearing the gray T-shirt I'd worn to lunch that afternoon, but I'd changed out of my skirt, into a pair of silk pajama pants. They were pale magenta with yellow thread sewn into a hieroglyphic pattern at the bottom. I'd found them years ago at the Rose Bowl Flea Market in Pasadena, and I always put them on when I worked at home. My hair was up in a knot but falling all over the place, and my face was bare. For a second, I panicked at my shabby appearance. I looked like I'd just had sex in the backseat of a car. But then I glanced again at my reflection and tried to see myself as Jacob might. I felt luminous.

As soon as I got to the door I saw Jacob. He'd parked across the street, about a block away, and was just locking up his car. He drove a dust-colored Land Cruiser that looked older than his coat, which he was still wearing. I watched him; I studied the way he moved. When he dropped his keys into his pocket, it gave him a weighted-down-on-one-side look. And he walked with his head bowed, as if it were cold and windy and he had to shield his face from the chill. When he was about ten yards from the gate, I stepped back toward the elevator so that he couldn't see me, and so that when he did, he would think I'd just come down. He paused and looked up at the building, like he was imagining which lighted window was mine. Then—out of the blue—he shook his head and laughed, as if he'd just realized where he was and what he was doing, standing in front of the apartment of a girl he hardly knew in the middle of the night. I saw him mouth something. I think he said "*Shit*."

Jacob picked a violet from the garden in front of the building and studied the names on the call box. Then he laughed again. That's when I opened the door. He saw me and his face lit up.

"I don't know your last name," he said, and pointed to the box.

"Jordan. 3E."

I heard him repeat my name to himself, as if burning it into his memory.

"Someone forgot to take down the Christmas lights," he said, and motioned to the trees as we walked inside.

In the elevator, Jacob fiddled with the flower in his hand. "I just picked it outside," he said.

"I know. I saw you."

"I know. I saw you, too."

"You did not." I was behind the wall. He couldn't have seen me.

"Well, I sensed you then. Anyway, I knew you were there. Now that I know you, I can feel your presence."

I felt a charge when he said that. Like he'd rubbed his

stocking-feet on carpet and touched my cheek.

"Here." He handed me the tiny stem and followed me off the elevator and into my apartment.

Jacob set his coat on the arm of the couch and wandered around slowly in and out of each room as if he could discover who I was by looking through my house. I waited for him in the kitchen, realizing it was the first time I'd seen him without the coat on. He was wearing a white v-neck T-shirt, black denim jeans that were at least a size too big, and heavy black boots. His shoulders were skinny; his forearms were covered faintly in chocolate-colored hairs; his skin was pale, anemic. He was raggedly, poetically handsome—to me anyway—I'm sure my mother would have thought he looked like a bum. Boxers or briefs, I mused. Maybe neither.

We stood in my kitchen and he glanced at the ad—the one he'd placed in the *Weekly*. I had it taped, eye-level, on my refrigerator.

Jacob read it out loud, ceremoniously. "Seeking a friend…for the end…of the world." He looked at me and rolled his eyes. "*Whatever*," he said. Then he opened the fridge, took out a bottle of beer, and meandered into the living room. He sank down onto the couch and I sat across from him on the floor, my arms wrapped around my knees.

"What does it mean?" I said, referring to the ad.

"I heard it in a song. I think it's about being lonely. It must have been a dark day for me." He took a swig from his bottle and puckered like it was tequila. "And here I am."

"Here you are," I said.

Jacob noticed the Miles Davis record on my turntable and asked me how I liked it. I told him it had inspired me all afternoon. He picked up the album jacket, shook his head, and said, "I fall in love too easily." He began humming.

I detected a note of quenched thirst in his drone. At first I thought he was trying to tell me something. Then it dawned on me that he was alluding to the song he liked so much, the third track on the record. Nevertheless, I studied the keen expression on his face and was certain he wanted me to wonder about the ambiguity of meaning caused by his choice of words. The statement, his coy smirk told me, was open to interpretation. We locked each other in a staredown and Jacob never broke face with me; he never looked away. We probably would have stayed like that all night had I not chickened out. I flinched and asked him how he liked Nick Drake.

"Majestic," he said, and laughed like he knew he'd won. "That guy's got it bad."

"He's dead," I told him.

"I know, I looked him up. He still has quite a following though."

A not-so-uncomfortable silence filled the room, thick with the kind of tension that made my mouth water.

"You're a very complicated girl, aren't you, Trixie?"

"I don't know what you mean," I said.

"Yes you do."

I took Jacob's necklace out of the felt I'd wrapped it in. It was an old piece of chrysoprase—a deep, Granny Smith green, with concrete-colored veins running throughout, which I'd carved into a primitively shaped arrowhead and surrounded by two pieces of onyx—one on each side. I beaded all that onto a black leather string. On the back of the arrowhead, I'd etched the Japanese character for love. You couldn't see it, but I'd always know it was there. It was my secret.

"You made this today?" Jacob said. He seemed touched.

"Will you put it on me?"

I raised myself onto my knees and reached around his neck. My face was an inch from his and I felt that gooey melting sensation again. When I closed the clasp, I let my hands brush against his hair and the soft skin on the back of his neck. I love the soft skin on the back of a man's neck. It gives me cannibalistic urges. I recognized, from our afternoon, the deep, woodsy scent of his skin, and the sweet cappuccino flavor of his breath.

He fingered the stone and asked me if I wanted to take a walk.

"*On va a la plage.* There's a full moon tonight," he said, rising and putting his coat back on.

"What?"

"The beach," he said. "Let's go."

"Right now? It's almost two o'clock."

As if he were making perfect sense, he said, "Yeah well, it's not orange, it's round."

I had no idea what the hell that meant, but it was supposed to convince me.

"Tomorrow's Saturday," he said. "You don't work on Saturday, do you?"

I worked freelance, selling mostly to small local boutiques and specialty department stores like Fred Segal and Barney's. My schedule was up to me.

"No, I don't have to work tomorrow," I said. I got up and grabbed my jacket.

Jacob took my hand. "I want to kiss you by the sea."

We walked west to Ocean Avenue, then down the walkway that crossed over Pacific Coast Highway and spiraled around to the beach. We could see the famous Santa Monica Pier in the distance: the carousel, the arcade, and the restaurants were all closed for the night. I'd never been on the beach at that hour; it was mystical, deserted. The sky was perfectly clear and the moon was a spotlight illuminated just for us, lighting up the water, turning it into a giant sheet of glass. The tide was calm; it flowed in and out in a slow rhythm, like lovers.

I ran straight to the water's edge. Jacob stopped about ten yards from where the waves ended and watched me. I took off my shoes and kept going forward, letting the water rise and fall over my feet, shrieking from the shock of the temperature.

"Cold?" he said.

"Come and see for yourself." It felt like glacier water.

Every time the waves inched closer to where he was standing, Jacob took a step backward. He raised his head and pondered the horizon. I tried to coax him my way, but the more I pleaded with him, the farther away he got.

"Come on," I said. "I thought you wanted to kiss me by the sea."

"I said by the sea, not in the sea."

"Don't be afraid," I said. At that point, the water was calf-deep on me. My teeth were chattering.

"You better get out of there. You're going to get hypothermia or something."

I walked another foot into the water as soon as he said that. It was up to my knees. Jacob stood with his hands deep in his pockets, biting the side of his cheek.

"Why did you want to come here if you're afraid of the water?" I said.

"Who says I'm afraid of the water?" he answered in a dry voice that made me believe him. That's when the look on his face changed from intensity to mischief. He peered straight into my eyes, dropped his coat, and took a step my way. He still had his boots on and refused to take them off. As the water seeped through to his feet, he sucked in a colossal gulp of air and leaped toward me. When he was standing in front of me, he wrapped his arms tightly around my body, and his lips cracked into a devilish, shit-eating grin.

"Fuck it," he said. "Let's go swimming."

He dove on top of me and we went under. It was like an ice cream–induced headache surging through my entire body.

When we popped back up, Jacob shook out his head and howled with joy.

"Holy shit," I said, and ran to the shore, shivering.

Jacob was no more afraid of the water than the fish. He dove back under, then surfaced moments later, floating on his back. All his exposed flesh was covered in chills, his eyes glowed, and his face looked phosphorescent. He was a pelagic angel, a merman. It was an image of him somehow I knew I'd never forget.

As the waves gently carried him back to land, I bolted in the opposite direction. He caught up to me and we tumbled to the ground. He pressed his body hard against mine. I felt his desire and it made me burn.

"That's pretty impressive in this temperature," I lauded.

He didn't say anything, he just devoured me with a freedom I never knew could be contained in a kiss.

"Let's go," I said.

We struggled to our feet, ran up what seemed like a thousand steps, then all the way back, groping each other along the way, leaving a path of saltwater and sand in our wake. Once inside the apartment, we dropped to the floor with a slippery thud—completely out of breath—and scrambled to take off our wet clothes. Jacob helped yank my shirt over my head and ripped out my left earring in the process. It spun around the floor like a top.

"Do you need to get that?" he said.

"No." I reached for his button fly.

Boxers. He was wearing pale blue boxers. They had what appeared to be little vintage airplanes on them, but I needed a closer look to be sure. I rolled over so that I was on top and I headed south.

"Oh. *Okay*," Jacob said.

Circumcised. Praise the lord, I said to myself. I prefer the snipped penis. It would have been just my luck for the man of my dreams to have had an elephant trunk in his pants.

Jacob moaned when I put his dick in my mouth. It tasted salty and, for a second, it made me think of Greg. Greg liked a blow job after a hard day of surfing, but I always made him shower first. I told him I didn't like the flavor of the ocean but apparently, I just didn't like the flavor of him; I could have sucked Jacob all night.

Jacob pulled me back up by my hair. He was rough and I liked it. "I need to be inside you," he said.

He flipped me over so I was on my back again. It dawned on me that the floor wasn't going to be the most comfortable place to go at it, but I didn't want to get sand all over the bed, and I had no intention of disrupting the current level of excitement to select a new location.

"Trixie?"

I looked up.

"Keep your eyes open," Jacob said. He moved deep in me, slowly at first.

"What?"

"Try to keep your eyes open the whole time."

"Why do you want me to keep my eyes open?"

"It's more intense that way. It keeps you present."

Jacob wasn't staring into my eyes, he was staring through them. I wondered what he saw there. He held on to the top of my head with his left arm. His right arm was pressed up against the wall. He stayed fixated on my face. I bet he didn't blink more than half a dozen times during the whole thing. It made me self-conscious at first. It was scary. I felt like there were waves washing up and over me. I knew I could explode at any second.

About a minute later, I did.

"Oops, sorry," I said, after realizing my eyes had involuntarily closed during the glorious burst of friction.

"My turn," Jacob said. He picked up his pace and I watched him. He squinted and threw his head back when he came, like he'd cut his knee open and was having it stitched up without novocaine.

Afterward, Jacob lay next to me. He reached for something over my head—my earring—and helped me put it back on.

"I've never done it that way. I mean really paying attention like that," I told him.

He let his hand glide up and down my body. "Did you like it?"

I nodded.

"I knew you would," he said.

Once we both recovered, we took turns taking showers, then we got into bed and did it again—backward that time— a position that allowed for eye-closing.

# FIVE

I woke up with the sun pouring over me like an invisible electric blanket. My room was so bright I could barely see, and so hot I could barely breathe. I blinked to adjust my eyes and thought about the twenty-four hours prior to that moment. For the first time in a long while, I was waking up happy. I reached for Jacob.

I was alone.

The clock said it was 9:30 in the morning, and even though I was still half asleep, a million thoughts raced through my mind. Thoughts like how Jacob probably wasn't his real name, and how he hadn't even put that ad in the paper, he was just some random insane person that I happened upon in the restaurant, and how he probably already pawned the necklace I made him. I thought, if last night was some meaningless one-night stand, then I'm the biggest fool who ever lived. I deserved any diseases he might have given me, or the demon love-child that might be growing inside me, and last but not least, I promised myself that as soon as it cooled off in my room, I was going to get dressed, hunt the bastard down, and kill him with my Exacto knife.

I got up and walked through the apartment whispering his name. Nothing. His jeans were gone, his shoes were gone, his jacket and shirt were gone, his precious blue boxers with the little airplanes were gone. If it hadn't been for my still-wet clothes in the doorway, and the sand all over the floor, I would have thought it had all been a dream.

I got in the shower and felt dizzy under the trickling of the water. I scrubbed myself clean of Jacob Grace, then I fell back into bed, smelled him on my pillow, and almost started to cry. I couldn't remember the last time I'd cried, but I had no intention of weeping over some freaky, seraphic asshole. I forced myself back to sleep, thinking, It figures. Mother-fucking, shit-ass, dick-head, piece-of-shit-for-brains, it figures.

# SIX

"Hey, Trixie, wake up. Do you mind if I open the window? It's like, nine million degrees in here."

I opened my eyes and turned my head and he was there, framed by the outline of the glass pane. He looked like a painting of Jesus with the light of heaven shining down around him. My savior. He was wearing different clothes: shabby army pants, and a once-white T-shirt that had become the color of a thirty year-old newspaper—it said Hanoi Dragon Café, and had a drawing of a fire-breathing beast with a smiley face on it. Jacob's face was stubble-free. He'd shaved.

"God, you sleep a lot. I must've really worn you out last night," he said.

He leaped onto the bed, full of energy, poised directly above me with a maniacal grin. "I brought you a present." He held up a small white bag that was filled with peaches. "From the Farmer's Market," he said.

Every Wednesday and Saturday, the city shut down a half-mile stretch of Santa Monica and held a Farmer's Market about four blocks from my apartment. Farmers from all over the state came to peddle the best of their crops. I liked going there because it made me feel like I lived in a civilized society from another time. I'd pretend I was a little peasant girl wandering the countryside, bartering for the sweetest tomatoes and the most fragrant basil. Sometimes I even wore a kerchief around my head for effect. I'd go with my best friend, Katrina. She calls me Blanca because I'm so white. I call her Katrina because that's her name. She's a Russian Jew.

"The Farmer's Market? You went to the fucking Farmer's Market?" I yelled.

Jacob must have thought I was demented. "I woke up early. I couldn't find any coffee and I didn't want to wake you."

I was impressed that he could be so lively after so little sleep, and that he even looked alluring with dark half-moons under his eyes, but I was too traumatized to compliment him. I tossed the peaches across the room. They hit the floor with a splat then rolled to a stop. I pulled Jacob tight into me and buried my face in his neck. About a minute passed and he pulled back, looking at me with his head cocked to one side like a dog does when you make a high-pitched noise. It was because I was crying. I couldn't hold it in that time; he felt the tears on his neck. Goddamn it, I cursed myself. Over the course of the night, I'd apparently turned into a Vermont Maple. I had sap oozing from all my glands and ducts.

I heaved away from Jacob and draped myself with the comforter, holding it down over my head.

"Hey…" he said.

"Go away."

"Beatrice, come on, what's wrong? What is it?"

That was the first time he'd called me by my real name. I hated my name, but it sounded like a piano sonata when he said it.

"Nothing. I thought you left. Leave me alone."

I heard him giggle. He lifted off his shirt and snuck under the covers at the bottom of the bed.

"What is so goddamn funny?" I said.

"You are. You're cute." He slithered up to me. "And I wasn't sure if you actually liked me, or you were just really horny last night, but now I know."

I wanted to tell him I didn't usually act that way. Ordinarily, I wasn't such a *girl*. But Jacob had seemingly used his dick as a knife and pierced right through my armor. I felt my vulnerability trickling down my legs, spilling out all over the bed, being replaced by an injection of his fresh new hope. A love transfusion. Like Keith Richards flushing out the heroin. I was clean.

Jacob spun me around so that I was facing him. "I'm sorry, I should've left a note or something."

He held my face in his hands and kissed me so deeply I thought he was going to draw blood. Then he slithered down the length of my body. He stopped when his face was between my legs. He used his tongue *and* his finger, and made all the pain go away.

"Oh, hey, I think I met your ex this morning," Jacob yelled from the kitchen. I was in the bedroom getting dressed.

"You what?"

"Surfer boy. I ran into him in the lobby. With his board, *dude*."

He mimicked Greg's voice exactly. I finished buttoning my shirt, ran into the kitchen and hopped up on the counter where Jacob was making something in the blender. Between tossing chunks of bruised fruit under the lid, he gave me the hang-ten sign.

"You know, you're kind of funny. For a writer."

"That guy's a real tool," he said. "A screw, no doubt."

"Don't remind me," I said, embarrassed that I'd ever touched Greg after the experience of Jacob. "What did you say to him?"

"He was coming back when I was. I had your keys and I think he recognized your keychain. He asked me where I was going. I told him 3E, and by the look on his face, I knew he was the guy. I said I'd just left you a couple hours ago, that you were still sleeping. I introduced myself to him as Henry Chinaski." Jacob howled, like this was the most hilarious thing he'd ever said in his life.

I didn't get the joke until he told me Henry Chinaski was Charles Bukowski's alter ego. Charles had used the alias in a bunch of books. Jacob clearly found it to be a highly amusing name. He handed me a frothy drink.

"What is this?" I said.

"A smoothie. We could've made a pie or something, but your little peach-throwing tantrum put an end to that," he said. "And by the way, it may be a little premature, but I told that Greg guy I was your boyfriend."

I paused. "You know how to make pie?"

# SEVEN

Sushi Night was a weekly event taken very seriously among Jacob's clan of friends. We went out with a group that included Jacob's best friend, Pete, a struggling musician with a round, jovial face and a beer belly, who made his living as a house-painter; Pete's wife, Sara, a pixie of a girl with flaming-red hair and a toothy smile; a drummer called Odie, who always wore leather pants; and Odie's girlfriend of the moment, Kristen, who went outside every ten minutes to smoke. She was a model.

Jacob introduced me to his friends as Beatrice. "But I call her Trixie," he said, and slouched into a seat at the head of the table. I took the chair to his right, and the rest of the gang scattered themselves around us. As soon as we were all in place, Pete whispered something to Jacob, who smiled and said, "I told you. My woman's got class."

"Yeah, well then what the hell's she doing with you?" Pete said.

Thus began a banter that continued all evening between Jacob and Pete. They finished each other's sentences and affectionately insulted each other's wit and manners. They were like children, like brothers; or what I imagine brothers could be like, since the only model I had were my own, and they didn't have that kind of rapport. Jacob told me how he'd introduced Pete to Sara after he met her at a salon. She cut his hair, he played Cupid.

"If it wasn't for me, you'd still be a miserable bastard," Jacob told Pete. "I take that back, you still are a miserable bastard."

Pete counter-offended by accusing Jacob of using him for frivolous entertainment.

"Let me tell you something," Pete said to me. "Don't let Jake give you his old 'I don't own a TV' bit, like it's beneath him or something."

"I *don't* own a TV," Jacob said.

"That's because you don't need one. You watch ours." Pete turned back to me. "He likes to pretend he's a real *arteest*, but he comes over our house for no other reason than to watch game shows and bad sitcoms."

"You two *are* a bad sitcom," Sara said.

Every so often, when Jacob was engaged in a conversation that didn't include me, he would reach for my hand and squeeze it, or he would just look over and smile, to make sure I was having a good time.

Kristen didn't talk much, she was too busy staring at the door every time someone walked into the place. I think she was waiting to be discovered. The homeless have more *amour-propre*. But she did like my jewelry, so I gave her a point for a decent sense of style. In the meantime, Sara and I got to know each other. I liked her a lot. She was soft-spoken and genuine. Jacob had told me all about her before we got to the restaurant, how she desperately wanted to have a baby. She and Pete had been trying for a couple years but, up to that point, had been unsuccessful, and she really took it hard. Early in the evening there was a family sitting behind us who had two small children making a lot of noise. Everyone at our table turned around at least once to see where the racket was coming from, except for Sara. It was like she couldn't bear to look.

Sara told me Jacob had stopped at their apartment that morning after he left mine. He woke them up to tell them about me.

"He was wearing damp clothes and he stunk like seaweed, but he wanted us to know he'd met someone really special," she said.

In the little basement-cum-restaurant, with cement blocks for walls, and browning Shoji screens as doors, we ordered more sushi than I thought was humanly possible to consume. During the process, it seemed like the men at the table each took a turn picking out something unusually wretched, like sea urchin, or gizzard shad. Everyone ordered with straight faces, but with the countenances of people trying to outdo each other. More than once I couldn't help myself, and made the mistake of expressing a negative sentiment regarding their extreme-sport version of sushi ordering, stating emphatically that monkfish liver wasn't going anywhere near my mouth. Pete and Odie looked at each other and raised their eyebrows, as if making mental notes. It was obviously an inside joke, and I didn't get it. When I asked Jacob what the deal was, he began to explain, until Pete silenced him.

"Hey! Hey! Hey!" Pete yelled. "That is *not* the way we welcome new friends!"

"Can I just advise her that it's in her best interest not to comment on the orders?" Jacob said.

"Absolutely not," Pete replied. Pete was the life of the party. He had the pleasantly crass manner of a Bostonian Irishman, even though he was originally from Burbank. He spoke a dozen decibels louder than anyone I knew, and I found it hard not to laugh at almost everything he said. I also noticed he drank saki like it was water. By the end of the night he must have consumed two bottles. It turned the tip of his nose pink.

"Try not to find my husband so amusing," Sara said. "It encourages his misbehavior and inflates his ego."

After everyone seemed to be finished eating, there were still over a half-dozen pieces of sushi left on the table—all the grotesque ones, I might add—and Sara was kind enough to explain to me the event that would take place next. They called it Roe-Sham-Bo. It was your basic papers-scissors-rock game, and everyone played until all but two contenders were eliminated, then those two would continue playing, with the loser of each round having to eat a piece of sushi—a piece chosen by the winner. The contest went on until all the sushi on the table had been consumed. At that point, it was clear to me why I'd made a big mistake commenting on the slimy ones. When they knew your Achilles heel, they made you eat it.

"Let the tournament begin!" Pete roared.

Kristen declined to play. "I'm stuffed," she said, even though I didn't see her eat anything but a bowl of miso soup and a couple bites of rice. The rest of us were game. Odie was an impressive competitor. He didn't lose a round and was out first, followed by Sara. I was horrible. I had a nervous habit of getting confused during the count and always playing paper.

"Strategy is very important, Trixie," Jacob said with serious conviction. "Think, then throw."

I was surrounded by professionals. They caught on quick to my weakness and nailed me with scissors three times before Jacob kicked me under the table.

"You might want to rethink the paper," he whispered. "It's getting you nowhere."

"Do you think we can't hear you?" Pete said. "No cheating or I'll kick your scrawny ass."

Immediately following Jacob's scant advice, I threw scissors. Pete was way ahead of me. Luckily, it was a best-out-of-three scenario. I managed to save myself by throwing paper a few more times, while Jacob kept throwing rock. I was pretty sure he'd done that intentionally.

That left Jacob and Pete.

"Why is it *always* Jacob and Pete who are left?" Sara said. "I swear they do it on purpose, just to torture each other."

And torture they did, forcing one another to eat things I wouldn't feed to a dog if I had one. Jacob desperately tried to avoid the giant clam. "It tastes like a foot that's been marinated in sewer-water for a week," he said. Pete was oddly petrified of anything containing avocado. "Rabbit diarrhea," he called it.

Pete ended up having to eat almost everything that was left on the table, including a small ball of wasabi. Jacob raised his arms in the air and declared himself the champion.

After dinner we all followed Pete and Sara to a seedy club in Hollywood, hidden in an alley behind Melrose Avenue, about two blocks away from Paramount Pictures. Odie said it was called Hearts, though I never saw a name or address anywhere on the building. It was one of those joints that, if you had to ask what it was called or where it was, you weren't cool enough to belong there.

The walls inside the tiny bar were painted the color of oxygenated blood. The air was foggy from all the cigarette smoke, and the place was packed with the typical mix of wanna-be's and already-are's. The music, however, was particularly memorable—a plump, middle-aged Jamaican woman known only as Pherbie, who slowly, soulfully belted out nothing but Led Zeppelin songs. Jacob thought she was the coolest thing he'd ever seen.

"This lady is *king*," he said.

We swayed on the dance floor while Pherbie sang "Whole Lotta Love" and "Fool in the Rain." Jacob stood close behind me, nodding his head to the beat, singing along, his arms around my waist. I got a strange, sort of surreal sensation there, mainly because it felt so natural and so new, all at the same time. I guess the events of the two preceding days had finally hit me. Technically, I hardly knew Jacob Grace. But I'd cried in front of him, I'd been naked in front of him, I'd had his penis in my mouth, for God's sake, and yet at that point, I'd been in his company for less than thirty-hours. Still, I knew that if an angel would have come down right then and there and given me the choice to spend all of eternity in his arms, listening to him sing in my ear, and feeling his warm breath on my cheek, I would have signed on the dotted line without a second-long thought.

When Pherbie took a break, Jacob asked me if I wanted anything to drink. He asked Pete and Sara the same, and walked off to the bar. Kristen was hanging out with some starlet friends in the corner, and Odie looked lost, so I wandered over to chat with him. We had to stand really close together to hear each other speak. I learned that he and Pete used to play in a band together, but that Odie had been doing mostly studio work since then. He eventually wanted to write soundtracks for movies. When he burped in the middle of a sentence, I got sushi-dinner deja-vu. I had to take a few steps back—I'm highly sensitive to smells.

I tried to keep my eye on Jacob while he was gone. I liked to observe him when he didn't know I was watching, even though I got the impression he always knew when I was. I saw a girl approach him—an attractive girl in a tank-top and a pair of studded jeans that seemed laminated to her legs. She bumped right into Jacob and tried to pretend it was an accident. I saw her touch his shoulder and attempt a joke. She tossed her hair around when she laughed like the glamorous android slut monster I knew she was. Jacob would never give the time of day to a girl like her, I told myself. Be that as it may, I focused on the ceiling panel above her head. I tried to will it loose. I wanted it to crash down and squash her like a villain in a cartoon. And I'm a pacifist.

Jacob, unfazed by the glamazon, walked back my way with a beer bottle in each hand, one for himself and one for Pete. Kristen stomped over to Odie and I heard her mention my name. I couldn't make out everything she was saying, but it sounded like she was mad because he'd been standing so close to me. She wanted to know what we'd been talking about. I think she even accused him of flirting. Odie hadn't flirted with me at all, still, I got a cheap thrill out of Kristen being jealous, since she was the future cover girl and everything. But then I felt sorry for her. She proved my point that beauty means nothing without the right attitude. Besides, why would she think I'd be interested in her boyfriend? He had Spicy Tuna Roll breath and Jacob was The Everything.

We stayed at Hearts for another half-hour. Pete said we couldn't leave until we heard "Stairway to Heaven."

Once that song was over, Jacob slipped his hands down into my hip-slung trousers and said, "What do you say we fucking blow this hotdog stand?"

# EIGHT

Jacob spent the next five nights with me. He came over in the evenings, we watched *Jeopardy,* made dinner, and fucked like rabbits. Except for when we went to work, we only left the house twice all week. The first time, we walked to the Promenade to catch a movie, but a detour in the bookstore cost us an hour and we missed it. The second time we had to go to a party for my friend, Katrina. And we only went to that because she would have killed me if I'd flaked on her. Literally, that's what she told me.

"I swear, I'll kill you if you flake on me, Blanca."

Katrina had a habit of saying that she and I were friends at first sight, but that's not entirely true. We studied art together in college. I met her the first day of school. Kat's a tall, broad-shouldered girl. At the time, she had electric-blond hair that was dyed black at the tips, like upside-down matchsticks, and she walked into the room wearing a shirt that she'd ripped the sleeves off of. Written on it were the words *Damn, I'm good* in what, to this day, she swears to me was blood. She sat down beside me, smelling like Fracas, and didn't say anything as we waited for the class to begin. I got bored and took out a book, some philosophical lexicon I was reading at the time. I think it was during my Ayn Rand phase. She peered at the book, then at me.

"So you're not as dumb as you look," she said. "Neither am I."

We've been friends ever since, even though we're polar opposites. She goes club-hopping almost nightly, only listens

to music made by DJs, and thinks Los Angeles is the greatest
city on the planet. Her father used to let his friends have sex
with her when she was a kid, so she's not the most emotion-
ally functional person I know, but she has a good therapist
and despite the childhood in Hades, she's doing okay—which
was why she was having a party—she'd just opened a trendy
little boutique on Robertson Boulevard called Chick. Besides
selling women's clothing and accessories, she got first dibs on
all my new jewelry.

When she called to remind me about the party, or really,
to make sure I'd be there, I was still in bed. Jacob answered
the phone in the kitchen.

"I think she's still sleeping," he said. "Can I take a message?"

Fifteen seconds into the conversation, I knew it was Kat
he was talking to.

"This is Jacob. Who's this?"

"My last name? My last name's Grace."

"Yes, it's my real name."

"No, I'm not Jewish."

"I don't know why you've never heard of me, maybe
because Trixie and I really haven't known each other for very
long….Sorry, I mean Beatrice….I met her through the
*Weekly*….She answered my personal ad….Yeah, I'm completely serious." Jacob chuckled.

I picked up the phone in the bedroom. "Buzz-off, Kat."

"See you later," Jacob said. After he hung up, Kat yelled,
"Blanca, you're dating someone you met through a *personal
ad*? Are you on *crack*?"

"It's not what you think," I said.

Kat and I talked about Jacob in our private code.

"Are you baking cookies yet?" she said. That was standard
for: have you fucked?

"Oh, yeah. We've made a couple dozen by now."

"What kind?" In other words, was Jacob any good.

"Chocolate-chip," I said. "And he not only likes to *bake* them, he likes to *eat* them, too."

"Congratulations."

I promised Kat that Jacob and I would sacrifice a few hours of our newlywed-like, hermit existence to attend her soiree. Before we hung up, she told me to try and make myself look presentable.

"Wear the Chloe, okay?"

She was referring to a dress she made me buy months before. It cost eleven hundred dollars and I still hadn't worn it yet. Kat was a bad influence. Normally, I would never spend that much on an article of clothing. Because that's what my mother does. She hasn't looked at a price tag in twenty-five years. I try to do the reverse of whatever my mother does. But when I was with Kat, I found myself in the dressing room wearing the pricey item, and soon thereafter at the counter, handing over my credit card.

"You can't take it with you, and I know you're not leaving it to me so you might as well spend it." That was Kat's theory.

The night of the party, I was grateful to her for making me buy the damn dress. It was the sexiest thing I had in my closet—a cap-sleeved, black silk number that hit just below the knee; fitted, not so tight that I looked like a hooker, but tight enough to see some curves. The neckline was made of lace and fell to the middle of my chest in a V. It was hot, but in a good way, not in the Notice-Me-Please-Mr. Hefner style that permeates the L.A. smog.

When I came out of the bedroom, Jacob made a deep, moaning noise. It was the same noise he made when he was hungry.

"That's a badass little dress," he said.

Jacob's idea of dressing up was a clean pair of pants, and any shirt that had buttons on it. He wore a pair of dark trousers, and his usual white T-shirt under a fuzzy, green, vintage cardigan that looked exactly like something my grandfather might have owned in his youth. On our way out the door, Jacob checked himself in the mirror. He ran his fingers through his hair, then flattened it back down with his palms. But he didn't need any more adornment than that; he had cheekbones.

We were late getting to the party because there was an accident on the freeway. A big-rig carrying enough spring water to fill a Great Lake had overturned and shut down the two left lanes. When we finally did arrive, it took us another fifteen minutes to find a place to park.

"Hey, this used to be Big Al's Brake and Alignment," Jacob said when we got to Chick.

The store was nothing more than a renovated old garage. The floors were cement, and there were oil stains all over the place, but Kat and I had dolled it up by painting the walls pink, bringing in fresh flowers, and throwing creamy shag rugs around the room.

As soon as I stepped through the door, the pungent aroma of the crowd made me want to vomit. Imagine a synthetic fusion of each and every fashionable perfume in existence, then mix that with hair spray, champagne, and cigarette breath. Not a good medley for a delicate nose, but definitely Hollywood at it's finest.

The first person I saw when I walked in was a bald-headed man who was standing near the door, talking into the cell phone wire that hung from his ear. He yelled into thin air and waved his arms around as if he were trying to hail a cab. He kept rubbing his head with his palm, like he was checking to see if any hair had grown back. He looked like a complete fool but I could tell he thought he was the coolest guy in the room. He winked at me when he walked by and, for kicks, I almost tripped him, but I held back. I didn't want Jacob to think I was mean.

The second person who caught my eye was a girl I recognized from a movie. She'd played some sort of spy, but she couldn't act her way out of a paper bag. She had ashen hair, eyes like a mantis, and she was wearing a leopard-print miniskirt that wrapped her hips like cellophane. She also had one of my leather chokers around her neck. She made it look cheap. I had a vision of ripping it off of her and running back to the car, but I contained that urge, too. I was good at containing most of my negative urges. As long as I breathed through my mouth, so as not to be suffocated by the stench, I knew I'd be all right.

Kat came running up to us as soon as she saw me. "You wore the Chloe, thank God! You look fabulous!" she said, as she twirled around to show me her new look. "What do you think? Is the hair too suburban?"

"It looks good," I said.

The last time I'd seen Kat, her hair had been strawberry blond. That night it was the same shade as a cup of espresso. It was a different color almost every time I saw her. Along with the crochet-knit dress, the platform-heeled boots, and the three layers of eye makeup she had on, the effect was well over-the-top. Kat always wore too much eye makeup, but she never listened to me about it so I stopped bothering to tell her. I introduced her to Jacob. She gave him a glass of champagne, then immediately dragged him off to the jewelry case. I saw her pointing out my work, close-talking into his ear. They were gone for quite a while, and every time I looked over, Kat's mouth was moving. Jacob saw me and smiled. I prayed that Kat wasn't telling him about the time we were on

Space Mountain at Disneyland, when she made me laugh so hard I peed in my pants. She liked to tell that story to the men I was dating.

"Everybody is *raving* over Blanca's jewelry!" she said when she brought Jacob back. He had no idea who she was talking about.

"She means me," I explained. "I'm Blanca. Apparently no one likes my real name."

"Why do you call her Blanca?" Jacob said.

"Look at her, she's the color of a cadaver. Although you're not exactly the Coppertone girl yourself, Grace."

Later on, when Jacob was off talking with some journalist he knew, Kat hauled me into a dressing room to gossip.

"Did you see who's here? Tom Hanks's wife…over there, the one with the curly hair. She said she's coming back tomorrow to buy the tourmaline ring."

"Doesn't she have a name?" I said, thinking it highly unfair that the seemingly lovely woman who liked my ring was known only as someone's wife.

"I don't remember her name. Mrs. Hanks, how's that? Anyway, never mind her, what's the scoop on Grace? I want all the details."

Before I got a word out, Kat shouted, "Rita!"

"What?"

"Her name. Tom Hanks's wife. Her name's Rita. Sorry, go ahead. About Grace. Amazing Grace. Can we call him that? Is he amazing? Go on, you were saying…"

*Amazing Grace how sweet the sound that saved a wretch like me I once was lost but now I'm found, was blind but now I see*

Amazing Grace. Of course. Why hadn't I thought of that?

"Hello? Earth to Blanca? You were saying?"

"I wasn't saying anything."

"Don't be shy," Kat said.

"What? I like him, okay?" I was unable, for some reason, to verbalize anything else, though I felt so much more. "You spent fifteen minutes with him. What did you think?"

"He's *so you*," Kat said.

"What the hell does that mean?"

"He talks funny. Spirit this, soul that. Like he learned how to chat by reading Deepak Chopra books."

"He doesn't read Deepak Chopra books."

"Does he bathe?"

"Kat!"

"I'm kidding. He's darling, I mean it. Sweet as pie and he can't take his eyes off you."

On our way home, I apologized to Jacob for Kat's moderately overbearing personality.

"She's a good girl who just needs a lot of attention," I said.

"Kind of like the female version of Pete."

By the time Friday came around, Jacob said he needed to write. He was getting behind on his work.

"You're like a Siren, Trixie. You keep luring me in. I know I have to go home but I just can't stay away."

We resolved to spend the weekend apart. Jacob was going to nail himself to his computer for forty-eight hours, and then we'd reconvene on Monday, ready to start the cycle again. I was so used to sleeping next to him that I tossed and turned all night long. When I finally did drift off, I had a horrible nightmare. Jacob and I were in a hot tub, a fancy one, in the backyard of what looked like a hideously swank Hollywood mansion. We were kissing and relaxing and everything was fine. But then a strange gypsy woman materialized out of nowhere. She stood above us and shook her head, and I recognized her immediately as the fortune-teller who I'd met when I was a kid. In a flash she vanished as fast as she'd appeared, and when I looked back down, the hot tub had become a whirlpool. The swank mansion was a jungle. I fought my way to the edge of the water and climbed out. I screamed for Jacob to grab my hand. He just smiled at me and swam straight to the center of the vortex.

He was about to be sucked under when the phone woke me up.

"Are you *okay*?" Jacob said. "You sound like you've been wrestling."

I told him I'd had a bad dream.

"Can you meet me for breakfast?" he said. "I need to talk to you about something *really important*."

"What about spending the weekend apart?"

"Fuck spending the weekend apart."

# NINE

We met at Anastasia's Asylum an hour later. Jacob ordered a turkey sandwich on sun-dried tomato bread, a bowl of vegetable soup, chips, and a double cappuccino. After surveying his meal, I felt the need to point out that, to me, it seemed more like lunch than breakfast.

"Anything eaten before noon counts as breakfast, no matter what the content," Jacob explained.

"Culinary wisdom from a man who ate a taco on his way to work last Wednesday."

"You know," he said, pointing at me, "you're a bit of a food snob. Tacos are very nutritional. They contain all four food groups. I don't understand why you won't eat them."

"It's not that I won't eat them, it's more like I can't," I said. "They make my hands smell like they've been shoved up someone's ass. Who wants hands that smell like that?"

Jacob sniffed his fingers, as if the days-old scent of a Taco Bell Grande still lingered. "You've almost got me convinced," he said.

All I ordered was a glass of orange juice. I was nervous about whatever it was Jacob wanted to talk to me about. I sat and watched him eat, all the while wishing we were back at my apartment. That's when I came to the pathetic conclusion that almost everything about Jacob made me think of sex. Even fairly prosaic things—the way his lips puckered into a pout when he bit into his sandwich, the way he said certain words—minor words, like the abbreviated *oll korrect*, also known as *okay*. I don't know what it was about that word, but he uttered it with a kind of needy resignation, a newly canonized saint irrevocably giving in to temptation. When he pronounced the last syllable, it sounded like ice smashing on concrete. I purposely asked him questions I knew he would answer *okay* to, just to hear it come out. And sometimes he would say it when I least expected it, or at a completely inopportune time, like right before we left for work, and I'd have to start reciting the alphabet to keep focused.

Funny thing was, the more sex I had, the more I thought about it. You would assume it would be the other way around. You know, the less you get, the more you want. Not with me. Everything I do is ass backwards. For a small instant, I actually contemplated the possibility that the whole Jacob affair was based on nothing but sexual attraction, that the spiritual connection I thought I felt was simply my imagination justifying it for me. Only I knew that couldn't be the case. I concluded it was a direct result of the fact that there was so much more than desire to our relationship that my lust flourished.

My lust never flourished arbitrarily.

Life had never been that easy for me.

I asked Jacob what he wanted to talk to me about, and I had knots in my stomach anticipating his response. I was positive he was going to say the last week had all been a big mistake and he never wanted to see me again. Thinking about it made me wonder what scared Jacob. He looked serenely brave almost all the time. Even in my dreams, when he was being vacuumed into the depths of the sea, he looked like a hero.

Jacob finished the last of his coffee and was about to say something when I cut him off. "What are you afraid of?" I said.

He raised his brows, which meant I should repeat the question.

"What are you afraid of?" I said again. "You know, what scares you? Spiders, heights, *girlfriends*, small spaces, *commitment*. What?"

"Are you *okay*?"

I pretended I didn't understand, so he'd say it again.

"Are you *okay*?" he repeated. "You seem edgy."

Jacob reached across the table, grabbed my glass, and took a big swig of juice while I asked him, point-blank, if he was breaking up with me. He laughed so hard that orange pulp came out of his nose. The lopsided table where we were sitting had a chair on one side, and a tiny red couch on the other. I was on the couch. Jacob came over and squeezed in next to me. He lifted my legs on top of his and pulled me close, so that we were perpendicular to each other.

"No, I'm not breaking up with you. What's up with that?"

"I don't know," I said, embarrassed. "I'm just afraid this is going to end." I couldn't believe I was telling him what I really felt. I rarely told people what I really felt. Especially boys.

"Don't waste your time with fear," Jacob said calmly. "Fear won't keep you safe from being hurt."

"It could," I said.

"I don't think so."

"What if you're scheduled to fly to Japan and at the last minute you chicken out, then the plane you were supposed to be on explodes into a ball of fire over the ocean?"

"You can't think like that. That's not living."

"Everyone's afraid of *something*," I said.

"*Okay* then," he said, trying to think of something quickly. "I'm afraid of sleeping another night without you. How's that?"

"That's good. Say 'okay' again."

"What?"

"Nothing. Forget it." A, B, C, D…

"Tell me what you're so afraid of," Jacob said.

Shit, I thought, this could take all day. My life was ruled by my fears.

"I'm afraid of everything. Fear of being alone, fear of being hurt, fear of being made a fool of, fear of failure. I even have a fear of being kidnaped, although I also have some perverse sexual fantasies associated with that one, stemming from a made-for-TV movie about Patty Hearst that I saw when I was a kid, so it doesn't really count. Still, I think all my fears bleed from one big one."

"What's that?"

"Death," I said. "As long as I can remember being conscious of existence, I've been conscious of death. Eternal rest isn't some abstract concept to me. It's real. It chases me down like a dog behind a bicycle. I'm faster than it is, for the moment, but I might pop a tire any second and it'll sink it's teeth into my heels. Or worse, into the heels of someone I love."

"I'm tempted to tell you that you think too much, but I'm not really one to talk," Jacob said. "Henry Miller wrote something about fear making you fearless. It's a very powerful emotion. Use it to get what you want. I mean if it's going to rule your life, it might as well rule you to freedom, right?"

"But no matter what, it won't make you immortal. It can't save you from the inevitable end."

"Nothing can save you from the inevitable end."

"Exactly. Doesn't that scare you?"

"I'm not afraid to die," Jacob said. "I look forward to finding out what's on the other side some day."

"But what if it's *nothing*?"

"Well, if it's *nothing*, then what's there to worry about? *Nothing* can't possibly hurt you. The way I see it, there's only two alternatives in death: you either get eternal bliss, you know, some kind of spiritual heaven; or you just *aren't* anymore. Neither of them sound too horrifying to me."

I asked Jacob if he believed in God. My mother always told me it was rude to ask people their views on politics or religion, but I figured since Jacob and I had ingested a dozen ounces of each other's bodily fluids, anything was fair game.

"Not in the conventional sense," he said. "I was raised with a belief in God. My mother's Catholic. But I saw through the bullshit of organized religion by the time I was old enough to piss standing up. I think we are God. We all have that inside of us. And I believe we go on after we've turned to dust. Our souls, I mean."

"I wish I believed that. To me, it's highly improbable. In my soul, there's just a big hole where God's supposed to be."

"That has nothing to do with God. The hole, that is. Everyone feels that void. Everyone who has the balls to look inside themselves, anyway. It's what life's all about."

"What?"

"A search. We're all searching for something to fill up what I like to call that big, God-shaped hole in our souls. Some people use alcohol, or sex, or their children, or food, or money, or music, or heroin. A lot of people even use the concept of God itself. I could go on and on. I used to know a girl who used shoes. She had over two-hundred pairs. But it's all the same thing, really. People, for some stupid reason, think they can escape their sorrows."

Jacob's words hit me deep in the gut. I could have never articulated it like he did, but I guess I didn't have to. What he said was exactly how I felt sometimes: like a bottomless pit.

"Jacob," I said, "do you think there's anything in life that can fill up the hole? And not only fill it up, but *keep* it filled?"

"That's the real trick, isn't it?" he said incisively. "It's easy to plant a seed and sprinkle it with water, but once the sun scorches the ground, and the earth soaks up all the moisture, you're left with nothing but a thirsty little flower trying desperately to make it out of the dirt."

I hadn't been arid since I set eyes on Jacob Grace.

Neither of us said anything for a long time. We both stared out the window, thinking, I suppose, about the emptiness of it all. I wish I could have read Jacob's mind at that moment. I wanted to know what had created the chasm in his spirit. Maybe it was a broken heart. Maybe it was the rejection of his father. Or maybe it had always been there, like mine. Because really, I could blame my existential sadness on a lot of issues, but the truth is, it's been a part of me since Day One. When I was four years old and my mother would come to my bed to say goodnight, she'd turn off the light and I remember feeling it even then—the sensation that your heart weighs more than your body—that it might burst out of your chest and splatter all over the wall. I suppose it's called loneliness.

Just thinking about it started to depress me. I rerouted my mood by concentrating on another one of the holes in my being that I wanted Jacob to fill. Father forgive me for I have sinned, it's been eighteen hours since my last orgasm.

"Are you ever going to tell me what you wanted to talk to me about?" I finally said.

"Oh, right. Sorry. You kind of got me off on a tangent." He had the check in one hand, and was digging through his pocket with the other.

"Trixie," he said, "how do you feel about moving in together?"

# TEN

Jacob lived in a building that, when it rained, smelled like worms. We decided to live at my place until the lease was up, then we had bigger plans.

"This prison holds not our destiny," Jacob said, shaking his head in a momentary fit of impatience. He wasn't referring to our apartment, but to Los Angeles County and all of its surrounding areas, and he repeated the very same conviction every day when he came home from work, worn out by the traffic nightmare that was the 10 freeway.

"We have to escape as soon as we get the chance, *n'est pas?*"

"*Oui,*" I said.

And thus began our obsession: we were going to leave California.

"The *minute* I sell the book," Jacob said.

We had no idea when that was going to happen. He had to finish it first. But if and when it did get published, we resolved, once and for all, to defect. It became what we lived for. It fueled our days, it pacified our nights. It kept us driving down the congested highways when all we wanted to do was pull over and fly away. To finally cross the state line and not look back would be our renaissance. I told Jacob that we didn't have to wait. I had enough money. Between my income and my trust fund, we could live comfortably for a long time.

"We can go now," I said. "We can buy that little house with a porch. You can finish the book there. I'll make jewelry and learn how to bake pies, and we'll have sweaty sex whenever we want."

Jacob sighed. "I could never let you do that. I need to be able to support myself. You understand that, right?"

Of course I understood. The man had integrity. It was admirable as hell. But it meant our dreams would have to wait.

The day he officially moved in, Jacob didn't have much to bring over. Almost all of his clothes were already in my apartment. Besides his sparse wardrobe, he had a few boxes of books, his music collection, an old Steel Case desk and his computer. Pete helped him haul everything in. He teased Jacob about co-habitating with a television.

"It's not mine," Jacob said.

"Just count how often he watches it," Pete begged me.

Jacob and I were unpacking in the office, and Pete was just about to walk out the door when somebody knocked.

"I'll get it," Pete said.

I figured it was Sara picking him up, until I heard the discordant shrill of my mother's voice. Pete said hi to her and she asked him, in the most embarrassingly indignant way, if this was still Beatrice Jordan's apartment and, if so, who was he. Of course it was still my fucking apartment, Mom, and did I forgot to tell you, I'm living with two men now. We all sleep together and we're going to have babies and start a commune and what on earth will you tell your friends?

I know that's exactly what she was thinking.

"Shit," I whispered, "it's my mother."

Jacob's face became effervescent. "Cool," he said, and headed for the door. I ran in front of him.

"Mom," I said, "what are you doing here?"

Her thin lips formed the shape of an artificial smile, which caused her frosted, perfectly coiffed, chin-length bob to rise up as a unit. The expression on her tanned face said she was relieved to see me. She eyed Pete, then Jacob. "Beatrice, is this a bad time?"

She always asked me that, every time she showed up, which she did the third Sunday of every month, when she would come down from Santa Barbara to go shopping and have dinner with my brother and his family. I'd forgotten what day it was, otherwise I would have been conveniently absent from the apartment.

"Actually, it is kind of a bad time," I said.

Pete exited as fast as he could. My mother, meanwhile, inspected my coffee table. She asked if it was new.

"It's not new, I just painted it," I said.

"You painted it black, Beatrice?"

The table was clearly black, so unless she'd gone color-blind in the last thirty days, I didn't know why she was asking.

"Mom, this is Jacob. Jacob, meet Diane." I knew she was going to ask, so I beat her to the punch. "Jacob and I met a couple weeks ago. He's moving in today. Isn't that great?"

She looked Jacob up and down. I was pretty certain her immediate impression of him would be unfavorable. He looked poor, and she didn't like poor people. Especially if I happened to be sleeping with them.

"I didn't know you were seeing anybody, Bea."

Jacob took my mother's hand with both of his and greeted her just like he'd done when I first met him. He immediately engaged her in conversation and asked her if she wanted some coffee.

"No, thank you," she said. She was so uptight I thought a cork might pop out of her ass.

"Oh, sure you do, come on," Jacob said, still holding her hand. He dragged her into the kitchen while her eyes darted all over the place, I'm sure to see what she could pick on next. She always picked on something when she came over. She thought my apartment was small and shabby, even though the rent was astronomical. She found it preposterous that I didn't hire a decorator, and, in her opinion, hardwood was tacky if you could afford carpet. She was wearing her weight in gold, which was the reason I refused to work with that particular metallic element, and I could smell her signature three squirts of Chanel No. 19 from where I stood. It made me want to regurgitate my lunch directly into her brand new designer clutch. I resented the fact that she was in my house and that she was, I suspected, judging Jacob, when she didn't know him and could never in a million lifetimes understand what he was all about.

Jacob and my mother came out of the kitchen a few minutes later with cups in their hands. My mother stared at me like she knew something I didn't. I swear I saw her smirk. And she looked completely disarmed, wandering around, making small talk—mostly with Jacob—until she finished her coffee. Then she picked up her bag and went to the door.

"Well, Beatrice, I must say, you've found yourself a charming young man."

If I'd been standing when she said that, I guarantee I would have fallen over. I can tell when my mother is being patronizing, and I can tell when she's telling the truth. She meant it. I didn't know what Jacob had spiked her coffee with, but whatever it was, it had taken hold.

"I guess we'll see you tonight," she said on her way out.

"Tonight? What do you mean?" I said.

"You're joining us at your brother's for dinner. Jacob said you would."

I looked at Jacob. He gave me a wide, gaping smile, like he'd put itching powder down my pants and was waiting for me to start scratching.

"Fuck you," I whispered to him behind my mother's back.

"Mrs. Jordan," he said, "your daughter has quite a foul mouth, do you know that?"

"Yes, I know. Now don't be late tonight. Beatrice has a tendency to be late for family functions." She took Jacob aside. "Why don't you ask her to fix her hair and put on something nice. She can be so pretty when she tries."

It was a good thing I didn't own a gun.

As soon as my mother was safe inside the elevator, I hurled a pillow in the direction of Jacob's head. He caught it just as it sideswiped his ear, then he threw it back at me. I ducked, and he tackled me onto the couch. He tried to kiss my neck but I was too distracted to keep still.

"Now do you see how she is? That's what I was talking about. She just shows up here, barely says hello. She didn't even kiss me or anything. She was nicer to you than she was to me. I haven't seen her in weeks and she treated me like I was her garbage man."

"I think you're a little hard on her. She needs to be placated, that's all." He was trying to unbutton my shirt.

"Jacob, did you *fuck* her in the kitchen or what? I mean what the hell was that all about? Don't take this the wrong way, but you are not the kind of man she would normally take to."

"I give off good vibes," he said. "Kids, dogs, and middle-aged divorcées like me."

"I'll bet they do."

"You don't give her enough credit. At least she was here. At least she tries."

"Whatever," I said. "Let's just do it and forget about her."

# ELEVEN

My younger brother, Cole, was off in Washington D.C. finishing up law school. Last time I'd talked to him he had political aspirations. My older brother, Chip, the one we had the pleasure of dining with, is a hot-shot film producer. He lucked out with a small-time action flick that ended up making millions at the box office and, consequently, scored a five-picture deal with Warner Bros. He thinks his shit smells like daisies because of it. I'd bet a g-note his shit smells more like month-old chili con carne.

Chip is fat; has black, greasy hair; and a black mole on his chin where a lone black whisker grows. He lives in the posh neighborhood of Holmby Hills with his wife, Elise, who is not fat, and his son, Chad, who is also not yet fat but has the propensity. Their twelve-thousand square-foot, Tudor-inspired abode is right down the street from the Playboy mansion.

I usually made it a point to only see Chip on holidays, and Thanksgiving was still over six months away. I cursed Jacob the entire drive to Chip's house. Jacob found my anxiety wholly amusing. I think he saw it as writing fodder. To Jacob, everything was writing fodder.

My mother's car was in the driveway when we pulled in. That meant we were late, even though we were ten minutes ahead of our scheduled arrival time. I gave Jacob one last chance to back out. He stepped in front of me and rang the bell.

Every time I walked into Chip's house, the formality of it made me feel like I was walking onto the set of *Dynasty*. I expected Linda Evans to swoop down the brass staircase and give me a coquettish little smile, like the one she gave in the TV show's intro. Instead, Elise answered the door for us. Elise was a petite blond, with lips pumped full of collagen. She was one of those failed actresses—the cutest, most popular girl from the Midwestern town she came from, who moved to Hollywood after high school expecting to become the world's next great thespian, but just ended up contributing another dime to the dozen. Elise never even got as far as hooking herself an agent, but as luck would have it, she met Chip at The Whiskey Bar one fateful evening. I guess she figured he was her best ticket out of the ant-infested, two-room bungalow she shared with a couple of bargain-basement strippers.

Chip ruled Elise's life. He instructed her how to talk, how to dress, and which charities she could support. I had a strong, ever-present notion to tell her to kick Chip in the balls and stand up for herself, but if she didn't mind, I figured it wasn't my business to do so. I got along okay with Elise. She was no Rhodes scholar, but she was nice; she called me the black sheep of the family and meant it as a compliment.

"Beatrice! I'm so glad you came," she said. "And you must be Jacob. Diane told us all about you. We hear you're a writer."

They probably had his social security number and shoe size, too.

My mother appeared from behind the door, took Jacob by the elbow, and with Chad in tow, gave him a tour of the house. Jacob couldn't have cared less about the damn house, but he appeased her nonetheless, pretending he was enthralled. While the three of them walked the grounds, Elise took me up to her closet to show me one of the new dresses she'd been given for an upcoming movie premiere. The garment was long, red, skin-tight, and had a strange green stitching around the neck and hem. It looked like a bloodstained mermaid, but I didn't have the heart to tell that to Elise; she was so riveted by it. She wanted to know if I would make her a bracelet and necklace to match.

"With star sapphires," she said. "I don't care how much they cost, I just want my accessories to be as unique as this dress."

"It'll be a challenge," I said. "But I'm sure I can whip something up."

Chip and Elise had a cook and a servant, and we ate in the dining room on the good china: roasted chicken, garlic mashed potatoes, romaine lettuce with rosemary vinaigrette, and fancy Italian wine. Jacob told Chip it was the best wine he'd ever had, and my brother immediately went off on a ten minute-long tangent about the year it was bottled, the region it came from, how rare it was, and how much the local hot spots charged for it when you ordered it there.

"I ship it in, right from Chianti," Chip said, mistakenly assuming he was impressing Jacob. "You're only allowed to bring in a certain number of bottles a year, you know, so consider yourself lucky." Chip's gruff, I'm-better-than-you snort shook the table. Jacob laughed along with Chip in a fake, Great Gatsby, old-money sort of voice, obviously mocking my brother. I was the only one who picked up on it, and I had to put my napkin in front of my mouth to hide my amusement. When Jacob took another gulp of his wine, I had visions of him squirting it like a fountain through his teeth. I'd seen him do that in the shower—he had quite a projectile range. I was disappointed when he swallowed.

Dessert was a heavenly concoction of ginger-flavored

crème brûlée—the highlight of the evening—and I contemplated sneaking a ramekin of it into my purse—an idea motivated by the quick fantasy I had that centered around my new roommate spreading it all over my body, then licking it off. The way in which Jacob slowly lapped it from his spoon told me he was thinking the same thing.

We were having coffee and brandy in the living room when my mother asked Jacob about his family.

"Tell us more about the Graces," she said.

I was about to order her not to pry into his life when Jacob cut me off and proceeded to give my mother a spiel I didn't follow at all. Apparently when he'd told her his last name that afternoon, she'd asked him what his father's first name was. He said Thomas, and my mother assumed that meant his father's name was Thomas Grace. What she didn't know was that Jacob went by his mother's last name. He was no relation to this Thomas Grace guy, a man whose social calendar my mother followed by reading *Town and Country* and *W*. Evidently, Thomas Grace was some big Internet mogul, owned a Renoir, attended every important gala in New York City, *and* had been recently divorced.

"Where is Thomas Grace now?" my mother asked Jacob.

"Oh, he's off on his yacht, cruising around the Greek isles for the next few months," Jacob said.

He was making the whole damn thing up, of course, and I assumed I finally knew why my mother liked him so much. She thought he was a dot-com kid. She thought I'd hit the jackpot.

"Why did you do that?" I asked Jacob on our way home.

"It was funny," he said.

"It was not funny."

"Then why are you laughing?"

I tried to curtail my level of entertainment. "How am I going to explain this to her, Jacob? Now she really is going to hate you."

"Tell her my father and I had a falling out and we don't speak anymore. That's not exactly a lie. By this time next year, we'll be gone and she'll never know the difference."

"Oh, yes she will. You don't know my mother. She's going to hound you until you invite her to the weekend spread in the Hamptons, trust me on this. And what if she meets your mother some day?"

"My mother will go along with it. She's a good sport."

I couldn't wait to meet Jacob's mother.

"I'm going to have to call her tomorrow and tell her the truth," I said.

"Why do you have to burst her bubble?" He was still chuckling.

"Jacob, I'm serious."

"This from a woman who once told a lover that her parents helped put Nelson Mandela in prison."

"The reason I told him that was because I wasn't planning on him being around long enough for it to matter and—" I froze. That thought gave me pause: what if this whole thing— what if I—was a big joke to Jacob? What if he was the best actor in the universe and I meant nothing to him? What if he had no intention of taking me any further south than Anaheim?

Jacob knew what I was thinking. He looked my way to try and get a reading on my expression, and almost swerved into the median.

"Watch the road, Slick."

"Do you think I think that?" he said. "Trixie, answer me. Do you think you won't be around long enough for it to matter?"

I didn't say anything. I just tried to look mopey.

"I have a surprise for you," he said. "Look behind me."

I reached under his seat and found something wrapped in aluminum foil. It was a dish of crème brûlée.

"Jacob, did you steal this?"

He howled. "No! God, ye of little faith. Elise gave it to me. I told her it was our first official night living together, that we wanted to celebrate. She thought it was romantic."

It was. It was fucking romantic as all hell. And I was an idiot.


Jacob called my mother the next day. He apologized to her and confessed that he was from Pasadena.

"I'm nothing but trailer trash," he said with pride.

He gave my mother the whole rigamarole about how his father deserted him when he was a baby, probably for sympathy points. And he kissed up to her a little more by claiming he only said he was related to Thomas Grace because of me.

"What you think is really important to Beatrice," he said. "She just wanted you to like me."

When he got off the phone, he said my mother laughed and thanked him for telling her the truth. She was still being nice to him.

"Her doctor must have her back on Valium," I said.

# TWELVE

All Jacob needed was a place to write. I gave him the spare bedroom in our apartment, and you would have thought he'd been crowned lord and master of the world, he was so happy. He'd just sold a story to a big travel magazine, loosely based on the time he spent in Costa Rica, and with the money he made on that he was able to retire from the *Weekly*, at least for a couple months, and work on his book full-time. I was at my studio during the day so he had the place to himself.

When Jacob was working, he had the dedication of a trained monkey. I would leave the house around nine and he'd already be at his computer. He kept his right elbow on his desk and his head in his hand, trance-like, unless he was typing. He typed like a monkey, too. When he was on a roll, it sounded like he was shelling out a thousand words a minute. I expected to see nothing but jumbled letters when I looked at the screen after one of his typing marathons, but I always found coherent sentences. He was the real deal.

When I came home, at six o'clock or so, he'd still be sitting there, either letting it pour like mad, or in fierce combat, desperately battling with wherever his words came from, to spit out something he deemed worthy. His hair would be even messier than normal, and there would be a random bowl, a browning apple core, or a bag of potato chips on his desk. That was the only evidence I had that he'd moved all day. Sometimes he'd stay like that late into the night, forgetting to eat, to change his clothes, or to shower. I felt like I actually spent less time with him once he moved in, but I could live with the fact that I didn't see him all day long, or barely speak a word to him. I knew he was there and that's what counted. For such a small human, Jacob's presence filled a hell of a lot of space.

Occasionally, Jacob left the house when he was done working. He'd wake me up and ask me if I wanted to steal around town with him.

"I need some fucking air," he'd say.

Sometimes I went, other times I just let him wind down by himself. If he felt like company and I was too tired, he'd call Pete. Pete was always good for a late-night drink and a game of pool. But Jacob's favorite place was the beach. More often than not, he came back wet, although he claimed he never actually planned on going in the water, he would just find himself there and not be able to help it.

A couple months after we'd been living together, I was lying on the couch, captivated by a *Jeffersons* marathon on Nick-at-Nite, when Jacob came out of the office. It was past midnight and he'd been working all day. I heard him take a quick shower, then he moseyed into the living room. His eyes were bloodshot, his face was vacant. He looked like a rag that had been submerged in water and wrung out until every drop of liquid had been drained from its fabric.

"Are you okay?" I said.

He rubbed his face and sighed. "Nine hours, and all I have to show for it are three lousy fucking pages of shit."

He disappeared into the kitchen. I heard him open a few jars and slam a few drawers. Five minutes later he came back with a peanut butter and jelly sandwich and a bottle of beer. After he ate, he lay down next to me. He buried his head in the curve of my neck and held me like his life depended on it. He smelled like soap and sweat and Skippy, and I could have died happy right there. I begged for us to be beamed up. A space-age Ascension. Heaven without the pain of passing on. God, if, by some slim chance, you actually exist, I thought, prove it to me by carrying us away because it can't get any better than this.

I stroked Jacob's hair while I watched George nag his neighbor, Helen. He was on her case about being married to a honky. It was the third episode I'd seen that night. I remember getting ready to comment out loud that Lenny Kravitz didn't look anything like his mother when Jacob started mumbling. His eyes were closed. My eyes were on Weezie. She was telling George to shut up and leave Helen alone. George acted like he wore the pants in the family, but he knew better than to mess with Weezie.

"Trixie?" Jacob said.

"Hmm?"

"Thanks."

"For what?"

"For understanding. For space. For not bitching at me because we haven't left the house together in a week."

I kissed the top of his head. "Don't mention it."

He repositioned his face up a little. Then he clung even tighter to me, opened his eyes, and outlined my profile with his finger. His lips barely touched my ear.

"I love you," he whispered. He said it so quietly I wasn't sure I was meant to hear it at all.

I wanted to say it back. Obviously, I felt it. I think I'd felt it since Day One. But I couldn't say it. I didn't want to jinx anything. I'd said "I love you" to boyfriends before, only I don't think I ever really meant it. It rolled off my tongue too easily, too unaffected to have come from any real, subterranean emotional region. Everything was different with Jacob. But I was afraid that if I told him how I really felt, he would go away—and I didn't mean leave—although that was part of it—I meant disappear. Vanish. Cease to exist. I hadn't forgotten the prophecy of that damn fortune-teller who cursed me when I was twelve. Not that I believed her, but it was a good excuse to feed my wimpy, once-abandoned heart. If I recognized Jacob as The One, who knew what might happen to him.

"Here's the thing," Jacob continued, "I feel like we grew in the same womb or something. Like we've been connected from the beginning by blood and veins. Siamese soul lovers, if there could ever be such a thing."

I looked down at him, wide-eyed and speechless.

"I know," he said. "That's weird as hell, I know."

It was the coolest thing anyone had ever said to me.

I opened my mouth—I was going to try to get the words out, I really was, but Jacob put his hand over my lips.

"You don't have to say anything. Just know how I feel, *okay*?"

He turned onto his side and watched the screen.

"Hey, *The Jeffersons*," he said. "You know, Lenny Kravitz doesn't look anything like his mother."

# THIRTEEN

Based on past experience, I held steadfast to the notion that mothers of my boyfriends gave me the willies. I assumed they were too judgmental, like when they looked at you they knew you were having sex with their kid, and that's what went through their minds. They saw it. They saw their darling little boys, the ones they used to change diapers for, just pounding away on some idiotic girl who came along to steal their baby; hogging his penis, his time, and everything else. That had to make a mother a little leery. Or maybe it was just me. But when I finally met Joanna Grace, I got a completely different impression. We'd spoken over the phone a few times, and talking to her was like talking to someone my age. She used the word "cool" and didn't sound like some hag trying to be hip. And I could tell she liked me even before she met me, just by her tone of voice. Jacob must have told her about some good character traits he thought I had, otherwise there would have been no reason for that.

Jacob and I drove to Pasadena to a neighborhood that was filled with tiny Arts and Craft–style homes. Joanna's was painted the color of a canary. When we walked in, she hugged Jacob for a good thirty seconds, even though she'd just seen him a few days before. It was obvious that she adored the hell out of him. After getting a closer look at her, I surmised she'd had Jacob very young—there was no way she was a day over fifty. And they only vaguely resembled each other, Joanna and Jacob. Her complexion was much darker than his, her face rounder. She wore her hair in a bun on top of her head like a ballerina. As soon as Jacob introduced us, Joanna hugged me too, with real gusto, and gave me a kiss. My own mother never greeted me like that. Not once in my whole life.

Then again, I don't think my mother ever really wanted kids, she just had nothing else to do. She tended to get pregnant every time my dad got a new girlfriend. She thought that would be some kind of lightning bolt to his dick, like it would make him come to his senses and love her or something. I guess after giving birth to three of his offspring, she finally figured out that was never going to happen. That's when she began investing all her emotions in Gucci.

Joanna touched my cheek and told me I had beautiful skin. "Like you've never seen the sun," she said.

She took my hand and led me into the kitchen, where she was making angel hair pasta, salad from spinach that she grew in her backyard, and a batch of cinnamon cookies still in the oven.

Throughout dinner, I quizzed her on Jacob. I wanted to know what he was like as a kid, and any other dirt she felt like digging up.

"Jacob was a daydreamer," Joanna said. She showed me a picture of his little league team and asked if I could pick him out of the group. It was easy. Even as a ten-year-old he had that intense, Jacob gaze—as if his river ran deeper than the oblivious tykes he was sitting next to.

"Jacob used to lose things all the time," Joanna said. "He was a selectively absent-minded young man. He could recite entire chapters from his favorite books in the middle of dinner, but ask him to stop at the market and grab a box of cereal on his way home from school, you could just forget about it."

After dinner, Joanna burned lavender incense. She told me she'd named her son Jacob because she loved Bob Dylan. She'd met Jacob's father at a Bob Dylan concert.

"And Bob named his son Jacob," she said. "But I think he spells it with a *k*."

I wanted to ask Joanna more about Jacob's father, since she brought him up, but I just wasn't sure he was an appropriate topic of conversation. Whenever Jacob talked about the man, which was rarely, it was always with a dark pain in his eyes, like he'd just stepped from sunlight into shade. He tried to mask it, I could tell. And not for my sake either, for his own, so I tried not to torment him with questions. But later on, Joanna showed me a photo album and there he was. I thought it was an old picture of Jacob until Joanna pointed to it and said, "That's Jacob's father."

His name was Thomas Doorley. And if Joanna had told me that she'd cut the man's head off and sewn it onto Jacob's neck, I would have believed her. It was almost eerie, the resemblance between father and son. They had the same eyes, the same hair, the same smile. Thomas couldn't have been much older than twenty when the picture I saw was taken. In it, he was sitting on a grassy hillside with a cigarette between his fingers, wearing a denim shirt and a sweet grin on his face. He looked like a harmless little hippy poet, his head tilted to one side, just like Jacob tilted his when he was thinking about something serious.

I learned that Thomas Doorley was a writer—a published writer of three novels and one book of short stories who had enjoyed mediocre, if not somewhat cult-like success, in the seventies. He lived in Northern California, somewhere outside of San Francisco, but they hadn't heard from him in a couple of decades. I pondered out loud why Jacob never told me his father was a writer.

"I don't know, I guess I don't really feel like I know enough about his life to talk about him."

"Why don't you use his last name?"

"Because I don't want it. I don't want anything from him, including his fucking name."

When we got home from dinner, we ran into Greg in the lobby. I'd seen him a dozen times since Jacob moved in, but never when we were actually together. Greg looked stoned.

"Hi Bea. Hi Henry," he said.

We made it into the elevator before we burst into laughter.

"You know, I've never read any of my father's books," Jacob confessed before we fell asleep that night.

"Would you mind if I read one?"

"Go ahead. There's one on the shelf. I've just never opened it." He cleared his throat and curled up around me. "Let me know if it's any good."

# FOURTEEN

Jacob and I had a date at the Getty Center. I was supposed to meet him there at one o'clock to see a visiting exhibit that made him foam at the mouth. Some front-line war photographer named Robert Capa.

"The guy had an eye for truth," Jacob said.

Capa was one of Jacob's favorite photographers. Jacob, I'd noticed, had a lot of favorites: people, places, and things he was passionate about, that he knew everything about, that he inhaled like oxygen. He wasn't one of those gray individuals. He either loved something, or his indifference bordered on autism. Jacob told me, with the utmost level of zeal, that Capa had been friends with Ernest Hemingway, and had died young after stepping on a landmine in Indochina.

"Legend has it, they found him with his camera still in his hands."

To Jacob, that made him a hero.

Jacob was the only person I knew in Los Angeles who actually used the public transportation system. He'd taken the bus to the museum and made it there on time. I was late because I drove from my studio and forgot to make a parking reservation. In Los Angeles, cars, not people, need reservations to go to museums. I had to flirt with the attendant to get in. After a little batting of the eyes, he finally agreed to give me a space, only he made me wait half an hour. I guess he thought I was cute, but not *that* cute.

The Getty complex sat atop a hill, high above the city, a gigantic maze of pure white geometric shapes and sparkling panes of glass the size of city blocks. Once I parked, I had to take a slow-paced tram up to the cluster of buildings that housed the various museums. The train was just as white as everything else, and riding it felt like being on mass transit to heaven, a simile which became all the more apropos as we started up the track, because as we ascended, I actually thought I was looking at hell below me.

It wasn't hell. It was the 405 freeway.

I saw Jacob as soon as I stepped off the train. He was sitting on a travertine bench with two little boys who had grape popsicle juice dripping down their shirts. One boy was sandy-haired and looked about six years old. The other had darker hair and, I guessed, was closer to eight. A pug-nosed woman I assumed to be their mother stood at close range, probably because she pegged Jacob as a child molester. Hell, he *was* wearing a mood ring on his finger—the one I'd given him a few days before. I made it for him as a five-month anniversary present. It was a dark gem, encased in textured silver, and it had the word *Grace* engraved on it's underside.

The three of them, Jacob and the boys, were deep in conversation. When I walked over, I heard the older boy tell Jacob that a shark could beat up a dog. His little brother told him no, a dog could beat up a shark. Only he said it like this: *shawk.*

"Sharks have bigger teeth," the older one said.

"But dawgs can wun. Shawks can't."

"Dogs can't swim," big brother told him.

"Yes they can. Dawgs can too swim. Jacob, can dawgs swim?"

"Yep, most dogs can swim," Jacob said sweetly. He must

have liked the younger one better, otherwise I'm sure he would have explained the aerodynamics of a shark's swim versus doggie paddle. It would be no match.

Jacob saw me and smiled. "Trixie, you made it." As soon as he said my name, the boys giggled.

"I see you made some friends," I said.

"Is that your weal name? Twixie?"

I lied and told him it was. He was the most adorable kid I'd ever seen. He didn't even look real. He had a sunny face and a lopsided smile. I was surprised mother-snot-face hadn't sold him to a television studio yet. He had the potential to be a millionaire by the age of ten and dead of an overdose by twenty.

"Hey, Jacob, is she your girlfwend?" he said.

When Jacob told them I was indeed his girlfriend, the older brother informed me that I was late and that I should kiss Jacob and say I was sorry. He said it with the voice of a drill sergeant. To put it bluntly, the kid was a brat—probably jealous because his cute little brother got more attention.

I apologized to Jacob for being late and planted a little peck on his cheek. The boys practically fell off their seats at that, like we were better than Saturday morning cartoons.

"Oh, to be so effortlessly entertained," I said.

Jacob and I decided to see some paintings before we dove into the photography. They had a small Van Gogh collection at the Getty, and I'd stopped to dwell on Vincent's irises when I heard Jacob call for me. He was standing across the hallway in front of a large canvas of a woman, looking into her eyes as if the two of them were conversing. Her dark hair was pulled back off of her face. She looked regal, mysterious, and sad. Her name was Princess Leonilla, or something like that. She was a Russian-born Parisian.

"She reminds me of you," Jacob said.

I wasn't at all flattered by the comparison. "She needs an eyebrow wax. I have better eyebrows than that."

"Forget her eyebrows. I'm talking about her gaze, about what's behind that façade. There's a lot going on in there."

"What are you saying?"

"Still water runs deep."

One of the many things I adored about Jacob was that he could see me in things like the painting of an ugly Russian princess. He did that all the time. A song would come on the radio, or we'd go see a movie, and he always managed to find some reason why they were all about me.

"You're the world's muse, Trixie."

"I just want to be your muse."

"Done."

Jacob was right about Capa. If ever photojournalism could be described as breathtaking, I thought, this man's certainly qualified. It was obvious to me why Jacob liked him so much. Capa was able to find the remains of beauty in the fractured, often ugly nature of truth and humanity. Jacob had that gift as well. The fact that he loved me proved it.

As we wandered the floor that displayed Capa's work, Jacob bombarded me with information about the photos, the same details that were written on the cards next to the frames, only he didn't have to read them.

"That's a loyalist there in the tree, he was killed hanging telephone wire," Jacob said. "This was taken in China, late thirties, I think. I love this one." It was a bunch of school children playing in the snow. "Hey, check it out. William Faulkner."

"I hate William Faulkner," I said. I walked right past that photo, not even bothering to look.

Jacob stopped in his tracks and glared at me as if I'd just threatened to behead his mother.

"What?" I said. "You have to read a page six hundred times before it sinks in. After one sentence, I break out in a cold sweat. I don't get it. And I was valedictorian!"

Jacob laughed, but with the laugh of a man who knew the punch line to a joke you were in the middle of telling.

"Wait until we move to the Mississippi delta," he said. "Then you'll get it."

We spent over two hours at the Capa exhibit. By the time we'd dissected each and every photo, Jacob was starving. Jacob was always starving. For such a skinny guy, he sure had an appetite.

"Let's head back into town. I know this great Italian place on San Vicente," he said.

I left Jacob at the coffee kiosk that sat in the museum courtyard. He wanted to grab a quick espresso before we got back in line for the train.

"Meet me in the bookstore when you're done," I said.

I bought one of Capa's books for Jacob, and another collection of photographs by a guy named William Eggleston— his pictures sent me into a complete tizzy. They brought more surreal exaltation to what only an idiot might refer to as mundane southern Americana than any other photographer I'd ever seen. I yearned to be there immediately: Greenwood, Huntsville, Knoxville, Montgomery, Memphis, anywhere any of the photos were taken. I wanted to live someplace sluggish and normal, near a truck-stop where we'd eat grits and drink coffee every morning. I wanted a little house with honey-colored walls and grandma-looking furniture from the seventies, maybe an organ in the living room, a cheap painting of a saint above our bed, and Formica countertops in the kitchen. We'd pretend we were Baptists so we could go to their church on Sundays and hear the choir sing. Jacob would write all day, and I'd work as a waitress. Pudgy, perspiring men would give me an extra dollar tip because I'd wear my uniform a few inches too short, but that's as far they would push it because the whole town would know about me and Jacob. We'd be recognized as the lovebirds—the sappy couple who held hands, kissed, and never mowed their lawn.

My heart ached for Jacob to finish his book so we could get out of the dazzling shithole we were stuck in and live happily ever after.

I looked at my watch and realized Jacob had been off getting coffee for almost half an hour. I couldn't wait to show him the book. When I went back outside, he was nowhere near where I left him. I wandered over to the train platform and saw him sitting on the same bench I'd seen him on earlier that afternoon. He wasn't drinking any coffee and he had a weird look on his face.

"Is it all right if we skip dinner and just go home?" he said.

I told him it was. "Is there something wrong?"

He stood up and took my hand. "Nothing I really want to talk about right now, if that's okay," he said soberly.

We drove home in silence. When we got back to the apartment, Jacob went into the office and didn't come out for hours. Finally I couldn't take it anymore. I knocked on the door and walked in. He had one elbow on the arm of his chair, and a pen in his mouth. His face had softened a little, but he still looked troubled.

"Hey," he said. "What's up?"

"I don't know. You tell me."

I sat on top of his desk. He put the pen down and set his palms on my legs. He rubbed my quadriceps gently with his thumbs, and stared at the blank wall, transfixed at nothing.

I sighed. "Jacob, what's wrong? You haven't said ten words since we left the museum. Please talk to me."

His brow furrowed. "It's Nina," he said.

Nina, I thought, this can't be good. "What about Nina?" I said, trying, I repeat *trying,* to stay calm.

"I saw her at the Getty today."

"You saw her? Why didn't you tell me you saw her?"

"I just did tell you."

"I mean while we were there."

"She saw you."

"What do you mean she saw me? How did she see me?"

"She saw us in front of the fountain."

I hardly thought it was fair that she got to see me but I didn't get to see her, the dyke-bitch. I rewound my memory fast and remembered that Jacob and I had stood in front of the fountain and kissed before he got in line for coffee. It wasn't just a little lip-smack either, it was a full-on, grand, public display of affection, with tongues and googlyeyes and everything. Art made us horny. I hoped Nina had seen that. I hoped she put that in her smack pipe and smoked it.

I got down off the desk and turned my back to Jacob. I stared out the window at the amusement park on the pier. I could just barely see the Ferris wheel. It was all lit up, going around and around. There was only a handful of people on it, and I wondered if it went faster when it was virtually empty. I had a feeling that if I watched it for too long, I would curse it and it would roll right into the water.

"Jacob," I said. "Why are you so upset about seeing her? I see Greg all the time, you don't see me moping around and locking myself in my room over it."

"I hadn't seen her since before I left for Costa Rica."

"So?"

"That was almost a year ago."

"So?"

"So, she's in bad shape. I shouldn't have just cut her off like that."

"Jacob, *she* dumped *you*, remember?"

"I asked her to come over tomorrow. I have to talk to her."

"You made a *date* with her?"

"It's not a date. She——"

"You have a time and a place? I'm pretty sure that's the definition of a date. You have a date with your ex-girlfriend tomorrow. That's nice. That's just fucking great!"

"Why are you getting so upset? You're not even letting me——"

"Do you *want* to see her? Was it your idea to get together?"

"It's not that simple."

"Just answer yes or no."

"You don't understand."

"Well then fucking enlighten me," I said, much louder than I'd planned. I smelled some kind of food coming from one of the apartments on our floor; it was buttery.

Jacob took a deep breath. "How can I fucking enlighten you when you're yelling and screaming and acting like a baby? Mellow out, will you? Then we can talk."

I stormed out of the room and slammed the door in his face. I didn't like being called a baby. I felt betrayed and deceived, and I feared I'd never get to be a William Eggleston character. Deep down, I knew I probably had no cause to be so upset, but my memory got the best of me. I flashed back to the day my father left. I saw him trying to get out the door while my mother held on to the arm of his shirt. He pulled his wrist up into his sleeve so that all she could grab was his cuff. Her grip slipped, and off he went—he just walked away, appendage-less. I pretended he'd been in a car accident and had lost his hand but would persevere over tragedy, just like that one-armed guy from Def Leppard.

After my father walked out the door, my mother ran to the window, her waterproof mascara shellacked to her lashes as tears ran down her cheeks. She shrieked so loud it sounded like she was being stabbed. Now that she has half of his fortune, she's reconstructed her poise, but back then she was just prideless and pitiful.

I heard a voice in my head. It said: I would rather be alone than ever be my mother. I will leave before I am left.

My intuition told me I was out of control but there was nothing I could do.

Jacob opened the door of the office and leaned against the wall. The smell of melted butter made my mouth water. I wondered if Jacob could smell it—he'd been hungry for hours.

"Beatrice, can we please talk about this? It's more complicated than you're allowing for and—"

"Shut up, Jacob. I don't want to hear it." I dug through my jacket for a set of keys. Jacob looked at me as if he'd never seen me before in his life.

"Did you just tell me to shut up?" he said.

Popcorn. That's what I smelled. Someone on our floor was making popcorn. Maybe it was Greg, I thought. Maybe I should knock on his door and have a handful of popcorn and fuck him. I wondered how Jacob would like that. He could fuck Nina and I could fuck Greg. Just like old times.

It was kind of ironic, actually. Greg had done infinitely worse things to me when we were together, but nothing he did ever hurt me. Because I didn't care, that was the core of the issue. I'd never cared before. I didn't know how to act like a normal person and be in love at the same time. Nor did I know how to process fear.

I was damaged goods. A cripple.

Pathetic.

I couldn't find my keys. I had to take Jacob's off the table. He asked me where I was going but I pretended like I couldn't hear him.

"Please don't leave right now, Beatrice. Please. I need to talk to you." He was that cute little boy from the museum and I was his mother running off without him.

"What do you care?" I shouted on my way out the door. "Maybe you can invite Nina over while I'm gone!"

"Hey!" he shouted back. "Maybe I will!"

It pissed me off that Jacob didn't follow me down the hall. I wanted him to run after me and grab my sleeve. I wouldn't have hid my hand like my father. I would have let Jacob take hold of me and he would have refused to let me go.

Instead, he just stood in the doorway and watched the elevator close.

# FIFTEEN

I had no idea where I was going. I thought about heading to Kat's, but she would have wanted to look Nina up and threaten her life or something, plus Kat lived in West Hollywood. To get to her apartment, I would have had to either drive down Wilshire, take Sunset, or get on the highway. Wilshire had too many lights; Sunset, too many curves; and California highways depress me the way bad smells do. I avoided the highways at all costs, even if side streets added an extra dozen miles to my trip.

The first place I stopped was the Third Street Promenade—an outdoor shopping mecca right around the corner from where we lived. It was nothing special, just a long boulevard of mass-produced, trendy clothing emporiums, lots of cheap, tourist-trap restaurants, and a bunch of movie theaters. I went directly to the Cineplex. I didn't want to see a movie or anything, but I was fixated on popcorn. The Cineplex had the best popcorn. It was the only theater on the Promenade that made it fresh. All the other establishments had it shipped to them in gigantic plastic bags. The girl in the ticket booth thought it was a strange request, only wanting the popcorn. She let me in anyway, and I got a bucketful with butter and salt, then I went back outside.

I sat on a bench with my popcorn and watched a rickety old man play drums in front of Banana Republic. He'd set up a full set right in the middle of the sidewalk, and he had a small crowd of fans congregated around him while he rocked-out, accompanied by prerecorded music on a boom box. He looked like a fossil and he was the worst drummer I'd ever heard. The erratic rhythm of his beats made me think of Jacob and Nina having sex. That's when I decided to go over to Pete and Sara's. They knew Nina. They could give me objective advice. Or at least tell me what she looked like.

When I rang the bell, Sara asked who was there, and she didn't seem at all surprised to hear it was me, even though I'd never dropped in on them before. She gave me a strong, maternal hug. It made me hope she'd get pregnant soon. She was going to be a good mother, I could tell. Even if Jacob was going to dump me and get back together with Nina, and I'd never see Sara again, or meet her future gamine child. Our never-quite-blossomed friendship would become a casualty of a breakup.

Pete and Sara's apartment was small. Their old wool couch had white stuffing peaking through the seams, the cushions on the dining chairs were plastic, and the window screens were fraying apart, but there wasn't a thing out of place, and the gray carpet on the floor had recently been cleaned, I could tell by the way the living room smelled. Like a new car.

"Pete just went to your place," Sara said. She shut the door behind me.

"Jacob called him?"

She nodded. I felt like I was back in high school. I hated high school, it was the most godforsaken four years of my life and the last place I wanted to return.

"Sara, what did Jacob say?"

"I don't know. All Pete told me was that Jacob bumped into Nina today, and that you freaked out about it and ran off for no reason."

"I didn't freak out." That was a slight exaggeration on Jacob's part. He was a writer, and writers exaggerate. "Besides, maybe if he would've talked to me first, instead of staring embryonically at the wall, I wouldn't have felt the need to freak."

I offered Sara some popcorn. She took a tiny handful.

"What's Nina like?" I said.

"A mess. And I'm not just saying that to make you feel better." Sara said she'd heard Nina's drug problem had gotten worse since she and Jacob broke up.

"She stopped by the salon once to ask about Jacob after he moved in with you. She wanted to know where he lived but I wouldn't tell her. She was so strung out she could barely walk."

"I thought she was a lesbian now."

"That was just a phase."

"Do you think Jacob still loves her?"

Sara gave good dramatic pause. "I've know Jacob for five years. I have *never*—and I mean *never*—seen him happier than he is now. With you. Do you want something to drink?"

"No, thanks."

Sara opened a bottle of red wine anyway, and we polished it off over the course of an hour. Sara was brutally candid when she was tipsy. Her voice got squeaky. She talked about how badly she wanted to have a child—she started to cry, telling me about all the doctors she'd seen, and all the poking and prodding they did to see if she was working properly. They promised her there was no medical reason she hadn't conceived yet. Then she said Pete had a small dick. She secretly thought that might be the problem, like the smaller ones didn't have as much power.

"How big is Jacob's?" she said, suddenly giggling.

"It's normal," I said. "Not too big, not too small. But he knows how to use it, that's the key." I told Sara about this special technique Jacob had. "Because he's kind of skinny, he can get his pelvic bone, or whatever the bone is that sits above the dick, he can get that bone right up against me, and he makes these little circles, round and round, until I'm nearly about to come. Then he just starts drilling. It makes me delirious."

"Pete can't do that. He's too chubby," Sara said. She looked disappointed.

When Pete came home, Sara was putting tiny braids in my hair, and we were in the middle of comparing notes on celebrities we'd spotted in Yoga class. I'd seen Cary Grant's daughter the week before. Sara one-upped me because she told me she accidentally farted in class the day Madonna was doing down-dog behind her.

Pete looked surprised to see me parked on his floor.

"You're *here*?" he said.

I smiled, trying to imagine just how small his dick was.

"Come on, *Trixie*," he said. "I'm taking you home."

"I don't want to go home."

"Yes, you do," Pete said.

"Jacob doesn't love me anymore."

"Yes, he does. Even though you're completely irrational, like all women are, he loves you."

"He loves Nina," I said.

"He doesn't love Nina. Nina's a disaster. Let's go." Pete pulled on my arm and I floated to the door with him, waving good-bye to Sara.

"Hey, Sara," I said before I left, "do you think I should cut my hair? I've never had short hair."

"I'll cut it for you. It'll be great!"

"Okay. Bye, Sara. Thanks!"

Before he took me home, Pete decided we needed to make a quick stop. He pulled in to a late night coffee shop, ordered me a double cappuccino on ice, and made me drink the whole thing. The instant brain-freeze did nothing but exacerbate my already excruciating headache.

"Let me tell you something about our little friend, Jake," Pete said. "He isn't like most guys, you know?"

"I know."

"No, but do you *really* know? I mean here's the deal, what do most guys want from a woman? I'll tell you what we want. We want a warm body to sleep next to, preferably one with a nice pair of tits, maybe someone who'll cook for us and fuck us on a regular basis. Pretty simple, huh? Now, what we *don't* want is someone who's going to come in and disrupt our lives and steal our souls. That's what we fear most. We call it our freedom, but it's our souls we're talking about. You following me?"

I nodded.

"Okay, good. Now forget it. Forget *all that*," Pete said. "Because Jacob's not like that. He's *never* been like that. He's a damn fool and he wants *the exact opposite* of that. He wants someone to obsess over, someone to possess his soul, and those are his corny words, by the way, not mine. It's what he lives for. It's what he thinks life's all *about*. Do you get what I'm saying?"

I nodded again.

"So there you have it. Do with it what you will. Just don't be so hard on him. Don't worry so much. Shit, if I was him, I'd kick your ass, running-off and slamming doors and all that."

"Pete," I said, "he didn't talk to me for hours. What was I supposed to think?"

"He's *Jacob*. He's *weird*, for Christ's sake. Believe me, I've known him a lot longer than you have. I lived with him back when our apartment was six hundred square feet, and sometimes he'd go days without talking to me. That's just the way he is. You better get used to it."

When I walked in the apartment, Jacob was lying on the couch watching *The Late Show with David Letterman*. The sound was muted but I could see the screen—Pete Townsend was the guest. I interpreted that as a good sign. Pete Townsend wrote one of my favorite lines of all time: *No one respects the flame quite like the fool who's badly burned.*

I wanted to whisper those words into Jacob's ear. I wanted to remind him that I'd been more than just burned, I'd been practically incinerated. And not by some random guy, either, but essentially by the one man in the world who was supposed to protect me. That's why I acted like a baby. I had scars. But my scars also served to instill a kind of reverence in me. Reverence that, during times of weakness, became shrouded in darkness.

I had a fleeting desire to ask Jacob to turn up the volume so I could hear Pete Townsend sing, but I thought better of that request. Jacob had a serious scowl on his face. I'd never seen him look so angry and I wasn't sure what to do.

After I shut the door, Jacob flicked off the TV, sat up, and crossed his arms in front of his chest. I stood frozen against the wall and decided to wait until he said something, or at least until he glanced in my direction.

He kept focused on the dead screen. He was waiting for me to talk.

I should have been nice and said I was sorry. That's what I'd wanted to do. That's what I'd intended to do prior to walking in, but his disposition caught me off guard and I changed tactics.

"Jacob, what's with the attitude?"

He looked at me, shook his head in disgust, then went back to the idle screen.

"Are you enjoying the show?" I said. I stepped in front of the TV to try and get his attention. "So what, you're never going to talk to me again?"

A sarcastic "nice hair" was all he could muster.

"Whatever. See if I care."

I spun around and pretended like I was going to walk out again. That got him up in a flash. And it was a good thing too, as I don't know where the hell I would have gone if he'd let me run off a second time.

I had the door cracked about an inch when he was upon me. "Oh, no you don't," he said, and slammed it shut. My back was against the wall. He straddled me with his outstretched arms.

"Why should I stay here if you're going to ignore me?" I said. I was trying to get around him. He wouldn't budge. He stood there for at least a minute, burning his silence into me with his eyes, as if I owed him an apology.

"Move!" I yelled.

"No," he said, simply and calmly.

"Let me go!"

I struggled to get away from him, but he was stronger than I was. I didn't have much of a chance. I was determined, nevertheless, to fight the good fight.

"Get out of my way!"

"You're not going anywhere."

"You can't control me!"

"Looks like I can."

"Fuck you!"

"Fuck you."

"Fuck off!"

"Suck my dick."

I bit him on the arm as hard as I could. Mature, I know. At least it opened up an escape route. Jacob grabbed his wound and I dove toward the bedroom. I thought I'd make it there and be able to lock him out for the night, but he was quick on my trail. He tackled me just as I got through the door and we fell, face down, onto the bed. In a frenzy, he flipped me over and held my arms flat. Before I knew it, his tongue was in my mouth—deep in my throat. I could hardly breathe and I loved it. I wanted to bite it off and swallow it and digest it and have its protein nourish me.

I wanted Jacob to be part of me forever.

I freed my hands and undid his pants. He ripped open my shirt, sending buttons flying across the bed. It was just like a movie. I know that uptight, pseudo-doctor woman on the radio tells the poor stooges who call her talk show that sex in real life isn't like sex you see in the movies, but she can just speak for her own sorry ass.

Jacob hiked up my skirt, forced my underwear over, and tried to get inside me. I wanted him—badly—but I resisted with all my strength. Partly because I was still pissed at him, but more so because I could tell he liked it. The more I struggled, the hotter he got.

"Fucking bitch," he said, trying to pry my legs apart.

"Come on, you can do better than that." I kept taunting him. I was trying to get him to haul off and slap me but he wouldn't do it.

"Don't pretend you don't want it," he said.

I drew my fingernails down his back, just like you're supposed to do when you're having rough sex. He winced, re-pinned my arms to the bed, and called me a whore. That's when I stopped fighting. I opened up and let him in and we went like mad, violently devouring each other like fucking food and we hadn't eaten in months.

Afterward, Jacob lingered inside of me, motionless, until the sound of a siren on Wilshire reminded us we were still alive. He shifted his body and I turned onto my side so that we were facing each other. He kissed me sweetly, almost brotherly, and brushed a lock of hair out of my eyes. He pulled the blanket up and covered both of us with it. We went to sleep without another word spoken.

I woke up in the exact same position about seven hours later. When I opened my eyes, Jacob's were on me. A thin strip of sunlight was slashing him diagonally in half; it made the whole left side of his face glow and gave his hair a coppery hue.

"What are you doing?" I said.

"Watching you." He took my hand and traced the lines of my palm with his finger.

"I'm sorry I acted like such a jerk yesterday," I said.

"You should be."

"I'm sorry I bit you."

"You should be."

"I'm sorry I'm neurotic and stupid and irrational. Don't you dare say 'You should be' again."

"I'm sorry I didn't talk to you when we got home. And I'm sorry I called you a bitch and a whore."

I told him that, in the heat of the moment, I didn't mind the name-calling so much. A wry smile pursed his lips, he looked away, and I swear I saw him blush. Jacob suddenly turning bashful could very well have been the cutest damn thing I'd ever seen.

"Do you hate me?" I said.

"I could never hate you, Trixie. Never."

"Jacob...," I took a deep breath and my heart started to beat in a quick rhythm, "I love you. More than I ever thought it was possible to love someone. Siamese twin lovers, identical wombs, whatever the hell you called it. All I want in life is to drive out of this horrible, soul-destroying state with you someday. Please don't leave me for Nina."

He smiled. "That's the first time you ever said that."

"I know."

"I say it at least twice a day. You have a lot of catching up to do."

"I know."

"Say it again."

"Don't press your luck." I picked a stray lash from his cheek and told him to make a wish. He closed his eyes tightly, then blew the tiny hair into the air. When he opened his eyes I asked him what he'd wished for.

"Trixie," he said. "Nina just found out she's HIV-positive. She told me yesterday when I ran into her. It kind of knocked me for a loop, you know?"

Faster than you can say "Elizabeth Taylor," I saw both of us lying next to each other, side by side in twin cots, with IV's sticking out of our arms and brown liquid dripping through tubes, while drug cocktails squeezed every ounce of life from our decaying veins. Jacob must have realized, by the look on my face, what I was thinking. He caught my fall.

"Oh, no. It's not *that*. Don't worry about me, I was tested months ago, long after she and I had been together. I'm fine. You're fine. Besides, she knows where she got it, from some dealer she was living with over Christmas. He even knew he was sick, he just didn't bother to tell her."

"Jacob, I had no idea…"

"She's alone right now and she doesn't know what to do." He paused. "I'm not going on a *date* with her, all right? I just need to try and convince her to get some help. That's all."

I felt like such an ass. "I won't say another word about it."

"You can say anything you want about it, just don't think I'd ever do anything to hurt you."

It was time to change the subject to a happier topic. I whipped out the book I bought at the museum—the

Eggleston. I showed it to Jacob and told him my silly fantasy about the house and the waitress job and the grits. He didn't think it was silly at all. Except the part about me being a waitress.

"I doubt that will be necessary," he said.

We studied each photo as if we were looking through a family album, all the while rhapsodizing about our future.

"I want us to paint the house ourselves," he said. "And we'll sand the floors and plant stuff in the yard. Maybe we'll even get a dog."

I asked Jacob if he ever wanted to have kids. He told me about a dream he'd had years before.

"I was pushing two little girls on swings. They were laughing and calling me Dad, and nothing else mattered in the world." He rolled onto his back and stared at the ceiling. "I can't believe my father didn't feel that. I can't believe he could just put down his kid and walk away." Jacob shifted his head to face me. "That's fucked-up," he said with sympathy. I wasn't sure if the sympathy was for himself or, oddly enough, for his father, nevertheless, I could see the clutter of years obscured inside his eyes.

"What did they look like," I said. "Your daughters?"

"They had a mess of black hair, just like you. And they had French names. Simone and Madeline, or something like that."

# SIXTEEN

Jacob had asked Nina to meet him at our apartment. He was on the phone when the buzzer rang. I had to let her in.

"Who is it?" I said, even though I knew damn well who it was. I was sorry Jacob had ever fixed that fucking buzzer.

"It's Nina. I'm here to see Jacob," she said with a raspy, chain-smoker voice. I was sure, at one time, Jacob thought that voice was sexy as hell, and I immediately hated Nina for it. When she knocked on the door two minutes later, I shuffled into the kitchen, to a spot where I could still see the entryway. I pretended I was washing dishes. Jacob opened the door with the phone still on his ear.

"Hey, come on in." He put his hand on her shoulder. "You *okay*?"

I wondered if that word had the same effect on Nina as it had on me.

Jacob wrapped up his call and started showing Nina around the apartment. He held her hand. I hated that, too.

Nina wasn't at all what I'd pictured. She was demure, doe-like; not the tough, streetwise chick I expected. It was obvious she had the potential to be quite attractive, but she wore the last year of her self-destructive life like a bad car wreck. Her hair hung in stringy pieces of flaxen thread, and her eyes were dark buckets of sludge. Still, she looked more like someone with a bad case of the flu than someone strung-out on smack.

"Nina, this is Beatrice," Jacob said when they walked into the kitchen.

"Nice to meet you," I lied in my most welcoming voice. When I shook her hand I got a whiff of something sweet and floral. Nina smelled pretty. Like rose water.

"Nice to meet you, too," she said. She looked at me with regret in her eyes. She thought I was the luckiest girl in the world, I could tell. I knew I was lucky. I certainly didn't need Nina to remind me of that. But the whole scenario struck me as perversely gruesome. Basically, Nina's loss, her downfall, was my salvation—a fateful technicality that made me strangely, unbelievably sad. It seemed cruelly unfair to me, even then, how fast your life can change before you have an opportunity to rethink your choices. We should get second chances on the big stuff. We should come equipped with erasers attached to the tops of our heads. Like pencils. We should be able to flip over and scribble away mistakes, at least once or twice during the duration of our existence, especially in matters of life and death.

I tried to think brighter thoughts: my little French daughters. They'd call me *Maman*. They'd eat escargot and not think it was weird.

I told Jacob that I was going out for a few hours, so he and Nina could talk.

"Trixie, you don't have to leave."

"It's okay. I don't want to be in the way," I said, which was true. I left out the part about not wanting to be in the same room with someone my boyfriend fucked on a regular basis for three years. I grabbed a book, wished Nina well, and said I'd be back later.

I went to the Cow's End, a two-story café in Venice that looked like a barn dressed up as a living room. It was like being in the house of a hippie relative. There was unpolished wood all over the walls and lots of plush couches with dingy upholstery—a perfect location to over-caffeinate myself and read all afternoon. I told the kid behind the counter, whose name tag read *Burn*, that I was going to be around for a few hours. He gave me my first latte at a discount.

"What kind of name is *Burn*?" I said.

"It's short for Bernard."

I think he mistook my curiosity for flirting. He asked me if I wanted to go to a keg party with him.

"How old are you?" I said.

"Eighteen. I'll be nineteen in a week."

"I think MTV is older than you are."

"I like your shoes," he said.

They were vintage Air Jordans. "I've had them since you were in third grade."

Burn called me Babe. And he used the word "party" as a verb. I thanked him for the offer and graciously declined his invitation for a date.

"Are you sure? It's gonna be a *rager*," he said.

I told him I had a boyfriend. Not that I would have gone with him otherwise, I was just trying to be polite. I wanted to let him down easy.

"So," he said, "I'm not exactly looking for a wife or anything."

I felt sorry for Burn. He had a lot to learn about women. And his remark annoyed me enough that I developed a strong, sudden desire to put him in his place.

"Bernard," I said, "the truth is, even though you think you're really cool, I'm pretty sure you couldn't lick a pussy to save your life." I waited for a retort but he didn't say shit. "That's what I thought," I said.

I picked up my coffee and found a warm corner to lounge in for the next few hours. I needed a quiet place to concentrate. I'd brought along a book I wanted to pay close attention to: a novel called *Morning Glory* by Thomas Doorley.

On the surface, Thomas Doorley's first novel was nothing more than a tale about a Vietnam vet who comes home from the war having had his right leg blown off in combat. I found the plot a bit predictable, in all likelihood because it was published in 1976, and I'd seen all the movies covering that topic. You know, *Apocalypse Now*, *Platoon*, *Born on the Fourth of July*. I remembered the news clips about the way the vets were treated, about the alienation, the post-traumatic stress disorder. However, curiously enough, the book contained an interesting allegory. I found the chaos of a man who'd lost part of himself, part of his flesh, and consequently felt like a part of his soul was missing. I saw the whole thing as a metaphor for something larger than a severed limb. Maybe I was reading too much into it, but I thought Jacob should read the book. I figured it might help him understand, might urge him to make contact with a man who, it seemed to me, was much more haunted by what he'd left behind than Jacob ever gave him credit for.

Before I went home, I stopped by the salon where Sara worked. I wanted to thank her for being so nice to me the night before. She made me sit down in her chair. I told her about Nina. She felt sorry, but she wasn't surprised.

"Are you ready for a big change?" Sara said, wielding the scissors between her fingers. She wanted to cut my hair. "Last night you said I could."

"I was kind of inebriated then." My hair had never been above my shoulders, not since I was a kid anyway.

"Come on, it'll look great, I promise. And if you hate it, it will always grow back."

"I'm scared," I said. As soon as my brain heard that word, *scared*, I ordered Sara to start cutting. A haircut was a stupid-ass thing to be afraid of. And Jacob said living in fear wasn't really living. It became a metaphorical experience of growth for me, a test of courage. Just like saying "I love you."

Sara led me to a big marble sink that practically gave me whiplash when I leaned my head into it. She shampooed my hair, then she took me back to her station and combed through my tangled mane.

"Do whatever you want," I said.

"Sit still," Sara begged.

I'd had way too much coffee. I couldn't stop fidgeting.

"Keep your head down," Sara said. "And don't look until I'm finished."

Big clumps of hair started dropping into my lap. Against the shocking blue color of the salon walls, the locks looked like dead crows falling out of the sky.

Almost an hour went by before Sara finally put the scissors down, but she still wouldn't let me look. She was rubbing my head with a goopy gel that smelled like pineapples.

"This is adorable," she said.

She shook the excess hair off of my face and lap, and had me stand up. My neck felt cold.

"Okay," she said. "You can look now."

My hair was maybe two inches long all over my head. Some of it stuck straight up in the air.

"What do you think?"

It was soft and fuzzy when I ran my fingers through it. And I could see my ears. "It's cool," I said. "I like it."

My first inclination was to go straight to my studio and make myself a new pair of earrings to celebrate the change, but I decided that could wait. I wanted to get home and show

Jacob.

I snuck into the apartment as quietly as possible and called his name.

"I'm in the bedroom," he said.

"Is Nina gone?"

There was a pause, then he said, "*Yes.*" I couldn't see his face, but the tone of his voice told me he'd just rolled his eyes. Like it was preposterous for me to think he'd be in the bedroom with Nina.

"Close your eyes, and keep them closed," I said.

I tiptoed in and stood next to the bed. Jacob's eyes were shut, he wasn't wearing a shirt, and he had the *New York Times* on his lap. We lived in Los Angeles but every day he read the *New York Times*. I took the paper out of his hands and repositioned myself so that I was in the best possible light.

"Okay, open," I said.

"Wow." He smiled, a bit startled. "You cut your hair."

"And the Nobel Prize goes to…Jacob Einstein!" I said, jumping up and down.

"You're a smart ass, you know that?" Jacob said.

"I know you are but what am I?"

"A smart ass."

"I know you are but what am I?"

"Trixie, did you have coffee today?" He pulled me down, rolled me over, and lay on top of me.

"Do you like my hair?" I said. "Sara did it for me."

He petted my head. "Yeah. You look like Jean Seberg from *Breathless.*"

I didn't know who that was. "Is she cute?" I said.

"She was beautiful. But not as beautiful as you."

"How was your afternoon?" I said.

"Long and depressing. Want to cheer me up?"

I knew exactly what he meant by that. I had to stop him

before he got carried away.

"Jacob, if you want the milk, you have to buy the cow a meal."

"Excuse me?"

"In the last twelve hours, I've had three lattes and a cookie. Put a shirt on. We're going to get dinner."

We walked to Second Street and, after ten minutes of deliberation, decided on Thai food. I ordered us Phad-Thai noodles, a spicy eggplant and basil dish, spring rolls, and a bottle of water.

"To go," Jacob said.

We hiked to the beach to eat and watch the sun set. Jacob wanted to tell me all about his day with Nina. Truth be told, I didn't care to hear it, but he seemed like he needed to let it out. The gist of it was that she'd just gotten out of rehab— some kind of month-long program in a halfway house where you have to wash dishes, do laundry, scrub the bathroom floors, and somehow stay off drugs at the same time. Jacob said Nina was trying hard to kick her habit and stay healthy, and he managed to convince her to go back east, where I gathered she was from, and stay with her parents for a while. I didn't pry any further because I wanted to seem unfazed. The last thing I needed to find out was that she'd tried to kiss him, or something that would make me jealous all over again. Besides, I had my own significant matter to discuss.

"*Jacob,*" I said theatrically.

"*What?*" he said quickly, imitating my melodrama.

"I read *Morning Glory* this afternoon."

It took Jacob a few seconds to figure out what that was. He'd just bitten into a roll, and he paused with his mouth full to watch a wave fold onto the shore. When he finished chewing, he swallowed hard and looked back at me.

"All of it?" he said.

"No, not all of it. I have about three chapters left."

"Well?" he said. "What's the verdict? Did I inherit my amazing talent, or am I a big fluke?" He played it off like it was no big deal. He didn't fool me.

"I'll tell you what I think. I think you should read it. I think you *need* to read it right away."

Jacob wanted to know why I thought it so consequential that he read the damn book. I told him my interpretation of the story, how I thought it was about him, about his father leaving him behind. He tried to be nonchalant, but I could tell he was curious. I could tell he was grappling with all the old, unresolved demons.

"I'm not sure I *can* read it," he said, eyeing the blue-orange glow of the horizon. It looked like the center of a flame and was one of the only things I liked about living in Los Angeles—sunsets on the Pacific.

I bet sunsets look just as beautiful on the Mississippi.

I didn't say anything else about the book. I knew Jacob would come around. He needed too many answers not to.

# SEVENTEEN

The first time my ass ever touched a public toilet seat was the day I made the reservations for Jacob's thirtieth birthday dinner. I should have recognized that as some kind of bad omen. I'm very particular about where I set my ass, so to allow that kind of mishap was beyond comprehension. It had never happened before, not even with those "for your protection" toilet-shaped tissues you're supposed to lay down before you go. They don't do a damn bit of good anyway—they just soak up the leftover pee that's already on the seat. So I squat. I've always squatted, ever since I was a child and my mother told me there were microscopic germs on toilet seats that could give you elephantiasis. I didn't even know what elephantiasis was, but it didn't sound like anything I wanted.

Two hours before I called the restaurant to make our reservation, I went to pick up Jacob's birthday present at the antique mart on Beverly Boulevard. I got him a clunky old silver watch, dated 1946. It wasn't glitzy or anything, just something special that he'd have for a long time—forever if he didn't lose it. I engraved it myself, but instead of writing something mushy, I put his name, address, and telephone number on it. Like a dog tag. Jacob had gone through three watches in the eight months I'd known him. I wasn't taking any chances.

I drank half a bottle of water before I left the apartment. By the time I got to Beverly, I really had to go. Somehow I miscalculated the distance from my butt to the bowl and there was contact. Only for a second. Nevertheless, contact was made.

Jacob's birthday fell on a Friday, so Pete and I decided to cancel our usual Sushi outing the following night and take him somewhere nice instead. It was a momentous occasion and we wanted to splurge. I called a pricey restaurant down on Ocean Avenue—the kind with amazing food and an unusual number of Mercedes in the valet—and I made a reservation for eight people.

"For when?" the lady said.

"Friday."

"What time?"

"Seven-thirty."

It was Monday. She acted like it would be no problem. She took my first name and my phone number, and everything was set.

Friday afternoon rolled around and I got a call from the restaurant. It was the same girl I'd spoken to before. She told me our party would have to be seated either at five-thirty or at ten.

"You can't do that," I said. "We have a reservation."

"I'm sorry," she said.

"You don't sound sorry."

"We have another group coming in. We made a mistake and can't accommodate you. But we'd love to offer you a complimentary dinner for two the next time you dine with us."

I told her to shove dinner for two up her vagina. That was the biggest bunch of bull I'd ever heard. After I hung up I ranted to Jacob about the injustices of Los Angeles, about how some people would sell their first born to kiss celebrity ass.

"Jacob, I'd bet your left testicle that some hot-shot actor called up and needed our table. There's no Academy Award-winning Beatrice to speak of, so they figured it was safe to dump us."

"Don't be gambling with my balls," he said. "So we'll find another place to eat. Big deal. What's a four-letter word for a baby kangaroo?"

Jacob was engrossed in his daily crossword puzzle. It was obvious that he didn't think restaurant politics were nearly as controversial as I did. To me, it was unacceptable. There was principal involved. That, and the banana split the restaurant served for dessert. It cost fifteen dollars and was worth every cent: three scoops of homemade ice cream surrounded by two bananas, a handful of fresh strawberries, blueberries, pineapple, a dish of almonds, and a dollop of whipped cream. On the side, they gave you two little pitchers. One was filled with hot fudge, the other one was filled with hot, gooey caramel.

It was foreplay. We *had* to have one.

"Trixie, all this fuss over ice cream?"

I nodded.

"I'll see what I can do," Jacob said. He looked up the number of the restaurant and dialed. "But let me just say, if this works, I'm going to lose all hope in humanity."

"Join the club," I said. "Joey."

Jacob spoke into the phone using his surfer voice. It was pretty close to his Greg impersonation, only a little deeper. He was extremely polite, telling the person on the other end of the line that he needed a table for eight people that night. He said he was getting ready to leave town to work on a film, and he really wanted to eat there before he left. He said his last name was Reeves.

"Uh-huh. Sure. Right on," he said into the phone. "Seven-thirty? Great, thanks very much." After he hung up, he said, "We've *got* to get out of here."

"I told you."

"Why did you call me Joey?"

"A baby kangaroo. Four letters. Joey."

# EIGHTEEN

When we got to the restaurant that night, Jacob announced us as "Reeves, party of eight."

The hostess picked up a stack of menus and immediately lead us to our table, only she looked at each person suspiciously, trying to locate the illustrious Mr. Reeves in our crowd. She was horribly dubious but she didn't say anything. What could she say without looking like a complete fool?

The walls of the restaurant were painted a pastel pink, all the dining chairs were made of wicker, and there were various ships hanging from the ceiling—a cruise ship, a battleship, a yacht, a catamaran, but miniature versions—the kind you can buy at a toy store and then build and paint in your basement. In the dim of the candlelight, the effect was nautically romantic. We were seated at a lovely table in the back, right across from a gigantic print of an old sailboat navigating rough waters. Across it said: Brave Men Run in My Family. It reminded me of the painting in the diner where Jacob and I first met, only this one was nicer. And five times as big. And it had a boat in it.

Not long after we sat down, Arnold Schwarzenegger and Maria Shriver came in with their kids. I heard Maria thank the maitre d' for squeezing them in on such short notice. I was positive they were the ones who stole our original table. I almost went over and told them the whole story. They looked like normal enough people, and I thought they'd get a kick out of it, but Jacob said if I ever wanted to eat there again, I shouldn't blow our cover.

"We're Reeves, remember? Not Beatrice."

The birthday party consisted of Jacob and I; Sara and Pete; Joanna Grace and her date, a shy schoolteacher with a heavy moustache, named Jim; plus Kat and her new boyfriend, Gopal. Gopal was a tall, lanky chap, originally from a small town in northern India. He spoke with a slight accent and was the only one at the table wearing a suit and tie. Kat said he never went out at night without a suit and tie on. She had a red rhinestone glued to her forehead, a pseudo bindi, obviously in his honor. Gopal had been in the United States for twelve years and he'd never heard of *The Brady Bunch*. Kat, conversely, spent practically every waking moment of youth watching television. She cited bogus lessons from the Brady family as mantras, and she knew every episode by heart. I guessed it would never last.

Pete was on his third gin martini by the time we were ready to eat. He wanted to order for everyone at the table. He asked each of us, in turn, what we thought sounded good, then he took it upon himself to decide what we were going to have.

"No roe-sham-bo tonight, all right sweetie?" Sara said.

"Pipe down. It costs too much to order shitty food here," he said. I didn't like the way he barked at her. I made a mental note to mention it to Jacob when we got home.

Pete ordered grilled salmon for the birthday boy. "Because grilled salmon is something a thirty-year-old would order," he said. He got me the grilled vegetable salad. He got Joanna and Jim pasta with vodka sauce. Kat ended up with a Cajun stew because Pete said she was spicy. Sara got lobster because it was an aphrodisiac, and Gopal got the mixed fish platter. I'm not sure why Pete ordered Gopal that, but I suspected it had something to do with the way Gopal pronounced the word *platter*. Pete got himself a T-bone. "Because that's what

Arnold's eating," he said.

For dessert, we ordered two of the famed banana splits to share. I pretended I had to go to the bathroom so I could ask our waiter to load them up with candles. Sara thought I really had to pee and she came with me—she did have to pee. Kat followed, so as not to miss anything.

On our way back to the table, I heard a strange, familiar voice.

"Beatrice?" he said.

When I turned around I almost hit the deck. He was sitting right there, had probably been sitting around the corner, about twenty feet away from me, all evening. A man with a face I hadn't seen in almost a decade.

My father.

It was kind of funny, really, that I hadn't run into him sooner. He only lived ten miles from my apartment. It was bound to happen eventually. But he didn't exactly frequent the places I did so I never worried about it. The last time I'd seen him was the day he walked out on my mother. He'd been fucking around for eons, and I think we all figured he would just keep fucking around and she'd keep taking him back, and that's the way life would continue to go, 'til death did them part. She would undoubtedly find divorce too embarrassing, and he wouldn't want to hand over too much of his net-worth, at least that was my theory. Then one day he came home and dropped the bomb—he'd just purchased a house in Malibu, he wanted to marry a twenty-six-year-old real estate broker, and that was it. He was willing to give my mother half of everything, plus a nice chunk of change for each of the kids, just to get rid of her.

He looked older than I remembered, mainly because his thick black hair had grayed a bit, but he was still in decent shape. My father was a handsome man. He was tall—well over six feet—and he had a geometric face, made of nothing but severe lines and sharp angels.

He was with a woman I assumed to be the one he married. All I knew about her was what my mother told me: she wasn't much older than I was and she had fake tits. That night was the first time I'd ever seen her. She reminded me of a Yorkshire Terrier.

"Beatrice? Honey, is that you?" my father said.

Please tell me he didn't just call me honey, I thought. Tell me I made that up.

I figured if I didn't respond, if I just kept walking, he'd think he was mistaken. Maybe I was just someone who resembled that girl called Beatrice. I think it would have worked too, had Kat not been there.

"Blanca, do you know that guy? He's calling you," she said.

I only vaguely remember the events that took place over the course of the next thirty minutes. Apparently I stared blank-faced at my father and walked back to our table, catatonic. When I sat down, Jacob told me I looked weird. He asked me if I was sick.

"You're white as a sheet," he said. I recall thinking that was a funny expression. Kind of cliché for a writer. And it didn't really hold water for me. The sheets on our bed were a minty shade of green.

Jacob put his palm on my forehead like my mother used to do when she was taking my temperature. "Are you sure you're *okay*?"

I didn't even enjoy the *okay* that time.

"She just ran into her father," Kat said. Kat had stayed and chatted with the stranger long enough to find out who he was.

"Beatrice, your Dad's here?" Pete yelled. "Hell, ask him to join us!"

Someone kicked Pete under the table.

"What? What'd I do?" Pete said. Sara yanked on his shirt and told him to shut up.

"Hey, Grace, here he comes," Kat shouted. "The good-looking guy in the beige shirt. Blanca, your dad's kind of *hot*."

Why was she shouting? Why did she have to say he was *hot*? And why did she always call Jacob by his last name?

I assumed that if I ignored my father he'd vanish as fast as he appeared. I saw the shape of him, like an apparition, floating toward the back of the restaurant. He was levitating my way. He was coming to haunt me. I turned away from him and tried to start a conversation with whoever was on my right. I faintly identified Joanna as that person.

When my father reached our table, he looked straight at me. I didn't *see* him looking—I never moved my head in his direction—but I felt him.

Jacob stood up from his chair and introduced himself as my boyfriend. My father was almost a head taller than Jacob. I saw it all through the corner of my eye. I saw them shake hands, as if they were shaking on me. Signed, sealed, delivered; she's yours.

"Jacob Grace," he said.

"Curtis Jordan," said the stranger. "It's good to meet you."

I'd forgotten my father's first name. I don't think I would have even been able to think of it unless he'd said it. He seemed a little uncomfortable, but he still sounded like a lawyer when he talked.

"This is my wife, Tara," he said.

Tara had followed him over. I bet she followed him everywhere. That's what little Yorkies do, I said to myself. I think Jacob shook her paw too, but I'm not sure because I still wasn't looking. My lips were moving and I was trying to say something to Joanna, only I didn't hear the sound when it came out of my mouth. It was too noisy there, in my head, where Bono was singing a song to me–a song about wanting so much, but being left with nothing.

Thank heaven for the wisdom of the prophets of rock 'n' roll. They're the ones who saved me back then, when my father ran off and my mother threatened to kill herself to make him stay, even though she never would have done it because my mother's a big coward and there's no way she would have died unless she'd given us explicit instructions regarding which designer we were to bury her in.

"Most likely Chanel," she always says. But it depends on who's at the helm, and during which season she croaks.

Jacob spoke to my father for a few more minutes. I didn't hear what they said, even though Jacob was right next to me, and Curtis Jordan was diagonal from my fucking face. It was all a big blur until Curtis and Tara wafted away. I saw them go. I saw them exit the restaurant. I saw Curtis hand his ticket to the valet guy. He looked back at me through the window as if he were looking at someone he loved laying dead in an open casket. Then he helped Tara into their brand new Jeep Grand Cherokee. She had a wide ass. From the front she looked small but her backside was a different story. I couldn't wait to tell my mother Tara was a yappy dog with a wide ass. I never had anything to talk to my mother about, but I knew she'd think that was the greatest thing since online shopping.

We all sang Happy Birthday and ate the banana splits. Jacob even opened a couple of gifts. Pete gave him some rare Miles Davis import record, Kat and Gopal gave him a bright yellow T-shirt that said Cheerios on it, and Joanna gave him a tattered, first edition copy of *Tropic of Cancer*. Jacob drooled all over that and told Joanna she shouldn't have, but she gave him a loud smooch on the cheek and demanded that he give her a break.

"My only son doesn't turn thirty every day, you know."

I don't remember any of this, mind you. It was all relayed back to me later, with the kind of intimate details only a writer could supply.

I didn't become conscious again until we got in the car. Jacob was in the right lane, getting ready to turn down our street, when I sprang back to life.

"Can we not go home right now?" I said.

Jacob floored it when the light turned green, and we zoomed past all the other cars. Then he swerved left, took the incline down to PCH, and drove north. When we got to Topanga Canyon, he made a right.

"Where are we going?"

"To the park," he said.

There's a state park in Topanga Canyon, right in the heart of the Santa Monica mountains. Getting there was like driving into another world—it didn't look anything like you picture L.A. to look at all. It was dry, woodsy land, filled with trees, and brush, and sprinkled with granola. I guessed the people who lived there pretended they weren't anywhere near Los Angeles. I was sure they played a lot of Crosby Stills and Nash records and let their kids walk around barefoot and acted like it was summertime in Woodstock every day of the year.

"Jacob, how much longer until you finish your book?"

"Soon," he said. "I promise."

He drove up to the park entrance. The sign said it was closed from sundown to sunrise, but there was no ranger around to stop us from going in. Instead of parking in the lot, Jacob hammered right onto the fire trail. We went up a mile or so and stopped on an overlook where we could see the Palisades to our left and the entire canyon on our right. We hopped into the backseat and huddled together to keep warm. The car smelled musty, like damp newspapers and stale cola.

Jacob's car always smelled like it needed a good cleaning.

We said and heard nothing for a good five minutes, until a couple of coyotes started howling. They sang back and forth, then together at the same time, like they were performing a tragic duet. I couldn't decide if it was a soothing sound, or if it reminded me of a horror movie, the moment right before the ax falls.

"Tell me what you're thinking," Jacob said.

I was thinking about a family vacation we took when I was in high school. The coyote cries made me remember it. The Honolulu Nightmare, that's what I called this particular holiday. The travelers included, in alphabetical order, me, Cole, my father, my mother, and some other woman my dad thought I was too stupid to notice because he got her a room on a different floor. Chip was already off at college so he was spared the torture.

For a week straight, I had the daily choice of sunbathing by the pool with my mother, golfing with my brother, or tailing my father. He claimed he had meetings, and he usually did, but not at seven o'clock in the morning in another woman's hotel room. Following him around was usually the most interesting option. It was also the most depressing. I blew it off after the second day and signed up for a scuba certification class instead.

The first time the instructor took me down, I'd been underwater for maybe ten minutes when the ocean started to echo with a blaring, high-pitched squeal. An aqua-opera. It sounded like the most beautiful music I'd ever heard, like a hundred babies with three-octave ranges. I had no idea what it was, but I prayed that it was a choir of sea nymphs coming to drag me to Atlantis.

When I surfaced, my instructor told me the sounds I'd heard were Humpback whales. It was mating season, and they were singing to attract their lovers. I asked him why we could hear them but not see them.

"They're a thousand miles away," the instructor said.

The coyotes went silent, and I wondered if they were screwing.

"Jacob, what did my father say to you?"

He explained the whole night to me, all the stuff I'd blacked out. My father asked him where we were living, and if I was still making jewelry, and how business was going. All the usual stuff a father would ask his daughter's boyfriend if he hadn't seen her in nine years. He noticed that I'd cut my hair and said he liked it. Before he walked away, he gave Jacob his business card. He told Jacob he wanted to have us up for Thanksgiving dinner the following week. They lived right on the beach. They always had a nice breeze. He said we'd love it.

"Has my father gone blind in the last decade? Did I *look* to him like I'd want to come over for a breezy little Thanksgiving beach party?"

I wondered if he remembered my birthday was coming up. He always remembered my birthday. He sent me a card every year. *Happy Birthday, Sweetheart.* That's what it always said. *I Miss You. Love, Dad.*

"He thought maybe I'd be able to convince you to come," Jacob said.

"He thought wrong. Why were you so nice to him?"

"Would you be mean to my father if you met him?"

The coyotes started up again. They must fuck fast.

"Jacob, Pete drinks too much."

"Your father wants you to call him."

"Oh, really? He has a phone. I'm listed. He can call me if he wants to talk. Didn't you think Pete was being rude to Sara at dinner?"

"Yeah, I noticed that. He can get a little belligerent. I'll talk to him. But what about your father?"

"My father can kiss my ass. Why are you taking his side?"

"I'm not taking anyone's side. But he seemed like a decent guy to me. If he wants to maybe, you know, patch things up, I don't think it would hurt to try."

"There's nothing to patch up. And by the way, you're one to talk."

"My situation is entirely different."

"No it isn't. I bet you cry every time you hear 'Cat's in the Cradle.'"

Jacob thought that was the funniest thing I'd ever said.

"I'll make you a deal, Jacob, when you call your father, I'll call mine. Stop laughing."

"Actually, 'Cat's in the Cradle' does make me cry," he said. "But only if it's dark out. And I like it. I like the suffering."

"You would," I said. Jacob was weird that way. He thought suffering was cool. He thought it made him a better writer.

"And your argument isn't fair, Trixie. Thomas Doorley left me without a trace. No support, no birthday cards, nothing. It was like my mother and I never existed. At least in Curtis's case," Jacob said, "he stuck around until you were old enough to *choose* to hate him. And really, you severed the ties, right?"

"He might as well have been dead for as much as I saw of him."

"Did you see him on Christmas morning?" Jacob said.

"Yes. But he related more to my brothers. He liked their toys better."

"Did he take you to the movies once in a while?"

"They were always movies his clients were in. He had to go."

"Did he ever go on a bike ride with you?"

"Maybe once or twice. Probably out of guilt."

"Did he have a picture of you on his desk at work?"

I remember the exact one he kept there. It was my fourth grade class picture. I'd insisted that my mother let me do my own hair that day. I tried to curl it with a curling iron, but I didn't know how to use one. I wrapped the hair around the wand in the wrong direction. Instead of curls, I got lumps. My mother was appalled.

"Beatrice, you can't leave the house like that. You look like you live in a trailer."

The picture was in a red plastic frame. I gave it to him for Father's Day.

"I've never celebrated Father's Day," Jacob said. "And Thomas Doorley doesn't know anything about me. He doesn't even know what I look like. I could walk up to him on the street tomorrow, ask him to spare some change, and he'd think I was just some no-good bum."

"Okay, you win," I said. "Your father is more pathetic than mine. But I'm still not calling him. When are you going to read that book anyhow?"

Jacob ignored my question.

What a couple of rueful souls we are, I thought. Whining in the middle of the night, just like a couple of horny coyotes.

Before we left the park, I gave Jacob his birthday present. I told him all about the toilet fiasco that accompanied its pick-up. He thought that was second only to my "Cat's in the Cradle" comment as the funniest thing he'd heard all week. He loved his watch.

"I promise I'll never lose it."

"I have one more present for you."

I wasn't in the mood for sex, per se. Seeing my father had zapped all that energy right out of me, but I thought Jacob deserved a little something on his birthday. I sucked him and let him come in my mouth. It warmed me from the inside out.

When we got home, we shared a glass of wine and fell

asleep watching an infomercial touting the healing benefits of juicing.

# NINETEEN

The day after I ran into my father, Joanna dropped by unexpectedly.

"Beatrice, you and I are going to lunch," she said. "Just the girls. Jacob's not invited."

She took me to an organic vegetarian restaurant on Santa Monica Boulevard that smelled like fresh-squeezed wheatgrass, and had sesame seed shakers on the tables instead of salt. Over tea made from Japanese twigs, and wheat protein with mushroom gravy that they called Salisbury Steak, Joanna said she was worried about me. She asked me if I wanted to talk about my father. She said she could tell I was angry with him—not that anyone with an I.Q. equal to my shoe size couldn't have figured that out. I proceeded to tell Joanna all about my fortunate young life growing up a child of privilege in the Hollywood Hills. I told her more than I would normally tell a person, actually, but something about the lines around her eyes inspired trust. She tried to persuade me not to hold a grudge against my father. She said it wasn't worth the trouble.

"People have reasons for what they do, Beatrice. And even if those reasons can't be justified, that doesn't make them bad people, just flawed. You have to remember," she said, "someone or something has hurt them, too."

Joanna sounded like my eighth grade religion teacher, Mrs. Chilton. That's exactly what she used to say when one kid would beat up another kid on the playground.

"That child must really be hurting inside."

Mrs. Chilton thought the kid with the bloody nose was supposed to feel sorry for the bully instead of hating him. She also said the weak and the poor would inherit the earth some day, while the rich and prosperous would suffer in hell. Even at thirteen, I found this an ironic morsel of insight to feed the class, being that we were all a bunch of bratty trust-fund kids. That's about the time I started giving up on God. I knew I wasn't going to sail down the river Styx just because I had a substantial bank account. Besides, I was suffering enough on earth. All the cash in the world wasn't going to make my pain go away.

Before Joanna had a chance to bring up God, I asked her how she felt about Thomas Doorley. "Do you forgive him?" I said.

"I understand why he left. We were young, too young to know how to be a family."

"But what about what he did to Jacob? Don't you think he should've thought about the consequences of his actions, and how those consequences were going to hurt his son? Even if he didn't want to be with you, couldn't he still have been Jacob's father?"

"I would never try to condone what he did to his son. Never," she said. Then she leaned in closer to me. "But I'm proud of the man Jacob is. I don't know that he'd be the same man right now had Thomas Doorley been part of his life, and I wouldn't want him any other way. Everything happens for a reason. That I do believe."

I wish I believed that. Joanna Grace was a fucking saint.

"I certainly don't think Jacob met *you* by accident," she said, and rested her hand on mine.

Jacob may have had one of the crappiest fathers known to man, but he sure as hell lucked out in the mother department.

I told Joanna that I'd read Thomas Doorley's book. I told her what my interpretation was, how I thought it was about Jacob.

"I know," she said. "Jacob will figure that out in his own time. For whatever it's worth."

# TWENTY

"Goddamn it, Trixie, it's a surprise," Jacob said as he chewed on the tip of a Twizzler and almost swerved off the road.

"Leave at least one hand on the wheel, why don't you?"

"Just give me the map," he said, trying to slide his hand under my ass—I was sitting on his map. I plucked a hair out of his arm so he'd let go.

"Ow. Shit."

"Tell me where we're going and I'll give you the map," I said.

"It's a *surprise*. Do you understand the meaning of that word? *Surprise*."

"Just tell me."

"If I tell you, it won't be a surprise, now will it?"

Jacob's birthday and my birthday were ten days apart. Except that he was two years older. Plus, he was a Scorpio and I was a Sagittarius. According to the little horoscope propaganda I bought at the famed astrological house of Chevron when we stopped for gas, that made Jacob a water sign and me a fire sign.

"That explains why you're drawn to the ocean," I said.

"That explains why you're so hot." He laughed at himself. Sometimes Jacob thought he was God's gift to the world of comedy.

"Water puts out fire. That's no good. You extinguish my

flame," I said.

"No, I squirt you with just enough to make a blaze."

I told Jacob what the paper supposedly said about him: that he was creative, intense, moody, the most passionate sign of the zodiac. So far, so good.

"*And* it says you have a knack for picking stocks," I said. "Maybe you should get on that. Then we can kiss Hell-Aye good-bye for good."

"What does it say about you?"

I looked up my sign. "I'm a philosopher. Very independent. I can also be curt and brash and irrational."

"Bingo," Jacob said, and pointed his finger about a millimeter from my cheek. "Does it say anything about how people born under your sign feel in regards to surprises on their birthday?"

My birthday wasn't for another few days, but Jacob decided that we needed a vacation. We left L.A. on Thanksgiving day, and planned to make a long weekend out of it. I hadn't quite recovered from my chance meeting with Daddy-o the week before, and Jacob thought a little trip would do me some good. We'd never gone away together, had never even fucked outside of our apartment before, so I was excited by the prospects the upcoming four days had to offer. I just wanted to know where we were going.

I threw a Hot Tamale at Jacob. It flew right past his head and out the window.

"Chill out, Trixie."

"Slow down, Speed Racer," I said. "Get it? Trixie and Speed Racer?"

"Yeah, I get it."

I threw another Tamale at him and it landed in his lap. He picked it up, smelled it, and tossed it in his mouth. After three chews he made a face like he'd just swallowed a fur ball. He coughed. "What flavor is this supposed to be?"

"It's cinnamon," I said.

"More like shit-a-mon." He spat the candy out the window, took a swig of his Coke, and put another Twizzler in his mouth, all the while trying to drive and seize the map at the same time. His attempts proved futile. He played the angry father: "Beatrice, don't make me turn this car around!"

He was just pretending to be mad, of course. Jacob was too content to be mad. The windows were down; his hair, which he hadn't cut in months and was longer than mine, was flapping around his face; the radio was up; the sun was out; his belly was full of junk food; and he knew I wasn't wearing any underwear. What more could a man want? In profile, he looked eighteen.

"It's like we're skipping school and sneaking off to some secluded hideaway where teenagers go to lose their virginity," I said. "Not that I would know exactly where that would be, since I never really had sex in high school, but I'm sure there is such a place."

"You never had sex in high school?" Jacob said. "That surprises me."

"Why?"

"Because."

"Because why?"

"I don't know. Because you're so…enthusiastic about it. I figured you'd been practicing a long time."

"In other words, you thought I was the class slut. Well, you couldn't be more wrong, buster. I did it once when I was sixteen, but I don't count that. It only lasted sixty seconds and it felt like a gynecological exam."

"I have news for you, if the horse made it through the gates, it counts."

"Not this horse. He was a friend of Chip's. He was sleeping over and he snuck into my room in the middle of the night, then he never spoke to me again. Looking back on it now, I realize I should have sent him to jail, or at the very least, lured him back into my bed and bit his dick off, but at the time, I figured, why add another headache to my life."

I'd never told anyone that story before. Not even Kat.

"How old was this asshole?" Jacob wanted to know.

"Twenty-two."

Jacob touched my cheek with the back of his hand. "That's really sad," he said. "I'm sorry."

I tried to play it off like it was completely trivial. I didn't want to hamper the festive mood. "I know," I said. "Being raised without a positive male role model can really fuck a girl up."

I wish I'd known Jacob back then. He would have been the kind of guy I could have actually liked. He probably sat in the back of the classroom with *Leaves of Grass* and *Ham on Rye*, wondering why the hell he was surrounded by so much stupidity. When I imagined Jacob in high school, I pictured him as this character from a movie I had to go see when I was a kid. One of my dad's clients was in the film, and my mother made us get all dressed up for the premiere. It was a story about a woman who had some really heavy problems in her life. Then, to make matters worse, she has a heart attack and somehow ends up back in the fifties, in high school. She befriends the cool, outcast guy that she was too popular to give the time of day to the first time around, and he teaches her about poetry. At least that's the way I remember it.

During the screening, my brother turned to me and said, "Hey Beatrice, that's who you're going to marry. Some freak who dresses in black and talks like a fag."

"He's not a fag, he's smart and sensitive," I said.

"Yeah, a fag."

"Cole, watch your mouth," my mother said, as if he'd insulted me or something. But I thought I'd be lucky to find a guy like that. Not a fag, mind you, just an intelligent, sensitive man. One who played a musical instrument instead of a contact sport.

"Jacob, can you play any instruments?" I had to shout because the radio was on full-blast, and Jacob was singing along with The Smiths as loud as his vocal chords would permit.

"Yeah, I can play a little guitar. Why?"

I suddenly thought my life was perfect. Or, at least, more perfect than it had ever been. It was as if all the melancholy I'd ever known, all the nights I sat alone thinking life sucked, had added up to our place in the world—finally a good place—and the spirit of that *rightness* was meant to echo on until the end of time. In one fleeting moment I believed, beyond a shadow of a doubt, that Jacob was going to sell his book someday, and that we were going to break free from whatever it really was that held us back. It had to happen. It was part of the order of things. It was the way the universe was supposed to work.

"Maybe the next time we take a road trip," I said, "we'll be driving east. For good." That prospect made me so excited I gave Jacob back his map.

He grabbed it quickly, pulled over, studied it for a few minutes, then headed back onto the highway. "I know exactly where we're going," he said. "You may now eat the map if you so desire."

"Smile," I said, camera in-hand. With licorice hanging out of his mouth, Jacob gave me his broadest grin—the one that made the apples of his cheeks pop up, the thin skin around his eyes crinkle, and his pouty upper lip spread out. I snapped his picture.

"Listen. Do you recognize this song?" Jacob said. He turned the radio back up.

It was a good song. Kind of gloomy. "I like it," I said. But I didn't think I'd ever heard it before.

"Does it ring any bells?"

I was about to deny any and all bell-ringing until I heard a familiar line, a line I still saw at least once a day, every time I opened the refrigerator.

"Hey…" I said, and listened:

*Call me now it's all right*
*It's just the end of the world*
*You need a friend in the world*
*'Cause you can't hide*
*So call and I'll get right back*
*If your intentions are pure*
*I'm seeking a friend for the end of the world*

"That's kind of morbid," I said when it was over.

"It can't be that morbid, it brought us together. We'll have to play it at our wedding."

That was the first time Jacob had mentioned marriage. Truthfully, I didn't think I would ever be dumb enough to get married, but if I did marry anyone, I said to myself, it would be Jacob. Jacob or no one.

I would never say no to Jacob.

For the rest of the drive we played a game called You Suck. We invented it when we got to the part of the state where the only music we seemed to be able to tune in to was classic rock. When a song came on, the first person to say the title, and/or the band who was performing it, got points. Extra points were given for additional pieces of trivial knowledge, things like the name of the album the song came from, or the names of band members—if they were obscure, that is—no points could be obtained by naming Kurt Cobain, or a Van Halen brother. But I did get one for a guy named Neil Peart—he's the drummer from Rush. Jacob thought it was funny that I knew the names of the members of Rush.

"What the hell is so funny about Rush?" I said.

"Nothing's funny about Rush. It's just that they seem like a boy band to me. You're the only girl I know who likes them."

"Their lyrics are very intelligent. Especially for Canadians."

The title of our game came from the habit of saying "You suck" every time the other person beat you to the punch. It also alluded to the winner's prize. The rule was we played to fifteen points. I won the first round by a landslide. By the middle of the second round, the score was thirteen to nine. I was in the lead again.

A new song began. As soon as he heard the first note, Jacob cried, "'Baba O'Riley!' The Who! *Who's Next!*" He thought he was a force of musical knowledge to be reckoned with.

"You suck," I said. I had two pieces of Ballistic Berry Bubble Yum in my mouth. That's the only reason he beat me on such an easy one. My teeth were stuck together.

"Twelve to thirteen. I'm on a comeback," he said with pride.

"Everybody knows this song."

"Did you know it?"

"Yes."

"Sure you did. But I knew it *faster*."

I knew the next song too, as soon as it began, but I waited to see if Jacob had any clue who it was. At the end of the first verse he shouted, "The Beatles!"

"Wrong," I said.

"Excuse me?"

"This isn't the Beatles."

"It is too."

"No it's not."

"Listen," he said, "if that isn't Paul McCartney, I'll eat the entire box of cinnamon shit candy."

"I hope you're hungry."

"Then who is it, smart-ass?"

"It's Badfinger."

"*Badfinger*? What the fuck is *Badfinger*?"

"One of the only acts to be signed by the Beatles's Apple Record label. The song is called 'Come and Get It.' Recorded August 1969. Written by Paul McCartney. Produced, I believe, by Paul McCartney. Performed, as I've already stated, by Badfinger."

"Are you making this up?"

I didn't have to answer. When the song ended, the DJ confirmed most of my story.

"You didn't get out much when you were a kid, did you?" Jacob said.

"Let's see, that's one point for the band, one for the writer of the song. I could even name two of the band members but I won't rub it in. I win again. Here, eat up." I handed him the Hot Tamales. "I'll make a deal with you. If you give me my prize the next time we stop for gas, you don't have to eat them."

The person with the most points always won the same reward: oral sex.

"You know, any way you look at it," Jacob said, "there are no real losers in this game."

My first destination hypothesis was that we were going to Big Sur because of Jacob's reverence for Henry Miller. I saw our entire weekend in a flash: a little inn overlooking the Pacific run by a couple of hairy-legged, lacto-vegetarian lesbians who sat around a fire singing folk songs in the evenings, cultivating the kind of place that made you want to go hiking with a notebook. Jacob and I would find a nice spot on the rocks to picnic and write sonnets to each other. Not that I was much of a writer or anything, but it was around that time I decided to start a diary. I had visions of becoming the twenty-first century's answer to Anaïs Nin. When I'm dead, I want strangers to read about all the awesome sex I had and wish they could be so lucky.

"Jacob, do you think I could write? I mean, keep a journal or something?"

He thought it was a great idea. "Everyone should keep a chronicle of their life." Easy for Jacob to say. His journals read like perfectly lyrical prose. He wrote truth in sharp sentences and concrete metaphors.

"You should do it, Trixie. It's good for your soul. If you have a desire to write, that means there's stuff in you that wants out. And if you don't write things down, you just forget them," he said. "Think of all the stuff you've forgotten over the course of your lifetime."

"How can I think of it if I've forgotten it?"

"My point exactly."

I bought a notebook in the next town. Jacob promised he'd make sure I wrote in it once a day. "We could do it before we go to bed. Fifteen minutes or so, that's all," he said.

"What if it's crap?"

"So, no one's going to see it. Except me, right?"

"If you're nice."

"Besides, you won't write crappy. You read too much. Reading is the best way to learn how to write."

"Big Sur?"

"What?'

"Is that where we're going? To Big Sur?"

"No, but that's a great idea. Next time."

When we finally turned on to the 580 off-ramp, I was pretty sure I knew where we were headed.

"San Francisco!" I said. I love San Francisco—it's the anti-Los Angeles.

I leaned across the seat and kissed Jacob on the neck. He looked pleased that I was pleased. But hell, he could have taken me to Bakersfield and I would have called it heaven.

# TWENTY-ONE

There was a six-month period, back in college, when Kat and I went to San Francisco once a month. We'd made this crazy rule for ourselves that we weren't allowed to date men who smoked, men who drove convertibles, or actors. That pretty much canceled out every penis in Los Angeles. We had to head north for our dicks.

The last time we'd gone, it was because Kat had insisted the party of the year was some big rave our lives wouldn't be complete without attending. It was in an old warehouse just south of Market Street, and supposedly, a world-famous DJ was hosting it. There are few things I hate more than fraternizing with large crowds of college-aged kids wasted on cheap alcohol and hallucinogenic drugs, so needless to say, I put up a fight.

"What else are you going to do all weekend? Sit in your room and *read*?" Kat said. "If you think I'm schlepping up there all by myself, you've got another thing coming."

Neither Kat nor I had boyfriends at the time, so the main goal of the trip became finding some. Kat, as usual, had the easier time. She picked up an advertising executive who lived in Noe Valley, drove a BMW, and seemed gay to me, but Kat said he was straight. Actually, what she said was, "He's straight enough." She never saw him again.

I ended up spending the night with a cute cyclist from Berkeley. We just fooled around a little and spent most of our time talking. I guess we liked each other and all that baloney, but the last thing I wanted was a long-distance relationship—I need way too much attention and immediate gratification to be content with an absentee boyfriend. I had a hard time getting rid of the guy. He called every day for three weeks straight. He even flew down once to visit me. The only thing I remember about him now is that he shaved his legs. I was surprised at how much I dug the shaved legs.

"Thanks for sharing," Jacob said.

I hadn't realized I'd been thinking aloud.

Jacob had booked us a room at the Ritz-Carlton—an elegant hotel that looked like the White House, and was within walking distance of Chinatown, North Beach, Nob Hill, and Union Square. The Ritz was one of those stuffy places where the staff looked at you like you won the lottery when you walked in looking the way Jacob and I did. I was wearing a skirt, but nothing fancy by any stretch of the imagination. It's not like I had diamonds on like everyone else in the lobby. And Jacob always looked like he'd just rolled out of bed in last night's clothes, which, on occasion, he had. I loved him for that, but some people can neither appreciate nor understand a holy lack of narcissism.

I knew the Ritz had to set the bank account back a few hundred bucks a night, but it had beds that felt like clouds, and there were chocolate-covered strawberries and champagne next to our bed when we arrived. I looked at the room service menu and almost fell over when I saw how much they charged for a dish of sliced bananas.

"I bet I could go to a nursery and get an entire banana tree for less than that," I said.

"Forget it, we're on vacation," Jacob said.

I didn't feel good about Jacob spending so much money on me. I asked him if I could help pay for the room.

"Are you fucking kidding me?" he said. "It's your birthday. You're not paying for the room."

He reminded me about the assignment he'd just been given by *Los Angeles* magazine. It was a going to be a three thousand word article, and at a dollar a word, he said, he could afford it.

"Let me blow half of my paycheck on you, *okay*?"

I tried to tell Jacob there were plenty of hotels in San Francisco that were cute, romantic, and nowhere near as fancy as the Ritz. He wouldn't hear of it.

"I don't want to stay in some trendy-ass place that caters to the hip, *People* magazine-reading, blow-snorting crowd," he said. "We'd stay in L.A. if we wanted that."

Jacob would have rather looked out of place at the Ritz than look like he cared to fit in anywhere.

# TWENTY-TWO

We ate Thanksgiving dinner with Jacob's Uncle Don. He wasn't really Jacob's uncle, not by blood anyway, he was just a guy that Joanna had lived with for a few years when Jacob was a kid. Don and Joanna went their separate ways when Jacob was in elementary school, but they all still kept in touch.

"He taught me how to catch a baseball and how to change a flat tire," Jacob said.

Uncle Don was the spitting image of the Boo Radley of my imagination—an obtuse-looking guy with wiry gray hair and a Jimmy Stewart stutter. He lived in a crummy duplex off of Polk Street and grew orchids in his spare time—he must have had twenty-five plants, all different varieties, all over the place. He had to keep the air warm and humid for them, and walking through his front door was like walking into Florida. Don had been a plumber for most of his adult life but, at the age of fifty, decided he wanted to be a chef. A week later he enrolled himself in the California Culinary Academy. He was six months into the program when we showed up for Thanksgiving. Don had no family in the Bay Area and was thrilled to have us, not only as company, but as guinea pigs.

"I'm experimenting tonight. Ha…Ha…How does a Pan-Asian Thanksgiving sound?"

We told him we were game, and he served us the most interesting holiday meal I'd had in a long time. Duck with citrus-coriander sauce, cucumber and papaya salad, garlic noodles, and vanilla bean ice cream with lychee for dessert.

"What exactly are lychee?" I had to ask because they looked like big, round bugs, and smelled like sugar-coated trash.

"It's a…a…a fruit. Though some people call it a nut."

Uncle Don hated Los Angeles more than Jacob and I did. All through dinner he listed for us the many reasons why we had to get out as soon as possible. He said it was the best thing he'd ever done.

"Los Angeles is a…a…a black hole. A Bermuda Triangle. A va…vast wasteland of vacant infidels."

When we told him our plan for leaving, he went on to explain his theory of people who lived there.

"As…as…as far as I'm concerned, there are three kinds of people who live in Los Angeles. Number one: those…those who love living there. Number two: those who love living there but pre…pretend they hate it because they know they'll be found out for the hollow shells they are if…if they admit how much they enjoy all the pointless drivel."

I was pretty sure Jacob had underestimated Uncle Don's influence. Undoubtedly, more than how to change a tire had rubbed off way back when.

"So where do Trixie and I fit in to your theory?" Jacob said.

"I'm…I'm getting to you," Uncle Don said. Uncle Don had beautiful, working-class hands. Strong and without mercy. Father hands. But not my father, of course, he manicured regularly.

"Then there's number three: you and…and…and this lovely young lady of yours. You're in the minority. You're part of those who want to escape but can't. Am I right?"

We nodded in agreement.

"And I bet it's not so much the smog, or the traffic, or

the…the fact that every night on the evening news, someone has been shot, run over by a car, beaten up by a member of the LAPD, or kill…killed by a natural disaster. No, it's more than that. It's the whole *vibe* down there. You don't fit into that world. I guess I can't speak for you, Beatrice, but you never did, Jake."

"We're moving to Georgia," I said.

"Mississippi," Jacob corrected.

Jacob and I had both been doing our southern research. I wanted to move to Athens, Georgia. It seemed like the kind of place that would offer small town southern charm, but with an art house movie theater and some decent restaurants. And I met a girl from Athens once—she had virtually no accent. I didn't want Madeline and Simone speaking French with a twang. Jacob wanted to live somewhere closer to the river, in a place where barbeque joints with greasy windows and our fantasy Eggleston diners were the most renowned culinary establishments within a twenty-mile radius.

"It should be noted, however," Jacob said, "that as far as we can recall, neither of us have ever set foot in the states of Georgia or Mississippi."

We told Uncle Don he could come and visit us when we moved to the Heartland.

"Whichever part of the Heartland we end up in," I said.

Before we left, we had Uncle Don take a photo of us holding the half-eaten duck carcass. It was the first picture we'd ever been in together.

Friday, Jacob and I spent our time doing silly touristy things. First we rode a cable car, but I was cold so we went back to the hotel to get the car. We drove down the crooked street, checked out the view from Coit Tower, and had shrimp cocktail smothered with red sauce and served in a cardboard cone at Fisherman's Wharf. After lunch we went to Steinhart Aquarium, where we spent the rest of the afternoon. The aquarium made me sad. I feel bad for anything that's locked up. Jacob loved it. He wouldn't leave until he'd seen everything: a poison dart frog, a living coral reef, dolphins, puffer fish. You name it, we saw it. Jacob got to touch a sea star, and for a price, even got to name a black-footed penguin. There is now a flightless aquatic bird in San Francisco called Trixie.

We had dinner that night at a Peruvian place in the Mission district, then found some live music at a bar on Valencia Street. That's where we met Ryan Chuck Montgomery. Ryan Chuck was a cab driver waiting outside for fares. He offered to cart us around town all night for twenty bucks.

"Thanks, but we have a car," I said.

Even if we hadn't had our own mode of transportation I would have told him that. Ryan Chuck scared the hell out of me. First of all, what kind of name is Ryan Chuck? Normal people don't have abbreviated middle names like that. His yellow, tobacco-stained teeth and the Confederate flag tattoo on his forearm didn't make my feelings toward him any fuzzier. When he warned us to watch out for all the Spics in the neighborhood, I saw Jacob's face begin to burn. He wanted to set the guy straight, I know he did. I squeezed his hand and pulled him into the bar. One doesn't need enemies named Ryan Chuck.

"Jacob, do you worry about guys like that once we move to the South?"

"Not really," Jacob said. "Ryan Chuck told me he was from Oregon."

On Saturday, we went bargain shopping in Chinatown. Jacob bought me a pair of slippers and a pink silk robe that had a dragon embroidered on the back. For lunch, we had vegetable chow mein and Kung Pao-something at a place called Nan King. I wasn't crazy about the way the restaurant smelled, kind of like a pet store, but our bill was nine bucks and it was the best Chinese food I'd ever tasted. We left there and walked down Broadway to browse the sex-toy shops. Jacob gave me five minutes and ten dollars, and told me to buy us something to play with.

"But you can't spend any more than ten dollars," he said.

I told him to go into the shop next door, which had virtually the same stock as the one I went in, and do the same. When we finished, we met on the sidewalk.

"I like this better than picking out records," I said.

"Here, happy early birthday." Jacob handed me a jar of chocolate body paint, and some battery-operated, bullet-shaped contraption called The Pocket Rocket. "Look what it says on the back." He turned it around and read it to me: "'For muscle relaxation.' Which *muscles* do you think they're talking about?"

I'd picked out a pair of handcuffs. The clerk wrapped them up like crazy in a plastic bag, and it took Jacob a while to get at them. He grinned when he realized what they were.

"They cost ten ninety-five. I hope that's okay," I said.

"It is."

"It is what?"

"It is *okay*," he said, exaggerating the last syllable.

Jacob had finally caught on to my *okay* infatuation. It only took him eight months, but he was wise to me. Still, he sated me nevertheless.

# TWENTY-THREE

City Lights Bookstore was right across the street from the sidewalk we were standing on. Jacob had never been there. I told him a writer's trip to San Francisco wasn't complete without a stop in City Lights. We put our toys away and walked over.

As soon as we entered the store Jacob went downstairs to nonfiction and history. He came back up ten minutes later with two books in his hand. One was a biography of Joe DiMaggio, the other was a collection of political essays by Noam Chomsky.

I was looking for a copy of a book called *The Road to Los Angeles* by John Fante. I'd loaned mine to Kat, and I rarely got back anything I loaned to Kat. I wrote it off and wandered over to fiction and literature to pick up a new one. I walked with my head tilted to the right so that I could read the books as I traced the shelves. I did that every time I went into a book store because I was afraid I was going to miss something, even though it made me dizzy and gave me a kink in my neck.

Passing through the Ds on my way to F, *Morning Glory* caught my eye. They also had another one of Thomas Doorley's books, something called *Tijuana Stories*.

"Hey, Jacob, come here for a second."

Jacob walked to me from the independent press shelf. His pile had grown by a book, but it was on the bottom; I couldn't see what the new addition was.

I set *Morning Glory* down on top of his stack.

"I already have that. Thanks though," he said.

"You said you wanted to spend the rest of the afternoon in the park. We'll go there and read. No stress attached. Come on, it's time."

He didn't say yes, but he didn't put the book away either. I interpreted that as a thumbs-up.

"Are you ready to go?" he said.

I found my Fante and we went to the check-out counter.

"This is a great book," the cashier said to me when he bagged my purchase.

"I know. I lost mine," I said.

When my transaction had been completed, Jacob set his four books down. As the cashier scanned Jacob's pile, one by one, he commented.

"Cool. Chomsky rules," the cashier said.

Jacob's additional purchase was a Mobil travel guide for the southeastern United States.

When the cashier got to *Morning Glory*, he chuckled and said, "Doorley, huh? He comes in here all the time. He's a real wacko."

Jacob took a terrified glance around the store and bowed his head down an inch, as if Thomas Doorley were hiding behind the shelves, about to jump out and say, "Boo!"

"Does he live around here?" I said.

"Trixie, let's go," Jacob said.

"No, he lives over in Marin County," the cashier said. "But he frequents the bar across the street."

I knew the bar across the street. It was called Tosca. I once spent a long weekend going to Tosca every night. U2 was in town and someone told me they liked to hang out there. I never saw them. Instead, I got hit on and harassed by a well-known actor who happened to be filming in the area. It was just like being in L.A. so I never went back.

The actor, who shall remain nameless, had dirty fingernails and smelled like he bathed in Heineken. When I turned him down, Kat's gay friend Doug cried fool and didn't talk to me for the rest of the night.

"Doorley practically lives in Tosca," the cashier said. "He drinks cheap whiskey, then comes over here all drunk and cranky and yells at us for not having more of his novels around. And he always buys *Lolita*. I don't know if he collects it, or if he just forgets he has it, but I've personally sold him three copies."

Jacob didn't say anything. He didn't even acknowledge the cashier was still speaking. He just picked up his bag and walked out.

"Do you know where in Marin Thomas Doorley lives?" I whispered to the cashier.

"He lives in Mill Valley, I think."

Jacob and I went straight to Golden Gate Park. We lay our coats down near the botanical gardens and read, hanging out like we had nothing pressing to attend to for the rest of our lives. We didn't talk much while we were there, but we always made sure some parts of our bodies were in direct contact. Jacob was like that. He wanted to be touching at all times.

It was almost dark when Jacob closed his book and stood up. "I'm hungry," he said.

We stopped at a crepe place on Cole Street for dinner. Jacob hadn't said anything about *Morning Glory*, but he'd made it halfway through without any breakdowns; only a few pauses when he would look up from the book and stare off into space.

"So, are you going to tell me what you think, or do I just have to try and read your mind?" I said.

A homeless woman wandered in to the restaurant. She was

heavy-set, wrapped in a blanket, and her thick green socks were bunched up around her fat ankles. She sat down on a bench inside the door.

"No more mashed potatoes, no more coffee," the woman mumbled. "Just eat hair." She grabbed a knotted chunk of her dirty mane and put it in her mouth. A waiter went over to her and asked her if she needed some help.

"I'm Mary," she said.

"Hi Mary, I'm Sam," the waiter said. Sam gave Mary a Styrofoam container of left-overs. I was glad he didn't make her leave. For his charitable gesture, Sam earned himself an extra few bucks tip from our table.

If we'd been in L.A., Mary would have been out on her ass.

"Well?" I said to Jacob, as gently as I could.

"Well," he said, "I don't know. It's weird. I have mixed emotions." He took a deep breath and peered into my eyes. I could see the vein on the left side of his forehead—the one that popped up when he was concentrating. He was looking to me for answers but, regrettably, I was the last person equipped to offer any enlightening familial words of wisdom. All I had was my opinion.

"Don't you think it's eerily familiar, metaphorically anyway?"

"Yeah," was all he said, while he trimmed the nail of his left index finger with one of his sharp teeth.

"You're a better writer than he is," I told him.

I saw the glimmer of a faint smile sneak onto his face as he spat the nail onto the floor. "I know."

While Jacob was still eating, I got up like I was going to the bathroom. I went to the pay phone and called information. I asked if there was a listing for Thomas Doorley. I spelled the name for the operator and requested an address.

Mary was still sitting at the door eating her dinner. I smiled at her but she didn't smile back.

"As soon as you're off the phone, I need to check my email," Mary said.

The operator came back a second later and read me Thomas Doorley's address. Then she connected me to a recording of his phone number. I wrote it all down and stuffed it into my wallet.

We attempted to play with our newly acquired sex toys that night, but Jacob's heart wasn't in it. I even tried ordering a skin flick from the pay-TV station to rile him up, something called *Naughty Nurses*, but that didn't do the trick either. Problem was, I found Jacob incredibly attractive when he was brooding. I got under the covers and climbed on top of him. Writhing my body on his dick made it hard, and once it was hard I could do whatever I wanted with it, even if Jacob wasn't in the mood. We always obliged each other that way.

He let me ride him until I came, and by then, between the porn and watching me get off, he was ready for a little something. Slowly, I slid him inside me. Usually he liked me to sit up when I fucked him, so he could see my body. That night he pulled me down close to his chest and didn't make a sound. No moans, no groans, nothing. He just let out a long exhale, like he'd been holding his breath, and he squinted for a few seconds. That's how I knew he was finished.

I fell asleep after that. Jacob didn't shut off the light for at least another hour. He stayed up and finished reading the book.

# TWENTY-FOUR

We slept late the next morning and splurged on room service for breakfast. I had a Belgian waffle with strawberries. Jacob had a mushroom and cheese omelet with hash browns, sausage, toast, and coffee. After my shower, I pranced around the room in the fluffy white hotel robe while we tried to decide what to do. It was our last full day in San Francisco and we didn't want to waste it. Jacob suggested that we stay in bed and watch movies, which wasn't a bad idea, except that it was a submission of avoidance rather than desire. He knew what I was going to propose. Deep down, I think he wanted me to say it, even needed me to. I waited until he'd ingested a sufficient amount of caffeine before I sprang it on him.

"So, did you know your father lived around here?"

"He lives in Mill Valley. That's north of the city," Jacob said. I didn't realize he was privy to so much information about Thomas Doorley's elusive life.

"How do you know that?"

"He's lived in the same place for twenty-five years. It's no big secret."

"Have you ever been there?" I said.

"No."

"Feel like stopping by?"

He tilted his head to the left and sighed.

I made him sit down and I apologized for being a pest about the whole situation, but, I told him, I could see how badly he wanted to make contact with the man. I could see it in his face every time I mentioned Thomas Doorley's name, every time I brought up the book. He was cursed. I even reminded him what he'd told me when we first met, that he hoped he would one day have the chance to speak to his father face to face. Those were practically his exact words.

"We're here. Why not just do it now?" I said.

"I don't know *exactly* where he lives or anything."

I took the secret piece of paper from my wallet and handed it to him.

"Next excuse," I said.

"Trixie, don't you think if he wanted to see me, he'd have found *me* by now?"

"Yes. But what difference does it make what he wants? Fuck what he wants. He doesn't deserve to have his wants respected. I mean, what about what *you* want? He's your father, for God's sake. You have every right."

"But he's not my father. I mean, *technically* he's my father, genetically. But beyond that, he's nothing."

"All I'm saying is that if you want to know this man, regardless of what he thinks, you should be able to."

Jacob rested his elbows on the room service table and held his fists together like he was praying. His mouth was covered by his hands and he mumbled something inaudible as he stared at the dime-sized red stain that stood out on the white tablecloth. It was from a strawberry that had fallen off his fork when he reached for a bite of my waffle. He sat there mesmerized by the little scarlet smudge. He looked scared. I'd never seen that much trepidation and helplessness on his face before, and looking at him made me ache like I did in high school when I was a volunteer at the animal shelter and my mother wouldn't let me bring home the dogs that were about to get the ax.

"But Mom, they're innocent."

"I don't care, Beatrice."

"They sense what's going to happen to them."

"I don't want to hear it."

"They don't want to die!"

"I'm not going to say it again."

I eventually had to quit. Being at the shelter was even more depressing than being at home. And I still feel guilty about not saving those fucking dogs. I should have protected them. Just like I should have protected Jacob. I should have kidnapped him and taken him to some perfect, southern, Eggleston-snapshot of an Elysian Field.

I should have locked him up instead of throwing him to the wolves.

I should have never let anyone or anything hurt him.

How many times in your life are you allowed to say, "*If only…?*"

# TWENTY-FIVE

Mill Valley was across the Golden Gate Bridge. How ridiculous, I thought, that I'd been to San Francisco a dozen times and had never crossed the Golden Gate. The sky was clear that day, the same color as the water, with a strong wind that drew our car to the left and filled the sails of the boats below us, sending them gliding across the bay. It was like driving right through a postcard.

"Isn't it beautiful?" I said. I was trying to distract Jacob with the view.

"Huh?" he said, a world away.

I took the Stinson Beach exit off of 101 and followed the signs for about three miles in to Mill Valley. There was a quaint town there, with a market, a vintage movie theater, little shops selling souvenirs and novelties, an unusual number of Italian restaurants, and a bookstore café called The Depot. About a dozen mountain-bikers were gathered in the square, and almost every person I saw was lugging either a dog or a kid behind them. The air smelled like eucalyptus. Besides all the cars and the fact that the whole town appeared to be overrun by yuppies, it seemed like a delightful place to live.

I parked in the lot behind the bookstore. Jacob stopped in for a cup of coffee and stalled for time by drinking it as slowly as possible. We wandered around, and the longer we wandered, the sweatier Jacob's hands became. Finally I asked a kid in a blue-and-yellow striped shirt who was standing in front of the bike shop passing out flyers where Lovell Avenue was.

That's the name of the street Thomas Doorley lived on.

"Right there," he said and pointed to the road behind us.

Jacob and I walked up a little hill, past a restaurant that served Indian burritos, whatever the hell those were, and checked the numbers on the houses. We were less than two blocks away.

The Doorley house was a tiny A-frame painted pale gray with white trim. There was a run-down old gate in front of the small yard and the hydrangea bushes were overgrown and unruly—Thomas Doorley was definitely not a gardener.

The house was right next door to a church, one with some sort of Sunday school in session. About a dozen children were scurrying around the basement classroom—we could hear them giggling through the open windows. Jacob walked over, looked in, and reported that the kids were having cookies and orange drink. Not orange *juice*, but orange *drink*, he specified. That concerned him.

"Kids need vitamin C," he said. "Not so much sugar. Remind me about that when we have kids. Remind me that our girls aren't going to a school where they get fed sugar to eat and sugar to drink."

"Our girls won't be going to school on Sunday," I said.

"Unless it's to sing with the Aretha Franklin clone who heads the choir in Greenville, Mississippi."

"Athens, Georgia," I said.

Jacob sat down on the steps of the parish with his elbow on his knee, his chin on his fist, and stared at the ground. I took a picture of him there. He looked like *The Thinker*.

"I need a cigarette," he said.

"Since when do you smoke?"

"Since right now."

I asked him how old his father would be and he tapped his fingers to his thumb, trying to figure it out.

"About fifty-one," he said.

I opened the gate in front of Thomas Doorley's yard, try-ing to see inside the house. There was a television and a couch in the small front room, but everything was turned off and there were no cars in the driveway. It didn't look like anyone was home.

I was about to prowl around to the back when I heard a woman's voice.

"Can I help you?"

I spun around. The lady who stood in front of me was probably in her mid-forties, kind of petite with frizzy red hair and freckles that covered every exposed inch of skin on her body. Beside her was a teenage boy, who, if I had to guess, was around sixteen. He had red hair, too; it came down almost to his shoulders. Something about his eyes struck me as familiar. I got a jolt when I figured out why.

They were Jacob's eyes.

Woman and boy were each carrying a bag of groceries, but they looked like the kind of people who might have shaken our hands had theirs been free.

"Um…do you live here?" I said to the woman.

When she said she did, Jacob stood up. He walked over slowly, curiously, but he didn't say anything. He just looked at her.

Standing face to face with those two people, it dawned on me that there was a greater than slim chance I hadn't thought our little field-trip through. Maybe it wasn't such a good idea after all. I'd pictured Thomas Doorley living alone. In a one-room cabin or in an old Airstream trailer. In the forest. In the middle of nowhere, cutting his own wood and growing marijuana in his backyard like some beatnik Unabomber.

Meekly, the woman said, "Is there something we can do for you?"

I introduced myself. I told her my name was Maureen

McCormick. I said I was a reporter from the *San Francisco Chronicle*. I don't know why I lied, but I figured at that point, it was the safest way to get information out of her. I had only a vague idea of who she might be, but I hadn't gone to Mill Valley to disrupt innocent lives; only guilty ones.

"Rhonda Doorley," she said. "This is my son, Eric."

As if he spoke another language and didn't quite comprehend Rhonda's words, Jacob mumbled, "Your son?"

I introduced Jacob as Barry Williams, hoping Rhonda and Eric weren't fans of *The Brady Bunch*.

"Are you looking for my husband?" she said.

I told her I was. I told her I was writing a story on artists living in Marin County. I told her the cashier at City Lights gave me their address.

The lies were coming to me in flashes and I thought, damn, I'd make a hell of a detective, because these two sponges have soaked up every drop I've spilled so far. I must have seemed honest or something. Then again, Jacob stared at me like I had birdshit on my face.

Rhonda spoke softly and told me that her husband wasn't home; that she didn't know when he'd be back. She was a bit of a shrinking violet. She struck me as the kind of woman who might let a man abuse her, simply because she didn't know she was being abused.

Eric's sweatshirt said Mt. Tamalpais Lacrosse on it. I remembered passing Mt. Tamalpais High School on our drive into town.

"You're welcome to wait if you want," Rhonda said. "But you could be waiting days. Tom lives in his own time zone. He was supposed to be back at noon."

It was after four.

"No, that's okay. Thanks anyway," Jacob said. "Let's go, Trixie."

If he'd called me Trixie one more time, he probably would have blown our cover.

"Have we met before?" Rhonda said to Jacob.

"No. We haven't," Jacob said regrettably. He took my hand and started dragging me down the street.

We were already to the corner when Rhonda paged us.

"Wait! Here he comes," she said. "That's Tom there!"

An old Mercury Montego painted a hideous, carnival shade of blue was just rounding the bend.

Jacob stopped dead in his tracks. Only his head moved. He followed the path of the car and made eye-contact with his father. Thomas looked at Jacob and Jacob looked at Thomas. If that guy is drunk, I thought, he's going to run right over his wife, crash through his gate, and flatten the hydrangeas. He wasn't paying one iota of attention to where he was going.

The car came to a stop in the driveway. Thomas got out and Rhonda tried to tell him we were a couple of reporters. He ignored her. He walked our way, peering at Jacob.

Once Thomas was directly in front of us, Jacob introduced himself. He said his name mechanically, as if he were participating in a spelling bee. He let the accent fall on his last name. It sounded like a slap in the face.

"I know who you are," Thomas said, smirking. "I figured you'd show up here one of these days. To be honest, I didn't think it'd take you this long."

Thomas was even smaller than Jacob, completely unkempt, and the fresh smile he'd worn in the photograph I'd seen of him had been replaced by dark impassivity. Underneath it all, though, his face was still just an aged version of my lover's. He was Jacob with deeper lines. Jacob plus twenty years and hundreds of bottles of Jack Daniels. Jacob plus the sixties, which, I judged, might have been part of the problem. The entire Decade of Love seemed shrouded inside of Thomas Doorley—like someone told him it had all been a myth—a myth he buried deep inside himself with the hope that it might sprout wings someday and finally fulfill it's promise of freedom.

"Who's the little lady?" Thomas said, looking me up and down like I was beef roast on a platter.

"The *little lady* is my girlfriend," Jacob said.

"Touchy, touchy…," Thomas stretched out his arm to greet me.

"Beatrice Jordan," I said.

He kissed the top of my hand. "It's a pleasure, Miss Jordan." Then he shifted toward his son. Jacob wouldn't take his father's hand.

"Fair enough," Thomas said.

Unless Jacob softens up, I thought, this isn't going to go well.

"Let's go get a drink," Thomas said. He led and we followed, while Rhonda's eyes trailed us. But Thomas offered his wife no explanations. He never even looked back at her.

We ended up at a place that was probably Mill Valley's most hopping scene at night, but in the middle of the day was empty save for us and the band that was setting up on the tiny stage. It was a sawdust bar called The Sweet Water, an inauthentic version of the kind of joint I was sure awaited us in any town below the Mason-Dixon line. I imagined our future hangout to have a jukebox instead of a band, with patrons who wasted their quarters on Lynard Skynard all night long. I would have had to bring lots of coins—to corner the market on better music, because I hate southern rock 'n' roll, especially the kind made by guys who cut down Neil Young in their songs.

"The yuppies must feel like they're roughing it in here," I

said without thinking. Thomas looked at me and laughed dryly, as if he agreed.

The bartender took our orders. He already knew what Thomas wanted: whiskey with no rocks. I asked for a glass of white wine. Jacob got coffee.

"Come on, drink with your old man," Doorley said to Jacob. The bartender paused and waited for Jacob to reconfirm his choice. Forcefully, and without a flinch, he reiterated, "*Coffee.*"

None of us said anything for the minute it took the bartender to fill our glasses. Thomas downed his drink in one gulp, then asked for another, all the while staring at Jacob. After his second shot, he spoke.

"Shit, looking at you is like looking in a fucking mirror. Only I'm looking at twenty years ago." Thomas turned to me. "I wasn't a bad looking guy, was I?"

"Damn straight," I said.

Jacob remained pensive. I felt like it was up to me to give birth to some sort of conversation. I told Thomas that I'd read *Morning Glory*. I asked him, artfully, where the inspiration came from for the story. He elbowed Jacob. "You better hang on to this one," he said. "Smart *and* she's got a nice ass. That's a rare combination in a woman."

Jacob gave his father a foul look. If Thomas had made one more crass remark, I truly believe Jacob would have belted him.

"Jacob's a writer, too," I said to Thomas, rattling off as much of Jacob's resume as I could remember. I even told him about *Hallelujah*, much to the dismay of my boyfriend, who I was sure, by the sneer he gave me, wanted me to shut up.

The look on Thomas's face made me think he was pleasantly surprised that his long-lost son made his living as a writer, even gratified by it, but he didn't question me any further. He was in the middle of asking me what I did when Jacob interrupted him.

"Is Eric my brother?" he said without looking up from his coffee.

Thomas answered yes to Jacob's question. He said Eric was indeed his half-brother. I think that hurt Jacob more than anything he could have imagined learning about the missing pieces of his life that day. He'd gone looking for a father, but a brother wasn't something he'd bargained for at all.

One of the guys in the band started tuning a guitar. It sounded like he was playing "The Star-Spangled Banner."

"Do I have any other siblings I should know about?" Jacob said.

"None that I know of," Thomas said.

"Does Eric know? About me?"

"He does now. At least he will, once I get home and have to explain you people to my family."

I found it heartbreaking that, when referring to his family, Thomas never once meant Jacob. I hated Thomas for that.

"I figured I'd tell him when and if the time came. I guess the time is now."

Thomas went on to explain tactlessly that Rhonda knew he'd "knocked a girl up" a long time ago, but nothing more than that. Evidently, Tom and Rhonda had been married for about sixteen years. She was his second wife. His first wife, who he was married to briefly in the mid-seventies, never had any kids.

"Accidents happen," Doorley said.

I didn't know if he was alluding to Jacob, to Eric, or to both of them. It was a pretty lousy thing to say, regardless.

"I was never cut out to be a father," Thomas said.

The band's singer, a bean pole with long, perfectly straight hair, joined the rest of his buddies on stage. He looked like one of the twelve apostles. He kept saying, "Check one, two, three," into the microphone.

"I had a pretty shitty father myself," Thomas said. "You were better off without me, trust me on that." He gulped down the remainder of his third drink.

"I think this was a mistake," Jacob said, and rose from his seat. "I'm sorry. I'm sorry if we bothered you, if we disturbed your *family* or anything." Jacob flipped through his wallet and slammed a twenty dollar bill on the bar.

With a deep, almost penitent sigh, Thomas said, "I don't know what you want from me, kid."

"I don't want anything," Jacob said, and walked away.

That's when I stood up. But I remained standing next to Thomas while he rolled an empty glass around in his palm.

"It was good to meet you, Mr. Doorley." I offered him my hand, and when he took it I held on longer than I should have. I squeezed hard. I tried to tell him, silently, all the things Jacob was feeling, all the things Jacob needed to hear to be complete. I begged him with my eyes to stop Jacob from walking out the door.

"I can't do it, baby doll," Thomas said.

When Jacob reached the door, he opened it and the afternoon sun flooded the dark room. I almost had to squint to see.

"I have nothing to give him," Thomas said to me. "I never did."

"I don't believe that for a second."

"Believe what you want."

"Jacob's a really good guy," I told Thomas. "You'd like him if you got to know him."

"I already like him," he said. "That kid's got heart. I can see it all over his goddamn face. But it'll be the death of him. He better toughen up or he's in for it. Life ain't no picnic, missy."

Where did he get the nerve? Did he think for one second that the last thirty years of Jacob's life had been some kind of fucking picnic? Did he think Jacob hadn't suffered, in large part, because of *him*? I had half a mind to grab Thomas Doorley by the shirt and shake the living daylights out of him. I had half a mind to slap him in the face. Instead, I just turned to go.

"Hey," Thomas said.

I spun back around.

"His writing any good?"

"Better than yours," I told him.

That made Thomas smile. Sort of. The corners of his lips rose anyway.

Quickly, I scribbled our address and phone number on a napkin and set it on the bar. "Drop your son a Christmas card or something. It's the least you could do."

Thomas didn't acknowledge my request, but he took the napkin. I saw him put it in his pocket.

Just to make myself feel better, I imagined a tear rolling down Thomas Doorley's cheek as his son walked away. Of course I knew that was a big lie. He never looked at us again after we left. I knew because I watched him.

As we drove back over the bridge, Jacob's gloom permeated the car like thick smoke. Thomas Doorley had broken his heart yet again. I felt like I'd instigated the whole event and, ironically, I of all people should have known better. But nobody ever really learns, do they?

There's nothing more pathetic than dreaming dreams you know can never come true.

*You'll never find your gold on a sandy beach*
*You'll never drill for oil on a city street*
*I know you're looking for a ruby in a mountain of rocks*

*But there ain't no Coupe de Ville hiding at the bottom of a Cracker Jack box.*

"Coupe de Ville?" Jacob said bitterly, speaking directly to the radio. "Hell, a Pinto would've been a prize."

"Two Out of Three Ain't Bad" was the last song in the world I felt like listening to. It was Jacob's day of pain. We had no time for any of *my* traumatic childhood memories. That one took me back to the night a strange woman named Violet Lyngstad called our house. I answered the phone and she said, "Hello, my name is Violet Lyngstad. Tell your mother that Curtis is in love with me. Violet Lyngstad is my name."

"I got 'Violet Lyngstad' the first time," I said. The whore didn't need to say it twice.

When I told my mother what Violet the Whore Lyngstad said, my mother threw a platter of pasta at my father, and dragged me and my brothers out the door.

"Curtis, I'm leaving! This is it!" she said.

As soon as we got in the car, Mom turned up the radio. That was so she wouldn't have to explain anything to us. While we drove down Mulholland, Chip complained about having homework to finish; Cole, who was only about four at the time, curled up next to me and sobbed himself to sleep; and over the airwaves, Meat Loaf tried to convince us that it was okay to settle for less than we deserved by accepting being wanted and needed, by just throwing in the towel on ever being loved. Groovy. Just what I always hoped life would hold for me: nothing special.

My mother checked us all in to the Beverly Hills Hotel for the night, and when we went back home the next day she thought Dad would be waiting for us, a changed man, but he'd just gone off to work like normal. He might have been an asshole, but he wasn't stupid. He knew we'd be back. Instead of being met with flowers and apologies when she returned, all my mother got was cold spaghetti and broken glass all over the kitchen floor. When I thought about the lack of rewards my mother reaped from her marriage, two out of three wouldn't have been half bad for her.

*I can't lie*
*I can't tell you that I'm something I'm not*
*No matter how I try*
*I'll never be able*
*to give you something*
*Something that I just haven't got*

Jacob reached over and slammed the radio off.

"Good move," I said. "With our luck, Harry Chapin would be next on the play list."

# TWENTY-SIX

Jacob was, understandably, in an extremely shitty mood. When we got back to the hotel he ripped off his boots, slammed the closet door, and brushed his teeth like he was scraping paint off the side of a house. Then he closed all the drapes so that it seemed like midnight in our room. He flinched with every move I made, making me feel like a complete and utter annoyance. He wanted to be alone. He wanted to write about what had transpired. I wanted to do the same thing, actually. At that point, I'd only been writing for a few days, and shit, did I pick an ideal weekend to start a journal. Two weeks prior, I would have been jotting down things like: slept until ten, mailed the rent check, had sex in the shower. This was in another realm altogether. But I knew I could write later. First and foremost, Jacob needed space.

I spent my time walking around, looking for a place to get take-out. I was sure Jacob would be hungry by the time I got back. I picked the cleanest sushi bar I could find and ordered a few rolls to go. They said it would take twenty minutes. I went back outside and searched for temporary entertainment. There wasn't much to see on the block. Basically, I had two choices: the empty laundromat next door or the card reader across the street.

I had no dirty clothes on hand.

The sign in the window read: Maria. Tarot. $15. I liked to say I didn't believe in mystics, but for fifteen bucks, I decided it might be worth something. I hadn't had my fortune told since I was twelve, and I pretended to deem that woman a complete charlatan. It was time for an update.

After three long knocks, an aloof teenaged girl finally opened the door and let me in. As I followed her through the living room, I realized I was in somebody's house. A little boy was sprawled out on the rust-colored carpet sucking his thumb and watching cartoons. He didn't even look up when I walked by.

The girl escorted me to the kitchen and told me to sit down. The room made me woozy. The walls were bright blue, the tiles on the counter were yellow and pink, and the little round table was red. I felt like I was inside a pinata. I focused on the three things I saw in the middle of the table: a votive candle, a dish of potato chips, and a deck of cards. The girl told me to help myself to the chips while she went to get her mother. Something in the oven smelled like burnt cheese.

"You want your cards read?" the middle-aged woman said when she came in.

"Yes, please."

She sat down across from me, grabbed a cluster of chips, and crammed them into her mouth. She was a good thirty pounds overweight—I could see her plump body outlined by the tight sweat pants and Oakland Raiders T-shirt she had on—and I contemplated advising her to opt for a lower-calorie snack while predicting futures, but I was afraid I'd offend her and she'd tell me something awful.

"Are you Maria?" I said.

"No. I'm Margaret. There is no more Maria."

That seemed weird. Maria was probably bound and gagged and stuffed in the coat closet.

Margaret shuffled the pack of picture cards and placed them in my hands. They were greasy and salty from the chip residue on her fingers.

"Hold them tight. Close your eyes. And make a wish. After you've made your wish, spread out the cards and pick five for me."

Jacob would have laughed so hard if he'd seen me there.

"You are not concentrating," Margaret said.

I tried to focus. All I could see was the look on Jacob's face the moment he made eye contact with his brother. Silently, I wished for Jacob to be happy. I opened my eyes, picked out a few cards just like Margaret instructed, and handed them to her.

She turned the cards over and studied them, shaking her head and picking at a zit on her chin.

"This is six," she said.

"What?"

"You gave me six cards. I asked you for five, but you gave me six."

"Shit. I never was very good at math," I said. "Is it bad? Does it mean something horrible is going to happen?"

"No. It's good luck. Did you make a wish?"

"Yes."

"It will come true," she said. "When is your birthday?"

"Tomorrow."

Margaret raised her head at breakneck speed and looked at me, like my birthday being the following day was monumental. She began turning the cards over, one by one.

"The World Card. This indicates you have chosen the right career. You will never want for money."

"Whatever," I said. I couldn't have cared less about money. All I cared about was love. "Can you tell me anything about my current relationship?"

"What I can tell you is that you have already met the man who should be your partner for life. Your soulmate. Whether or not it's the man you are with, I do not know."

"It is," I told her. Not that she cared, that was obvious.

She turned over another card. It was something called the Knight of Wands. She said it indicated a change of residence in the next twelve months. If I bought even a word of her crap, that meant Jacob was going to sell his book and we'd be off to Georgia within a year. Good news. I wanted to kiss Margaret.

The next card was the Nine of Swords. With a straight face, she said, "This is a vision of impending doom." I immediately changed my mind about kissing her. She was a bitch. It didn't bother her one bit that I was doomed.

"What does *that* mean?"

"It means be careful," she warned. "Don't let your loved ones wander."

I asked her what she meant by wander.

"The cards say there is risk in wandering. That is all I know."

"Come on, this is important," I said. "Don't you *see* anything? Try closing your eyes or something."

She did—she closed her eyes just like I asked. "I see a water tornado," she said.

At first I didn't know what the hell she was talking about. Then I tried to picture it.

"The whirlpool!" I gasped. Just like in my dream. Jacob was now officially banned from hot tubs for life.

"What else?" I said.

The next card was the Empress. Margaret said it represented fertility, something maternal. I was afraid she was going to tell me I was pregnant, but she said, in laymen's terms, it could imply that I had to mother someone, which was true. Sometimes Jacob needed mothering.

The next two cards were the Three of Swords and the Ten of Swords.

"What's with all the swords?" I said.

"They suggest an inevitable ending. Something you have

no control over. But remember that there is light at the end of the every tunnel. Every end promises a new beginning. Okay? Thank you. That is your reading."

"That's it?" I said. My reading was too vague and wrought with cliche. I should have threatened Margaret. I should have told her I knew about Maria's decomposing body in the closet, and unless I got a more concise vision of my future, I was going straight to the cops.

I was already in the doorway when I asked one last question.

"Can you at least tell me if I'm going to live in Georgia or Mississippi?"

She looked at me like I was insane. "I don't see you in a warm climate." Then she shut the door in my face.

When I got back to the Ritz, Jacob was sitting on the bed with his back against the headboard. He was on the phone with Joanna. I put down the sushi, took off my shoes, and curled up next to him. Across the front of the black notebook on his lap, he'd drawn the word TRAVELER. Jacob had dozens of notebooks that he kept strewn about our apartment, and he named them all like that. He had one he wrote in first thing in the morning, he kept it by the bed for dreams, it said *phoenix*. The one he wrote poetry in he called *The Juggernaut*. My favorite was the one he jotted story ideas in, that was *Father, Son, and the Holy Toast*. He'd drawn a picture on the cover of it, a cartoon of a crucifix, only the crucifix was spread out over a piece of bread, but the bread wasn't just bread, it was the earth shaped like bread. What I mean is, it had all the continents drawn around it, and the parts that were supposed to be the oceans were shaded with a blue pen. He also had another little pad he kept in his coat pocket— that was *Roy*.

I wanted to draw some cool word or phrase on my notebook too, but I couldn't think of a good one.

"I missed you," Jacob said when he got off the phone. He touched my hair. That's the way he greeted me sometimes—he petted me.

"How are you?"

"I've been better," he said. Then he flipped through half a dozen pages of chicken scratch in his notebook. "But there's nothing like a little heartbreak and pain to inspire."

I asked him if he was sorry he went to Mill Valley and he said no, he had to go. "I just wish…" But then he stopped, as if it wasn't worth it.

"Tell me," I said.

"I don't know, I just feel like all these years I kind of gave him the benefit of the doubt. Even through my anger, I made excuses for him. Like he said, he didn't want a kid, didn't want the responsibility, the whole family thing. And for some stupid reason, I think that would have been acceptable. But he didn't not want a family, he just didn't want *our* family. My family. He didn't want *me*."

I didn't agree with Jacob's assessment of his father and I told him so.

"First of all," I said, "Thomas Doorley didn't appear to be any more into his current family than he was into you. The fact that he lives with them seems completely inconsequential. Second, from my perspective, the man is just totally lost. Maybe he's one of those people who never fit in. Maybe he's not so different from me and you. Only he goes about dealing with his pain in the worst way possible—by drowning it with whiskey. He puts up walls. He shuts people out. Not just you, Jacob, but everyone. It's like what you always say about that hole we all have in our souls. Your father has a big one. And instead of trying to fill it up with anything real, he left it empty and day by day, year after year, it started to swallow him from the inside out. That's what I think."

Jacob planted a gentle kiss on my shoulder. "That's pretty good for a woman who spends most of the day working with metal."

I could tell that in between the rock of Jacob's anger and the hard place of his disappointment, lay a glimmer of hope that shone directly above Thomas Doorley's head, a glimmer that no amount of mistreatment was going to make disappear. I admired Jacob for having even a tiny bit of that faith. I didn't think I was strong enough to feel an emotion like that. If I were, I said to myself, I would have been in Malibu for Thanksgiving.

# TWENTY-SEVEN

"We can't spend our last night in San Francisco all cooped up like a couple of chickens," Jacob said. He got claustrophobic when he was stressed out. If we'd been at home, he would have wanted to go to the beach. Luckily, the bay was too cold for a midnight swim.

"Let's go grab a beer," he said. He already had his coat on.

We went back to the bar on Valencia. There was no Ryan Chuck outside, and no live band inside, just a crummy DJ who spun a load of half-assed pop songs from the early eighties. Jacob neither cared nor noticed. He hadn't gone for the tunes. We were barely through the door before he had a seat at the bar and a bottle in his hand. He ordered us both beers, even though I said I didn't want one, and we sat there like a couple of lonely sots. I tried to get him to dance but he was unequivocally glued to his chair. He finished his beer in five big gulps, had two quick shots of tequila, then started drinking from my bottle.

"Thirsty?" I said. He ignored me. "Jacob, why don't we just go back to the hotel?"

"I don't want to go back to the hotel," he snapped. "If I go back there, all I'm going to do is sit around and think about it."

I assumed *it* meant his father, as well as the brother he never knew he had. He sucked on my beer and gazed at his reflection in the frosted mirror behind the bar. He stared straight into his own eyes, and I can't say for sure what he saw, but I would have bet my inheritance he wasn't looking at himself. I found it funny that he thought going back to the hotel was going to make him think of *it*, because there he was, sitting on a barstool, thinking so hard on *it* that he couldn't even recognize his own goddamn face.

I spun my chair around and watched the small crowd dance. When the DJ took a break, everyone swarmed the bar for refills.

A guy in crisp blue jeans and a bomber jacket stepped between me and Jacob, and ordered a rum and coke.

"Omar?" I said.

The guy did a double-take. Jacob looked over to see who I was talking to.

"Beatrice?" Omar said. "Are you kidding me? What are you doing here?"

I stood up and he threw his arms around me.

Omar's girlfriend, Valerie, and I were roommates our last year of college. We stayed friends for a while after graduation, until he and Valerie moved up to the Bay Area and I lost touch with them. Omar was a dark, lanky theater actor with a dusty presence. I always had a crush on him.

"You look great," he said. "How are you?" He kept his arm around me.

"Good," I said. I introduced him to Jacob and the arm came down.

Omar gave Jacob a quick overview of our past, explaining how long it had been since we'd seen each other. Jacob vacantly acknowledged Omar and never really tuned in to the conversation.

"He had a bad day," I said.

There were no empty seats at the bar. Omar had to stand close in front of me as we talked. I saw Jacob watching him in the mirror, as if there were some imaginary line in the floor Omar had mistakenly crossed. Jacob was being unusually rude but, like I said, he'd had a bad day; I wasn't going to hold it against him.

Omar told me he was working with a theater company up the street and was considering moving to New York. I asked him about Valerie. They'd broken up a few years ago, he said. She was married now and lived in Boise.

"You know, I still have that ring you made me," he said.

Back when Omar and Valerie thought they were going to live happily ever after, they had me make them a set of rings. It was my final project in metalsmithing; I got all the materials for free.

Omar wanted to know what Kat was up to. As I filled him in, the DJ started spinning again.

"You guys want to dance?" Omar said. "Come on Beatrice, I know how much you like to dance."

"How much does she like to dance?" Jacob mumbled.

Jacob and I had never gone dancing. It was hard in L.A. The older I got, the less tolerant I became of establishments with bouncers at the door and C-grade celebrities as the main attractions inside.

I invited Jacob to join me but he said no. He told me to go with Omar. His eyes were getting glassy, and I asked him one last time if he wanted to leave.

"No. Have a good time. I'm fine."

"Just for a few minutes," I said. "I'll be right back."

I followed Omar to the middle of the crowd. After the first song ended, I said I'd had enough. He pleaded with me.

"One more," Omar said. "Come on, I haven't seen you in years."

The next song was slow. Omar wrapped his arms around me and started whispering in my ear. His neck smelled like a citrus tree.

"You know, I never told you this before," Omar said, "but I really had a thing for you back when you lived with Valerie. Did you know that?"

"No," I said, which was a lie. Of course I knew, I just never acknowledged it. I felt the same way and didn't want to get into trouble. Believe it or not, I have boundaries. Valerie was my friend.

"It started when we all went up to Tahoe together," he said. "I was driving and you were sitting right behind me. Everyone else was asleep and you gave me a shoulder massage. Do you remember that?"

"I remember that you had to throw your jacket over your lap so I wouldn't see the bulge in your pants."

Omar laughed. "You haven't changed at all, Beatrice." Little did he know. He kept pulling me closer. Too close, I thought, but I didn't pull away. "What's the deal with you and that guy?" he said.

Omar slid his palm down the curve of my lower back. He was a centimeter away from having my ass in his hand. I realized what was going on and I stepped back. I hadn't been that close to another man since I met Jacob, and the truth is, I would have had to use a calculator to count how many times, over the course of the year I lived with Valerie, that I'd thought about what Omar's dick looked like, or what kind of cereal he'd offer me for breakfast if I ever spent the night with him. I used to walk around the apartment wearing black lace bras under thin white T-shirts, just to give him a glimpse of what he was missing. And oddly enough, if it had been any other time prior to meeting Jacob, I probably would have taken Omar home, fucked his brains out, then ended up dating him for a year or so before he would have realized what a head case I was and dumped me.

I turned around to check on Jacob and didn't see him

above all the people. I walked back to where I'd left him. He was gone.

I asked Omar to look for Jacob in the men's room. When he came back to report the search futile, I darted out to the car. Omar followed. Before I got in, he tried to kiss me. After a brief hesitation, I pushed him away.

"Keep in touch, okay?" he said.

Compared to Jacob, Omar's *okay* sounded like a violin getting run over by a lawnmower.

I sped back to the hotel in a panic. I felt like a heel. Jacob needed me and I'd let him down. I'd gone off and danced and flirted while he wallowed in misery and as a result, he was *wandering*. Margaret said he wasn't supposed to *wander*.

I took the elevator up to our floor and ran down the hallway. As soon as I got to the door, I realized Jacob couldn't be there—he didn't have the key. And he rarely carried identification. I'm not even sure he had identification. I knew he had a credit card and an ATM card, but I'd never seen his driver's licence. In the inebriated state I knew he was in, I highly doubted the hotel would have kindly unlocked the door for him on his word alone.

Our room was pitch dark. I turned on the lights, sat down on the bed, and contemplated what to do. I considered going out to look for Jacob, but I wanted to be there when he got back. I stayed up as long as I could by writing in my diary. I don't know how long it was after that, I was awakened by the sound of my name being called. At first I thought it was someone at the door. Once I sat up, I realized it was coming from outside the window. I pushed the curtains aside and looked down into the hotel courtyard.

Jacob was in the pool. He was shirtless, but still in his jeans and boots. I saw his jacket and his T-shirt bunched up on a lounge chair near the shallow end. I remember wondering why he'd bothered to take off his shirt but not his boots. He had a few other shirts to wear, but he'd only brought that one pair of shoes. They were going to be wet for the rest of the trip.

"Trixie! There you are. I've been waiting for you, Trixie!"

He looked so small from where I was. "Shhh!" I said. "People are sleeping." It was two o'clock in the morning.

"Why won't you swim with me, Trixie?" he said. "Why won't you ever swim with me?"

By the time I made it downstairs, the concierge on duty, a dapper lad named Simon, had somehow managed to get Jacob out of the water. Jacob was sitting on the edge of a hot tub—it was right next to the pool—dangling his boots in the warm current. His teeth were chattering.

"Get away from there," I said, and yanked him to his feet.

Simon gave me a weak smile and handed Jacob a towel. I'd never seen a man with posture more perfect than Simon's. His spine must have been shaped like a ruler. He was completely vertical.

I pushed Jacob in the direction of our room.

"I'm really sorry about this," I said to Simon. "He thinks he's Keith Moon." I was trying to be funny, but Simon's blank face told me he had no idea who I was talking about.

Jacob was still shivering when we got upstairs. I turned the shower on hot and told him to get in. When I tried to help him undress, he shoved me aside and slammed the bathroom door in my face.

He came out a few minutes later wearing a pair of shorts. He just fell into bed. I tried to curl up next to him but he turned his back to me. When I touched my feet to his, he jerked them away.

"Jacob…"

"Don't talk to me, Beatrice. You're the last person I want to fucking talk to right now, *okay*?"

Fifteen minutes earlier he'd wanted to swim with me. It took a quick shower to make us mortal enemies.

I had the dream again that night. The one where Jacob got caught in the whirlpool. Only this time I *saw* him get pulled under. He had that same weird look on his face, where he was smiling, but his eyes were filled with panic. I bolted upright in bed and purposely made a lot of noise around the room. I like to live by the rule that if I'm not sleeping, nobody's sleeping. Especially if it's the person indirectly responsible for keeping me awake. I turned on the TV, then I ordered a large pot of coffee and a basket of pastries from room service. After it arrived, I filled two cups, one for Jacob and one for myself. I didn't usually drink coffee in the morning, but the Ritz served what Jacob called "the good shit." It was creamy and sweet, and I sopped it up with a croissant, imagining that's what Anais did at breakfast while she was in Paris screwing Henry Miller.

Jacob drank his coffee in silence. He looked like he'd been hit by a truck. After he checked his watch—twice, to make sure he was seeing it right—he rubbed his eyes and said, "Why, pray tell, did you wake me up at such a ridiculous hour?"

It was a little after six.

"I couldn't sleep," I said.

The TV was tuned to The Weather Channel. There was a huge storm over North Carolina, and a high pressure system in the northeast.

"Did you have fun last night?" Jacob said, running his hands through his ransacked hair.

"Oh yeah, I had a ball. You?"

"Fuck you, Trixie. I went to Tosca last night."

"You did? Why?"

"Why do you *think*? I thought maybe I'd run into him. I figured we'd get along better if I leveled the playing field a little, you know, if I was drunk out of my mind."

"Well, you definitely accomplished that goal."

He gave me a look that said he'd just about had it with me.

The anchorwoman in the tweed pantsuit and the perfectly coiffed up-do said there was a chance of thunderstorms in the southeast. I-85 between Greensboro and Atlanta could be dangerous. A flood warning had been issued.

"Jacob, I was worried about you."

"Oh, really? You could've fooled me."

"What's that supposed to mean?"

"You were too busy hanging all over that *Oh-mar* guy to be worried."

"I wasn't hanging all over him."

"Beatrice, you could've picked your feet up off the ground and not fallen down. That's how all-fucking-over-him you were." Jacob slammed his spoon onto the table. It crashed into the porcelain cream pitcher and made a horrible clanging noise. He got up and stood by the window.

The weather lady said it was partly sunny and unseasonably humid in the western half of Mississippi. I wondered if Jacob heard that—if he was thinking what I was—perfect weather for sweaty sex in the middle of the night.

"Did you fuck him, Trixie?"

"What?"

"You heard me."

"Come on, be serious. He's just an old friend."

"A pretty good friend, I imagine. When I left he practically had his hands down your pants and his tongue in your ear. Not that you seemed to mind."

"I didn't fuck him."

"Not last night, I mean ever."

"No."

"Did you want to?"

I thought about my answer before I gave it.

"No," I said. "A long time ago I did, but not now. Not last night." I got up and stood next to him. I pushed his bangs off his face. "I'm sorry. I should have never left you last night."

He wouldn't let me kiss him.

Prissy-pants on TV said, "Stay tuned for your local forecast," as if it were the prize we'd been waiting for all hour.

"I feel like shit," Jacob said. "I need some aspirin or something." He reached for his jeans and grimaced. "Why the fuck are my pants wet?"

"You don't remember being in the pool last night?"

"I was in the pool last night?" He hesitated, trying to recall the hour he was missing. "Damn." He shook his head and cracked a tiny smile.

I took the jeans from him, let them drop to the floor, and got back in bed. "It's too early to put pants on. Come here," I said.

"No."

"Please…"

"Don't think this means I'm not still pissed at you," he said when he finally gave in. I pulled the covers up over our heads, to pretend it was still dark, and got as close to him as I possibly could. I apologized a few more times. Then I told him about the rest of the night, everything from Omar trying to kiss me to Simon's posture. I even confessed to the face-off with Margaret, and the reoccurrence of the whirlpool dream. I made him promise me he'd never wander into another hot tub.

"You don't really believe that stuff, do you?" he said.

"No. But just in case."

He crossed his heart and swore over his mother. No more hot tubs.

"Speaking of impending doom," he said. "I saw him at the bar last night. I saw my father."

"And?"

"And nothing, really. We drank half a dozen Irish coffees and talked about books. That's it. We just sat at the bar, shooting the shit on books. I think he was jealous when I told him I used to gamble with Bukowski." Jacob seemed pleased that he'd impressed the man.

"So, that's something, right? At least it was civil."

"I suppose. It's just that…" He took a deep breath. "I didn't feel like I was sitting with my *father*. Not what I thought it would feel like anyway."

"What did you expect?"

"I don't know," he said mournfully. "An apology would have been really nice."

He toyed with the buttons on my shirt—his shirt, actually—that I'd worn to bed. "And you know what else? I always thought if I ever met him, that we'd have some kind of a bond, that I'd feel a connection to him. I didn't. We were like two strangers who happened to be sitting next to each other."

"A connection takes time. At least you have a memory of him now."

"Cold comfort," he said. "Don't have a father, just *imagine* that you do."

"It's the first step," I said. "You never know."

Jacob nodded, like he craved that to be the truth, but frankly, I highly doubted Thomas Doorley would ever come around.

The local forecast told us to expect another cold, windy morning filled with lots of sun.

182

"Hey," Jacob said, "no more talk about asshole fathers for the rest of the day, *okay*?" He unbuttoned my shirt and reached for the handcuffs on the bedside table. "Happy Birthday…"

# TWENTY-EIGHT

It was during what they called the rainy season when Jacob finally finished *Hallelujah*. The year's rainy season in Los Angeles was, of course, one particular week of spring when all the thirsty plants turned green for a few days, all the houses near the water braced for floods, all the hillside highways closed due to rock slides, and all the native Californians drove their cars like blind men.

Jacob and I had officially been together a little over a year and the book was, at last, complete. I remember when Jacob and I met, he said then that he was almost finished with it. Almost finished must mean a year to go on the internal clock of a writer.

One might accuse me of bias, as I automatically categorize anyone whose semen tastes like lemon meringue pie as extraordinary, but sex aside, I was wholly impressed. Of course, I knew Jacob was talented. I'd read the articles he wrote, the short stories, but he never let me near the book until it was done so I had no idea what to expect. It was funny, that was the first big surprise; although it shouldn't have been because Jacob was funny—not nearly as funny as he thought he was sometimes—still, his wit translated well onto the page.

Thematically, however, *Hallelujah* was a bleak, solemn story, probably even more so for me. I likened it to a kind of autobiography of spirit for Jacob. The circumstances and the characters were completely made up, but the truth was there in the emotional undercurrent. It was like getting a little glimpse into the darkest corner of Jacob's soul, into some parallel universe where his name was Jackson Grayson, and he was a seventeen-year-old trumpet player living in a tenement building in Hollywood, with a mother who wanted to be a Vaudeville singer; an alcoholic father who wanted to be a Brooklyn Dodger; and a neighbor he was in love with who faked her Southern accent and went by the name of Scarlett O'Hara, even though her mail came addressed to someone named Eleanora Schwartz. Meanwhile, there was a drought going on, and all Jackson wanted in the world was to see it rain.

It was a story about people with dreams. Dreams that never come true.

Jacob pretended he was watching television all weekend long while I read in the bedroom. Whenever he heard me chuckle at something, he came in to see what page I was on.

"You really think that's funny?" he'd say.

"Yes."

"Why?"

Halfway through the book I had to lock him out so I could read in peace.

To me, *Hallelujah* was more than just a novel, it was the catalyst for our future. Jacob and I were explorers and the book was the *Nina*, the *Pinta*, and the *Santa Maria*, all rolled into one, and it was going to carry us to the new world. As I read, I allowed myself to daydream about what our life was going to be like: would we have the kind of summer storms where warm mist rises off the pavement, and the thunder and lightening make you think the earth is going to crack in two? Will cotton grow wild in our backyard? Will we have fireflies? How about a peach tree? Jacob loved peaches.

"Well?" he said late Sunday afternoon when I finished.

I knelt down to match his eye-level on the couch and kissed him as slowly and as deeply as I could. I was at a loss for words so I tried to speak with my body instead. And, interestingly enough, Jacob heard what I was saying. After the long lip-lock, he said, "You *really* liked it?"

I nodded. I felt myself getting teary over the whole thing, but I did my best not to act too girly. "Are you going to dedicate it to me?"

"You'll see," Jacob said. Light oozed from behind his eyes. "But tell me the truth. Are you *sure* you liked it?"

"Jacob, I loved it, I swear. And you know it's good so don't give me that phony-ass, doubt-infested face of yours."

He did know it was good. He just wanted to hear it come out of my mouth. One thing Jacob never truly questioned was the quality of his work. He was well aware of his skill as a writer, so if he poured his heart into something, and then other people didn't like it, he thought it no fault of his own. To Jacob, the act of critiquing art was essentially imprecise. That's why he didn't read reviews on anything he liked, be it a book, a movie, or a record. He believed that any work an artist puts forth which contains the truth as he or she sees it is worthy of consideration, and any commentary of the work beyond that is nothing more than pure individual opinion and should not be considered relevant to the work itself.

I bet I could recite that damn speech backward, Jacob delivered it so often.

"Pack your bags," I said in my best southern drawl. "Joe-ja, here we come."

"Tennessee." He pulled me onto the couch and beamed. "Tennes*see*."

Originally, Jacob had been all gung-ho over Mississippi, but after much research he'd decided, once and for all, that we had to live in Tennessee. For a few reasons. First, he was supposedly born in Gallatin, a small town outside of Nashville. Both Joanna and Thomas Doorley were from New York, but they left there after she got pregnant. They roamed around the country before finally arriving in Southern California. Jacob hadn't been back to Tennessee since he was a few months old.

Second, Jacob said the music was better in Tennessee than it was anywhere else in the South.

"Memphis is practically the birthplace of rock 'n' roll. We'll be able to wander down to Beale Street any night of the week and be *inspired*," he said. "Plus, they have casinos nearby, a zoo, and, as far as I know, the only civil rights museum in the country."

According to Jacob, we were going to live somewhere near Graceland. But not because of Elvis, mind you. Neither of us were fans of The King.

"Supposedly, there are signs all over town that lead to Graceland," he said.

This entertained his imagination, being that his name was Grace.

"How can you not feel like you belong in a place where your name is all over the goddamn town?" he said.

Jacob sent *Hallelujah* off to his agent the next day, and she took us to dinner to celebrate its completion. Jacob's agent was a sixty-one-year-old ex-editor originally from Long Island. Her name was Ardelene Gladstone, but Jacob affectionately called her Adrenaline because she talked faster than an auctioneer, and almost louder than Pete, if that was possible. She thought the book was fabulous.

"I mean posi*tively* fabulous," she said.

To Adrenaline, everything was fabulous, so the word kind of lost meaning for me halfway through the salad course. The

Caesar was fabulous. My necklace was fabulous. The shoe department at Barney's? You guessed it. And Jacob, of course, that went without saying, but she said it anyway.

"*Fabulous.*"

Adrenaline surmised that with Jacob's credible list of published work, she'd be able to negotiate a price for the book somewhere in the mid five-digit range. Nothing that was going to make him a millionaire, but more than enough to put a down payment on a house and get us out of town.

Adrenaline promised us that Los Angeles County would be a memory by the fourth of July.

"Have I ev-a let you down, Jacob?"

He told her no, she hadn't. And she damn well better not start now, I thought.

# TWENTY-NINE

"Do you sweat more when you're having your period?" Kat said.

She stood next to me, her face an inch away from the compact mirror in her hand, and rubbed her armpit in between re-application of the maroon eyeliner she was putting on her lower lids. Kat had bleached her hair again, and the crimson make-up made her look like a polar bear dipped in Kool-Aid. I'd spent three days with her, working at Chick in the afternoons while one of her sales associates was out sick, and it seemed as if each night, instead of taking off her make-up and reapplying it the next day, she just kept adding to it. It never faded, it just got more vivid. A Lite-Brite face.

Working in the store was enthralling for the first five minutes. I'd begged for the job of ringing people up—Kat had one of those old-fashioned cash registers, the wooden ones with the heavy buttons and bells, and I thought it would be fun to play with. But the novelty of servitude gets old fast, especially when you have to wait on snot-faced rich people like my mother, or celebrities who think they deserve special treatment above and beyond the common man just because they emote somebody else's words and ideas in front of a camera. I'd be happy to give special treatment to a dedicated school teacher, or even someone like William Faulkner if he was still alive, because despite the fact that an exegesis of his prose completely eluded me, I had to admit, especially when Jacob held me down and made me say it, that the guy was a kick-ass architect of the ever-elusive sentence. But some silly TV star? I don't care how much money they make, I won't bend. More than one customer had complained to Kat about my attitude. Both times she yelled at me right in front of them, screaming, "You're fired!"

Behind their backs, she egged me on and gave me an air five.

"I don't know why, but I sweat more when I'm having my period," she said.

"It's probably hormonal," I told her. "I think estrogen makes you sweat. Do you smell bad?"

She took a whiff of her pit and grimaced. "I smell like cumin. Gopal says it smells yucky in India and no wonder. Those wretched spices seep through your pores. In that heat, forget about it."

Kat and Gopal had, miraculously, managed to hold their relationship together for over six record-breaking months. He cooked for her, he brought her flowers once a week, he even watched *The Brady Bunch* on a regular basis, only he thought it was a modern TV show. Syndication was a concept he didn't yet grasp. All the positive attention started to drive Kat crazy. She began to hate him for it.

"When he lathers up his face in the morning, before he shaves, he puts the foam over his mouth as well as where the hair actually grows. He ends up shaving his lips," she said. "It's like kissing a girl. A girl who smells like curry."

"You belong on a talk show," I said. I occasionally watched late night reruns of *Oprah*, so I knew. Oprah had a guest on once who lectured for half an hour about women being pussies with men who are assholes, and then being assholes with men who are decent. I tried to get Kat to watch that one, thinking she'd learn something, but Kat's idea of self-improvement is a good bikini wax. I'd even been tempted to write to Oprah about Kat. I had it all planned. Oprah would

have had Kat on her show, and the theme would have read
something like this: Women Who Hate the Men Who Love
Them. We would have all been there in the audience—Jacob
and I, and some of Kat's other friends, like an intervention.
Kat would have told her whole life story, all the stuff about
her father pimping her out to his poker buddies, and her
mother putting pot brownies in her lunch box. Everyone
would have felt sorry for her, and all the attention would have
made her realize how lucky she was to have people in her life
who really loved her. She'd finally appreciate Gopal, except
she'd be devastated when it dawned on her that she blew it
because by the time I got all this shit to happen, she would
surely have dumped his ass. Gopal, however, would have been
hip to my master plan. He'd have been in Chicago too, hiding in the Green Room. At the end of the show he would
have run onto the stage with an engagement ring and made
everyone in the audience cry. Even Oprah would have cried.

"If I'm going to smell like cumin for the rest of my life,
this relationship is doomed," Kat said. "Think I should dump
him, Blanca?"

"Kat, what would Oprah say?"

The store was quiet during lunch. While Kat did inven-
tory, I tried to finish beading a set of bracelets that she'd
promised a customer I'd have done by the end of the day. A
woman had come in and noticed the one I was wearing on
my wrist. She bought it right off my arm and asked me to
make two more.

"My daughters will go mad for them," she said.

The total cost for materials was about thirty-five bucks.
There was little intensive labor involved. Kat told the woman
they'd be $150 each.

"They're special order one-of-a-kinds," Kat explained.

The real reason Kat charged her so much was because the woman was wearing cowboy boots. Kat was prejudiced against people who wore cowboy boots as a fashion statement. "I don't have a problem with them on a ranch or something, but you know, not in *El Aye*. Only Heavy Metal people wear cowboy boots in *El Aye*."

"What are you going to do when I leave?" I said. "Who's going to make bracelets on command for you? Who's going to harass your customers? Admit it, your going to miss me."

Kat didn't like it when I talked about leaving town. Every time I brought it up, she thought of something new to worry about. Her worries were hilarious. So hilarious, in fact, that I started to write them down.

"Blanca, promise me harder than you've ever promised me anything that you're not going to start saying *y'all*, okay?"

I grabbed my new spiral notebook out of my purse—I'd taken up Jacob's habit of carrying one around with me—a Bantam 3x5 size, just in case something struck me as worth remembering.

"Why the hell does your note pad say *mango* on it?" Kat said.

I still hadn't named my daily journal, but my portable one had been christened upon purchase. I took a Sharpie to it and wrote the word *mango* in thick black letters.

"You really want to know?"

"I do now," Kat said.

The day I bought it I'd had to leave the apartment early in the morning to put in a few hours at the studio and then be at Chick by noon. I'd sliced up a mango for breakfast, and Jacob was awake but still in bed. I carried the dish into the bedroom to see if he wanted a piece. I fed him a sliver and he said something corny about how the sweet stickiness of the fruit turned him on.

"It reminds me of something," he said.

He tried to get me back into bed, but I had to decline the offer. I was already showered and dressed, and I didn't want to walk around the rest of the day with gooey underwear.

"How much time do you have?" he said.

"About five minutes."

"*Okay,* then just keep eating the mango exactly like you're doing. But not too fast."

I sat down next to him and, as seductively as possible, I kept eating and sucking and letting Jacob lick the juice as it ran down my fingers. I felt kind of silly about the whole performance, but Jacob didn't seem to notice. He watched me, and while he watched he jacked off. Come shot up across his chest, far enough that it almost hit the wall behind him.

"Have you ever tried to get that in your mouth?" I said.

"Uh, *no*…" He rolled his eyes and shook his head. "*No.*"

Before I left, I cleaned him up with a paper towel. For the rest of the day all I could think about was that precious fruit. The mango, that is.

"So, Grace is a shooter?" Kat said.

"Mm–hmm."

"What in the name of God does that have to do with your pad of paper?"

"Nothing."

"You know, if you think you're going to get fresh, sexy mangos in Tallahassee, you've got another thing coming."

"Tennessee," I said. "Not Tallahassee."

"Whatever. Same thing. I can't believe you're going to leave California for some crummy hick town."

Kat was one of those people Uncle Don preached about. He would say there was something wrong with her because she couldn't comprehend a person not liking L.A. Of course, he'd be right. There was something wrong with her.

"Grace sell his book yet?" Kat said.

"Not yet, but he will."

It had been almost three months since Adrenaline began shopping the book, and there had been no takers. Since she originally told us it would be sold by the fourth of July, which at that point was right around the corner, I determined she'd exaggerated a little.

"Nothing to be concerned about," she said. "It's not going to happen overnight."

Jacob was concerned, naturally, but he'd gone back to work at the *Weekly* so he was too preoccupied to dwell on it. Oddly enough, I wasn't worried at all, I was just impatient. Days feel longer when you know there's something beyond the eternal here and now of Los Angeles to look forward to, even longer than if there's nothing to look forward to, because at least then you're not biding valuable time. That's why I always thought if I ever had to go to jail, I'd rather get thrown in for life as opposed to say, thirty years. With life, you just sit back and chill and get on with whatever it is you do inside of a prison for the remainder of your days. Thirty years, and you're counting the years by the months, the months by the days, and the days by the minutes. That's what I'd been doing and trust me, it fucking took forever.

I left Chick early that day. I had an appointment at Helen Nail's. My monthly ten dollar pedicure.

"Listen, Trixie," Jacob said to me not long after we moved in together. "I wouldn't trust a place that doesn't understand how to correctly form the possessive of a noun."

Helen Nail's was right down the street from our apartment. That particular day, I had them paint my toes a shiny lavender shade that matched the underwear I had on. The color was called *Fetish*. Just the sight of that word spelled out on the bottle brought flashbacks of the mango episode. On my way home, I took a detour to the market for another one. I was excited as hell until I walked through the front door of our apartment and my joy came to a screeching halt.

Greg was sitting on the living room floor with a cheeseburger in his hands and ketchup on his chin. Jacob was across from him on the couch, stuffing french fries into his mouth. They were chatting away like long lost brothers.

"What the *hell* is going on here?" I said.

Apparently it went down like this: Jacob was coming in that afternoon just as Greg was heading out to ride the midday waves. He asked Jacob, or Henry, as he still called him, if he wanted to come along. Jacob had never been much of a surfer, and figured, What the hey, if you're going to learn, you might as well learn from a pro, even if that aforementioned pro used to use his massive shlong to bonk your woman.

"You should've seen me," Jacob said. "I was riding the waves, baby. I was *flying*."

"Dude, Henry's a natural," Greg said. I'd never noticed it before, but Greg looked like a frog. A blond-haired, imbecilic frog. I wanted him to get out of our apartment immediately. But since he didn't look like he was leaving, was too stupid to pick up on how annoyed I was by his presence, and because Jacob got a kick out of provoking me by keeping him there, I was the one who had to go. First, though, I made a trade with Jacob—the mango for the rest of his fries.

"Nice toes," Jacob said.

"They match my underwear," I whispered. "I'm going to take a nap. Wake me up when he's gone. And bring the mango."

Jacob clamored after me with his mouth full. "Oh, hey Trix, your mom called this morning. We're having a family portrait taken tomorrow. Call her back before six."

"Her mom?" I heard Greg say. "Isn't her mother dead?"

# THIRTY

Our family hadn't taken a picture together since before my father left. My brother, Cole, who was just out of law school, was visiting for a few days, and my mother thought the circumstances called for a professional photograph. Jacob had already told her we'd come. When I called her back, it was simply to get all the gory details. Jacob and I were both on the phone when my mother described for us the get-ups we were expected to wear.

"Khaki pants and white shirts."

I heard Jacob try to stifle a laugh on the other end of the line.

"You're kidding, right?" I said.

"Do I sound like I'm kidding, Beatrice?"

"Mom, I'm not wearing khaki pants."

"Honey, don't be difficult," she said. "Jacob…"

My mother turned to Jacob for help because, for reasons I still couldn't fathom, she adored him. She thought he'd take her side.

"Sorry Diane, but I'm going to have to go with Beatrice on this one. Khaki's not a good color for me. It really washes me out."

I was surprised she was even letting Jacob be in the goddamn picture. Normally it would plague her to allow a pseudo family member into an official photo. I thought maybe she'd grown until I found out Cole was bringing his fiancée home. My mother originally told Cole that his future wife couldn't be in the photograph because they weren't married yet. Besides, she'd never even met the girl. Cole said he wouldn't do it unless Mom changed her mind. I guessed that, to avoid another argument, she decided not to put up a stink about Jacob.

We eventually came to a compromise with her on what we were going to wear. It was futile trying to convince her how queer everyone would look if we all wore the same things, especially khaki, but we managed to talk her into black pants and white shirts. As long as the shirts were long sleeved, because, she said, "Too much skin is vulgar in a portrait."

When Jacob walked out of the bedroom the next morning, I was glad we were going for a photo. He needed to be captured on film in his chosen outfit. He had on his black Levi's, paired with a white shirt he got in Costa Rica. It was long sleeved, per mother's command, with a sort of lattice embroidery on opposite sides of the buttons, like one of those shirts the old president of the Philippines used to wear in press photos—the guy who's wife had all the shoes. Jacob also wore the necklace I'd given him, and a funky bowler hat that made the sides of his hair flip up like wings. He looked like a cab driver.

"The hat will never make the final cut," I said.

"Sure it will," Jacob said. "I've got Diane wrapped around my finger. She'll let me wear whatever I want."

"Wanna bet?"

"The usual?" Jacob said.

We shook on it.

I wore black slacks, black boots, and a fitted white cashmere turtleneck. Jacob told me I looked like I should be editing *Vogue* magazine. Somehow this turned into a sexual role-playing game.

"You can be my fare and I'll be your cabbie. Except this cabbie carries handcuffs."

"Cool your jets, Ferdinand. We have to go."

I was sweating my ass off in the sweater, and I contemplated changing before we left, but my mother hates turtlenecks. I figured a little suffering would be worth the thrill of annoying her.

"I don't know why you have to torment her all the time," Jacob said.

"She wears me out."

Chip, Elise, and Chad were all dressed and ready when we arrived. They had on matching Armani outfits and looked like doormen from the Mondrian hotel. I picked up a weird vibe between Chip and Elise as soon as I walked in. While the photographer fiddled with the lights, Elise went outside and I followed her. I asked her if everything was okay. I barely had the question out of my mouth when she began a discourse, feigning the detachment of a court-appointed arbitrator, regarding the humiliating state of her marriage. Evidently, over the course of a few months, she'd been getting suspicious of Chip. All the stereotypical signs: lack of interest in sex, short temper, unexplained late nights out. So she did what everyone in Hollywood who thinks their spouse is cheating does: she hired someone to tail him. Elise had pretty much come to the conclusion that Chip was having an affair and, strangely enough, I sensed she was willing to accept that.

"I mean, if it was an actress or something, I would understand," she said.

Elise thought that if a person was famous that meant they were better than she was, and why wouldn't Chip deserve to fuck someone better than his nobody wife? Much to her dismay, however, Elise discovered that once a week Chip booked a suite at the Four Seasons Hotel, where he stopped in to meet up with some high-class call girls.

"How long has all this been going on?" I said.

"Probably close to a year."

I told her to divorce him and she laughed as if I'd made a joke.

"Divorce him?" she said.

"Like father, like son," I told her. If Elise didn't get out fast, she was going to end up like my mother. Except this was worse. At least my father didn't have to pay for his bimbos. Not by the hour anyway.

"What are you going to do?" I said.

"Look on the bright side, I have an excuse not to have sex with him anymore." She saw my face drop. "Don't look at me like that, Bea. You're in love now so you don't understand. But I was in love once too, you know."

This was a thirty-four-year-old woman with an eight-year-old son talking as if she were standing on the pitcher's mound watching the batter rounding third and heading home. The ball was in her hand but she had no intention of throwing it to the catcher. As if life and love just weren't worth the out.

The way I saw it, if Chip wanted to screw hookers, that was his problem. It was Elise's disconnection and selflessness that infuriated me.

"Committing suicide so as not to be murdered is the worst reason I've ever heard of to die," I said.

I walked away.

My mother showed up for the photo in a long black skirt, a white blouse with gold buttons, and a pair of black and gold earrings that looked like satellite dishes hanging off of her ears. Jacob used those earrings as leverage when negotiating for his hat, but to no avail.

"Jacob, please," my mother said. "You're starting to sound just like Beatrice."

"Better start warming up that tongue," I said to him.

"Sit and spin, baby."

When Cole came in I almost didn't recognize him. I hadn't seen my little brother in almost three years and everything about him seemed different. He didn't look so Republican anymore. He hadn't even worn a tie. And I immediately identified the smell of his deodorant. It was Regular Scent Speed Stick—the same deodorant Jacob used. That won Cole bonus points right off the bat. Jacob thought Cole and I looked alike. "Except for the eyes," Jacob said. Cole was the only Jordan kid who got my mother's blue eyes. Last I'd heard, Cole was planning a career as a congressman. He'd done a complete turnaround since then. He told us about the job he'd just accepted in Montgomery, Alabama, working for a non-profit law firm famous for fighting hate crimes. This from a man who used to think Richard Nixon was the greatest president of the twentieth century.

The change in him was overwhelming and I credited a lot of it to his fiancée, Toren. She was a natural blond from Massachusetts who worked at the Smithsonian Institute and had a tattoo of a beetle on her arm. Luckily she'd brought a sweater with her. My mother would have had the photo airbrushed if the tattoo had been showing. Toren told me she loved my hair and wanted to know if I could recommend a place for her to get a trim while she was in town. I called Sara and made an appointment to take her to the salon, then lunch and shopping the next day. We told Cole he could join us, but the plans didn't seem to thrill him. He liked Jacob's invitation better. Jacob and his new pal, Greg, had a date with the waves at the crack of dawn.

"I don't know why you bad-mouthed your brother," Jacob said when we all met up for sushi the following night. "I like him."

"I take it back," I said. "I like him, too. And not because he's my brother but in spite of it."

I sat next to Cole during dinner and for the first time in our lives, we related to each other not only as adults, but as brother and sister. We talked about our childhood, our parents, our significant others. Cole told me how much he liked hanging out with Jacob all day.

"I approve," he said.

I didn't know my brother cared enough to approve and I told him so. He laughed and said, "I always knew you were going to end up with a guy like that."

I asked him about his wedding. He and Toren had been engaged since Christmas and were getting married the following summer on Martha's Vineyard.

"Promise me you'll come," my brother said.

Jacob swore we'd make plans to be there.

I once saw an actor on TV doing press for a movie. I don't remember the question he was asked, but I remember his answer, word for word.

"You wanna know how to make God laugh?" he said. "Tell him your plans."

"Boy, did he turn out to be a real prick," Cole said after I told him about Chip and the hookers. But here's where Cole and I differed: Cole didn't judge Chip. He didn't judge our father either. Neither of my brothers had cut off contact with our father like I had. Cole was even spending the rest of the weekend with him in Malibu. But Cole was like Joanna, so willing to let go of the past. I wished I could be like that. It's easy to say all it takes is a little forgiveness, but forgiveness is a concept I've always had a hard time grasping. First of all, you need faith for forgiveness, and as far as I knew, I had very little of that. Second, why should you excuse someone who's hurt you deeply? I mean sure, it's great in theory. If someone is fifteen minutes late for dinner, or borrows your car and brings it back with a dent in it, okay, I can see where a little understanding is in order.

But there's a limit to how long you can starve a hungry person before they're going to bite your leg off. Even if I did decide to forgive my father, and we became best friends, would that erase all the years he was off gallivanting with some worthless floozy instead of being at home helping me with my homework, or some other Norman Rockwell bullshit like that? I assumed I'd need amnesia to have a relationship with my father after the debauchery he'd made of my youth. I'd have to be like one of those heroines from daytime television who gets hit over the head with a big rock, hard enough to knock me out for a few months, maybe years, so that when I woke up I wouldn't remember a thing. Then, when I came to, the nurses would tell me all about how my father had stayed by my bedside day and night, reading me *The Giving Tree*, holding my hand, and trying not to cry. When they let me out of the hospital, we'd all go to Dad's breezy *chateau de la plage* to lounge around in our flip-flops. We'd barbeque hamburgers and hotdogs on the grill, put our arms around each other and rattle on about how lucky we were to have such a great family.

It was weird talking so honestly with Cole. It gave me an urge to grab his hand and tell him I loved him. I'd never told him that before, but I held back. I knew if I said it I would have started bawling in front of everyone.

"All right, enough deep conversation, you two down at the end of the table, it's time to let the games begin," Pete yelled. "But first I have an announcement to make!"

Once Pete had our attention, he said Sara wasn't allowed to play Roe-Sham-Bo, and, as a matter of fact, in case we hadn't noticed, she didn't eat any raw fish either, because her doctor told her pregnant woman weren't supposed to eat raw fish.

Sara blushed and glowed and giggled.

"Holy shit, you did it!" Jacob said, cheering his friends.

We all screamed and applauded them. Jacob took Pete's head in his hands and planted a big wet kiss on his forehead, slapping his face. "I told you your little guys were fighters."

The baby was due in February. "We'll be in Memphis by then," Jacob said. "But we'll come back to meet him as soon as he's born." Jacob put his face near Sara's belly and whispered something to the little embryo.

"Maybe it's a she," I said.

"Not according to Pete."

"All the men in my family have sons," Pete said. "My grandfather had two sons, my father had two sons, that's just the way it goes."

Sara said Pete wanted to name the kid Blaze. She thought that sounded like a race horse. "I'm going to call him Nicholas," she said.

Between the baby news and bonding with Cole, I was completely distracted during the game. I paid absolutely no attention to what I was doing and lost almost every round. In the end it came down to me and Pete, and that was no contest. I had to eat all but one of the leftovers, including something that looked like a soggy almond on a bed of rice. It tasted like spoiled milk, and was some kind of fish organ, only I'm not sure which one because no one would tell me. Whatever it was made me sick. I threw up as soon as we got home and beige mucus dripped out of my nose.

Jacob wiped my face and made me drink Ginger Ale on

the bathroom floor.

"You may be a lousy player, but you're a hell of a good sport," he said.

# THIRTY-ONE

"Die mother-fucker, die!"

There was a bug on the windshield of my car and I was trying to end it's life with a parking ticket. I figured the City of Los Angeles deserved a dead bug in the mail for giving me the damn thing in the first place. My meter ran out less than thirty seconds before I got back to my car, but the parking Nazi who wrote up the violation completely ignored me as I stood there pleading with him.

"Look, I have two quarters right here," I said. He didn't even look up from his clipboard. "Hello? Sir? Hello?"

He was short, had tiny hands, and a wide, bulbous nose.

"Hey, Napoleon," I said, once I was safe inside my car. "It's okay, I understand. I'd be hostile too if I were a meter maid."

Between the heat of the midday sun and the pagan glitter of tinsel town, I couldn't tell if the bug was inside or out. Luckily, the car was barely moving, otherwise I'm sure I would have swerved hysterically into one of the oncoming lanes. I turned on the wipers to discover the truth, and the guts of the innocent insect, thick and green, told me all I needed to know.

Needless to say, I was in a highly agitated state of mind as I inched my way down Sunset Boulevard. Between the traffic, the bug, the ticket, and the general vibe of The Strip, it was enough to make me stop my car in protest. I actually pulled over, got out, and walked the rest of the way.

"This will never happen in Memphis!" I screamed to the

sky, and to whoever else was listening as I marched down the street.

I was on my way to a boutique called Tracy's in West Hollywood. I'd been to Tracy's before. It was one of Kat's favorite haunts until she opened Chick. The last time we'd stopped by, some curvy bimbo with long fuchsia nails stole the T-shirt I wanted. It was white and it said *Emily didn't search to belong, she searched to be lost* on the front of it. If ever a T-shirt was fated for someone, that one was mine, only Playmate of the Year got to it faster than I did. Obviously, she was a big liar. She didn't deserve the shirt—she absolutely looked like a woman who searched to belong, when all I wanted was out of there.

Tracy was also the name of the shop owner. She had seen my jewelry on one of her customers, tracked me down by way of Kat, and asked me if I would drop by to show her some of my new pieces. She was interested in my latest line of rings. I started making them because of all the compliments Jacob got on the one I'd given him the summer before—the chunky silver band with the irregular-shaped black opal in the center. Black opals, in the right light, look a bit like mood rings, except they don't change color with the temperature of your skin, they just stay a trippy shade of ebony, so I called them Bad Mood rings. I also made a more petite version, with a more traditional-colored opal. I called those Good Mood rings. Photos of them turned up in a local magazine. After that they were the rage about town. The best part of the ring was, naturally, the part nobody noticed. If you flipped it over, it said *Grace* in a dark, Medieval font. I showed Tracy that little distinguishing mark. She thought it was cool, the word Grace. But I didn't tell her why I put it there. Some things I liked to keep to myself.

Tracy wanted to know if she could sell the rings

exclusively from her store. After I made sure Kat wasn't going to feel ripped-off, I accepted her proposal.

Word of the rings spread faster than the legs of a struggling starlet, as word does in Los Angeles, and a national fashion magazine ran a little snippet about how Julia Roberts was seen wearing one of them. Tracy started getting calls from all over the country, and I had to hire an assistant to help me keep up with the demand. It was my most successful creation to date and, of course, I credited it all to Jacob.

# THIRTY-TWO

I knew Jacob was home from work. I saw his car in the garage when I pulled in, but he wasn't upstairs when I got there. I figured he walked to the market or down to the Coffee Bean for a pre-dinner pick-me-up. I changed into a pair of jeans, sorted colors from whites, and threw a load of laundry into the washer. I checked to see if anyone had called and there were three messages on the machine. The first one was from Mike, Jacob's friend from the *Weekly*. He called to say the staff meeting the following day had been changed to ten o'clock. The second message was from Uncle Don in San Francisco. He asked Jacob to call him as soon as possible. The last message was from Joanna.

"Honey, please call me," she said. "I know you spoke to Don. I hope you're okay."

Uncle Don and Joanna both sounded peculiar. I tried to phone Joanna back but she didn't answer. I looked up Uncle Don's number in San Francisco and got him on the line. I asked him if something was wrong.

"Ta…ta…Thomas Doorley died," he said.

"*What?*"

A heart attack, Uncle Don explained. He'd read about it in the paper. Only fifty-two years old. What a shame. Uncle Don said Jacob had seemed pretty shaken by the news.

"I'm sorry I had to…to…to be the one to tell him."

I got off the phone with Don and racked my brain trying to figure out where Jacob could have gone. Then I realized, if I knew Jacob like I thought I did, there was only one place he'd be—the place he always went to either amplify his happiness or to wallow in misery.

I put my shoes back on and ran to the beach, crossing the overpass and bolting down the steps like a madwoman.

I stopped to catch my breath when I saw him. He was sitting on the sand, spitting distance from the water, his arms wrapped around his legs. The wind had blown his hair forward and he was sustaining an apocalyptic focus on the line where the water met the sky. "The threshold of the sea." That's what Jackson Grayson called the horizon in *Hallelujah*.

When I got close enough to touch him, I heard him humming. It took me a few bars to figure out what song it was: Bob Dylan's "If You See Her, Say Hello." An unusual choice, I thought at first, upon the death of one's father. But really, it's a song about loss. And regret. I'm sure it made perfect sense to Jacob.

As quietly as possible, I called Jacob's name. He turned and looked up at me with the face of a needy child and the eyes of an ancient shaman.

I fell down to my knees and cradled him in my arms. He didn't say anything. He just rested his head on my shoulder and cried. I'd never seen a grown man cry like that before, so unself-consciously, so unashamedly. I didn't know if he was crying for what he'd lost, or for what he'd never had, but there was a beauty in his tears that moved me more than I could ever explain with words—a beauty in the honesty of his sadness, in the grace of it's purity. It was holy water raining down from the clouds in his eyes, falling to the sand then being carried back to the source from which it came—his blessed sea.

My fingertips were wet with his mourning, and I had a perverse yearning to genuflect and make the sign of the cross on my forehead.

We stayed like that for a long time, long enough to watch the sun go down and the moon fade in. Finally, when the weight of the day had been absorbed, we headed home. As we walked, Jacob gripped my hand so tightly that my knuckles cracked, but I didn't tell him he was practically breaking my fingers because for God's sake, the guy had to hold on to something.

Jacob called Rhonda Doorley that night. He wanted to attend the memorial service, he wanted to say good-bye to his father, and she was the only person he knew who could tell him where and when he'd be able to do that. He still had the piece of paper I'd given him in San Francisco, the one I wrote Thomas Doorley's name and number on. He dug it out of his address book and dialed slowly. The jawbone on the right side of his face pulsated while he waited for an answer.

Someone on the other end picked up and Jacob asked for Rhonda. When she got to the phone, he spoke apprehensively.

"Mrs. Doorley?" he said. "Uh, you don't really know me but…well…I knew your husband…"

Jacob uttered a winded paragraph of condolences, after which he asked Rhonda about the funeral arrangements. He wrote down whatever information she gave him. It was the name of a church, Our Lady of Mount-something, in Mill Valley. The services were to be held the following afternoon. I think Rhonda thanked Jacob for calling—he told her she was welcome. Then she must have asked him his name. I was hoping he'd fall back on Barry Williams if the question arose, but he made the mistake of telling her the truth.

He blinked three times in quick succession and squinted. "I understand where you're coming from, I do," Jacob said. "But—"

Those were his exact words, only he didn't look like he

understood. Finally, with defeat, he said, "Right. Good-bye, Mrs. Doorley."

He didn't put the phone down until he was sure Rhonda had hung up, after which he slammed it so hard the earpiece snapped off. Then he kicked the wall with his boot.

"Jacob, what did she say?"

He turned away from me. "She doesn't want me there. She said she knows who I am and she thinks it's better, after all they've been through the past few days, if I don't show up and make it worse. That's what she said. That I'd make it worse. My father's dead and I'm not even allowed to go to his fucking funeral."

The minute Jacob learned his father's life had become what, in relation to him it had been all along, an apparition, is when I saw desire begin to fade from his eyes. Jacob searched harder than ever for meaning in his being. His body had been orphaned long before, but this time, Thomas Doorley had taken his soul. Because a soul never truly loses hope until hope has turned to ashes, or has been buried six feet underground.

I know that better than anybody.

Jacob became a bastard of confusion. He saw himself as a once fertilized union of bodily fluid that should have been sucked from the womb instead of made to endure the existential question of why.

# THIRTY-THREE

Jacob lay in bed that night, fully clothed. I don't think he slept at all. He just tossed and turned above the sheets, spreading stow-away grains of sand that drained from his pockets and dusted the bed. When he finally rose after the sun came up, without a shower or a change of clothes, and in a sleep-deprived haze, he said he was going to work.

"Why don't you call in sick?" I said. "You need some rest. We can spend the day together."

"Thanks, but I'm fine."

Before he walked out the door, he caressed my face and said, "I don't know where I'd be right now if it wasn't for you, Trixie."

I drove over to the *Weekly* office at lunchtime, to see how Jacob was holding up. Mike told me he hadn't been there all day. He'd missed the staff meeting and had yet to call in.

Night came and went, and I didn't hear a word from Jacob. I was pretty sure I knew where he'd gone, still, by the middle of the next afternoon, I started to panic. I considered going to San Francisco after him, but at that point the funeral had been over for twenty-four hours. I couldn't very well wander aimlessly around the city assuming I'd run into him.

Late that night, he called collect.

"Trixie? I'm sorry, Trixie. I'm sorry if I woke you up."

He'd been drinking, I could tell by the way he slurred his words and said my name over and over.

"Jacob, are you okay?"

"Can you come and pick me up?"

"Where are you?"

"The airport."

"The airport? Where's your car?"

"It's here," he said. "It's here, but I don't think I can drive it. I love you, Trixie."

Part of me was on the verge of exploding at his lack of consideration, for taking off and disappearing without a word. I wanted to scream at him. My other half told me to bite the bullet, to go rescue him and shut up. At least he was safe. And it's not like fathers drop dead every day; the cutting of a little slack might be acceptable.

I called Pete and asked him to come with me, to drive Jacob's car home. Jacob was sitting on the curb outside the United terminal when we pulled up. He could barely stand, and he looked so trashed I couldn't believe they even let him on the plane. He fawned all over me, still muttering, "I'm sorry, Trixie, I'm sorry," as Pete eased him into the back seat. We drove around the parking garage for forty-five minutes looking for his car. By the time we found it, Jacob was completely passed out.

Pete carried Jacob up to the apartment for me. "He'll be all right," he said. "He's a tough kid. Don't worry, okay?"

After Pete left, I went straight to bed. Jacob's head was at the wrong end of the mattress, his feet were on his pillow, and he was curled up in a fetal position. He smelled the way kids do when they've been playing outside all day. Like dirt. I lifted his arm and it just fell when I let it go. I lifted it once more, wrapped it around me, and held on to it for the rest of the night.

Jacob was in the shower when I woke up the next morning. He spent a good fifteen minutes there, coughing and sniffling like holy hell. When he came back to the bedroom to get dressed, I pretended I was still sleeping. I'm not sure why I did that, but it didn't work anyway.

"I saw you blink," Jacob said.

He'd combed all of his wet hair back off his face. It made his forehead look really high and rectangular. His skin was the color of a raw oyster.

"What did you do, drink gasoline for two days straight?" I said.

He sat down next to me and ran his index finger up and down my shoulder.

"I was in San Francisco," he said.

"I figured as much."

"It rained the whole time." He pointed to his nose, to explain his pneumonia-like symptoms.

I didn't say a word, I just let him talk.

"I never went into the church or anything. I just stood outside. I watched them take the casket in and I watched them carry it out....Nobody saw me....I had to go....Are you going to say anything, Trixie? Are you mad at me?"

I took a deep breath. "I'm trying not to be. I understand why you needed to go. I don't blame you for that, but you should have told me. You should have let me come with you. You can't just vanish like that and expect me not to be worried. Would it have killed you to call and tell me where you were going?"

"I know," he said. "I wasn't thinking straight. I had every intention of going to work, I really did, but on my way there I saw the exit for the airport and something told me to take it. For closure."

I stood up. "Get your ass back in bed. I'm going to make

you some tea, or chicken soup, or something."

"Hey…" He held on to my arm. "Don't worry, it's all over now, *okay*?" he said. "It's *over*."

# THIRTY-FOUR

It's never over. How can something be over that is the essence of what it means to go on in perpetuity—the vicious familial line that runs on an invisible string, linking us to our past and to our future, to what we embrace and to what we try to deny? Take the proverbial scissors and snip at it if you dare, but you're snipping into thin air because the thread lies inside. To sever it would mean the end of breath and the end of life, which, to some, is just another beginning. Thus the cycle continues.

So it wasn't over.

It never is and never will be.

Jacob remained sullen for days following his return from San Francisco, and I felt him retreating from me, but only incidentally. What he was really backing away from was life; I was simply a part of that. He hadn't mentioned his book in weeks. He hadn't even returned any of Adrenaline's calls.

"It's just more bad news, I can tell by her decibel level," he said.

Adrenaline's sell-by date had come and gone, and there had been no strong leads. Maybe Jacob didn't think he was ever going to sell the book, and even if he did, I surmised there was a part of him that didn't care anymore, a part of him that had built an illusion around what would have happened upon the publication of *Hallelujah*. His father would have undoubtedly read it. His father would have been proud of him. His father would have called him up and said, I'm sorry, please be my son because you're everything I always wanted to be but never could become.

Surely Jacob hadn't spent the last decade of his life writing solely for the acceptance of Thomas Doorley. Deep down I know he knew that, but he'd buried his passion under his grief, and someone or something had to either dig it out, wait for it to spring back up, or watch it turn to dust.

# THIRTY-FIVE

The last straw came about a month later, in the form of a phone call from an attorney representing Rhonda Doorley, a local guy named Sanford Wilcox, who arranged a meeting with Jacob. He suggested that Jacob bring legal representation.

"What's this regarding?" Jacob said.

Mr. Wilcox told Jacob he preferred to discuss the matter in person. Jacob put on a suit and tie for the meeting. I'd never seen Jacob dressed like that. It made him look like a rock star moonlighting as an insurance salesman. He declined to bring a lawyer along. He took me instead.

The law offices of Samuelson, Wilcox, Bergman & Klein were on the seventeenth floor of a gleaming Century City high-rise. All the walls were glass, the carpet was the color of bamboo, and the furniture was made of that slippery kind of leather your ass can't get a grip on when you sit down.

The receptionist offered us beverages as soon as we arrived, then she escorted us to Mr. Wilcox's office.

Sanford Wilcox stood up from behind his massive desk when we walked in. He was a thick man, with the shoulders of a linebacker. "Thank you for coming, Mr. Grace. I'm glad you brought an attorney."

"I'm not his attorney, I'm his girlfriend," I said. "Beatrice Jordan."

His handshake was respectably firm, so I didn't hate him

right off the bat like I usually did when I met a lawyer.

"Any relation to Curtis Jordan?" he said.

For Christ's sake, I thought, can we never escape?

"He's my father," I said, albeit reluctantly. I was going to lie, but I changed my mind because Jacob looked at me with eyes that said, Trixie, it's neither the time nor the place to make up something stupid.

"Curtis and I go way back. He's a good guy. And a great attorney," he said. "I'll have to tell him I ran into you."

"You do that." I feigned a smile.

Mr. Wilcox gave Jacob a small pile of papers which, he explained, was Thomas Doorley's will. Except instead of saying Thomas Doorley, he kept saying "your father" in a way that made me think he didn't know anything at all about Jacob's relationship with the man.

Jacob shifted nervously in his chair and paged through the documents, perplexed. "Mr. Wilcox, what does this have to do with me? Why am I here?"

"Call me Sanford," he said.

"Sanford," Jacob said, "what's this all about?"

"Let me get right to the point. You're being sued by my client, your stepmother."

"My *stepmother*? Do you mean Rhonda?"

Sanford nodded.

"She's suing me for what?"

Sanford asked Jacob to turn to the third page of the file. He read paragraph C to us. It stated something to the effect that, in the unlikely event of the death of Mr. Thomas Charles Doorley, Jacob would inherit the Lovell Avenue property, located in Mill Valley, California, zip code 94941.

"He left me his *house*?" Jacob said.

Sanford explained that Thomas Doorley had only two valuable assets in his estate. One was a bank account containing close to two hundred and twenty-nine thousand dollars. The other was his house. He'd left the money and all other incidental possessions to his wife and son, Eric. He'd left the house to Jacob.

Thomas Doorley had apparently been even more of a screwball than I originally gave him credit for.

"Your father paid sixty-five thousand dollars for that house when he bought it back in the seventies," Sanford said. "I don't think he had any idea of it's current value, but today, it's estimated to be worth close to five hundred thousand."

Jacob didn't know what to say.

"Mrs. Doorley is suing you for the house. She lives in it, she wants to keep it, and she believes she has a right to it. But she's willing to offer you a settlement. One hundred-thousand dollars cash, and you sign the house over to her."

"One hundred grand?" I said. "What a rip off."

Jacob shook his head, and I tried to interpret his expression. All I could decipher was shock. A moment later he read something in the will that stopped him in his tracks and drained every drop of blood from his face.

"Mr. Wilcox," Jacob said, "when did Thomas Doorley *make* this will?"

"Back in the late eighties. The most recent date, the one you see there on that page, is the date the will was amended. He executed the original years ago, and in it he'd left everything to Rhonda and Eric. He changed it just last year to include you."

I saw what Jacob saw. The date the change was made. The first week of December. Thomas Doorley changed his will the first week of December—the week after he'd met Jacob.

"I guess you can see why you need counsel, Mr. Grace."

Jacob continued to page through the documents. When he looked up, calmly, but regrettably, he said, "I don't need counsel. Tell Rhonda she can keep her house."

"Mr. Grace, surely you want to think about it before you make a decision—"

"I have thought about it. Let me know when you get all the paperwork ready and I'll sign it."

"So you're accepting my client's offer?"

Jacob ripped a small corner of paper from one of his documents. He scribbled something on it and handed it to Sanford Wilcox.

"Joanna Grace, that's my mother," he said. "That's her address and phone number. I want the check made out to her."

The first thought that popped into my head was this: we could leave Los Angeles tomorrow if Jacob kept that money. I knew, however, that a discussion on the subject would be futile. If Jacob wouldn't let me buy us a house in Memphis, there was no way in hell he'd let his father's guilt buy us one either. Besides, Joanna deserved the money as much as anyone.

Jacob closed his file and stood up. "I guess you'll be in touch," he said to Sanford.

"I'll be in touch."

I found it fascinating that Thomas Doorley never took the time to send his first-born son a Christmas card like I'd asked him to, but he'd taken the time to leave him the house his family inhabited. I couldn't even begin to unravel the meaning behind those actions.

# THIRTY-SIX

Driftwood. Jacob just floated around like driftwood. Everything was copacetic but nothing really mattered. If I was simply confused by Thomas Doorley's posthumous revelations, Jacob was positively spellbound, and he sought no constructive outlet for the chaos he felt. He barely acknowledged my presence when I came home. He'd taken to drinking midmorning, sleeping it off in the afternoon, sometimes disappearing in the middle of the night and not coming back until late the next day. On more than one occasion, he'd snuck out of bed at one or two A.M., unable to sleep, and quietly left the apartment. Jacob explained his absences by telling me he'd been driving around all night—an excuse I found highly suspicious until I checked the odometer on his car. One night he drove to Vegas and back. I asked him if he'd gambled and he said no, he just stopped to ride the roller coaster at the state line.

"The thought of the city up ahead, the lights and all those people, it made me feel rotten. I just turned the car around and came home."

Another time he took off to Joshua Tree National Park, where he allegedly slept on the desert floor with nothing but his jacket, Dante's *Inferno*, and a bottle of cheap red wine to keep him warm. The afternoon following that excursion, he stopped in to see me at the studio, looking like a sewer rat, to tell me that another publisher had turned down his book. His hair smelled like vomit, and he kept babbling on about not wanting to end up alone.

"Promise me you won't leave me, Trixie. Promise me."

"I promise."

"Wanna go to Disneyland?" he said.

"Right now?"

Things had been crazy around the studio since the mood ring frenzy. I couldn't just take off on a whim like I used to. I told Jacob I had to work and he sulked away, accusing me of not loving him anymore. It was an unfair tactic but it did the trick. I had two choices: either go to Disneyland with Jacob, or let him go home, drink a bottle of Wild Turkey, and pass out on the couch.

Jacob made me stop at Pete and Sara's on our way to the park to see if they wanted to come with us. Sara was awash in morning sickness.

"Just the thought of greasy food and the Mad Tea Party is enough to send me running for the bathroom," she said. Pete was off painting a house somewhere. I was glad they couldn't tag along. Jacob and I needed to be alone. We had to talk.

We went straight to Fantasyland. Since it was during the middle of the week we didn't have to wait in line for anything. We walked right onto It's a Small World and stayed there, riding the little boat over and over, our own jolly cruise around the globe. I loved all the dolls, with their native outfits and smiling faces.

"They're freaking the living hell out of me," Jacob said.

It was peaceful inside the tunnel. Except there was an eerie chill in the air, as if we were floating on dry ice.

I took Jacob's hand and begged him to tell me what was going on inside his head. Motionless, he stared at the water and said he didn't know what was wrong with him.

"The last few weeks seem like a blur," he said. "I wish I'd done so many things differently. I wish a lot of people had done things differently, things it's too late to change or ever take back."

Jacob might have been right about the dolls. I knew I was going to be kept awake all night by plastic munchkins singing that sunny fucking song. The amount of faith in their voices eventually made me want to set their little heads on fire.

"This is going to sound supremely ridiculous," Jacob continued, "but I really feel like I lost something when I lost my father. And I didn't even *know* him."

The Eskimo boys and girls went by. For a second I forgot they weren't real, and I accidentally waved at them. "That's not ridiculous at all," I said, "but don't let it consume you, Jacob."

The thing was, everything that interested Jacob consumed him.

"Maybe things could've been different. Maybe I could've helped him, Trixie. Obviously, the guy needed help. I was so busy thinking about myself and what I wanted from him, I never got the chance to find out what he may have needed from me."

"Jacob, whatever you do, don't paint your father as the victim here just because he's dead. He's the one who made the choice to obliterate you from his life thirty years ago, remember?"

"So why did he leave me the fucking house? I'll never know why he did that. I'll never understand."

"Why don't you think of it as a peace offering instead of a riddle?"

"Because," Jacob said, "that makes it worse."

It was time to switch rides. After Space Mountain and Pirates of the Carribean, we ended up on the Monorail. Jacob gazed out over Orange County and tried desperately to clarify his thoughts.

"It's like I'd been missing something my whole life, but I didn't know it wasn't there until it was too late. I mean, I always knew I was missing a *father*, but what that really meant, I didn't know. How could I?" He paused. "It's more than just someone to watch you play little league and teach you how to ride a bike, it's part of your history. It's half of who you are. It's how you find your place in the world, from what comes before you and, ultimately, what you leave behind. Without that, how do you know? You're empty," he said. "I'm empty."

The hole, I thought. That ever-present, God-shaped hole. Having a father doesn't necessarily mend it, I wanted to tell Jacob.

"You're not empty," I said vehemently. "You're the least empty person I know."

"Tell it to my soul."

I wish I could have. I wanted to be enough to fill the universe inside of Jacob Grace. But I guessed that no matter how strong it was, love alone couldn't turn a speck of dust into a galaxy of stars.

I asked Jacob if he still thought about Memphis. I told him that the best thing we could do would be to just pick up and go. "Immediately," I said. "We'll start all over."

"What's the point?" he said, and just shook his head back and forth, as if it were impossible. "Don't you get it, Trixie? To go right now would be the *worst* thing we could do. It would be an admission of defeat."

Joanna insisted that Jacob take half of the money she received from Thomas Doorley's estate. He refused, of course. But after bartering for days, she finally convinced him to accept a measly ten grand so he didn't have to go back to the *Weekly* for a while. The money made Jacob feel even worse.

He said it was like cutting the course in a marathon when you were the fastest runner there. He said it was cheating.

I was scared when we left Disneyland. I knew Jacob and I hadn't solved anything. I knew nothing was going to change. I also knew that I couldn't sit around and watch the slow disintegration of his spirit. For so long I'd been able to read Jacob. I could look at him and know, without a word spoken, exactly what he was thinking. I always saw a man who longed to *live*; a man who, unlike most of the automatons that crossed my path, was actually conscious of his existence and felt there was something else out there, something *more*. It was still all I wanted. It's what got me out of bed in the morning. But when I began staring into Jacob's eyes, seeing nothing but two puddles of mud, I wasn't so sure it was ever going to come to pass. Either I wasn't equipped with the knowledge to help him, or I was afraid of getting too deep in the muck.

That's what happens when you're raised around a lot of static.

You learn to tune it out.

# THIRTY-SEVEN

I hated socializing in Los Angeles. The whole Hollywood scene of frighteningly beautiful creatures posing as long lost friends was something to be avoided like the plague. Thus, under normal circumstances, I wouldn't have been caught dead at a black tie charity gala in Beverly Hills. Namely one being hosted by an ever-important style publication acting as the foremost authority on fashion trends. But I made an exception for philanthropy. They were auctioning off one-of-a-kind pieces of jewelry, clothing, and handbags from various local artisans, the proceeds of which went to a summer camp for kids with terminal illnesses. I couldn't say no to that. I'm a sucker for a sob story and a good cause. Most of the other artists involved in the auction were much ritzier designers, but a couple of us anti-flash renegades made the cut. As usual, there were a bunch of celebrities in attendance. Chip and Elise came. As did my mother—she'd suffocate a baby before she'd miss an opportunity to extol the talents of one of her children. Even if it was the misfit child—the one who found herself dubiously flirting with the mainstream. To have so many obnoxious people appreciate my work felt like a small failure to me. My mother acted like it was the biggest occasion of my life, some pivotal turning point of success and social status.

I just wanted to eat and go home.

Originally, Jacob told me he had no intention of coming with me. He liked the aforementioned crowds less than I did, and he wasn't too thrilled about having to dress up. I didn't blame him, but I was hurt by his lack of support. I told Kat she had to be my date. She was so appalled at Jacob's attitude that she stopped by our apartment the day before the event just to let him have it.

"Hey, Grace," she said, kicking the bottom of his foot with the tip of her pointy shoe, "what the hell's your problem?"

Jacob was laying on the couch with *Slaughterhouse-Five* on his lap and a bottle of beer beside him on the floor.

"Don't you care that Blanca will have to walk around alone? She's going to look single. Cheesy Hollywood rich guys are going to hit on her while their wives are off powdering their noses. Is that what you want?"

"Get off my case," Jacob said.

"I swear, every time I see you lately, you have a scowl on your face. Snap out of it already."

"Fuck off," he said. He was in no mood for her.

Kat looked my way. "Did you hear what he said to me?"

I just shrugged.

"Fine," Kat said to Jacob. "I'm going to search out the cutest guy there, one who happens to be able to recite poetry. And listens to weird music. And wants to move to Tallahassee. And I'm going to make sure he sits right next to Blanca. Then you'll be up shit creek, won't you?"

Jacob slapped his book down. "Didn't you hear me the first time? I said fuck off, Kat. Just *fuck off*."

"Bite me," she said.

"No thanks, I don't eat leftovers."

"Enough!" I yelled, just in time to stop Kat from screaming another obscenity.

Kat bent down really close to Jacob's face. "Just don't say I didn't warn you."

Jacob only got jealous when he was depressed. When he

was down, he thought everything that could possibly go wrong would. And I suppose some of what Kat threatened him with had germinated in his brain overnight. The morning of the party, he said, "All right, I'll go," and I had to scramble to get him a tux.

The soiree was held in an enormous, swanky hotel ball-room that echoed with the incessant cacophony of bad orchestral music. It was the kind of sound that foreboded disaster. I felt like I was on the *Titanic* right before its little run-in with the iceberg.

The walls of the room were papered in a pale gold fabric that I swore was gift wrapping. And hanging from the middle of the ceiling were the two ugliest chandeliers I'd ever seen. They looked like upside-down champagne glasses, dripping with crystals that left freckling fragments of light on a number of the already glittering faces below.

The only thing I looked forward to all evening—the food—was impressively disappointing. The alleged four-star chef threw soggy Feta cheese on half the meal and called it a Mediterranean feast. Nobody noticed or complained about it though, except me and Kat, probably because nobody else in Beverly Hills eats.

Less than thirty minutes after our arrival, Jacob began asking me how long we had to stay. I couldn't leave until the auction was over, or at least until my piece was sold. Jacob's anxiety and inability to even attempt to conceal his indifference drove me mad. Hell, it wasn't my idea of a pleasant evening either, but I managed to masquerade as a person having a good time. Jacob looked on with a mix of repulsion and detachment, as if he were watching an appendectomy. Moreover, whenever I was introduced to new people, I would, out of common courtesy, begin to introduce Jacob.

Before I could get his name out, he'd chime in with, "Henry Chinaski. Of Chinaski and Sons. Good to meet you." Then he'd shake their hands at warped speed like some kind of maniac.

"And what do you do, Mr. Chinaski?"

"I'm a mortician," he'd say. "You kill 'em, I fill 'em. Ha! Ha! Ha!"

Finally, I dragged him into a corner. "Jacob, are you going to act like a jerk all night?" I said. "You're embarrassing me."

"You used to think I was funny."

"You used to be funny."

After that, he stopped talking to me altogether.

Most of the designers who had been invited to participate in the festivities made tasteless necklaces and broaches, things normal people with any real style would never wear. I designed something just as impractical, but with much more class—an intricate little tiara that turned out to be the most talked-about piece of the evening. It was a sprinkling of tiny diamonds set in platinum, but had been carved in a rough vein to resemble a rose stem. A metallic crown of thorns. It probably could have retailed for about twenty grand, but after a lot of back and forth bidding, a young, Oscar-nominated actress ended up scoring it for ten. She told me she was doing a big feature with *Vanity Fair* and wanted to wear it on the cover. My mother was orgasmic over the whole deal. She went around bragging about me to everyone she made eye contact with.

"That's my daughter. She made the tiara. Isn't it an amazing piece of artwork?"

The irony was, if my mother had seen the tiara in a magazine, she would have scoffed at it and called it trashy, or avant-garde, or some other word she didn't understand the definition of.

I guess I should have been excited over the attention, but something about all the phony hoopla made me sad, and rendered the evening completely inconsequential in my mind.

"Where's Jacob?" my mother said toward the end of the night. She was trying to make up her mind about what to bid on, and she wanted his opinion. She'd narrowed down her choices to a dragonfly pin with emerald eyes, or a diamond tennis bracelet.

"I don't know where he is," I said. I tried to act like it was no big deal because if she thought Jacob and I were having problems, she would have blamed it all on me and asked me what I'd done to mess everything up.

# THIRTY-EIGHT

I never saw Jacob again that evening. He wasn't at the apartment when I got back from the party, and he didn't come home the next day, or the next day, or the day after that. I worried myself into a frenzy, and I had no idea what the hell to do about it. I ended up fretting around without being capable of accomplishing a thing. I didn't sleep, I barely ate, I couldn't work. I was like a truck driver on speed. All I did was motor around town staring at street people, expecting to find Jacob hunched beside a garbage can with a beard, no shoes, and dirt all over his face.

I didn't hear from Jacob for five days. That's when he decided to call and say hi. He left a message explaining he was at a place called the Sage and Cedar Motel, somewhere outside of Needles, California. I didn't even know where Needles was. I had to look it up. It's past the Mojave desert, right at the Arizona border, out in the middle of nowhere.

Jacob rambled on like a crazed schizophrenic away on a business trip.

"Trixie, I totally lost track of time, otherwise I would have called sooner....It's so fucking hot here....I drove eight miles on the old Route 66 yesterday. It was really cool and weird. You would've liked it....I swam in the Colorado river....I saw a ghost town....Indian hieroglyphs....Now I'm just holed up in this dump, writing a shitload of thoughts. Thoughts are king, Trixie. King," he said.

He left his number and asked me to call him. "I need you.

I need to hear your voice."

I pressed the delete button. There was no way I was calling him back.

He phoned every day for the next week but I never answered. I refused to play the dutiful wife. When I thought about Jacob, I wasn't worried about his safety anymore, if he was eating enough, or getting enough rest, if he was happy. I just pictured him on a big vacation, hanging out at some crappy bar, drinking beer that tasted like piss, spewing all his withering-soul philosophies while women swooned and begged for the chance to mend his broken heart. He'd get too wasted to see straight and go home with some voluptuous barmaid named Rosalita. She'd have shiny skin and a flirty Mexican accent, and when she asked him if he had a girlfriend, he'd just laugh.

"*No se preocupes*," he'd say, in his half-assed high school Spanish. "She's far away."

Maybe he would promise to take Rosalita to Memphis, too. Maybe he was already on his way there.

I began to hate Jacob. I couldn't think about anything else, just hate.

This is the kind of stupid shit my mother must have gone through while she waited up for my father, I thought. Like the times she pretended she wasn't tired, even though she could barely keep her eyes open, because she wanted to be in the living room, right in his face, when he tried to sneak in quietly in the middle of the night. Sometimes she'd still be there in the morning, as if she'd just dozed off watching TV. Those were the mornings we didn't ask questions, and she didn't look us in the eyes because she couldn't. When I thought about those days, it made me feel sorry for my mother. Then I felt sorry for myself, for allowing myself to be in a position to identify with her. I swore I'd never do that.

# THIRTY-NINE

Jacob was gone for a total of fifteen days. When he came home, he waltzed in the apartment like nothing was wrong, like he'd been down at the market picking up a carton of milk. He told me he'd left Needles and from there had gone to Big Sur, where he sat on a cold, stony beach and pondered the meaning of his life.

"Big Sur isn't anywhere near Needles," I said.

"I know. Here, I brought this for you."

He handed me a magnet. It was a cartoon of a wave over-taking the words Big Sur, with a thermometer attached to the right side. It was seventy degrees in our apartment.

That same morning, there was a TV show filming on the street outside of our building. The monotonous noise of their trailers and generators below the window more than got on my nerves, and gave a slow, insipid rhythm to our whole con-versation. Once in a while I'd hear "Action!" or "Cut!" But mostly it was just those damn motors.

"We were supposed to go to Big Sur together someday," I said.

Jacob told me he was sorry. He was looking for Henry Miller's grave. He couldn't find it.

"He wasn't buried there," he said. "Or if he was, nobody would tell me where. Did you know Henry Miller's first wife's name was Beatrice?" Jacob seemed to think that had some momentous significance in our lives. "Did you?"

"No, I didn't know that."

He didn't even seem drunk, so he had no excuse for walking around in such a thick fucking fog.

"Trixie, this is important, you'll get a kick out of this. Henry Miller was healthy and happy when he lived in Big Sur. For years and years. And then you know what happened? He moved to Pacific Palisades and he *died*. He came to Los Angeles and it *killed* him."

Yeah, about twenty years later, I thought. It's not like he dropped the day he arrived or anything. He was old.

"Jacob, I don't care about Henry Miller right now."

"*Okay.*"

It had been a while since I heard him say that. I pretended it didn't move me at all.

There was a quick hammering noise on the set below us. I tried to walk past Jacob, to look out the window and see what they were building, but he pulled me over to where he stood. He slid his hand up my shirt.

"I missed you so much," he said.

His mouth was on mine and his tongue was slowly, gently trying to break through. I kept my lips locked tight and wondered if he kissed Rosalita like that. I pushed him away.

"I need to talk to you," I said.

For the first time since he walked in the door, he sat down. He kept flipping the Big Sur thermometer upside-down and then right-side up again, as if it were an hourglass. He waited for me to speak.

I heard the assistant director outside calling for the actors. Three times he said, "First team to the set, please!"

I rehearsed in my head what I was going to say. I didn't know why I was going to say it, but at the time I didn't think I had a choice. I hadn't convinced myself it was the right thing to do, but I was scared. I made up my mind that it was my only option. To save myself from the pain.

I wished for a sudden, catastrophic earthquake. One big enough to tear the building off its foundation and toss us like corn kernels in hot oil, popping about the room, ending everything right there. Jacob and I would have died synchronously and been together for all of eternity.

I thought the magnet was wrong. It seemed much warmer than seventy degrees in our living room.

Outside, someone said, "Roll camera!" Another guy yelled, "Speed!" Then the director called, "Action!"

"Trixie, what's wrong?' Jacob said.

"*What's wrong*?" I said. "How can you ask me that? How can you not know what's wrong?"

"Well, you're obviously upset, and—"

"I want you to leave. Now. You need to go." I turned my back so that I couldn't see his face.

"Go? I just got back. What's the matter with you?"

I spun back around and said, "*Me?* What the fuck is the matter with *you*? You think you can just disappear for a couple weeks and then come back here and be my boyfriend and act like nothing's happened? I'm sorry but it doesn't work that way."

"I had a lot of thinking to do. I needed to get my shit together. I didn't want to be a drag."

"Jacob, I'm supposed to *help* you get your shit together. That's part of the job description of a girlfriend, whether you're in Big Sur or Needles or Timbuktu." I paused. "Then again, God knows where the hell you *really* were." What I actually meant was, God knows who you were with.

"Hey," he said. "You do. You know where I was because I told you. And anyway, I called you a million times but you never called me back."

"Why didn't you take me with you?"

"Beatrice, you're the one who kept telling me how

fucking busy you were. I was trying to do you a favor by getting out of your way."

"Give me a break. How stupid do you think I am?"

"*What?*"

"You were gone for over two weeks. Am I supposed to believe you weren't out fucking around, having a grand old time?"

That made Jacob mad. Irrationality always pissed him off. "Yeah, actually, you are supposed to believe that! Is *that* what this is about? Were you really concerned about me at all, or did you just think I was off fucking someone else?"

"Can you prove to me that you weren't?"

"I shouldn't have to! God, Trixie, you can be so fucking warped sometimes!"

"You're one to talk," I said. I had a quick childhood flashback. I pictured the time my father said he was going to Chicago for business in the middle of winter, then came home with a tan.

The little devil on my shoulder whispered: Jacob *does* look more golden than usual.

He did. He looked like he'd been frolicking around the beach with some cheap trollop.

"It's over," I said.

Jacob didn't know whether or not to believe me. I had to repeat myself, simulating conviction. "It's *over*," I said again. "I mean it. The end."

The light in Jacob's eyes dimmed. "Trixie…," he whispered, "why are you doing this?"

"…And cut!" the director yelled. "Let's go one more time!"

"I won't let you walk all over me, that's why. I won't sit here and be made a fool of."

"Oh, *okay*. Are you talking to me or your father?"

"Get out!"

Jacob sat on the couch with his head in his hands and looked at the floor. He rubbed his face. "What about Memphis?"

I thought he must have gone off the deep end to ask me a question like that after the way he'd behaved.

"Memphis? What *about* Memphis?" I said. "How can we move to Memphis when you don't even talk to me anymore? When you're never here, and when you are, you just float in and out like this is some weigh station where you stop to sleep and shower and fuck once in a while. No wonder you didn't know Nina was on heroin. I probably could've shot up right in front of your face and you wouldn't have seen me!"

Jacob told me I was being selfish and cruel, that I didn't understand what he'd been dealing with, and that I didn't even try. "I'm sorry about running off, Trixie. I'm *sorry*. But I had some really serious stuff I needed to sort out. In case you forgot, my father fucking *died*, all right? And one of the reasons I left was because you were making me feel like an inconvenience. Like I was in your way or something. You didn't want to deal with me any more than I wanted to deal with myself."

"Oh, so it's my fault?"

"It's no one's fault."

"Don't act like I gave you license to abandon me."

"I didn't abandon you!" He got up and held me by the shoulders. "Listen, you have to stop assuming that every man who says he loves you is going to run off and disappoint you someday."

"Every man who's said he loves me *has* run off and disappointed me."

That hurt him, I could tell. But that's why I said it. I wanted him to hurt. I wanted to get even with him for hurting me.

Jacob was supposed to get down on his knees, right then and there, and promise to put the shattered pieces back together. He was supposed to reject my command to leave, drag me into the bedroom, and order me to start packing. We're leaving right away, he'd tell me. Forget California once and for all, it's tearing us apart. I'll sell the book from Memphis, it will all be *okay*. Graceland is waiting, my love. Los Angeles killed Henry Miller but it won't kill us. We're gone!

That's what was supposed to happen. Instead, Jacob said, "You know, I'm not so sure you ever really understood me at all."

That's when I told him I didn't love him anymore.

"You don't mean that," he said.

He was right, I didn't mean even an ounce of it, but I wouldn't take it back. I didn't want to go through all the shit anymore—the feeling of being so fucking in love every single day that it hurt like a gunshot in your gut. Who the hell would want to feel like that for the rest of their life?

"You promised you wouldn't leave," Jacob said quietly. "Remember? You promised."

"I'm not leaving. You are."

Someone outside yelled, "That's a wrap."

"Please don't do this, Trixie. Please."

"By the way, my name's not Trixie."

Jacob didn't say anything else after that. He just stormed into the bedroom, grabbed a handful of clothes, a couple of notebooks, threw them into a bag, and left. It was that easy. He didn't even say good-bye. And I had to elicit the aid of every power source in my body to resist the crushing urge to run after him. Because when I caught him, I would have told him the truth—I would have told him that when he came in, all I wanted to do was rest my head in the curve between his shoulder and his neck, breathing in his scent, listening to him chant his crazy dreams in my ear.

But I didn't move a muscle.

My feet were glued to the floor by the past and there wasn't a prayer in hell that was going to pry them loose.

I couldn't sleep that night. I stayed up and watched the news, because there's nothing like watching the local news in Los Angeles to cheer a person up. I saw a story about a woman named Lucille who had been car-jacked somewhere in the San Fernando Valley. Lucille was in the backseat with her son, James, while her friend Nancy drove. Nancy was on TV, too. She had a perm.

The afternoon of the crime, Nancy made a pit-stop at a pharmacy. She went in to pick up a prescription and, in the meantime, some sixteen-year-old thug with a handgun hopped into the driver's seat of her car and took off with Lucille and James along for the ride. Lucille screamed and begged the guy not to hurt her baby. But, this is the kicker, she had the wherewithal during the whole ordeal to secretly dial 911 on the cell phone laying at her feet. She cried directions into the phone, things like: "Mr. Carjacker, sir, please don't hurt us. Just pull over into that Whole Foods parking lot right next to the Ford dealership there on the corner of Ventura and Canoga and let us out!"

From her prattling, the police were able to locate the car, speed to Lucille's rescue, and save her life and the life of her son. After Lucille told the whole story in vivid detail, I thought, Hell, that's pretty quick for a woman with Lee press-on nails. But then the news anchor had to go and ask her how in the world she thought to call 911 and talk like that in such a time of crisis. You know what she said?

God.

That's right, that's who got all the credit.

"God gave me divine grace to be strong and think fast. God saved my life and the life of my son," she said. "It was all part of his plan."

I was insanely jealous of Lucille. More jealous than I'd ever been of anyone in my entire life. Because she truly meant it. All I could think was, why can't I be as stupid as Lucille? Why can't I blame all my successes and all my failures on The Lord Jesus Christ Almighty? I would be so fucking happy if I lived like that. I could have said God told me to break up with Jacob, and if God told me to do it, it must have been the right thing. I would have been able to fault God for taking Thomas Doorley away from Jacob. And for letting Jacob go to Big Sur without me. And it would have definitely been all God's fault that Jacob hadn't sold his book yet, because if God has the power to let wide receivers on one team score touchdowns against the apparent sinners on the other side like they seem to think he does, surely God could have made Simon and Schuster stand up and take notice of how brilliant a writer Jacob was.

My true point of view goes like this: *If there really was a God, Jacob and I would be in Memphis right now.*

Meanwhile, if Lucille's God heard her yapping, I'm sure he laughed his ass off. He laughed so hard, he peed his big, God pants. Because if, between the billions of people God had to baby-sit, he happened to be in the Rite-Aid parking lot in Woodland Hills, California, just in time to whisper commands of salvation into Lucille's perky ears, then God needed to get a fucking hobby.

# FORTY

Sara called me a few days after Jacob left and told me he was staying with them, in case I was worried.

"I'm not," I said. I was lying. Again. I'd become quite a master prevaricator.

Sara wanted to know if there was anything she could do to help.

"Is Jacob there now?" I said.

"No, he went to Chez Jay's with Pete and Odie. To watch the Dodger game. Why don't you stop in and see them?" Chez Jay's was a bar that happened to be about a mile from my apartment. I told her I couldn't go.

"I'm really busy," I said. I would have bet my life that Jacob had asked Sara to call.

"This is stupid, you two belong together," she said. "Jacob's really getting his head back on straight. Everything will work out. I know it will."

"I'm glad one of us is optimistic." I asked her what Jacob had been doing all day, if he'd gone back to work or what.

"No," she said, "he's just been sitting around reading and fiddling with Pete's guitars. Can I tell him I spoke to you, Beatrice? Can I tell him you want to see him?"

"Please don't do that, Sara."

I said good-bye to her so she didn't try to change my mind.

Jacob started phoning me every day. I had to screen my calls.

"Trixie, you have to call me back. Please. I'll be around all afternoon."

He always talked to the machine like it was a real person.

"Listen, why don't you just come over when you get home. We'll take a long walk on the beach and we'll figure all this out. I'm not going anywhere tonight. I'll wait until you get here."

The next day, he said, "Trixie, you should have come over last night."

Once he called just to say he hoped I was keeping up with my journal.

"Remember to write what you feel. And don't read it over too much. Don't make corrections." He was referring to the time he caught me rewriting. He'd been looking over my shoulder and thought I'd written the wrong date at the top of the page, until I told him I was fixing an old entry; you know, revising punctuation, spell-checking. He said you weren't supposed to do that.

Another time, Jacob sang to me.

"Listen to this." I heard him put the phone down and start strumming on a guitar. "I've been practicing," he said. "I used to know how to play pretty well. I'm a little rusty, but Pete taught me a few songs. This one's about us."

I only heard the first verse because the machine cut him off. It was the story of some barfly who was really smart, who could build things, and could seemingly grasp every riddle in life except why his girl had left him.

It was just another fucked-up love song, but Jacob turned it into the truth. His truth. Jacob was the only person I'd ever met, besides myself, who believed music was a cosmic language that spoke directly to our souls—to ease our pain, and to remind us we weren't alone.

"A good song can save your life, Trixie. Don't ever forget it."

He was going to write a book about it someday.

After the serenade failed to win me back, Jacob made one last attempt to reach me. That's when he said he wasn't going to call anymore.

"I get the hint," he said. "I'm coming over tomorrow to get my computer. I'll be there around noon. I'd really like to see you."

I made sure I was gone all day. And I left Jacob a note asking him to leave me his key. When I got home late that night, I knew Jacob had been there—even before I looked in the office to see if his computer was gone, because I smelled remnants of him in the air.

He'd left the key on the desk.

When I tried to spell out the whole mess for Kat, she told me that even if I was unhappy with Jacob, which we both knew was a big, fat, juicy lie, it couldn't be any worse than what I was without him. She spat me the hocker of advice I usually spit at everyone else.

"Blanca, you can't commit suicide so as not to be murdered, *right*? That's the worst way to die, *right*?"

It drives me crazy when people know me well enough to remind me what I believe. Kat said I had a future with Jacob. "And you're fucking it up for no other reason than you're a stubborn idiot who's afraid to be happy. But if you want to be a baby about it, so be it. I didn't want you to end up in Dogpatch or Tallahassee or wherever the hell you wanted to go anyway."

# FORTY-ONE

"Dude, where's Henry been? I haven't seen him in a while."

Greg was standing in the middle of the hallway, barefoot, when I walked out my door. His feet looked like he'd been dancing in coal. He was the last person in the world I felt like talking to. I prayed to my non-existent God for the elevator to arrive as quickly as possible.

"Henry's on assignment in Borneo. He's writing an article on albino orangutans."

"Right on," Greg said. I pushed the Close Door button a dozen times. Greg's voice echoed down the shaft. "You look really nice, by the way."

I didn't want to hear that. I didn't want to look nice for the pathetic evening I was in store for—the one I blamed all on Kat. I guess you could have called it a date, but I didn't. It was only *dinner*. I was having *dinner* with some friend of Gopal's that I met at a cocktail party. After scheming in the corner with Kat for half the evening, the bloke walked right up to me and wouldn't stop talking. I refer to him as a bloke because he was English, but not the cool, working-class Englishmen you see in independent films. This one talked like he hadn't taken a shit in days. He told me all about his consulting firm, and how he liked to walk Nigel, his Rottweiler puppy, to the dog park in Laurel Canyon. He also informed me that he was allergic to penicillin. He took it once when he was a kid and his throat swelled up like a balloon.

"I almost died. Fortunately, my mother was a nurse. She gave me a shot of something, and things turned out brilliantly."

Lucky me, I thought. Why couldn't his mother have been a telephone operator?

"Give him a chance," Kat said. "He's cute. He looks like royalty. Maybe he's a lord or something."

"I don't see it."

I went home feeling so unbearably alone I actually thought there was a possibility I could drop dead before the night was over.

Without consultation, Kat gave the lord my phone number. He called me the next day and asked me out for dinner. I told him I'd just been diagnosed schizophrenic. He didn't fall for it.

"Katrina said I couldn't take no for an answer."

I had two choices: dinner with the royal pain-in-the-ass or sit at home and proofread my journal.

"Come on, a free meal with a cute limey won't kill you," Kat said.

That was debatable.

His name was Steven, and rest assured, he was no lord. He arrived at my door wearing a white shirt that he'd buttoned all the way up to the collar, and pleated khaki pants. The fact that he was dressed for a Jordan family photo was the first red flag. Jacob wouldn't have been caught dead in that costume. Nor would Jacob have combed his hair like Steven combed his, neatly to one side. Jacob would have never driven a car that smelled like baby powder either. Or listened to bubble-gum pop music. As a matter of fact, Jacob would have probably rather been shot by a firing squad than made to listen to bubble-gum pop crap.

If the car hadn't been moving, I'm sure I would have jumped out. As we drove down my street, I hoped Jacob had been stalking me. I kept an eye out for his dirty Land Cruiser. I waited for it to pull up behind us. I wanted a chase to ensue. I wanted Jacob to try and run Steven off the road. I wanted Steven to speed down the freeway, bank a turn, roll his car and break an arm, or maybe crack his snotty British nose. Nothing life-threatening, just enough to immobilize him and allow me to escape. I would have jumped into Jacob's car and we would have driven off, never stopping until we reached the Memphis city limits.

Steven took me to an Italian restaurant on Rodeo Drive. He asked me what I was going to have, and when I told him I wanted the spaghetti pomodoro, he ordered it for me. What I mean is, the waiter came over and asked if we'd decided on dinner, and Steven proceeded to say, "The lady will have…" I could tell by his asinine smirk that he thought he was being impressively chivalrous, but in all actuality, he'd just hammered the final khaki-colored nail into his bubble-gum pop crap coffin.

If only I'd had some penicillin, I could have ended it real quick.

I called Kat the minute I got home. I told her to shove Lord Steven up her ass. Then I spent the rest of the night writing in my still-nameless diary. I filled an entire page with a sentence I remembered from *Hallelujah*. It was one of my favorite lines in the book:

*Our love became a casualty of my family tree.*

I wrote it ninety-three times, until there was no more room on the page.

On the next sheet of paper I wrote every possible version of my name if I would have married Jacob. *Beatrice Grace.* That sounded good. *Beatrice Jordan Grace*. Also good, but I knew I wouldn't keep my maiden name if I got to pick up a lovely new one like Grace. *Beatrice Casimir Grace*. I crossed that out. Casimir is my middle name. I don't use it because it's my mother's maiden name, as well as Chip's real first name. In Poland, it's loosely translated as "One who makes peace." Go figure.

I wrote my nickname, too. *Trixie Grace*. That kind of looked like the name of a stripper, but in Tennessee it might have gone unnoticed. How about the kids? *Madeline Grace*. *Simone Grace*.

It would have been perfect.

# FORTY-TWO

Dawn makes a sound. If you listen closely, right as the sun starts to come up, you'll hear it. It's like the echo of birth: silence, followed by a gentle push, followed by moans, then the sloppy deluge of new life. On good days I like it because it reminds me that I'm alive. On bad days it makes me feel like dust.

Los Angeles without Jacob made me feel like dust. Los Angeles without Jacob was a giant mortar and pestle that ground me down finer and finer until I started to become nothing but powdery particles about to float off into a vacuum.

To put it in plain English: I was highly unproductive after Jacob and I split. I still went to the studio every morning and tried to work, but my heart and my hands refused to cooperate. Kat called constantly to check up on me. Anytime she thought I sounded like I was about to jump off a tall building, she'd con me into coming over.

"Get your ass down here, my salesgirl called in sick again."

I always went. And not so much because Kat was good at cheering me up. I just didn't have the energy to do much else.

"Beatrice, telephone," Shelly said. Shelly was my ponytailed little assistant. She was supposed to help me make jewelry, not play secretary, but I don't like to talk on the phone when I'm gloomy. I'm distrustful of people when I can't see their faces.

I pretended to be busy drawing rings. "Who is it?"

"It's Jacob," she whispered.

He'd stopped calling me exactly fourteen days and sixteen hours earlier, and we hadn't spoken or seen each other since the day we broke up. I desperately wanted to talk to him. As a matter of fact, I'd called Pete and Sara's apartment a dozen times in as many days intending to admit what a fool I'd been, but every time someone said hello, I'd get scared and hang up.

With pangs of regret, I shook my head. That meant Shelly was supposed to tell Jacob I wasn't around, even though I'm sure he'd heard my voice.

"He wants you to call him," Shelly said. "He said it's *really important*."

I could tell, by the tone of her voice, that she was on his side.

I picked up my purse. "I'm going to Chick."

I walked into the store and told Kat she had to help me make a list of all the reasons why it would have sucked to live in Memphis. She started to itemize immediately.

"Number one: It's humid in Memphis."

"No," I said, "that's no good."

"What do you mean? It gets *hot* in Tennessee."

"I know. But that was a positive for us."

"Why?" She cringed, anticipating a ludicrous response.

"Sweaty sex," I said.

"Oy-vey, Blanca!"

Kat felt sorry for me and said I could work the cash register for the rest of the day. Then she had an idea. "Let's pretend we're one of those uppity Beverly Hills stores that give poor people dirty looks when they walk in. Like the way they treated you in Gucci."

I was always treated like trash when I went into fancy

stores. I didn't dress rich enough. The last time I'd gone to Gucci I was with Kat and Gopal. He needed to pick up a pair of shoes, and he had on one of their suits so they were nice to him. I was wearing hand-me-down pants from the Army/Navy store, along with Jacob's Love Motel T-shirt. I didn't look like I had a pot to piss in. The sales girl, who I swear had a fishing pole up her butt and chicken cutlets in her bra, followed me around like I was going to steal something. Kat begged me to pull a *Pretty Woman* maneuver and buy up the place, but back then I still thought I was moving to Memphis, and what kind of shithead wears Gucci in Memphis?

Kat wanted to conduct an experiment based on that incident. "We'll fawn all over the scrubby-looking people, and treat the ones who think they're important like they have leprosy."

As for celebrities, it went without saying that most of them got the shitty treatment, no matter how they were dressed— they cared too much and we didn't like them for that. Credible musicians were our one exception.

"Because we respect them," Kat said.

"This is reverse discrimination," I told her. "And lucky for you, I'm in the right mood to go along with it."

"New number one," Kat said. She was still working on the Memphis list. "Did you really want to live in the same state as Dollywood?"

There was no arguing with her on that.

A lanky supermodel wearing a crushed-velvet hat walked in not long after we'd decided to torture patrons such as herself. Kat said hi to her as a test. She returned neither a word nor a smile.

After examining the jewelry case for a few minutes, the girl spoke to me without looking up. "Can I see that necklace? The one with the pink and purple stones."

They weren't pink and purple stones, they were amethyst and rose quartz.

"Excuse me, *Miss*?" she said a little louder.

I pretended I was deaf and didn't even raise my head. The model chick sashayed out, more confused than offended.

"Should I call him?" I said to Kat. I picked up the phone, then I put it down quickly and shook my head. "No, I can't."

Kat started lecturing me. "*Call* him already. I mean really, do you think you're ever going to find a guy more perfect for you than that freak? Someone who loves you like he does? He's fucking whipped. And you're doing exactly what you talked me out of doing to Gopal. Why is it that you can con me into keeping a decent relationship going, but you can't hold on to your own, huh? What would Oprah say about them apples, Blanca?"

A skinny little girl with diamond stud earrings bigger than her ass walked in. She asked me for help finding a pair of jeans in her size.

"Try the pre-teen department at Sears," I said.

Kat went back to her mannequin and the list. "Number two: Inbreeding," she said. "Number three: Ducks in the hotels."

"Did you say *ducks*?"

"It's true. Gopal told me there's some hotel in Memphis that lets a bunch of ducks march through the lobby, like, once a day or something. They hop into a fountain, take baths, then march back out."

"Back out to where? Where do they live?"

"How the hell would I know?"

Fixated on the clicking of the cash register buttons, I thought about Jacob and rang up a phantom purchase costing sixty-nine dollars and sixty-nine cents. I was adding on the tax when I asked Kat one more time if I should call him.

"Not going to be necessary," she said.

I glanced up. Jacob was standing right in front of me. He looked unbelievably happy. Maybe he hadn't missed me at all, I immediately thought, because he looked better than I'd seen him look since his father died. He was wearing a new shirt. It was too big for him, like everything in his closet, with short sleeves, buttons down the front, and a paisley design that made me think of sperm. He'd had his hair cut, too. The thick locks that used to brush his collar were gone, making him look cleaner and younger. And he had the most ridiculous coyote grin on his face.

"Let's go," he said. He grabbed my purse off the counter.

"I'm not going anywhere with you," I said indignantly, just to give him a hard time.

"You have no choice. You either get up willing, or I'm going to pick you up and drag your ass out of here."

"Oh my God, that would be just like *An Officer and a Gentleman*," Kat cried. "Pick her up, Grace! Do it!"

I sat there, arms crossed, and stared at him. I could be a real bitch when I wanted to, even when I wasn't trying that hard.

"Come on, Trixie. An hour of your time is all I ask. Then you never have to see me again if you don't want to."

Funny, that struck me as the most horrible thought imaginable—to never see Jacob again.

"I'm counting to three. One…Two…" He started around the counter for me.

"All right!" I stood up and took my purse from him, trying my hardest to act annoyed. "Where are you taking me?"

"It's a surprise," he said.

# FORTY-THREE

"Give me the keys," Jacob said when we got to my car. "I'm driving."

"Please tell me where we're going."

"You'll see."

We headed south down Robertson, turned onto the 10 freeway going east, and drove. After passing the La Cienega, Fairfax, and La Brea exits, Jacob finally signaled and got off at Crenshaw Boulevard. There was a guy in heavy trousers and no shirt standing on the corner selling roses. Jacob seemed to contemplate stopping for a flower, but the light turned green and we kept moving.

"We're going to the Hood?" I said.

"South Central, baby."

I was sure the senile grin on his face meant he was taking me to the home of some gold-toothed gang lord where he was going to watch with glee as man named Booger chopped me up into little pieces then stuffed me in a dumpster.

"So, how's it going?" he said blithely. "How have you been?"

I didn't answer his question and that made him laugh. He kept glancing over at me as he drove. I focused my gaze out the window. I didn't want to make eye contact with him—I was too weak for that.

We passed pawn shops, dilapidated buildings, and tons of gas stations. It seemed like there was a gas station on every block.

"Do a lot of people get shot around here?" I said.

"Yeah, so you better behave yourself." Jacob made a quick left and parked the car.

"Are you sure this is safe?" I said.

"It's fine. Don't be such a baby."

We walked across the street to a tiny restaurant that said "Chef Lulu's" above the entrance. There were bars on the doors and windows.

"It looks closed," I said.

"It's not closed." Jacob opened the door and we went in.

The restaurant was the size of a small living room, the metal tables and chairs bordered on decrepit, and the dark purple carpet on the floor was stained with grease, but I hadn't eaten for hours, and the smells coming from the kitchen made my stomach growl. Still, I couldn't figure out why Jacob had brought me there.

A sign at the back of the restaurant boasted, "Best Oxtail west of the Mississippi." I wondered what the hell we were going to eat. I certainly wasn't going to feast on some ox's ass.

Jacob sat me down at a table and went to the pick-up window. The woman standing there happened to be Chef Lulu herself, at least that's what her apron said.

"What can I get for you?" Lulu said to Jacob.

He ordered fried catfish with cornbread, collard greens, and a side of macaroni and cheese.

"And give us a slice of sweet potato pie for dessert," he said. "For my girlfriend. Because she's being so sweet to me today."

Lulu poked her head out the window and examined me. She was a strong woman with big, dangling beads on her ears and a white scarf tied around her head. Her skin was the color of creamy milk chocolate.

"I'm not his girlfriend," I told her.

"She will be by the time we're done eating," Jacob said.

At that, I rolled my eyes. Jacob said, "Trixie, stop being such a brat."

There was an ancient TV on in the corner of the restaurant. It had a pair of rabbit ears on top that you had to play around with to get a clear picture. The only other patron in the place, a hunchback man in a velour jogging suit, sat in front of it, fiddling with the antenna and watching a fat Texan explain the proper way to catch a fish. Lulu gave the man a bag of hot food and he wandered out. The Texan on TV said the most important decision to make when casting your line was depth. Don't be afraid to ask the fisherman in the boat next to you how far down he caught his fish, he said. Sometimes he'll actually tell you.

Lulu informed Jacob that they'd bring our food out when it was ready. Before he took his seat, Jacob helped himself to the self-serve refrigerator of soft drinks. He brought us each a can of orange soda.

An older African-American woman came in right after Jacob sat down. She was tiny and she held her head up high. Lulu greeted the woman with respect and asked her if she wanted her usual, red beans and rice. The woman nodded, then she made herself comfortable at the table across from us. I said hi to her and tried to start up a conversation, mainly because she looked interesting, but also because I was afraid to face Jacob. I knew he wanted to *talk*.

"I'm Mrs. Morris," the woman said. "But you can just call me Morris. Everybody does." She told us she used to have a soul food restaurant, too. "It was famous for awhile. We even got written up in *Gourmet* magazine."

Mrs. Morris claimed she was eighty-four years old. Her face didn't betray her age as a day over sixty, but her hands were history books. If I'd had a camera, I would have taken a

picture of her hands and hung them on my wall to remind
me that you can't put life on pause and then catch up with it
later when you have more energy to give. You have to play it
all the way through to the end.

Morris said, "I'm the only woman in town besides Lulu
who knows how to cook beans. My grandmother taught me
how to make them back in Arkansas more years ago than I
care to remember."

I knew it. I knew she wasn't a native. They didn't grow
very many people like her in the cement soil of Los Angeles.

When her beans and rice were ready, Morris carefully
lifted her bag and said good-bye. My heart hurt to see her go.
She was exactly the kind of person I dreamed we would have
had as a neighbor if we'd ever moved South—a surrogate
grandmother who would invite us over for dinner once a
week, complain that we were too skinny, and keep feeding us
until we were ready to burst. We'd go to the market for her
when she needed groceries, and she'd apologize for being a
burden, but she'd love us and know we'd do anything for her.

"Isn't she great?" Jacob said after the door closed behind
her. "I ate in her restaurant once a long time ago. I tried to
order mac and cheese but she yelled at me and said only a
white boy would order that in the middle of the week. She
said I had to eat something else. It was a Wednesday afternoon. Mrs. Morris thinks mac and cheese is a completely
inappropriate side dish anytime except Sunday."

Jacob had never told me that story before, but it sounded
incredibly familiar. It took me a few blinks to figure out
why—there was a bent version of it in *Hallelujah*.

"You just don't meet people like that west of La Brea," I
said, quoting Jackson Grayson.

Jacob didn't even try to hide how charmed he was that I'd
remembered a line he'd written verbatim. He sat at the table

with his chin in his hand, the way he always did, and watched me. I wanted to tell him not a second had gone by since we'd broken up that I didn't wish things were back the way they were before Thomas Doorley bit the dust. I didn't say it though. Not that I needed to.

"Trixie, I have a lot of things to say. Can I start?"

I nodded.

"First of all…," he said, "I'm sorry. I'm sorry, I'm sorry, I'm sorry. Should I say it again? I'm sorry. For acting like such a dick after my father died, for pushing you away, for leaving town, for thinking you wouldn't understand, for anything and everything I may have done wrong. I did exactly what I said I'd never do. I became like him. But I'm done with that."

A teenager who looked like he might be Lulu's son brought us our food. In the meantime, the Texan on TV spoke in baby talk to the fish he'd just reeled in. He called the fish "Boy." I didn't like the Texan. He struck me as the kind of guy who drove around with a shotgun in the back of his pick-up.

"The second thing I want to say is this," Jacob continued. "I know I made some mistakes, for which I've just apologized, but I want to point out—free of malice—that you weren't exactly winning any Good Samaritan of the Year contests. You just gave up on me. On us. What's up with that?"

My first impulse was to get defensive at Jacob's insinuation that I had anything to do with the collapse of our relationship. I curbed it. I knew better. Jacob was right, I'd been a horrible friend to him. I didn't even know how he could stand to be around me after the way I'd acted.

"I didn't give up," I said. "I copped out." I was disappointed in myself. More disappointed than Jacob was in me, I could tell. "Why do you even want me back?"

"Because I'm in love with you, that's why. And you had your reasons. You were motivated by fear, not by how you felt about me. At least that's what I think. Anyway, I've got it all figured out."

"Oh, you do, huh?"

"Yeah. I went through all these emotions. I was mad at you, I was mad at me, I was mad at *him*. Basically, I was just mad at the world. Bottom line: we both screwed up. But it's *okay* to screw up as long as you keep trying. The key is to keep trying." He stopped to take a swig of his soda.

"Are you done?" I said.

"No. I need to ask you some questions. And you have to be honest. You have to tell me the truth. *Okay?*"

"Okay," I said. I had to squeeze my legs together to stop the tingling between them.

"And give me simple answers, *okay?*"

"Do me a favor, don't say *okay* so much. It's very distracting."

"*Okay.*" He laughed. "Did you mean what you said that day—the day you threw me out on my ass—or do you still love me?"

I began dreaming up a long dissertation until he reminded me, "The *simple* answer, Trixie."

That put me in a predicament. There was only one simple way to answer the question.

"Yes," I said.

"Yes, what? Yes you meant what you said, or yes you still love me?"

I stared at the tablecloth and mumbled, "I still love you."

"Can you speak up?"

"You heard me."

"Do you love me a little, or more than a little?"

I sighed.

"Come on, just answer. Without thinking so hard," Jacob said.

"More than a little."

He smiled mischievously. "As I suspected," he said. "*Why?*"

"*Why?* I don't know, I just do." I felt like I was blushing.

"I *need* to know *why.*"

"Jacob, there are a lot of reasons."

"Then give me a few."

I tried to do a quick survey of my emotions. "Well," I said, "I guess the biggest one is because you're not like anyone I know."

Jacob looked at me as if my words held the cure for cancer. "Can you explain that?"

"I thought you wanted the simple answer."

"I changed my mind. Complicate." He raised his brow like he was waiting for something deep and meaningful to come dancing out of my mouth.

"I think it has something to do with the way you feel things," I said. "Everything matters to you. And you aren't afraid to show it."

"What do you mean?"

What, when, why. Sometimes talking to Jacob was like talking to a four-year-old.

"Remember the night your father died?" I said. "When I found you on the beach and for an hour you cried in my arms? It might sound totally sick and twisted, but that was one of the most beautiful hours of my life. I loved you so much for being able to do that. I wish I could be that honest."

He shook his head. "You underestimate yourself. I know you think you hide so much, but I can see right through you."

He could. He was the only one.

"That's why *I* love *you,*" he said. "You try and act so tough, you think you're so damn hopeless and godless and faithless, but you don't fool me. People without hope aren't tormented by the world the way you are. People without hope don't give a shit. But I see it in you, in the way you look at things, even in the way you look at me sometimes, like I'm the coolest fucking guy in the universe, and I know it's in there. Reverence. Belief. *Something.* You have a lot more faith than you own up to. You just don't want to be let down. But I'm not going to let you down again. Not if I can help it."

Jacob extended his left hand out across the table. He wanted me to take hold of it, but there were too many things I needed to say first, things I'd been thinking about and writing in my journal for weeks; things that were finally becoming clear to me.

I slammed my soda can down and rolled my eyes. "Goddamn it," I said. "That's it."

"What?"

"*That's* why I love you. Because you say ridiculous fucking things like that. Normal people don't *say* things like that, Jacob. All my life I waited for someone who would say things like that to me. And for someone I didn't feel alone in the presence of. Someone who *understood.* Someone who would make me feel like it wasn't just me against the world. Even when we're not together. Even when I think you're having rough, dirty sex with Rosalita the barmaid in Needles, California, I'm still comforted by the fact that you're out there. Just knowing you exist changed the world for me. No one has ever made me feel like that, except maybe Howard Roark from *The Fountainhead*, but he doesn't count because he's fictional."

Jacob looked like he was going to say something profound, then he froze. "Wait a second," he said with a crooked face. "Who the hell is Rosalita?"

"No one. Forget it."

He picked up a piece of fried fish, squirted it with lemon, and shoved it in his mouth just as the Texan began to show the camera how to de-bone the catch of the day. Before Jacob swallowed, he said, "We belong together. You know we do. Taste this."

He held a spoonful of macaroni and cheese in front of my face and I took it.

The young waiter came back out to check on us. Instead of asking if everything was all right, he said, "Everything *cool*?"

These are good people, I thought. Not like the west side losers who say things like, "Is there anything else we can get for you today, Ma'am?" as if they're auditioning for a role on a sitcom.

Jacob said, "Listen, I love you. You love me. I am not, nor will I ever be, the heartbreaking scoundrel you think your father was. You have to get that through your thick skull. You have to let go. Don't be so afraid. That's all I can say. The rest is up to you."

I took a bite of the cornbread. It tasted like yellow birthday cake. Jacob was right about the food, but I still didn't understand the significance of our visit to Chef Lulu's. And I knew there had to be significance. Jacob would have never orchestrated something so specific without significance involved.

"This ain't no game," the Texan said, explaining the finer points of reeling in a fighting bass. He yelled at his Billy Bob cohort. "Pull back! And keep your tip up," he said. "Set the hook! Set the hook!" He could barely talk around the big wad of chew in his mouth.

"Jacob, why are we here?" I said. "Why did you bring me all the way out to this place to talk? And why now?"

"Why? Because this is the best soul food in Los Angeles, that's why." Then, acting like what he was about to say was completely beside the point, he continued, "And because I want you to get used to the kind of food you'll be eating if you come to Memphis with me next month. We probably should've ordered something barbequed. They're big on that down there. They char everything. Especially pork. I don't even like pork, to tell you the truth. We're going to have to buy a grill. Do you like pork, Trixie?"

He crammed a giant forkful of collard greens into his mouth and tried not to smile.

"*What did you say?*"

"I don't know about you, but come next month, I'm outta here," he said smugly.

I wish I knew how to explain the phenomenon that came over me after his words sunk in. If he said he was moving, it could only mean one thing.

He'd sold the book.

My entire body became paralyzed. I'm not exaggerating, I couldn't feel my arms or my legs, only the rushing of blood through veins.

"Jacob?" I stuttered slowly, "Did you…"

He grinned like a proud papa.

The idea of the book finally being sold, the possibility of what it promised, was almost too much for me. When I regained control of my motor skills I stood up, probably to make sure I still could. I didn't say a word. I just walked out the door. I needed air.

There was an old, run-down house across the street from the restaurant. Half of the building was lopsided, it had plastic paper flapping where the front windows should have been, and most of the yard was covered with rusty car parts. To the left of the door was a tiny flower box filled with dandelions.

Nine out of ten people walking by would have called them weeds. They were the most breathtaking bunch of yellow weeds I'd ever seen, as if the sun had given birth to a dozen babies.

I sat down on the curb and burst into tears.

A moment later I felt Jacob's hands on my shoulders.

"Hey," was all he said. He lifted me up, turned me around, and engulfed me in his arms.

That made me cry even harder. I put my lips to his lips. To say I kissed him would be inaccurate. I tried to consume him.

"Control yourself," Jacob said. "According to you we're not even dating, remember?"

I buried my face in his chest and inhaled. I'd missed the smell of him almost more than I'd missed anything.

"Our food's going to get cold," he said.

I asked him to give me a minute. I wanted to look around. I wanted to take notice of everything. All of a sudden, I felt the need to completely absorb the place in which I stood.

Before he went back inside, Jacob handed me a piece of paper. It was folded up into a cube, the size of a square inch. On it he'd written me a note:

*Dear Trixie,*

*Will you come to Memphis with me?*

*A) Yes*

*B) No*

*C) I'd go anywhere with you because you fuck like a goddamn fire hose.*

*D) You're an asshole and I never want to see you again.*

*Circle ONLY ONE and give it back to me when you're done eating.*

*Love, J*

When I went back inside, Chef Lulu was spying on us from her window. She saw me wiping away the tears. She shook her head. "See what my food does to people? Makes 'em fools," she said.

I sat down, next to Jacob instead of across from him, and made him give me all the details of the book sale. He explained how Adrenaline ended up getting two separate publishers to vie for it.

"And then something called 'a floor' got going," he said.

"What's that?"

"I'm still not exactly sure. It's *fabulous* though," he said. "I think it's something like an auction maybe, but different. One of the interested publishing houses throws out a bid, and if that bid isn't upped by the other house then they get the book. I think that's what happened. All I know is that she finalized it yesterday. It's done. There's no turning back now."

We were in the middle of eating the sweet potato pie when the waiter brought us our check. I asked him if I could borrow his pen. I unfolded Jacob's note, circled my answer, and handed it to him. Jacob looked at it but manifested no reaction. He just nodded like a judge reading a verdict, feigning indifference.

"You ready to go?" he said.

On our way out of the restaurant, Jacob pressed his body against mine, lowered his voice and said, "Speaking of fire hoses…"

We considered stopping at the Exxon across the street for a quickie, but Jacob feared the smell of a service station bathroom would compromise the purity of my enjoyment.

We made it home in record time.

"I hope you're ready," Jacob said as we wrestled with each other's clothes. He felt the need to apologize beforehand, predicting the imminent session wasn't going to take very long.

"Contrary to what you seem to think, *Rosalita*, it's been a while for me."

# FORTY-FOUR

Jacob was making breakfast when I woke up the next morning. The sight of him standing over a frying pan with bed-head wearing nothing but a pair of baggy shorts made me feel like Mary Magdalene the day after Jesus's resurrection.

We ate banana pancakes and made a list of all the things we had to do before we left. There were myriad minor details to iron out, a lot of loose ends to tie up, and not all that much time to do them. One month—that's the window we gave ourselves. We wanted to be ex-residents of California by mid-November. No, I take that back, it wasn't simply that we *wanted* to be, we *had* to be. Once our exodus was imminent, it was all we could do not to get in the car and go.

"Beatrice," Jacob said. I knew he meant business if he was calling me by my real name, "why haven't you ever left before? I mean I had self-imposed mind games, not to mention financial constraints, keeping me here. You could've gone a long time ago. How come you didn't?"

"I don't know," I said. "Maybe I never really believed it was an option. And I didn't want to go alone."

Jacob smiled impishly. "What do you say we leave everything we can't fit in the back of the car and take off now. Today," he said, barely able to keep still. I watched him doodle over his pancakes with syrup. First he drew a bird, then he smeared that with his fork into a sticky Rorschach blot and tested me.

"What do you see?" he said. "I see B.B. King. Do you

know B.B. King has a bar in Memphis? Come on, what do you see?"

"I see a Herman Miller ball clock."

He turned his plate sideways, entertaining that possibility, then he nodded and looked up. "So, what do you think? You wanna go tonight?"

"Jacob…" I said. I hated to burst his beautiful little bubble of joy, but one of us had to be practical. We had commitments, work to finish, people to say good-bye to. We couldn't just *go*. Once I finally convinced him of that, he said, "*Okay* then, let's leave a few days before my birthday. That way we can take our time driving across the country and still be in Memphis by the end of the month. How's that?"

"Sounds like a plan."

We called everyone who cared and told them the good news.

Pete and Sara decided to throw us a big going-away party the Saturday before we left.

Kat told me I was the best friend she'd ever had. Then she freaked out. "Y'all have a good time now," she said in a pissy voice, and hung up. Jacob called her right back.

"Hey, butt-face," he said. "We're not going into the witness protection program, you know. We're just moving."

"This is all your fault, Grace. Don't think I don't know it." Click.

Joanna congratulated us and promised she'd visit as soon as we got settled.

My mother wanted to know why we couldn't wait until after the holidays to move. "Nobody moves *during* the holiday season," she said.

I told her we'd waited long enough.

Jacob and I got back into bed with his beat-up road atlas and started planning our drive.

"Can we camp the whole way?" Jacob said.

"Camp? You mean like sleep outside?"

"No, I mean dress in drag," Jacob said sarcastically.

"I guess," I said. But I was skeptical. I'd never been camping before. Certain aspects of it concerned me. "Won't it be cold?"

"Not if we bring the right gear."

"Where do we go to the bathroom?"

"In the woods. I'll dig you holes."

"Holes?"

"Come on, don't you want to make love under the stars?"

He didn't have to ask me twice. Fucking under the stars more than made up for having to shit in a hole.

Jacob planned on showing me where he stayed in Needles, which was sort of on the way. He wanted me to get a good look at the barmaid there.

"To ease your mind," he said.

I pretended I didn't know what he was talking about. Moving on, we'd go through Kingman, Arizona; make a fleeting stop in Flagstaff; from there we'd keep heading east to Albuquerque, speed through Amarillo and Oklahoma as fast as possible, then hit the fringes of Dixieland. Little Rock, Arkansas, would be the last real city we'd see before finally glimpsing the banks of the Mississippi river framed by the Memphis skyline. Depending on how much time that took, we were planning a quick detour down to Montgomery to spend Thanksgiving with Cole and Toren. I called Cole and he said we were more than welcome to stay with them as long as we wanted. He thought we might even like Montgomery enough to live there.

"We have our hearts set on Memphis," I said.

Jacob and I decided to pack up most of our stuff. Then we'd have movers store it for us until we found a house. That way we wouldn't have to lug a U-Haul across the country.

Jacob was going to sell his car, and we'd keep my Jetta for the drive.

We surfed the Internet to get an idea of housing prices in the Memphis area. According to the real estate website we browsed, there was a two-story Victorian fixer-upper waiting for us. It had three bedrooms, a vaulted ceiling, a living room, charm, and "other features" that included hardwood floors, a fireplace, and the symbol of freedom itself—a porch. It was everything we wanted. But the best part was, the mortgage would be *half* of what we currently paid in rent.

"Hell, people spend more on cosmetic surgery in Los Angeles than we're going to spend on a whole *maison* full of charm," Jacob said. He was looking at my journal. "Still haven't named it yet, huh? It's been almost a year."

"I'll probably be done with it by the time I think of one."

Jacob went through journals faster than I did, obviously because he wrote more. And he bought those small composition books. I had the four-subject, college-ruled mother. I'd finished English, science, and math, but still had all of history to fill up. Jacob's current journal, which he pulled out of his coat pocket and handed to me, was called *La Corbeille*.

"It means 'trash can' in French," he said.

*La Corbeille* contained most of what he'd penned while we were apart. "Read it when you get a chance. So you know how much unnecessary pain you caused me."

"Shove it," I said.

Jacob stumbled across the page in my book where I'd scribbled my current and potential surnames, along with the names of our kids. I saw him chuckle.

"Hey!" I said. I tried to grab it from him, but he spun around and held it above my reach. "Did I say you could look at that?"

"This is *so cute*, Trixie."

I flung myself down onto the bed and hid my face. Jacob put the book aside, knelt down on the floor, and waited until I looked up. He didn't say anything, he just kept his eyes fixed on me. It reminded me of the day I met him, when I sat down at the table in Fred's diner and he stared at me for two minutes straight without talking. I thought he was a total nut job, and I'm sure it was in those 120 seconds that I first fell in love with him.

"What?" I said. "What are you looking at, you shithead?"

He glanced at me sideways. "Do you want to get married?"

"Jacob…" I sighed. "What the hell is *that*?

"What?"

"I mean, is it a question or a proposal?"

He laughed. "It's only a question. I just want to know for future reference. If it was a proposal I'd be more prepared. You know, maybe a ring and what not," he said. "So, do you?"

"I don't know," I said. "Do you?"

"I like the way your name looks with mine."

Jacob and I both agreed that marriage was something we'd neither planned on nor longed for all our lives like some people did, yet we weren't outlandishly opposed to it anymore.

"Deep down," Jacob said, "I know that calling you my girlfriend for the rest of my life is never going to do our relationship justice."

I concurred with him on that point.

"Maybe after we get settled we should consider making this thing legit," he said.

We both wanted a small ceremony. In a cotton field or on the Mississippi river shore. Then we'd go off to Paris for a honeymoon. We'd eat Brie and baguettes and stare at Rodin sculptures by day, and lick *mousse au chocolat* off of each others toes by night.

# FORTY-FIVE

It was as if the Red Sea had parted and was about to lead us to the Promised Land. That's what we started referring to Memphis as—our promised land. Rand McNally was Moses.

The first article of business I took care of was giving notice on the apartment. We'd been going month to month for a while, so it was no problem getting out of the lease. I was going to lose a bit of my deposit by not providing the required sixty-day heads-up, but I wrote that off. Getting even half of the deposit back would pay our Memphis mortgage for a couple months. Jacob took care of arranging for the cessation of our phone, gas, and electric services. The only other thing I had left was to close down operations at work. I finished up what I'd been working on, filled the last of my orders, and moved out of the studio. I told all my vendors and private customers that I wouldn't be debuting anything again until spring. I wanted my next collection to be a reflection of my new surroundings, and of the perspective I would have once I began to see the world through the eyes of Memphis, Tennessee. Taking a few months off would also give me extra time for all the home improvement projects Jacob and I envisioned in our little Victorian charmer.

I still couldn't believe it was really going to happen. If someone would have asked me then, I might have slipped and said maybe there was a God after all. Maybe there was a slim chance he did exist, and he'd started to feel sorry for me and Jacob. He was finally willing to give us a break. Hell, it wasn't as if we'd been asking to rule the world, or anything diabolical like that. We didn't want to be presidents, or astronauts, or Bill Gates. We had pathetically simple dreams: to do meaningful work that we could be proud of, to be together, and to be happy. That certainly wasn't too much to ask.

Or was it?

Jacob spent the entire month leading up to our impending departure awash in *Hallelujah* responsibilities. He was either on the phone with his editor, or at the computer retooling and perfecting his masterpiece. I ran out of things to do after a week, and spent most of my time with Kat and Sara, planning the big bash. We opted to have a barbeque, in honor of the alleged River City staple, at Sara and Pete's house. They lived on the bottom floor of a white-washed duplex in Venice, one with a small, grassy front yard. Their whole block was closed to cars, only a few streets over from the beach. We booked an ex-con named Ronnie the Rib Tickler to come and cook for us. I was worried about all the noise we might make, but Sara said as long as we offered the neighbors some food we could hang out all night, be as loud as we wanted, and nobody would call the cops.

Jacob thought it was mean that I wouldn't invite my mother, or Chip and Elise, to the party. In my defense, I knew my mother wouldn't have stepped one toe in Venice, especially for a barbeque. Even if I had convinced her to come, she would have been paranoid about bugs, thinking they were crawling on her all night. She doesn't like to be outside unless she's lounging by the pool in her over-exterminated backyard. As for Chip, he would have spent the evening asking people if they were in the movie business, bragging about his latest box office gross. We didn't need that kind of crap permeating the mood of the celebration. I made plans for us to have dinner with all of them the night after the party. It was simpler to say good-bye on their own turf.

"What about Greg?" Jacob said. We were trying to make sure we hadn't forgotten to invite anyone.

"Don't even think about it."

Fifteen minutes later Jacob looked up from his crossword puzzle and said, "Trixie, don't you think you should call your father?"

"You want me to invite my father to the party? Are you *high*?"

"Not to invite him to the party. Just to call him and tell him you're leaving. To say good-bye."

"No," I said. But truth be told, the thought had crossed my mind. I didn't want to leave Los Angeles with bad karma. I had visions of, maybe a decade later, the phone ringing in the middle of the night. Chip or Cole would be on the other end, waking me out of a deep sleep, in the arms of my charming husband, in my charming house, in the promised land of Memphis, to tell me my father was dancing with the grim reaper and I'd never see him again. Maybe I'd even helped kill him. Maybe he was so distraught over not having me in his life that he couldn't take it anymore. I know I said I hated him, but I still, for some curious reason, found solace in the idea of him. I mean I *had* a father. Even if he was useless. Even if I refused to talk to him. Even if he caused me inexcusable angst, it was still nice to know he was there. I told Jacob all of this.

"I hear ya," Jacob said. "But you made me see Thomas Doorley."

"Yeah, and look where that got us."

"Trixie," Jacob said, "I distinctly remember you telling me the night of my birthday last year that if I called my father, you would call yours. I kept up my end of the bargain."

"I recall saying no such thing."

"I'll call him for you," Jacob said. He picked up the phone.

I grabbed it from him and put it back on the receiver. "You can't call him. He's *my* father."

"That doesn't make any sense."

"What's your point?"

"How about this," Jacob said. "I'll call him to tell him we're moving. I'll suggest that maybe he invite us over before we leave. I'll tell you don't even know I'm asking. Then, if he calls back, we go. If not, fuck him and you never have to see him again."

I sat there nervous and worried. I knew exactly where the conversation was going to end up.

# FORTY-SIX

He called. Less than an hour after he got Jacob's message. Three days before our party. While Jacob and I were in the middle of deciding what music to take with us on the drive and what to pack, the phone rang. I picked it up and heard my father say my name. I mouthed the words *dick* and *head* at Jacob, for getting me into the whole mess in the first place. He grabbed a pen and, in his architectural, left-handed Jacob font, scribbled: *Give him a chance, Trixie.* He even put in the comma and the period.

I played dumb with my father. I pretended I had no clue his call was even a remote possibility.

"I know you're probably going to say no," my father said, "but I heard you were moving. I'd really like to see you before you leave."

Just to test how big a liar he was, I asked him how he knew about the move. I figured he'd say Chip told him. Instead, he said, "To tell you the truth, honey, Jacob called me. And I was glad he did."

That's when I agreed to the visit.

"I'm *very* proud of you," Jacob said after I hung up.

"Fuck off."

# FORTY-SEVEN

My father's house was a flat, modern, cardboard-colored rectangle built high above the sand on Pacific Coast Highway. It looked like a big box that had been stepped on. Inside, the walls were the same drab shade as the exterior, all the floors were made of dark slate blocks, and the furniture was sparse and cozy. It made quite a statement, like something you'd see in *Metropolitan Home*, which is more than I could say for my mother's house. She was fond of gilded mirrors, floral patters, and chintz up the wazoo. Much to my surprise, my father had taste—taste he apparently wasn't allowed to express when Diane was in charge of the decor.

The back wall of my father's living room wasn't a wall at all, but a big glass door that opened up to a deck overlooking the ocean. He walked us out to show us the view and I spotted a hot tub in the corner. It was bubbling and making an awful sucking noise. I took hold of Jacob's hand and pulled him back inside.

My father shuffled off to get us some wine. "Red or white?" he said.

"Red," Jacob answered.

Jacob and I stood over the fireplace and examined the dozen or so photos that sat on the mantle. A few of them, I immediately noticed, were of me. I couldn't believe my father had pictures of me in his house. He even had one I'd never seen. I was probably about six years old in the particular snapshot. It looked like it had been taken at a zoo. I was petting some kind of wild cat, and I had on a bright orange-and-pink plaid jumper.

"Nice threads," Jacob said.

I recognized myself in the photograph but, oddly enough, I had absolutely no memory of ever being there.

"I bet he put these up today because we were coming over," I whispered.

Jacob sighed, barely moved his lips and said, "Trixie, what did I tell you?"

To behave, that's what he'd told me, right before we got out of the car.

My father handed us each a glass of wine. He staggered nervously around me, like he wanted to hug me but didn't know whether or not he was allowed. After some hesitation, he settled on a firm grip of the shoulder. "It's really nice to see you, honey."

I saw my father nod to Jacob, as if to say, This is all thanks to you.

It was, the bastard.

Jacob and I both shook hands with Tara when she came in. I still thought she looked like a dog, but I decided it wasn't a Yorkie after all, it was a Maltese, just like the one she and my father had. They called him Truffles, and he was out of control. He bounced all over the place, from couch to chair to lap without a break. Truffles was the spitting image of Tara. I've heard it said that dogs look like their owners, and if that's an actual topic of discussion, Tara and her canine companion could have been case study number one to prove it. Tara wore white cotton pants that had elastic around the ankles. They were the same color as Truffles's fur. And she had a gold chain around her waist, just like her dog's collar. I wished Kat could have seen her. Kat would have taken one look at that get-up and called the fashion police, or just gone ahead and made a citizen's arrest. But I tried not to harp on Tara too much. She went out of her way to be nice to me. She complimented me, she asked me questions about my life, and not so much in a bogus way either, more in a way that made me think she simply saw me as the one with all the power. She just wanted me to like her.

"I see your jewelry in Barney's all the time. It's really beautiful," Tara said. "I bought these there." She pulled her hair back and showed me her earrings. She had on what were known as the Cursive Cs. They were little platinum curls I'd actually made to look like waves, but everyone thought they looked like the handwritten, lowercase *c*, so that's what they were called.

"C for Curtis," she said. I thought that was sweet, in a dumb kind of way.

The art of conversation seemed to be lagging between me and my father. Neither of us wanted to say anything too revealing right off the bat. Awkward small talk was all we could manage. And Tara babbled nervously. Jacob was the only one who was even remotely at ease—more than that, he was enjoying himself. He thrived on my familial tension.

"The dynamics are fascinating as hell," he said. "I couldn't make up shit like this if I tried."

Truffles was having a good time too, circling the dining table like he was playing duck-duck-goose, hoping to find someone who'd give him a morsel or two. I saw my father slip him bites every other lap. Once the treats stopped, however, Truffles jumped directly onto the table.

"Your father taught him that trick," Tara said to me as she grabbed the dog and set him back on the floor.

My father laughed. "I didn't teach him that," he said. "I just didn't discourage it."

If my father would have let an animal jump onto the dinner

table back when he lived with my mother, she would have ripped him a new asshole and given him a ten-minute lecture about germs.

To sort of break the ice, I think, Jacob asked my father a bunch of lawyer questions, which led to conversations on things I didn't know Jacob had any knowledge about, like interest rates and the Dow Jones industrial average. When I wondered out loud where Jacob got all the stats, he said, "I read the *New York Times*, Trixie."

My father thought it was cute that Jacob called me Trixie.

"When Beatrice was little," my father said to Jacob, "I used to call her Honey Bee."

Jacob caught my eye when my father said that. I knew he was thinking of some sort of sexual innuendo to tease me with later. I had to look away so I didn't laugh. I didn't want my father to know how perverted I was.

I'd forgotten all about that nickname. I'd forgotten a lot of things about my father. Like how a deep dimple formed on the left side of his cheek when he smiled, and how the aftershave he wore smelled like sweet Vermouth.

I thought it best to stick with meaningless chit-chat for the evening, but once Jacob got my father loosened up, he was ready to reminisce.

"Did Bea ever tell you about the time we were in London?" my father said. "We drove for hours out to the countryside, to see one of those famous castles, and her mother was furious with her because she wouldn't look out the window."

"I was reading," I said.

"She was sixteen," my father explained.

"I'd just discovered Ralph Waldo Emerson."

"During the trip, Beatrice picked up a new motto."

"'To be great is to be misunderstood,'" I said.

"She said it thirty times that day if she said it once."

I heard my parents' voices in my head: "Beatrice, if all you wanted to do was read, you should've stayed home."

"For Christ's sake, Diane, leave her be."

I found it weird that my father recalled that particular trip so fondly. I remember feeling completely tormented the entire time.

My father looked at Jacob. "Back then, Beatrice thought that dead writers and angry musicians were the only people in the world who could comprehend what she was going through."

"That's because they were the only ones who were ever around," I said, much more abrasively than I'd meant to. A silence befell the table.

My father looked down at the dog. "Go get your ball," he said, trying to hide the regret in his voice.

Jacob tilted his head and lifted his brow at me, like I'd broken a promise. Shit, I said to myself, with the vengeful, burning pain of memory somewhere in my chest. Why was I the only one whose recollections never grew any fonder with time? Why was I the only one who seemed to look back on all those yesterdays as being so bad? Had the stories my father told actually been good times, or did he just choose to believe they were?

I allowed for the possibility that hindsight could reconcile one's perspective on the past. But I leaned toward the likelihood of complete distortion.

It's never the truth that changes.

Truffles barked at the edge of the table with a tennis ball in his mouth. My father took the ball and threw it into the kitchen. Twenty seconds later the dog was back, tail wagging for more. Halfway through dessert, after watching my father throw that stupid ball a dozen times, I came to a historic diagnosis. As

I looked at him, at his house, his dog, his relaxed rapport with his wife; at how much he'd changed since I last spent time with him, it dawned on me that he and my mother may have been nothing more than a match made in Hell. I always saw my mother as the pathetic victim in the fiasco they called a marriage. I wasn't so sure about that anymore. What I was sure about was how my mother and father didn't belong together. They never did. It was finally obvious to me that they had nothing in common. I don't know, maybe they loved each other at one time, but it was also quite possible that she only married him because she wanted to live in that chintzy house of hers, and wear her chintzy rings, and lunch with her chintzy friends at the chintzy fucking country club. The poor thing. She had no idea what the consequences of her aspirations were going to turn out to be.

"It really was nice to see you," my father said again before we left. He hugged me that time. Tightly. And I hugged back. I wanted to tell him I was sorry for what I'd said at the table, I just didn't have the guts.

"If you ever need anything," he said, "please call me. Well, call me anyway, just to say hi sometime. How about that?"

I told him I would. Then he tried to give us a check. "Buy yourselves a house-warming present," he said.

"Dad, I can't." I had enough of my father's money. I refused to take anymore. He didn't argue with me. He just shrugged and told Jacob I'd always been stubborn.

"Really? I hadn't noticed," Jacob said.

The two of them shared a knowing laugh that made me feel like we were all part of a big, happy family, if only for an instant.

My father put his arm around Jacob's shoulder and they shook hands, "You take care of her, okay?"

"I will," Jacob said.

Driving away, the headlights on the cars going in the opposite direction hypnotized me. They were unearthly eyes that never blinked. I got a sinking feeling that they were trying to tell me a secret, to forewarn me. It was like deja-vu without the recollection of details. They sang to me through the radio, and they had the voice of my father, if my father had been Cat Stevens.

*If you wanna leave, take good care I hope you make a lot of nice friends out there But just remember there's a lot of bad and beware...*

"You want to go for a walk?" Jacob said after he saw the effect Yusuf Islam had on my mood. He nodded toward Will Rogers State Beach.

"No, I just want to go home."

Jacob took my hand to his lips, kissed my palm, and something swelled up inside of me.

"Did I do that?" he said.

I glanced down at my arms. Every hair was standing on end.

"Yeah, you did that," I said.

# FORTY-EIGHT

"Learn how to drive, asshole!" I shouted at the car that almost ran us off the road. I was about to continue my tirade by spouting off a few more obscenities, but Jacob put my window up.

"Hey," I said. "Did you see the way he cut you off? It would be a very bad omen to get in a wreck on the way to our own party."

"It would be an even worse omen if that guy pulled out a gun and shot you."

The menacing vehicle, a custom-painted, chartreuse-green Riviera with gold-plated hubcaps, whizzed past us like a bottle rocket and swerved so far into our lane he almost took off our passenger-side mirror. We caught up to him at the next red light and that's when I saw the TV—it was smack-dab in the center of his dashboard.

"Oh, this guy's a real gem," I said.

Jacob couldn't see much while he drove, but I was able to look right in and give a full report. "He has a bottle of Budweiser in his hand *and* he's watching television."

"Television?" Jacob said.

I did a double take. I saw boobs—big, fake ones—the kind that probably felt like turtle shells. "Holy shit, he's watching porn!"

"Wanna drive?" Jacob said.

I looked one more time. Then I screamed. "Oh my God! Jacob, there's a German Shepard on the screen. And its dick is bigger than yours!"

Jacob almost crashed into a garbage can trying to get a glimpse. "I need to see it to believe it," he said.

Once Jacob confirmed my story with his own eyes, we decided that of all our years in that crummy city, of all the crazy things we'd seen, a video of a woman getting fucked by a German Shepard—on TV in a car—was definitely in the top three. Maybe even number one.

"Well, *that's* a good omen," Jacob said.

"I'm tempted to ask why you think that starting off the evening of our going-away party with doggie porn is a good omen, only I'm not sure I want to hear your answer."

"Trixie, could we have asked for a clearer sign that getting out of California is absolutely the best decision we've ever made?"

Pete and Sara's house was only a couple miles from our apartment. Imagine what we could have seen if they lived in, say, Glendale.

We got to the party just as Ronnie the Rib Tickler had finished setting up. The whole yard smelled like roasted, greasy meat. Ronnie was a stout guy with a belly that hung a few inches below his waist. He had barbeque-stained fingernails and a face that looked hickory-smoked. Jacob became obsessed with Ronnie the minute we walked through the gate. Word on the street was Ronnie had done time for manslaughter before he became a cook. His business card said he was a three-time runner up at the International Barbeque Festival, which happens to be held in Memphis. Jacob talked Ronnie's ear off, notebook and pen in hand.

Inside, Joanna was predicting the sex of Sara's baby. "It's a boy for sure."

"Tell me something I don't know," Pete said.

Joanna explained her theory to me. "When a pregnant woman grows by width, when her hips are the first to broaden, it means she's having a girl. When she gets a pouch protruding from her lower abdomen, it's a boy."

Sara was about six months along and she had the pouch. From the back she looked baby-free. From the front she looked like a mother kangaroo.

Not long after Jacob and I arrived, everyone else started sauntering in. Shelly, my ponytailed little assistant, came with her ponytailed boyfriend, Rob. Odie brought his newest model girlfriend. Her name was Claire, and she spent the entire night fawning all over Mike from the *Weekly*. Pete's brother, Gary, was there too, with a bunch of his friends. I'd only met Gary once before. He was two years older than Pete, about three inches taller, twenty pounds heavier, and he worked as a bartender. We put him in charge of the drinks. The first thing Gary did was to stir up a batch of Kamikazes, which he passed around on a plastic tray.

"To get things started off right," he said.

Gary was disappointed that Jacob wouldn't take one. Jacob had made up his mind to stop drinking while he was in Big Sur. It was all part of his plan to be the anti-Thomas Doorley and he was sticking to it.

"I'll take Jacob's share," Pete said, and downed a second shot.

I walked back outside. Jacob came over to tell me what he'd learned from The Rib Tickler.

"I was mentioning to Ronnie that you make jewelry. He told me about this place in Memphis, it's called the Museum of Ornamental Metal. Have you ever heard of it?"

"No."

"Apparently they have a rotating display of all things metal. Teapots, sculptures, even jewelry. It's on the top of some hill Mark Twain supposedly called 'The best bluff view south of St. Louis.' You wanna know how Ronnie knew about it?"

"How?"

"He tried to rob it once." Jacob laughed. Then he spotted Joanna. "Is that my mom in the kitchen?"

Jacob tiptoed inside. He snuck up behind Joanna and grabbed her waist. She jumped, spun around and swatted him in the chest with her purse. I watched them talk. Jacob's face shined and his whole body seemed weightless. Like he hovered a foot above the ground. I'd never seen him look happier than he did then.

"Kiss me," I said when he came back.

Kat stuck her face in between us, with Gopal on her arm, just as Jacob's tongue was reaching the back of my throat. "Get a room," she said.

"I reckon y'all are late," Jacob teased. He and Kat had developed a habit of harassing each other whenever they could. It was all out of love, of course, but it never stopped.

"Shut up, Grace," she said.

"Shut up, *Grace*," he mimicked.

Kat looked him up and down. "I see you decided to dress up for the party."

Jacob had on what he always wore: jeans, boots, and a T-shirt.

"You don't like my outfit?" he said.

"You look like you fell down a flight of stairs."

Gary came over and asked Kat and Gopal what they wanted to drink. "How about a lovely little aperitif to wet the whistle before the meal?"

Gopal said he needed food first.

"I'll take a dry martini," Kat said.

Ronnie rang his cow bell. "Chow time!"

After we finished eating, and after everyone had an opportunity to whine about how much they were going to miss us, Pete asked Jacob and Odie if they wanted to form a little trio and play a few songs. As we all relocated inside, Pete rummaged through a closet and pulled out two guitars and a bongo drum.

"Save me a front row seat," Sara said. She ran into the bedroom, then came back a minute later with her video camera.

Joanna tapped me on the shoulder. "I hate to miss the concert, but…" It was getting late and she had to drive all the way back to Pasadena. I stole Jacob away from the band and we walked Joanna to her car. She pretended to be all bubbles and cheer, but we could see she was fighting the tears.

"Not yet, Mom," Jacob said.

Joanna hugged us quickly and wiped her eyes. "I know, save it for Wednesday," she said. We were going to have breakfast with her the morning we left; she wasn't allowed to consider it good-bye until then.

We took our time walking back to the party. Jacob suggested we veer west. He wanted to stop at the beach.

"Once more," he said. "For old time's sake."

"Later," I told him. "Everyone's waiting for us."

Standing outside Pete and Sara's door, Jacob stopped, turned to face me, and clutched my hand tightly. He looked like he needed to tell me something.

"Trixie…" he said. But then he froze.

"Are you okay?" He had goose bumps, I could see them all over his arms. "Did I do that?" I said, echoing his words from the night before.

He shook his head apprehensively. "I don't know. I just had this really weird feeling."

Gently, but with painstaking intention, Jacob put his hands on the sides of my face. He held me still and pierced me with his gaze, as if he were taking a photograph with his mind's eye. Something about the sudden tightness of his features made me think he was frightened, but only for an instant, then the tension gave way to a faint glow of tranquillity that washed over him in the form of a subtle, pacific grin.

"I love you," he said. "You know that, right?"

I nodded. "I love you, too."

Pete was tuning the guitars when we got back to the house. Odie sat patiently at his drum, somehow oblivious to Claire, who, along with Mike, was nowhere in sight.

"Hey Beatrice, your friend Kat's got a Buttery Nipple," Gary said. He shoved a plastic cup in my face. "Here. Have one."

"I already had a beer."

"You're no fun," Gary said.

Jacob made himself comfortable on the couch. He sunk into the flimsy cushions with a shiny black guitar on his lap. It made him look slight and vulnerable. After strumming a few chords, he stopped, took off his ring, and tossed it into my lap.

"Hold that for me, will you?"

I put it on my thumb.

"*Any day now!*" Pete yelled. He was sitting right next to Jacob but he yelled anyway. Odie was on a stool beside them.

Once Jacob finally looked settled, Pete said, "All right, now that everyone's too drunk to really hear us, are their any requests?"

The whole party was gathered around them on the floor of the tiny living room, packed in like a kindergarten class at story time. Except for Gary—he was still at the makeshift bar, which was actually the kitchen table, whipping up some hideous concoctions.

People started blurting out random songs. Kat, who'd

gulped down everything Gary put in her hand, kept yelling, "Sleepy Jean! Sleepy Jean!" She meant "Daydream Believer." It was one of her favorite non-electronic songs, but she was too hammered to remember what it was really called.

"Free Bird!" Gary shouted.

"Forget it," Pete said. "We'll just play."

Gary walked around with a towel on his head and a tray in his hands, yelling, "Tom Collins! Get your Tom Collins here!"

"What's a Tom Collins?" Shelly asked before she took one.

"Why, it's a choice beverage," Gary explained. "Perfect for this hot summer evening."

"Hey, Gary," Jacob said. "It's November."

"Right." Gary nodded. You know the old saying, three sheets to the wind? Gary had a dozen sheets flapping in the breeze.

By the time the new batch of drinks had been passed around, Jacob, Pete, and Odie were ready to play, and they actually managed to pull a few impressive numbers out of their hats. The first song they did was an acoustic version of the AC/DC classic "You Shook Me All Night Long."

Jacob tried to sing, but Pete kept making obnoxious gyrations to go along with the lyrics and he couldn't keep it together. By the end of the second verse, all three of them were cracking up.

Sara turned to me. "They're so weird," she said.

The second show-stopper was a song called "Like A Hurricane" by Neil Young.

"I *hate* this song," Sara said as soon as she heard the first note. "Ask me why I hate it, Beatrice."

"Why do you hate this song?"

"Because when you wouldn't talk to Jacob, when he was living here, he played it all day long. I mean *all day long*."

"Sorry," I said.

Next, the guys did a raucous cover of "I Wanna Be Sedated" by The Ramones. Pete attempted to sing that one. I finally knew why he usually stuck with the string instruments. They followed that with a dazzling rendition of The Rolling Stones's "Sweet Virginia." Jacob smiled at me when he sang the part about California's bitter fruit.

At the end of that song, Pete and Odie both wanted another drink, so Jacob played one by himself. He was a little clumsy with some of the chords, but his commitment made up for what he lacked in skill. It was a tune called "Shock Me," originally recorded by Kiss, but Jacob did the version he'd learned from listening to a somewhat obscure San Francisco band called Red House Painters.

Once he'd finished, Jacob set the guitar down at his feet. I squeezed in beside him on the couch and he eased his left hand under my sweater, resting it on my midriff. I felt the pulse in his wrist. It seemed to be beating in time with mine. We were synchronized.

Gary marched around the room with a bottle of something that looked like vinegar and smelled like disinfectant. He poured a splash into every cup he saw.

"What is that?" Gopal asked, while he covered the top of his glass with his hand.

"Everclear," Gary said. "Just a drop or two really rounds out a drink nicely."

"Don't anybody light a match," Jacob said dryly.

Sara turned her video camera on us. "Look, here's the two lovebirds," she said. "Say something philosophical."

"*Something philosophical*," we said in unison.

"Attention! To whom it may concern, we're running short on libations!" Gary yelled. Which explained why he'd resorted to spiking the drinks with firewater.

"The night is still young," Pete said. And if the party was going to continue, he told us, he had to go for reinstallments. "When Muni's calls, I answer."

Muni's was the neighborhood liquor store. It was three blocks away.

"You're not going anywhere," Sara said to Pete. "Nobody in this room needs any more alcohol."

Gary booed.

"Hey, Sara," Kat said. "Just because you can't drink doesn't mean we should all suffer."

"It's all right, Trixie and I will go to Muni's," Jacob said. He looked at me and winked.

We unglued ourselves from each other and got up. Pete, who'd seen Jacob's eye gymnastics, said, "Everyone might as well say good-bye to them now, these two aren't coming back."

He was only half right.

# FORTY-NINE

Jacob wanted to create a moment. That was the reason he gave for leading me to the beach instead of to the car after the party ended. One last romp with the life we were leaving behind. Something to put in the back pocket of experience like a souvenir.

"It's all about *now*," he said. "Let's always try to remember how we feel *right now*."

When we got to the sand I stopped to take off my shoes. Jacob turned around to face me as I ran to catch him, and walked backward until the water was up to his knees. Then he just lay down into it.

"Isn't it cold?" I said.

"It is a tit nippily." He laughed and tried to splash my shirt.

It was dark outside, but the moon was almost full, the sky was cloudless, and to the south, the lights of Palos Verdes were bright enough to illuminate the beach with a shadowy, amber glow that gave me the faintest impression I was on another planet.

I walked in until the chilly water was above my ankles. The surface was smooth, but there was a strong undertow that pulled on me and quickly buried my feet with sand. Jacob swam around as the ocean rolled underneath him. It would lift him up for just an instant and then fall my way, making ripples that broke into foam across my legs.

"Hey," I said. "Don't go out so far."

A bigger wave was growing behind him, but he flipped

over and dove into it, then popped up on the other side, smiling. He tried to coax me into joining him.

"Come on," he said, doing a sort of backstroke in place so as not to be carried toward the shore. "Come dance with me."

There was another wave coming in and I told him to turn around. I recall thinking, in the way your mind replays long stretches of time in a split second, about the first walk he and I had ever taken to the beach, when he'd pounced on me and took me underwater, and I ran back to the shore, shivering, while he stayed in and floated around with the moon wrapped up in his hair.

That's exactly how he looked the last time I saw him— floating around, entangled in the moon.

The wave wasn't even that big. It just broke sooner than he'd expected, right on top of him, and pulled him under.

I waited impatiently, thinking he was just fooling around.

"It's not funny," I yelled.

Nothing.

I opened my mouth and shouted Jacob's name again and again, but felt as if no sounds were coming out. Then I began screaming for someone to get help, only there wasn't anyone in sight.

"Jacob, I'm going to call someone!" I said, but I didn't know who the right person to call was. A policeman? The Coast Guard? Christ?

I ran to the first pay phone I saw. It was about seventy-five yards behind me, near the bathrooms. It smelled like dead fish and trash near the bathrooms, and I had to hold my nose so that I didn't retch. I dialed 911 and told the lady who answered that Jacob was in the water, that he'd disappeared. I gave her my exact location, and then I started mumbling Jacob's name. I couldn't stop saying his name.

The lady wanted to have a goddamn conversation. She asked me how old Jacob was, whether or not he knew how to swim, and how long he'd been missing.

"There are officers in the area. They'll be there as soon as they can," the lady said. Then she continued to chit-chat.

"Is anyone else there with you, Ma'am?"

She was trying to keep me on the phone.

"I have to go," I told her.

"Try to remain calm. And stay out of the water," she said, or something stupid like that.

I dropped the phone and bolted back to the shore, thinking I was going to find Jacob, thinking I was going to save him. I ran into the water until it was up to my waist, then I dove down and opened my eyes. I couldn't even see my hand in front of my face. When I came up for air, a wave hit me head-on and threw me back to the sand. Coughing and gagging, I stood up and tried to move but my legs were like cement blocks. I stared out at the water. It seemed so much darker than when Jacob and I had first arrived.

My head began to shake uncontrollably. My mind began screaming and cursing itself. *Why did you let him go in?* it said. *Why didn't you stop him?*

*Rewind! Do over! Take it back!*

And then I did what any desperate fool would do. I started to pray.

The only bona fide prayer I could remember was the Our Father, and I recited it over and over, in the hopes that a supreme being, if one did indeed exist, would never be cruel enough to take Jacob away from me, especially if I begged.

I was on my twenty-ninth invocation when two cops showed up and asked me if I was the girl who had called for help.

"Yes," I answered quickly, because my head was still shaking and I didn't want them to get the wrong idea.

One of the cops was tall. The other one had dark skin and pale eyes. The tall one told me his name was Officer Tim Hopper. He wrapped me in a blanket and helped me sit down. The dark, pale-eyed one didn't tell me his name, but he knelt beside me and in a gentle, fatherly voice, started interrogating me. He wanted to know my name, and Jacob's full name and address. He wrote it all down on a pad of paper.

"Now," he said, "tell me exactly what happened."

I grabbed him by the shirt. "What the fuck is the matter with you? Forget the questions and get in there and find Jacob!"

"Search and Rescue's on their way," he said sympathetically, reaching for my hand. "If anyone can find him, they can. But you *need* to tell us what happened."

With as much coherency as possible, I explained the entire night to him.

"Had Mr. Grace been drinking?" he said. "Had he been doing any drugs this evening, that you're aware of?"

"Jacob quit drinking," I said. "He quit drinking because he doesn't want to end up like his father. Because we're moving and he's happy. So happy, he hovers a foot above the ground."

The nameless cop looked at me with pity in his eyes. He patted my shoulder and walked over to Officer Tim Hopper. They began discussing the situation. I tried to listen but I couldn't hear all the words. I got the feeling they didn't want me to hear them. Then Officer Tim Hopper raised his voice, probably by accident. He said it didn't look good. I had no idea what that meant.

I sat on the sand and waited. I was completely, unnaturally calm, still staring out at the water, shaking my head and trying to process the facts. I couldn't do it. Reality had ceased to exist. I no longer felt like a participant in the world and I no longer cared.

I remember wondering what it would take to get the nameless cop to whip out his Glock 40 and fire a round of hollow-point bullets into my chest.

What felt like hours later, but in reality had only been a few minutes, Officer Tim Hopper came back over and helped me to my feet. "I'm going to take you home now, Beatrice."

I shook my head harder. It didn't seem right to leave without Jacob.

"There's nothing you can do here," the nameless cop said. "We'll call you as soon as we know anything."

Officer Tim Hopper put one hand under my arm, the other around my waist, and with a slight force, began guiding me away from the water. Looking back, I saw the lights of a boat and heard the sounds of a helicopter.

When we got to the pavement, I pointed down the street, to Pete and Sara's house. I told Officer Tim Hopper to take me there.


Pete opened the door dressed in a pair of blue pajama bottoms. He reeked of alcohol.

Officer Tim Hopper introduced himself to Pete and with a somber, practiced expression, started telling him what had happened.

That's when I passed out.

# FIFTY

It was mid-morning when I woke up on Pete and Sara's couch. The sun was burning through the window and I let my eyes wander around the room. There was a black guitar at my feet, Sara was half asleep in a chair across from me, and Pete was in another chair against the wall. Joanna, who had rushed over after a middle-of-the-night phone call from Officer Tim Hopper, was standing in the kitchen looking out the back door.

Sara saw that I was awake. She came over, put one arm around me, spit some saliva onto her fingers and wiped my face.

"You were born to be a mother," I told her.

"We're waiting to hear from the police," she said. "They went out again this morning. They're going to call soon."

Joanna sat down next to me. She held me and told me everything was going to be all right. Then she started jabbering on about God.

"He never gives us anything we can't handle," she said. "He knows what he's doing."

I realized she was struggling to find meaning and justification for what was happening, so I refrained from telling her what a bunch of bull that was. I wondered how Lucille—the woman on the news who got car-jacked in the Valley—would have rationalized our situation. If I'd remembered her last name, I would have called her up and asked her where her benevolent God was while I prayed for someone to toss Jacob a lifeline.

I started rambling. "They'll find him," I told Joanna. "Jacob does this all the time. You know, he just takes off, but he'll be back. He has to be back by Tuesday. That's when the movers are coming. They're coming to take our stuff. They're going to hold it for us while we find a house in Memphis. Then Jacob's going to call them and give them our new address and they'll bring us our furniture and they'll fill our charm-laden house with it. Because that's what movers do. That's their job."

Thick tears dripped from Joanna's eyes like wax from a candle. "Beatrice, he's gone," she said quietly. "He's gone."

She pronounced it like she knew it as fact. As if, just because she was his mother, because he'd grown inside of her and fed off of her body for nine months, that gave her some kind of holy right to intuit his extinction. I had news for her, he'd been feeding off my body for twice as long as he'd fed off hers, and I didn't feel it. Not a thing. If Jacob was really *gone*, I thought, I'd feel it. For Christ's sake, *I'd know*.

That's the moment I became conscious, for the first time in my life, of clinging boldly to the sensation of hope; of wishing desperately for something I had absolutely no control over; of having faith. But it wasn't the superfluous blind faith of miracles I was believing in. It was a metaphysical perception that an end could never come to a person who was more alive than anyone I'd ever known.

Still, I had yet to shed a tear. Because tears come from the eyes and eyes are of the body. I was imploding in spirit. Exteriorly, I was perfectly composed. Inside, a bomb was discharging, but in slow motion.

It was just a matter of time before the shrapnel began to rip my guts to shreds.

Real annihilation happens from the inside out.

# FIFTY-ONE

The police didn't call until 5:29 that night. I know exactly what time it was because right before the phone rang, Sara asked if anyone was hungry. No one had eaten all day and she said it was time for dinner.

It didn't feel like dinnertime to me. I looked at the clock to see if Sara was telling the truth.

5:29.

Pete picked up the phone on the table, but he walked into the kitchen before he answered it. We didn't hear him say much to whoever was on the other end of the line. He just mumbled a few inaudible responses and then said good-bye. The phone was still in his hand when he came back into the living room. You could have heard a flea land on a dog while we waited for him to speak. Only he didn't have to. We all knew, by the look on his face, what he was going to say.

In the quietest voice I'd ever heard Pete use, he said, "They, uh…they think they found him." He stared at the phone, bewildered, as if all the fault lay inside that little plastic rectangle.

Pete turned around and gazed out the window. About a minute later, his back still to us, he said, "They need someone to go down there. Someone has to identify the body."

If I had been teetering on the fence of denial, the tangible image of the word *body* began to push me right over the edge, face-down into reality.

Pete was the one who went to the morgue. I thought maybe I should have gone with him, but I couldn't do it. I didn't want to see Jacob like that.

That's not what I wanted to remember.


As soon as Pete came home, the minute he walked through the door, I shot up from the couch, sort of involuntarily, and moved his way. Pete's face was blank, the color of cement, and when he opened his mouth to speak nothing came out. He just stood there, jaw agape, like he was waiting for a dental hygienist to scrape plaque off of his teeth. Then he took hold of my left hand. He turned it face-up, reached into his pocket, and pressed Jacob's watch and necklace firmly into my palm.

"I thought you'd want these," he said.

He grabbed a half-empty bottle of vodka off the table, went into the bedroom, and shut the door.

From where I stood, in the middle of the living room, I heard Pete crying.

The second hand on Jacob's watch was still moving. Something about that seemed painfully, nefariously wrong to me. I flipped the watch over and checked for the engraving behind the face. Seeing his name there, his address and phone number, and smelling the ocean between the metal was like a right hook to the jaw.

I tucked the jewelry into my pocket.

"I have to go home," I said.

Later on, I thought about how the party didn't turn out the way I'd imagined at all. But I guess nothing ever does.

# FIFTY-TWO

I've heard it said that when a person drowns, a strange and pleasant euphoria comes over them before they die. Supposedly it's kind of like going back into the womb. Once you stop fighting for air and your lungs fill up with fluid, there's only peace. With all my heart I hoped that was true. The idea that Jacob could have suffered, even for an instant, hurt me so bad I thought I might expire just thinking about it.

I wondered if Jacob had been scared in those last moments. I wondered what his final thoughts had been. Did he think of me? Of Memphis? Of all the sorrow he'd leave in his wake? Of his father waiting with open arms at the pearly gates? Did he think of making love under the stars? Of Madeline and Simone and the charming porch we'd never sit on?

I hoped his last sensation was the euphoria. The peace. The love.

I *had* to believe it was the love.

I walked into our apartment and all I saw were boxes. Almost everything we owned was buried inside cardboard. The first realization I had was that my closet was empty—I didn't have anything to wear to the memorial service. I dialed Kat's number and left her a message. I asked her, if it wasn't too much trouble, could she please find me something nice. Then I told her to call Pete and Sara for an explanation. I couldn't bring myself to say any more.

I examined all the rooms and observed evidence of life everywhere.

Jacob's *New York Times* crossword puzzle was spread out on the table, five clues away from completion, next to a cup of day-old, muddy coffee. Looks like the Mississippi river, I thought. Not that I knew what the Mississippi river looked like. Not that I'd ever know now.

There was an envelope on the couch. It was filled with the cash Jacob got for selling his car. He'd drawn a dollar sign on the front of it.

"Food and gas money for the drive," he said.

Jacob's computer was still on.

"Why don't you just let the movers take that?" I'd said a few days earlier.

"Trixie, what if some brilliant story strikes me in the middle of Oklahoma?"

"You'll have your notebooks."

"What if I need to *type* the story?"

Jacob's screen-saver was the image of a deformed clock, a`la Salvador Dali. It made a ticking noise every second.

"Doesn't that drive you crazy all day?" I once asked him.

"I like it. It reminds me that time is always moving."

The razor Jacob left on the sink formed a small puddle of water, crusty foam, and tiny hairs.

His olive-green cut-off shorts lay at the foot of our messy bed. It was the same pair he'd taken off the day before when he came into the bedroom looking for me.

"What are you doing?" he said, a child looking for a play-mate.

"Taking a nap." I'd gotten up early and didn't want to be tired for the party.

"Shouldn't you be sucking my dick?"

He was only teasing, but it sounded like a good idea to me.

"Whip it out," I said.

An adolescent grin spread across his face. "You're one badass girlfriend, you know that?" He slipped off the shorts.

I had to get out of the bedroom. It smelled too much like us in there.

In the kitchen, the first thing I saw was that fucking piece of paper on the refrigerator.

*"If your intentions are pure*
*I'm seeking a friend*
*for the end*
*of the world"*

I was certain that no one, with the exception of myself, could ever comprehend the magnitude of the unequivocal truth contained in those four little lines. I tore the ad down and ripped it into as many pieces as I could. I threw the shards in the disposal and ground them up. I turned on the faucet and let the water carry the words straight into the bowels of the city.

Then came more questions: Why didn't I feel it when it happened? Weren't Jacob and I soulmates? Weren't we connected by blood and veins? *Siamese soul lovers?* Then why didn't I know when he was gone? Why didn't I lose my breath as he gasped for his last one? Why didn't I sense his departure from the world like a strike of lightening surging through my nervous system? Why did it feel like Jacob was still out there, somewhere?

I demanded an explanation; a sign. "I'll wait forever for a sign," I shouted, even though I knew damn well no one could hear me.

And that's when it hit me. I collapsed down onto the floor and at a sluggish, Memphis-in-August speed, my whole body started to tremble uncontrollably. My lungs tightened and convulsed in my chest, and the tears began to flow. Jacob's never coming back, I tried to tell myself. I'll *never* see him again. That didn't make sense. Nothing did. And I knew nothing would for a long, long time. I cried so hard that the tears stung my skin like cat scratches down my face. Only it wasn't tears, but the sandy fluid of the Pacific that scraped my cheeks as the water gushed up and over my lids, just like the waves Jacob had danced on the night before.

The ocean was a thief. A murderer. A soul-snatcher.

Too petrified to move, I cried myself to sleep on the kitchen floor with the faucet still running and the computer clock still ticking. I stayed there until the next day, until I was awakened by my mother knocking and yelling at my door.

"Shit," I whispered. "Who the fuck called her?"

# FIFTY-THREE

"Beatrice, open up this door right now," my mother cried. She had obviously been out there for a while. It sounded like she was mad at me.

I heard Kat's voice in the background. "Do you think anyone else has a key?" she said.

"Jacob," I said quietly. "Jacob had a key."

They pounded harder.

"Go away," I pleaded. "Please just go away."

My eyes were dry and burning from all the tears, and my body was stiff from the ten-hour siesta on the kitchen floor. I was barely able to get up, and found it almost impossible to blink.

"We're not leaving until you let us in," my mother said.

"I have clothes for you, Blanca."

They continued to clamor while I shut off the tap.

"All right. I'm coming." It took forever to walk the eight short steps to the door. Another minute went by before I got it open.

My mother stood in the hall, her mouth forming the shape of a perfect circle. She raised her sun-spotted hand, along with the charm bracelet that hung on her wrist, to cover it. I focused on the bangles: a cable car, a yacht, a tennis racquet, a high-heeled shoe. My mother was a walking, twenty-four-carat Monopoly game. Her eyes were wide and they welled up with tears when she saw me. I wondered if she was crying for Jacob, or if she was crying because I undoubtedly looked like I'd been raped and mugged. Maybe she was crying for some other reason only she knew. Whatever it was, I didn't want her in my apartment. I didn't want either of them in my apartment.

My mother came toward me and I stepped backward. Eventually she sped up, arms outstretched, jingling like a tambourine. She grabbed me. I wasn't used to being so close to her and I had an almost overwhelming urge to push her off, to see her fall to the floor. Then I remembered what Jacob used to say.

"Don't be so hard on her, Trixie."

No one was ever going to call me Trixie again. Trixie had ceased to exist the exact moment Jacob had.

Kat was still standing in the doorway. I looked at her over my mother's shoulder and, upon eye-contact, she burst into tears. Between the two of them, it was like having a couple of rain clouds in the house.

"I'm going to take a shower," I said.

Once clean, I dressed in Jacob's clothes. I wore the shorts he'd left on the floor—I had to belt them so they didn't slide off of me—and his blue shirt, the one with the squiggly, sperm-like design.

My mother was in the kitchen making sandwiches. When I walked past her she took a double-take at my ensemble but she didn't say anything.

Kat was doing her best to get the lights on in the living room. She tried the switch, then the button on the lamp. Nothing worked.

"Did you forget to pay your electric bill?" Kat mumbled through her sniffles. She also pretended not to notice my attire.

I listened for the ticking of Jacob's computer clock. Silence. Time had stopped.

"What day is it?" I said.

"Monday."

"Jacob had most of our utilities shut off today."

"That explains why your phone was—" Kat caught herself. "—Why your phone wasn't working." I'm pretty sure she was going to say *dead*. It would have been the first time I'd heard the word uttered since before the party. I was glad she had enough sense to refrain. I wasn't ready for that.

I know Kat wondered why Jacob had our utilities shut off two days before we were supposed to leave, but she didn't ask, and I didn't feel like explaining his logic to her anyway. I didn't feel like telling her that he did it for me, to get me ready for the great outdoors; that he thought it would be fun to live without modern conveniences for a few days. Except for water. He let the water stay because, he said, "I can't dig you a hole in the apartment."

Kat pulled out the clothes she bought for the memorial service. "It's the best I could do on such short notice," she said. "Everything was either fall leftovers or cruise wear."

She had two options for me to choose from. The first one was a long, black, A-line skirt with a cream-colored silk shirt. It looked like basic, puritanical funeral garb. She knew there was no way I'd ever wear it. I couldn't say good-bye to Jacob dressed like a dowdy fucking housewife.

"I told you it was slim pickings," Kat said.

The second choice was a straight, almost geometrical black suit with a black mock-turtleneck to go underneath. I looked at the label—Calvin Klein.

"How much did this cost?" I said.

"For God's sake, Blanca, don't be frugal at a time like this," Kat said, and began sobbing again.

I sighed. "Please stop that." I couldn't take any more tears. "I'm only going to wear the damn thing once. It's a complete waste of money."

"Your mother paid for it," she said. "Shut-up and try it on. Make sure it fits." Kat wiped her nose with a soggy pink tissue that she pulled out from under her sleeve. One more wad of snot and I was sure it would disintegrate in her palm.

The suit was nice. It was simple and mod. Jacob liked when I dressed that way. He said I looked like the girls who used to hang out in Montmartre, drinking Absinthe and discussing Jean-Paul Sarte and the nonexistent meaning of life.

My mother came out of the kitchen to offer her invaluable fashion opinion. She liked the skirt outfit.

"I'll wear the suit," I said.

"Honey, your stove doesn't work," my mother said. She obviously missed the conversation about the power being shut off. "Eat something, please. You're too skinny." She set a tuna sandwich down in front of me, and one in front of Kat.

I didn't think I wanted any food, but after the first bite I realized how hungry I was. I scarfed down the whole sandwich, plus the four baby carrot sticks that were also on the plate.

Kat sat next to me on the couch and picked at her lunch in silence. My mother, meanwhile, stood hypnotized by the photograph that sat on top of the TV. It was the picture I took of Jacob on our way to San Francisco. He had a piece of red licorice hanging from his mouth and he was smiling like a king. My mother stared at that picture for a long time, like she was going to miss him.

"You know, I still have a copy of the family portrait for you. I keep forgetting to mail it," she said. "With Jacob in that silly shirt."

"Mom," I said, "why did you let Jacob be in that picture with us?"

She didn't answer me; she just shrugged.

"I mean it, I need to know. Why did you like him so much?"

Her back was to me and she kept it that way. "Because he liked you so much," she said, wiping dust from the glass inside the frame. She was gentle when she cleared it from Jacob's face, as if he could feel it or something ridiculous like that.

"How do you know how much he liked me?" I said.

She put the photo back down in the exact same spot she found it, nervously straightening her skirt. My mother hated to talk about personal things, even if they weren't necessarily personal to her. It made her fidgety to discuss anything she kept hidden below the surface of her collagen-injected facade. I guess she felt just enough pity to humor me a little.

"He told me," she said. "Remember the day I met him? The day he was moving in? He was so sweet to me. He took me into the kitchen and made me coffee, and he told me all about how wonderful he thought you were. Then he *thanked* me."

"What do you mean he *thanked* you?"

"He *thanked* me. For *creating* you, or something like that. I can't remember the exact word he used, but he gave me at least half the credit for how you turned out." My mother paused. "I don't usually get much credit for anything, you know."

At that, Kat started to gush again.

I looked out the window and shook my head.

Jacob sure knew how to butter a girl up.

# FIFTY-FOUR

The memorial service sailed by me like a blurry ship in some strange, Impressionistic movie. I caught vague pieces of words and phrases, but nothing concrete ever really materialized.

Joanna called the event "a celebration of Jacob's life," not a funeral. She said that sounded happier and, for some reason, she thought the whole thing was supposed to be a joyful experience. She held the festivities in a little wooden church in Pasadena; one that had hand-painted cherubs on the ceiling; a rustic crucifix with a handsome, emaciated Jesus behind the altar; and a different station-of-the-cross covering each stained-glass window. No actual mass took place, Joanna knew that's not what Jacob would have wanted. Instead she invited the people who cared the most about him to talk. Everyone who spoke gave their own weepy interpretation of what made Jacob so special.

I remember Uncle Don. He read a passage from Whitman.

Pete started off with an impressive speech on what it meant to be a friend. He said Jacob was the epitome of the word. Then he told everyone about the time Jacob made him a birthday cake. Jacob had used olive oil instead of vegetable oil as a joke. He wanted to see how long we would go on eating it before we told him it sucked. I only swallowed one bite before I put my fork down. Sara did the same. Pete followed each mouthful with a gulp of gin and ate three-quarters of his piece, until Jacob started laughing and brought out the real cake. Pete said the reason he told that story was because it was easy to think of Jacob as this really soulful, moody guy, and he wanted people to remember that Jacob knew how to have a good laugh, too.

Joanna was last to speak. She rambled on for twenty minutes with an entire overview of Jacob's life, but I never got the gist of what she said because by then I'd started to zone out. I heard Joanna mention my name a few times at the end. Apparently she said a lot of nice things about me. I wish I'd paid more attention, but it was too painful to listen closely to all the memories, especially if I wasn't in them. I resented the time other people had with Jacob. In most cases, it was more time than I got, and I knew, deep in my heart, that meant something in the universe had gone seriously awry. The earth was off-kilter. The fates had royally screwed up. I remember thinking, over and over, *This isn't the way it was supposed to turn out.*

Thank God Joanna didn't make me talk. She asked me if I wanted to, but I politely declined. The way I saw it, Jacob's life amounted to much more than any sugar-coated sentences I could have put together. He was more than the sum of the parts I observed looking around the church: the grieving faces, the lachrymose anecdotes, the jar of ashes he'd been reduced to. I didn't know how to be poignant and moving and clever on the face of that, when all I felt was hollow. I was still trying to reason it all out. People lose loved ones all the time. It happens everyday. It's just a part of life. That's what I tried to tell myself. The difference was, everybody didn't lose someone like Jacob. They lost uncles they didn't particularly like all that much, or a friend of a friend they hardly knew, or an elderly grandparent who'd already had their chance at this big joke called life. What's more, I could have easily named a hundred people the world would be better off without. Jacob wasn't one of them. And it wasn't just my selfish sense of loss, or simply a loss to every person in that church. The way I saw it, the permanent absence of Jacob Grace was a cruel, savage blow to the whole goddamn planet.

Once the service ended, a hairy ape of a guy in a dark cloak, who Joanna called Father Joe, led us to an old brick building behind the church. It smelled like moth balls inside, and there were signs advertising Sunday Night Bingo on the walls. A buffet was set up in the middle of the room and a dozen stainless-steel food-warmers, filled with various kinds of meats and vegetables, lay sprawled across the long table. Everything edible was covered in either tomato sauce or brown gravy, with a layer of butter floating on top. The whole scene made my stomach turn. To make matters worse, nobody would leave me alone. Everyone in attendance, even Joanna's friends, and other people I'd never met, came over to touch me and offer their condolences. They whispered stupid comments about me as they walked away, comments they thought I couldn't hear.

"The poor thing."

"She looks lost."

"And such a pretty girl."

"Oh, she's young, she'll be okay, it's Joanna *I'm* worried about."

"What did she say her name was?"

"I think she's wearing Armani."

I wanted to shout, Calvin Klein, you shallow L.A. nimrod!

I was the little widow in the cool outfit. Nothing more, nothing less.

Adrenaline was the first mourner to grab me when I walked in to the reception hall. She was already in line for food, and she blew her nose so loudly she practically cracked the windows. She held me by the shoulders and, with tears in her eyes and saliva bubbling in the corners of her mouth, told me that *Hallelujah* would be released in the spring exactly as planned.

"I'll make Jacob Grace a legend," she said. "You have my word on that."

Yeah, sure. If her fabulous word was good for anything, Jacob and I would have been long gone and he'd be safe. Or, at the very least, he'd *be*.

"If the book does well," Adrenaline said, "we should think about maybe publishing some of Jacob's journals."

In your dreams, I thought. I ventured a guess that Adrenaline had already discussed the whole thing with an editor and a marketing department. No doubt books by a dead guy are a PR dream come true.

I was pretty sure that the day I walked into a bookstore and saw *Hallelujah* staring back at me was going to feel a lot like making it to the summit of Mt. Everest and then being stabbed in the heart with an ice axe.

As if all the strangers weren't bad enough, Jacob's memorial service was like a Jordan family reunion. My mother came. Chip and Elise came. Toren couldn't get off work, but Cole flew in all the way from Montgomery. My father and Tara had shown up too, but they had to hide behind the *Weekly* staff. I never saw them.

"Dad wanted me to tell you he was thinking about you," Cole said. "He just didn't want to run into Mom."

"Damn," I said. "I would've liked to have seen that, actually."

Nina was there. I hadn't noticed her during the service, Sara said she was on the other side of the aisle about five rows back, but she came over to talk to me while I was eating. In a slow, pharmaceutical-induced rhythm, she told me how sorry she was. She had on a floral-printed dress, glasses, and an old cardigan sweater that made her look more like a school teacher than an ex-dope fiend.

"I can't believe it," she said, along with a few other trite phrases that I let go over my head.

Nina didn't look sick but I envied her anyway. Odds are she's going to die before I do, I thought. That means if there is life after death, she'll see Jacob again first.

"Do you think you can have sex in the hereafter?" I said to Kat.

Her eyes widened and she stared at me. She didn't know how to respond to a question like that.

"I don't want Jacob and Nina to get back together in paradise," I said.

I wanted to trade places with Nina and suffer with her disease. I wanted to be with Jacob. And I'm absolutely certain that if I weren't so fucking afraid of what lay in wait for me on the other side, I would have tried to follow him to wherever he'd gone.

All day long, during the service and then later on at the brunch, I kept having a dreamy sensation that I was plummeting off a tall building, but, as if I'd just fallen asleep, the feeling would be followed by a quick jerk back into consciousness.

"Let's take a walk," Cole said. "You look like you could use some fresh air."

"There is no fresh air in Pasadena."

Cole took my hand. On our way outside we heard Chip and Elise chatting in the foyer. They were talking about Jacob. Chip must have asked Elise if she'd managed to dig up any details about the accident.

"He was just swimming, I guess," Elise said. "They think he got caught under a wave and because it was dark, he got disoriented and didn't know which way was up or something."

Chip was glancing at the program that Joanna had made for the service. There was a photo on the cover. In it, Jacob was looking straight into the camera, his head was tilted slightly to the side, he had a transcendent gaze in his eyes and just the slightest trace of a smile on his lips. He was wearing an old flannel shirt, and something that looked like keys around his neck. The dates of his birth and death were under the picture. Below that it said: We'll miss you.

"It was midnight, for Christ's sake," Chip said, attempting to whisper. "What kind of idiot goes swimming at midnight? And with all those clothes on? It was reckless, that's all. Just stupid and reckless. Or who knows, maybe the guy was trying to off himself."

Cole saw me sour. He squeezed my hand. "Let it go. It doesn't matter," he said.

But it *did* matter. In the name of everything Jacob was, it mattered.

I charged around the corner, grabbed Chip by the arm, and dragged him out the door. I took him to where I wouldn't make a scene. He looked like he had a hard-boiled egg stuck in his throat. Cole and Elise followed quickly behind me. Kat and Gopal were standing on the steps and they walked over to see the commotion.

"You are such a fucking asshole!" I said to Chip, poking his bloated chest with my finger.

"Beatrice, I didn't mean—"

"I know *exactly* what you meant, you fat fuck, but you don't know shit. You with your servants, your summer blockbusters, your surgically attached cell phone, and your two-bit hookers, you don't know shit."

"Word," Kat said.

Cole covered his mouth and tried not to laugh.

Elise scampered up next to me, "Honey, please. He didn't mean what he said. He just likes to hear himself talk, you know that." I ignored her.

"Let me tell you something," I said. I looked Chip straight in the eyes until his face got pasty. "I want to tell you a story." I took a quick breath. "Last spring, Jacob and I went to Catalina for the day. We hiked about three miles up a trail, to a bluff overlooking the whole island. We snuck off the path and made our way into this tiny meadow that was covered with wild flowers. Jacob spotted two butterflies there, right at the edge of the field. They were just hanging out, fluttering from one flower to another, and he couldn't take his eyes off them. I mean he was *mesmerized* by the damn things." I paused to regain some composure—remembering a day like that had the power to thoroughly wreck me. "We followed those two stupid insects around for over an hour, and do you want to know *why*?" I wiped my nose with the sleeve of my fifteen-hundred dollar suit. "Because Jacob was curious about what butterflies *did*, that's why. So don't tell me Jacob was *reckless*. Jacob was *not* reckless. Jacob just wanted to *feel* things. He wanted to *live*, something you wouldn't know the first thing about."

I stormed back inside. Kat followed. Cole brought me a Styrofoam cup filled with black coffee. The smell of it reminded me of Jacob's breath and I couldn't drink it. I tried to give the cup back to Cole in a hurry but it slipped out of my hand and crashed to the floor. Seeing the splash on the linoleum broke something in me. It was my life spilt, the dark liquid of my sorrow being released. I completely lost it.

"It's okay," Cole said. "I'll clean it up."

"Are you all right?" Kat said. I noticed Kat wasn't wearing

any lipstick. She looked weird without her lipstick.

"Am I all right?" I cried hysterically. "What kind of a question is that? Of course I'm not all right. And can I tell you why? Because Chip is probably going to live to be a hundred years old. A hundred fucking years old. But Jacob will never get to see the sun rise again. He'll never see his book in print. He'll never push two raven-haired daughters on a swing. He'll never paint his little Victorian house and he'll never pull into Memphis and see the goddamn signs for Graceland!"

A moment later Kat whispered, "Graceland," as if the connection had just dawned on her.

"Jacob wasn't stupid," I said to whoever was listening.

"We know that," Cole said.

"He didn't go into that water to test fate. He didn't go in thinking there was a chance he might *die*. He went in because it reminded him of the beauty of being alive. Does *anybody* understand that?"

"*Grace* land," Kat said again.

# FIFTY-FIVE

"My heavens, Beatrice, where are all your *things*?"

I left the brunch in a bit of a state, and my mother stopped over that night to check on me. By the time she arrived the apartment was empty, save for my backpack and a box of Jacob's notebooks—I wanted those with me at all times— they echoed with the sound of his voice.

"The movers took everything," I said.

"*Movers*? What are you talking about? Surely you're not still *moving*?"

"I'm leaving tomorrow." Before my mother had a chance to squawk, I cut her off. "Don't try to change my mind, or tell me it's dangerous, or that I don't know what I'm doing, or that I need time to think it over. I've made up my mind and I'm leaving as planned. End of discussion."

And I had thought it over. I'd spent hours thinking it over. I came to the conclusion that if I stayed in Los Angeles, I would be relegating myself to the equivalent of life in prison without the possibility of parole. If I didn't leave then, I knew I never would.

You can't wait forever for something, and then say it's too late when the time finally comes, even if every shred of incentive inside you has been lost.

Jacob would have been disappointed in me if I'd stayed.

"Well…" my mother said. "May I ask one question?"

"What?"

"Where are you going?"

I knew I wasn't going to Memphis. There was no way I could go anywhere near the state of Tennessee without Jacob.

I took my mother's hand and walked her to the door. "I don't know where I'm going. I really don't," I said. "But I promise I'll call you when I get there."

That afternoon, when I bid farewell to my friends, it was with the understanding that I wouldn't be seeing them for a long time. Kat was in her own category—she wasn't part of the Jacob contingent and I knew she wouldn't let me slip away. The others were different. I told Pete and Sara I'd keep in touch, but I knew there was a chance I wouldn't—that I couldn't. They were going to have a new baby soon, their lives would be refilled with life. Hell, I thought they might even do something enormously touching and name the kid after Jacob. They would never forget him, but they would get over him. They had to. And I'd become nothing more than an afterthought. I'd be that girl their dead friend used to date. They probably wouldn't even remember my name in five years.

As for Joanna, I planned on calling her regularly, to see how she was holding up, and to keep some sort of blood-connection with Jacob going. I needed that. But Joanna wouldn't understand the incredulity of my grief. The *unfairness* of it all. Joanna had God to help her make sense of things, so she was better off than I was right from the start. And she would have the strength to remember all the good times. She would thank her lord that she'd been blessed with her precious son, even if it had only been for a short while.

Meanwhile, I'm left with nothing. Sure, I had Jacob's clothes, his books. I could even push Play on a machine and watch him sing and joke and play a guitar. I should have been grateful for that. I hated it. I hated that I had to go on without him. I hated the future I saw before me. The thousands of showers, the meals, the mindless conversations, the sleepless nights, the complaining about traffic; the hours spent making beautiful, unimportant rings and necklaces; and in the meantime, Jacob Grace is history. He no longer *is,* he just *was.*

I don't even know what that means, let alone how I'm supposed to endure it for the rest of my life.

"At least you have the memories, right?"

That's what some dickhead from the *Weekly* staff said to me after the memorial service. Memories, my ass. In *Hallelujah,* Jacob wrote that memories are the patches that make up the quilt of our emotions. A beautiful way to put it, but wrong. If that were true, then memories would blanket us, they would keep us warm. My memories were chilling me to the bone.

I took a long walk that night, my intended destination being Venice Beach. I was going to find the spot where Jacob disappeared. I'm not sure what I planned on doing once I got there, but my legs refused to take me in the right direction. I ended up in a dark, empty church instead. The air smelled like frankincense, and the only illumination in the place was at a little alter in the back, just to the left of the pews. I knelt down there, in front of a black iron tray that held dozens of burning candles. I dropped nineteen dollars and sixty-six cents—all the money I had in my pocket—into the offering slot. I lit a candle and decided to give God one more chance. I asked him to do me a really big favor—to let me forfeit the next thirty or forty years of my life. I was willing to skip right to old age if I could see Jacob one more time, even if it was only for a minute. I promised God I'd never doubt him again if he'd honor my one request.

When I didn't hear back from God, I wheeled-and-dealed with the smaller people: Mary, Jesus, Joseph, Saint Anthony, Saint Frances, Saint Joan, Saint Michael, Saint Christopher, Adam, Eve, Matthew, Mark, Luke, John. I even tried Moses and Noah. I cried out to every stupid holy person I'd ever heard of. And I don't know, maybe I half-expected one of them to show up and bargain with me a little, but, as usual, I didn't get shit.

# FIFTY-SIX

I ran into Greg the next morning. I'd just shut the door of my apartment for the final time, and I could taste my heart in my throat as I walked down the hall with my backpack.

"Hey, Bea. You guys are leaving today, huh?"

He said *you guys*. He didn't know. I wanted to live in Greg's world, the one where Jacob Grace was still a person.

"Yeah," I said. "We're leaving right now. Ja—I mean Henry—he's waiting for me in the car. I have to go."

Greg misinterpreted my melancholia. He thought I was going to miss his sorry ass. He hugged me good-bye.

"Have a nice life," he said.

Going through the California desert in a car was like being inside a kiln. But the desert was no different to me than Los Angeles. It was forsaken land. Scorched, unconquerable, and crawling with phantoms who perished trying to quench their thirst for gold.

For the first hundred miles or so, all I could think about was how shitty life was. And how sometimes you stumble upon things—good things—that give everything meaning, and when you do, you should get to keep them. They shouldn't be taken away. They shouldn't be swallowed alive and then spewed back out, limp and lifeless. Not the good things.

Maybe I was just stupid.

I wondered about the omens, the warning signs.

I like to say I don't believe in mystics. I don't believe in fate. I don't believe in destiny or kismet. I don't believe in God. I don't believe in anything.

But I believe in the *possibility* of *everything*.

The whirlpool dream—I'd interpreted that all wrong. The whirlpool was a fucking metaphor. The water will show no mercy, that's what it was trying to say. If I believed that crap.

It was a coincidence, that's all. A random chance, an accident, a fluke.

And then there was Margaret. She said no wandering. But she was a walking sham. Nobody sells the truth for fifteen bucks.

The one that irked me the most was Madra—that damn fortune-teller who cursed me when I was a kid. She couldn't have made it any clearer for me if she tried. For Christ's sake, Warren Beatty had four kids. His wife practically popped one out on national television during the Academy Awards—the same month Jacob and I met. We'd watched that show together, it was right after he moved in, and we laughed about how bad it would suck to have a seventy-five-year-old father when you were in high school.

"Then again," Jacob said, "beggars can't be choosers. In the father department, I'd have taken whatever I could get."

I looked out across the wasteland and my soul ached.

I knew *whatever I could get* would never be enough for me now.

I didn't make it out of California that first night. I stopped in Needles to see if I could find traces of Jacob there. I checked into the infamous Sage and Cedar Motel—a horizontal, one-story building made of aluminum siding, with a hunter-green roof, fake wood paneling for walls, and spider webs in the corners of the ceiling. A dump, just like Jacob said.

The man behind the desk was a tawny old totem pole

who greeted me like he wasn't sure I was really there. I told him I knew someone who'd stayed at the motel. I gave him the exact date Jacob would have arrived.

"I'd like the same room you gave him," I said.

The man put on a thick pair of bifocals and scanned the registry. After a minute, he said, "Sorry lady, we had no Grace here."

I knew I had the right place.

"Try Chinaski," I said. I spelled it for him. He spun the book around and pointed his bony finger at Jacob's scraggly signature.

"Chinaski stayed in room seventeen," he said.

"Is it available?"

He handed me the key and I thanked him like crazy. I could tell he thought I was a little off my rocker.

Room seventeen had tacky, prehistoric carpet on the floor, a decrepit floral bedspread, and it reeked like bug spray. In his journal, Jacob had described the room as stinking like shoe polish, but my sense of smell was more acute than Jacob's. I knew Raid when I detected it in the air.

After I got cleaned up, I called all my family members, the ones I was still speaking to, and asked them if they remembered Madra.

"Beatrice, I was nine in 1984," Cole said.

"I know, but think. Please. It's important."

After a moment, he said, "I'm sorry. I really am. The only thing I remember about that party is sitting next to Fernando Valenzuela."

My mother told me I'd imagined Madra.

My father was the last straw.

"The lady with the big earrings?" he said. "Sure, I remember her. She gave me the creeps. She cornered me near the men's room and told me to be careful. She said your mother wasn't using birth control. If it wasn't for that woman, you'd probably have another brother or sister."

# FIFTY-SEVEN

I had no visions that night at the Sage and Cedar Motel. No out-of-body experiences. No dreams of Jacob professing his eternal love from beyond the grave. He didn't appear to me in the reflection of the mirror, or float an ashtray across the room, or cause the TV to spontaneously combust, or anything else I'd asked him for out loud. I waited up as long as I could for something to happen. Nothing did.

I was back in the car not long after the sun came up. Within ten minutes I passed a sign that said: YOU ARE NOW LEAVING CALIFORNIA.

I only looked back once.

I drove east for most of the morning, but as soon as I got to Flagstaff, I realized I was on the exact route Jacob and I had planned. Over a long lunch I reevaluated my direction. I flipped a coin, turned left, and proceeded north.

By mid-afternoon I found myself at the edge of a giant canyon in southern Utah. I detected an unyielding vibe in Utah. There was something about the way certain people looked at me that gave me the impression they had four right angles in the corners of their heads. I was wearing an old pair of Levi's and a crisp, white cotton shirt that buttoned down the front, but I didn't have a bra on—I just didn't feel like wearing one that day—and I got stared at like I was some kind of flower-child sinner. I liked the canyon though. It was weird and immense. The majesty of the rock formations, worn down by the wrath of the past, made me feel completely insignificant. I parked on a turnout and, with my journal in-hand, I walked about a hundred yards, to a place where I could sit and look out over the entire gorge.

I stayed there for a long time, to watch the sunset and write down a lot of corny thoughts about Jacob.

"Thoughts are king, Trixie. King," he'd said.

When the sky burned pink like a flower on fire, a soft gust of wind brushed my shoulders and gave me chills. There wasn't another human being in sight, yet in some inexplicable way, I sensed I wasn't alone. I'm sure it was nothing more than wishful thinking on my part, but for the first time since I lost Jacob, I thought I felt his presence. I even convinced myself that I smelled him in the air. I guess the feeling that came over me could be described as joy, but only if joy can be profoundly painful. It rushed like a river down into my abysmal emptiness, but no matter how long or how far it flowed, I knew it could never reach the bottom.

I missed my unforgettable friend.

The days will always be brighter because he existed.

The nights will always be darker because he's gone.

And no matter what anybody says about grief, and about time healing all wounds, the truth is, there are certain sorrows that never fade away until the heart stops beating and the last breath is taken.

It was there I wrote in my journal that the colossal chasm below me seemed to reach deep into the soul of the earth, identical in dimension to the hole inside of me.

I closed my notebook and scribbled three words on the cover. Finally, it had a name. I wondered if Jacob could see it, and if he approved. I wondered if anyone else would ever know or understand what those words really meant.

I stayed there and pondered my future for a while longer,

but it was getting dark and I wanted to make it out of Utah that night. I wasn't sure what kind of place I was looking for, but Utah wasn't it.

I put away my notebook, stood up, and went back to the car.

I had to keep going.

# A SELECTION OF NOVELS AVAILABLE FROM JUDY PIATKUS (PUBLISHERS) LIMITED

THE PRICES BELOW WERE CORRECT AT THE TIME OF GOING TO PRESS. HOWEVER JUDY PIATKUS (PUBLISHERS) LIMITED RESERVE THE RIGHT TO SHOW NEW RETAIL PRICES ON COVERS WHICH MAY DIFFER FROM THOSE PREVIOUSLY ADVERTISED IN THE TEXT OR ELSEWHERE.

| 0 7499 3363 1 | The Dive From Clausen's Pier | Ann Packer | £6.99 |
| 0 7499 3336 4 | Girls' Poker Night | Jill A. Davis | £6.99 |
| 0 7499 3333 X | It's How You Play the Game | Jimmy Gleacher | £6.99 |
| 0 7499 3307 0 | How to Cook a Tart | Nina Killham | £6.99 |
| 0 7499 3314 3 | Flesh Tones | M.J. Rose | £6.99 |
| 0 7499 3334 8 | Blood | Patricia Traxler | £6.99 |

All Piatkus titles are available by post from:

## www.bookpost.co.uk

or by contacting our sales department on

## 0800 454816

Free postage and packing in the UK
(on orders of two books or more)